RESTORING HOPE

by

Valerie Knupp

OTHER BOOKS BY VALERIE KNUPP

Finding Faith – The Jack Tyler Series Vol. 2
Creating Chance– The Jack Tyler Series Vol. 3

Available on Amazon.com for Kindle or in paperback

www.thrillersbyknupp.com

This is a work of fiction. Names, characters, places, and incidents either are the product of the author's imagination or are used fictitiously, and any resemblance to actual persons, living or dead, events or locales is entirely coincidental.

Copyright © 2013 by Valerie Knupp

SBN-13: **978-0989902908**
ISBN-10: **0989902900**

Printed in the United States of America

Table of Contents

Dedication

This book is dedicated to my father, Billy Mike Knupp, the man who gave me a twisted outlook and the gift of quick thought, making writing a free flowing process. I only wish he were still on this earth to read it. I think he would have enjoyed seeing his daughter's name in print.

Prologue

He had no idea what day it was, much less the month. His eyes didn't want to open, and even if they did, he questioned whether they'd see the way they should. Even with his eyes closed, he knew that the room was spinning around him, the world turned upside down, making the room appear to be a fog. The only certainty was that his head, his heart and his body were in terrible pain.

How long had he been here? Where *was* here? That thought brought more clarity with it, and his memory started to return. How much had he had to drink last night? Had he hurt anyone? He wasn't certain, but for the moment all he could think about was how could he 'kill' the pain. He tried to rise and forced his eyes open; slowly glancing around, his nostrils filled with the smell of ... what? What was that smell? It was putrid, whatever it was ... like old cigarettes, the copper of dried, yet fresh blood, and old fermented wine. Realization poured over him; it was he who smelled like this. The room around him was nearly dark. Still, his eyes struggled to adjust to the low light and dust particles that hung in the air, evident even through his hang over. He needed to pee. That was going to take precedence over his unwillingness to move. He swung his legs over the side of the dirty mattress, sheets askew and sticking to his sweaty body, then tossed the blankets aside. Struggling to his feet, he began to make his way through the room, tripping over clothes and piles of food bags with names like McDonalds and Burger King on them, stepping on the newspapers headlining the latest killing spree. What was the name they were calling him now? He wondered, sparing a glance at the newspapers, averting his eyes toward the window not really interested in what the media thought of him anyway.

The curtains hung off the rod slightly, allowing for a small amount of light to seep around them and into the hotel room. The effect made the scene around him even more unsavory, as the glow merely displayed the chaos of his life. This life – not the one he had cherished, but this new ugly one. The life he was living now made him want to do these ugly things, driving him to think those thoughts again. This life drove him into the darkness looking, hunting…, this life would no doubt win, consume him, unless. *Unless what?*

He made his way through the clutter to the bathroom and stood in front of the dirty toilet, hands trembling as he relieved himself. He slowly zipped his pants, flushed, and watched his fluids spin around and then down, out into the city sewer. He moved to stand over the chipped and stained sink, which was as rundown as the rest of the hotel room. As rundown as his body felt. Rusty water stains snaked from the faucets into the drain, making a trail that seemed to naturally disappear into the pipe and from there into the dark city. He found this ironic, as those rust stains and his bodily fluids were much like him, finding their way back out into the dark city.

Looking into the mirror through his blood-shot eyes, now he realized that he saw only pieces of the man he used to be. His eyes – once blue and sparkling, hinting of a happier day – were now gray and dull. The lines in his face once there from smiling where deep and taunt, his shoulders once held high and proud stooped and ached. Looking at his reflection through the cracks in the mirror, which had most likely been delivered by some hooker or drug addict during a few hours of paid-for passion, he started to see the way. The answer was there right in front of him, he realized, though it was in pieces, parts, and fragments. But he had a chance to have it all again, if he could put all those pieces together. If he could just change, focus, and plan. His life – this one that consisted of pain and chaos – must end, and a new one – a happy one – could replace it.

He just had to make some minor changes. In his mind, a plan began to form.

Chapter One

The Jackie Cooper Mercedes Benz lot was displaying balloons and incentive signs for the special of the month. The signs flapped frantically in the Oklahoma wind, seemingly begging a buyer to come in and see what deals were being offered. As he pulled the black SL550 convertible onto the lot, he thought that the dealership must have just opened; there appeared to be no other customers in sight. It was Wednesday, though, and perhaps that meant it was a low volume sales day.

If that was true, then this should be easy.

He pulled into the parking lot and pulled into one of the spaces near the front steps. Before he could even get his long frame out of the car, a sales person was bounding down the stairs from the showroom floor. The man was obviously the typical, car salesman; flashy, and sporting a gold chain necklace. Thick, and probably fake. He had on a cheap – but shiny – pair of black, loafer-style shoes, and had the overly whitened smile to match.

"Good morning, sir," he called out, waving. "My name is Ben, but most folks remember me as Benz. How can I help you this fine, sunny morning?"

It was difficult not to notice the partial comb over flapping in the wind, seeming to dance in unison with the signs, and even harder not to laugh at it. This was the first step to regaining his life and it was time to begin to act like Jack again; he straightened his face and answered politely enough.

"Well Benz, my name is Jack, and I need to swap out my convertible here," he said, pointing to the car he'd just exited, the door still standing open. "I'd like to get a more practical car, as my wife and I are planning on settling down here."

"Okay, well I am sure we can work out a deal. That is one beautiful car you have there. I'd hate to part with it if it was up to me, but what are you thinking? A sedan, wagon, SUV? We have them all," Benz said with a gleam in his eye. He swept his arm out across the air, gesturing to the lot, which shone with all of the newest models.

Jack nodded, humored by the man's stupidity. Benz had clearly ran out when he had seen Jack pull onto the sales lot thinking this would be a big sale based on the current vehicle Jack was driving. It was obvious Benz didn't realize the plan was to move out of the luxury vehicle and into a practical one. It was necessary to eliminate this vehicle and settle into something less noticeable with a good sized cargo area. "I was thinking maybe a Honda or Toyota from your used car sales lot, actually," he answered quietly.

"Ohhhh," Benz exclaimed, trying desperately to hide his disappointment in the request. "Are you certain? I would think after having the finest in luxury, you might be disappointed in such a choice." Noting the darkness that fell over Jack's face, Benz continued, "But we aim to please all of our customers. Let me walk you back to where the used cars are, and we can see if any of them interest you."

He set off toward the back of the lot, and Jack followed, seeing that Benz had a slight imperfection in his gait. It appeared that one leg was shorter than the other. Mentally noting that this minor disability might be helpful later, Jack followed him having no problem keeping up with Benz, but found he was struggling to pay attention as Benz rattled on about how long the dealership had been in business, his years of service, and the numerous monthly awards he'd received over the years for top sales performance. Jack's mind, instead of listening to the salesman, had already wandered on to his next steps. He would eliminate Benz, so that there would be no witnesses and, well, because it had been two weeks and the need was raging. After that, he would begin working towards the day that he could settle into this new life with his wife, his love, and everything else. Benz would be a necessary casualty so that he could move forward. Jack knew he must succumb to the darkness while he put the rest of his plan in place. Benz would help him get through.

Benz stopped suddenly, spinning around to face Jack again, interrupting those thoughts. "As you can see, we have a pretty wide assortment of used cars. Why don't you tell me what style you're looking for and we can narrow down the selection?"

Jack looked around at the cars in front of him. As Benz had said, there was a good assortment. While his preference was actually to keep the car he had, he realized his life could only be good again through numerous personal sacrifices. Giving up a luxury automobile would be nothing compared to the reward he would have in the end. He noted a few cars that would meet the 'look' he was striving for – not overly successful, a subtle color, with minimum to moderate mileage on the odometer. Appearances were going to be incredibly important; being low key and blending in were a primary part of the plan.

"I think a mid-sized or large SUV will do," he said, thinking that the additional trunk space might be useful. "And anything with around 50,000 miles should be satisfactory. I'd prefer a silver or beige color. You know, easy to clean," he explained. What he was really thinking, of course, was that those colors would blend in on the road. He looked back at Benz and smiled, knowing his smile was difficult for anyone to resist. If he played his cards right, the guy would be in the palm of his hand within minutes.

By the age of five or six, Jack had learned that he had something special – a charm that, when applied, could easily win over anyone. At about the same time, he'd discovered his darker side and realized that he had the ability to apply looks which could immediately invoke feelings in others. Feelings of fear, joy, seduction … they were all quickly within his reach, just through an adaptation of his facial expressions. Over the years Jack had crafted this skill to encourage people to behave as he desired them to. He could quickly gain trust or was capable of easily making someone uncomfortable. Most people would say he had charisma and charm. Jack thought of it as a means to manipulate necessarily, and this was one of those times.

He'd also realized that he could make these changes so quickly that most people didn't even realize what happened. They never knew that anything had changed, until it was too late.

Once he recognized this incredible ability, he had worked diligently to hone it to perfection. Over the years, he'd gotten really good at adapting to the situation or the personality he was trying to manipulate. On almost every occasion, he got exactly what he wanted.

Benz looked at Jack a bit quizzically at the request for the SUV, and then turned to look at the sea of cars, trucks and SUVs. "Okay, then let's take a look at this one over here. This is a Toyota Sequoia, it has …" He paused for a moment, as he leaned over the windshield to see the details on the tag, 58,520 miles on it. Came from a single owner, a single mom from right here in Tulsa. Her youngest went off to college this year, and she traded this in for her dream car."

Walking over to the silver full-sized SUV, Benz used his dealer key to pop open the lock on the key storage device. Opening up the driver's side door, he stepped to the side and clicked the door opener to unlock all the doors. Then he dropped the keys into Jack's hand and walked around the rear bumper to the passenger side.

Jack reached in and moved the driver's seat back to accommodate his 6-foot frame and climbed in to settle behind the wheel. Benz joined him in the passenger seat and began to show Jack the features of the SUV, covering everything all the way down to the nine cup holders. Then, jumping back out of the car, Benz walked to the rear of the vehicle. Jack joined him as he pulled down the seats and showed the cargo space.

"Great for vacationing with the missus. In fact, my wife and I had a vehicle similar to this a few years back." Suddenly, looking somber he continued, "That was before the cancer took her, of course. You should definitely take the missus on lots of trips," he finished, a look of sorrow filling his eyes. Then, returning to his sales pitch, he continued to explain how the seats folded completely flat.

Jack looked into the back of the vehicle, wondering to himself how well Benz would fit in there later. When he spoke, though, it was to offer platitudes. "I'm sorry to hear about your wife. You alone now, or are your children in the area?

"Ah thanks, it's fine. Kids are all grown and busy with their lives. Just me these days," Benz answered, plastering on a smile.

Looking at Benz with his most sympathetic face, Jack decided he knew more than he'd hoped for and needed to change the subject. He didn't want to get personal with Benz, nothing good could come from it. Tipping his head towards the car, he said, "I think this will do just fine."

Benz barely contained his surprise at this sudden sale, but recovered gracefully. "Okay, well let's take her for a spin."

But Jack shook his head, his mind already made up. "That won't be necessary. I think this will do nicely for me and my wife. I see there's a dealer warranty, and I'd like to go ahead and do the deal on this car. Why don't we talk to your manager about trading in my car?"

Suppressing a sigh, Benz looked up at Jack, taking in his expensive clothes, nice shoes and manicured hands. "Of course," he said. "I'll have the car pulled around and cleaned for you while we work out the details." Benz suppressed his obvious disappointed, the deal being made was not going to be a favorable one from a commission perspective as he had originally hoped. The car being traded far out priced the car being bought.

"Don't bother," Jack stopped him. "The car seems to be in quite good condition." Secretly, Jack was smiling at the red nail polish spots on the carpet inside the car—an obvious spill from the prior owner. How much more perfect could that be? Closing the hatch he followed Benz into the showroom to meet the finance manager.

An hour later, Jack was pulling out of the dealership in his newly purchased used SUV. The dealer had provided him with a note to pick up a cashier's check for $60,000 in two days. A fair deal, he felt, though he had paid well over $100,000 for his car just a little over a year ago. Had it been that long since his life had been turned upside down? He hadn't expected the dealer to be able to write him a check and realized that once the money cleared, he would have completed everything necessary before eliminating his current identity. Dr. Jack Tyler would no longer exist. Then he could begin the rest of the plans necessary to restoring his true life.

Pulling out onto the street, Jack made a right turn to head north on Memorial Avenue. He had already conducted an Internet search for schools offering programs that would teach him a new profession. It was all part of the next phase of the plan. It was show time, time for him to begin his transformation. While he didn't relish the idea, he knew he had to leave himself behind for now.

If there was even a chance for Hope, it required a metamorphosis. He had to learn to live in a world that held little to no interest for him.

He'd already started exploring the programs and realized that he could complete them and be in his new profession in just three months. This timing was perfect, really, as it gave him the time he needed to practice his new lifestyle. That new life would provide cover and the perfect place for finding and putting the pieces all back together.

Chapter Two

"Agent Wells, it's a pleasure. How was your flight?" Chief of Police Harding asked, greeting one of the FBI's finest agents. He grasped the man's hand and pumped his arm fiercely, noticing the agent's tall, muscular frame, and thinking to himself that the guy could obviously hold his own.

The agent returned the greeting, sweeping his eyes over the large parking lot and the police headquarter building in one glance, and just as quickly returning his gaze to the chief. "Chief Harding, thank you for the invitation to work with you on this case. How can I help?" he asked.

Harding faced Wells, with the sun glinting off the dark pupils of his eyes, standing 5'10", with thick arms, broad shoulders, and a slight paunch around the midsection that came with too many greasy meals, late nights, and passing the age of fifty. He looked up at the younger man, who he guessed was mid-thirties, stood 6'2" and obviously only ate healthy, high-protein foods. Harding immediately respected the Agent, knowing he would have the type of discipline to remain focused under pressure. The necessary attributes of a good person to have on your side. Making eye contact, he started laying out the high-level details.

"We have six bodies, all same MO. The method of killing is always the same. There's a lot of rage, violent deaths all of them. Either a knife or saw was used with an unusual skill level, very clean, though we haven't yet identified the weapon of choice. He leaves nothing behind, and the bodies were all carefully cleaned with bleach afterward. No specific victimology, and this is where we're stuck. We're not going to be able to catch him until we know who he's going after. We need your help on the profiling." The chief shifted his eyes away as the roar of a motorcycle came racing into the parking lot, abruptly stopping about 25 yards to the east of them.

"Perfect timing," Harding stated, nodding to where the motorcycle stopped. "That's Detective Max Nichols, lead investigator on the case. Nichols can fill you in on all the case files, victims, and evidence, or lack thereof."

The two men started heading towards where the motorcycle had come to rest in one of the motorcycle parking spaces near the front entrance of the police department. As they got near the cycle, Wells began to take in the bike – an impressive ride that any man would love. He knew little about sports bikes, but admired the details of the silver and black Kawasaki Ninja ZX-14R. As the rider dismounted, propping the bike up expertly on its kickstand, Agent Wells prepared to shake hands with the rider. He drew back when that rider removed the helmet, freeing handfuls of long, rich, flowing, dark auburn hair.

"You must be Agent Wells. Max Nichols. Call me Max. Welcome to beautiful, sunny California," the woman under the helmet and attached to the hair stated, extending her hand and offering a firm handshake.

Wells quickly recovered from his surprise and returned the handshake, replying, "Mark Wells." He dropped his gaze slightly, taking in the beautiful, confident creature that was Detective Maxine Nichols.

Watching the exchange the chief smiled to himself.

Wells collected himself and brought the meeting back to order. "Detective Nichols... Max, my pleasure. I understand you have a serial on your hands. Chief Harding tells me I might be able to assist in profiling your un-sub. I hope I can help. I'm at your disposal for the next forty-eight hours. Ready to get started when you are," Wells stated, staring into the detective's rich emerald green eyes.

Max returned the gaze, sizing the man up in a similar fashion, noting his all-American good looks, excellent physical shape, blue eyes, and dark, thick, hair, which swept slightly to the left across his forehead. He had a sharp jawline that exploded into a perfectly white smile. *Okay, he'll do,* she thought to herself. Quickly pulling her hair back and nesting it into a pony tail, she pulled off her leather jacket and nodded towards the entrance. Climbing the steps two at a time, she arrived at the double doors and turned back to the two men who seemed to be falling behind. As she entered the building, her mind drifted to the case. She had six dead bodies on her hands, and while she wasn't originally thrilled about the FBI swooping in, she knew she needed input, and fast, if she was going to catch the killer. She hoped like hell that dreamy, Agent Mark Wells would be able to see something, anything, that she had missed, so she could lock the bastard away forever.

Chapter Three

Jack smiled to himself as he continued down the street. The sun was shining, though the news had called for rain. He didn't care for rainy weather, but he did have to admit that rain had some advantages. Everything needed water to survive, after all. Rain also did useful things like destroying evidence in a murder. That was a *major* advantage. The day was sunny, traffic was light – the benefit of middle-of-the-day travel, though it didn't much matter, as Tulsa never really suffered long traffic delays. The worst he had seen was over on 71st, where it seemed every business was packed into one area. The uncongested traffic patterns allowed him to be nimble in his activities, and that made him feel safer and at ease in his surroundings.

When he had been looking to relocate, one of the allures of this area was the city for hunting and the country for disposal, having little to no traffic issues was an added benefit. As he slid down the street, and pulled into a Walgreens, he was making a mental list of supplies he needed. He'd already spent some time planning and practicing the look he needed. He'd even gone to night clubs in California before leaving to make sure he knew how to behave in the situations he would likely face. It was imperative that the persona was believable.

As he approached the store, the automatic door slid open, and he felt the draft of wind caused by the external air forcing in against the heating system. Grabbing a small basket by the handle, he immediately headed over to the cosmetics department and began putting items in the basket. The Internet was a very helpful device, he'd realized, and very important for his plans. He'd spent quite a bit of time studying the cost and variety of mascara, face creams, lipsticks and eyeliners, and he put that research to good use now. Once he started school, classmates or – hell – even newfound friends might be close enough to notice that sort of thing, and he needed to make sure they stood up to the critical eye of a woman.

His persona, after all, had to be impeccable, or he'd be caught.

With his items selected, he headed to the checkout counter, where a plump woman stood smiling, her face pleasant, but lost behind acne. Paying with cash and thanking her, Jack collected his bag and returned to the car.

His next goal was the school itself, but first he'd stopped by the house. When he first arrived in Tulsa, he'd sought out a modest home with a few specific requirements. It had to have a basement and some privacy, but not enough to cause suspicion. He didn't want anyone wondering why a man like him would want to live too far from the ease of the city. He ended up buying a ranch style home just outside the city in a connecting town called Catoosa. His house sat on two acres with a private driveway and a basement, which had been separated into two rooms. He hadn't required the basement design, but he sure had been pleased to discover it. It appeared the prior owner had designed the rooms for specific purposes – one a family room and the other for canning fruits and vegetables.

He had much different plans, of course, but the layout was perfect.

Turning into the driveway, Jack slowly pulled the SUV into the garage. As the door closed behind him, he got out of the 'new' car and walked through the sparsely decorated garage, absent of the normal tools a man would have displayed in the space. The only masculine things here were the paint cans and brushes in the corner, under the built-in workbench. There was also a shovel and some gardening gloves in the corner. It was all quite intentional to not have much in the garage; he did not want to seem overly manly to any potential visitors. That was necessary to support his new image and the overall plan.

Entering the house through the door just off the kitchen, he headed left past the living room and guest bedroom, entering the master bedroom. From there he continued on into the bathroom. The area had his and her sinks; he smiled at that. They would not likely live in this home together for very long, but knowing that they would be back together soon made a sense of warmth begin to burn in his stomach.

Setting the bag on the counter in front of the mirror, he began peeling open the packaging, tossing the torn cardboard in the pink waste can against the wall. Moving back into the bedroom he opened the door to the double mirrored closet, and stood briefly admiring the contents. It wasn't so much that he actually appreciated the items neatly organized on the hangers inside. More that he appreciated the cleverness of his plan. This was real, and it was all beginning today.

Selecting a light pink tank top and a white button-up dress shirt, he closed the closet door and laid the clothes out on the bed. Now he removed the polo shirt he was wearing, pulled on the tank, and slid his arms into the dress shirt. Returning to the mirror, he admired the look as he fastened the shirt. The jeans were tight fitting and allowed just enough masculinity to make him look attractive rather than ridiculous. Considering his shoes, he opened the door again and took out a pair of Andrew Dyker wing tips in gray suede. He'd picked them up on Melrose before leaving California, along with most of the clothing inside the closet; he thought today would be the perfect time to try them out. Sitting on the edge of the bed he pulled on the shoes admiring the fit. He stood to slip on a gray belt then took in the whole ensemble, smiling. Perfect.

Back in the bathroom, he applied some gel to his hair, spiking it up on top. Next he applied a single fine line of eyeliner on each eye. He hand was steady, his mind completely focused on completing the task. A thin layer of lip gloss completed the look he was striving to achieve. The subtle change was perfect for where he was going today. The other makeup items would be for a more dramatic effect if needed.

He stood back and stared at himself in the mirror. Was it convincing? Realistic?

Yes, he decided. He looked at the rest of the items on the counter and then scooped them into his vanity drawer, arranging them in straight lines. Then he grabbed up his keys from the counter and retraced his steps through the house, glancing at the clock on the wall and noting that it was only two o'clock.

Perfect, he would be at the school before three o'clock.

Returning to the garage he climbed into the SUV. Pulling out of the garage and heading back down the driveway, he glanced in the mirror instinctively, verifying that the garage door had closed. A moment later he was turning the SUV back out to the highway. Passing the Hard Rock Casino, he noticed the neon sign indicated that Diana Ross would be playing there soon. This made him wonder for a moment what had happened to her, not having heard anything of her in years. In fact, he'd nearly forgotten that she existed. Shrugging to himself, he returned his focus back to the road.

He followed the road to the split at highways 412 and 44, listening to Pink piping through the speakers and watching for the Broken Arrow Expressway. From there Jack followed the highway past Clary Sage Cosmetology School getting off at Sheridan and looping to the right to pull into the parking lot.

Show time, he thought, taking a quick, approving glance in the mirror. As he got out of the vehicle and locked it, he inserted a slight sway to his gait. He exaggerated the sway as he walked across the parking lot, the excitement building inside of him. It wouldn't be long now.

In front of him, the school was polished and bright, with lots of windows and doors. He walked in and immediately gave his million dollar smile, bright teeth flashing at the two girls behind the counter. Glancing up, they both immediately returned his smile, though theirs seemed genuine.

"Hi there, welcome to Clary Sage. How may we help you today?" a blonde with short cropped hair the tips painted a light red, said, glancing at the girl next to her.

Jack took in both girls without allowing them to notice even the slightest display of male to female interest. The fact was that his interest in them was only how they could help him. That made the pretense he was presenting much easier to be convincing.

"I'm interested in applying for classes for mani and pedis," Jack replied with a slight bat of his eyes, giving the first hint as to why a strapping, handsome man such as himself would ever want to take those classes.

"Oh, of course," the blonde replied, seeming to suddenly understand. "My name is Mandy, and I can help you with all of the details, including any financial aid needs you might have." She reached out and handed him a brochure, and continued, "I'd love to give you a personal tour and answer any questions."

"Mandy, that would be wonderful," Jack replied, laying on just the right amount of excitement.

"Fantastic." Mandy smiled and held out her hand. "What is your name?"

"It's Thomas. Thomas Jennings," he lied, returning her handshake with a weak grip. Coming around the counter, Mandy began explaining the layout of the school, taking him through the expansive lobby the various rooms, explaining all of the training programs offered at the school. She was thorough, covering the school's accreditation and attendance policy, and even describing the final testing requirements upon course completion. Then, leading Jack into a small room that looked more like an office, she offered him a seat and asked if he would like a bottled water or herbal tea.

Accepting an herbal tea, he settled into the chair.

Mandy left for a moment then returned with the tea, handing the cup to Jack. She settled into the chair opposite him and put a file folder on the table between them. She opened it and started going through each of the papers inside. There was a cover letter welcoming the potential student to Clary Sage, the school mission statement, an enrollment application, and financial aid documentation.

"Now the hard part – money. How do you think you'll be paying for the program? We do offer financial aid, which can fund all or part of the program. Once school is over and you're working, earning an income, you can set up a repayment program at a very low interest rate. Almost all of our students get at least some of their school covered through financial aid. It's a very simple process, and we offer assistance in filling out the paperwork."

Jack clearly did not need the money, but he also did not want to stand out. He needed to fit the role of the person he was presenting himself as. He listened intently as Mandy explained options to him.

Mandy stopped and smiled, allowing Jack, aka Thomas, to take it all in. Not seeing any confusion on his face, she continued on. "We also have grants that can help cover some parts of the program completely. I really like to encourage all students to apply for these, as it's a great way to get a good portion of the program taken care of without any repayment required."

Jack let his eyes drift over all of the forms. Looking up, he put on what he hoped was his best glow. "I'm so excited. Once I fill out the application, how long before I can get started?"

Mandy returned his excited gaze, "Well, your timing is very good. We happen to have a new class starting the week after next, and it still has two openings in it. I should tell you, though, that it's an accelerated program, for full-time students only, and completes in just over eight weeks. If we had your application back no later than tomorrow afternoon, we could get you started in that class. Or we have a part-time class that starts in four weeks."

Mandy seemed just as excited as he was, she was apparently pleased that he was ready to enroll immediately. He assumed class vacancy was frowned on and that her boss would be thrilled that she had enrolled another new student.

"Were you considering full time or part time?"

"Oh, I want full time for sure, and I think I could have my application back tomorrow to be sure I get it in on time. Will you be here tomorrow morning?" Jack was struggling to contain his real excitement. He truly thought he would have to wait much longer to get into a program. Being able to complete this part of the process in such a short period of time was even better than he had imagined. This was setting the timeline for the entire plan, and he could not have been more pleased. *Soon, he thought. Soon.*

She blushed, flattered at the fact that he'd asked. He was adorable, and though she was certain he was not interested in her in *that* way she still could hardly take her eyes off of his. "Yes, I'll be in starting at nine o'clock. If you bring this back to me, I'll make sure we get you started, Thomas. You're going to love our school. The program goes quickly, and the instructor, Melody, is excellent. You'll love her!"

"Okay, fabulous," Jack beamed. "I'll be here first thing, then, just to be sure it all gets processed on time." He jumped up, giving Mandy a quick hug. "Girl, you have no idea how excited I am."

Mandy returned his pats on the back, clearly comfortable with him. Walking Jack back through the lobby, she waved her fingers at him as he bounced out the door, and then said to her co-worker who had just come back into the room, "Why do all the super cute guys have to be gay?"

When he got back to his SUV and closed the door behind him, Jack let out a sigh. *Well, that went well,* he thought as he tossed the folder on the seat next to him. His stomach was telling him he had missed lunch. Later there would be some unfinished business with Benz. Benz was someone that knew him as Jack and that was not acceptable. Besides, the darkness was starting to rage within, and he needed something to tamp it down, so he could keep his focus.

Replaying the meeting with Mandy in his mind, he thought it important that he apply for some sort of funding. Having credit run on his new identity wasn't his favorite idea, but she did say that almost all the students did it. He didn't want to stand out in any way. He certainly didn't want to march in there and act like he could pay for the whole thing himself. This definitely didn't go with his new persona. Sighing at that, he moved on to thinking about where he wanted to eat.

Chapter Four

Max and Agent Wells had spent several hours going through the six case files, working diligently with all the victim crime scene photos lining the table between them. They'd discussed each victim, where they were last seen, financial records, and family information. Finally, deciding that it was time to grab a bite, they both stood, stretching their legs and backs. Max tossed the Styrofoam cups that had held their numerous refills of the burnt station house coffee in the trash, "I know a great place to grab lunch," she said as she turned to face Agent Wells.

"I'd like to see the first victim's house and the dump site," he said as they walked out the doors and down the steps. Pulling keys from his pocket, he dangled them at the detective. "Looks like I'll be driving."

She smirked. "Of course, while my ride could hold you, I'm not sure you could hang on tight enough. Besides the Federal Government has deep pockets and they seldom share," Max smirked, pushing a rogue strand of wavy hair behind her ear. "We can go visit the dump site on the way to the first victim's house, AFTER we eat." Leaving the lot, Max smiled, knowing she could have checked out a police cruiser. The fact that she didn't even offer made her feel like she'd pulled one over on Agent Wells, and for some reason that made her happy. Though she had no idea why, she wasn't going to investigate it any further. For the moment, being happy about it was enough.

Leading him out towards Venice Beach, she began to recap what they knew. Six bodies – two males, four females, two black, four white. Was this meaningful? Doubtful, she thought, but it was still something they had noted together. There was no sexual assault on any of the victims and no appearance of sexual motivation or failed rape attempt. So whoever killed them wasn't doing it for sexual satisfaction. The victims were from various social areas, all seeming to have been grabbed from random locations and from what they could gather from the witnesses – those last seen with the victims – there hadn't been any trophies taken. All personal items were left with the victims.

From there, it was a matter of detail. Each victim had been stripped of all their clothes, cut from just below the throat to the

21

pelvis, and internally explored. They were cleaned excessively with bleach before they were dumped, this final act wiping out any possible evidence. The clothes had been deposited into the grave with each body. Nothing appeared to have been kept.

Max pointed Wells toward a diner near the Santa Monica pier, and they circled the block once before finding a place to park the rental car. As they walked the half block to the diner, Max could feel Wells watching her. She knew he was checking her out. For a moment she wondered what he was thinking about the physical attributes of his newfound colleague. She knew she had Hollywood looks, yet she seldom thought about it. She suspected that he was wondering how she'd ended up chasing killers, that always seemed to be the first question people wanted to know the answer to.

As they entered the diner, a few heads turning briefly in their direction. After assessing the attractive pair focus returned to their dining mates, newspapers, phones, or food. After asking for a table for two, Max followed a young woman to a booth at the back of the room. The diner was what you might expect – walls covered with photos of movie stars personally autographed in thanks to the place for great food or service. The pair took their seats and accepted the menus offered by the hostess.

Max was absorbed in the menu for a moment, then tossed it down and blurted out, "So, Wells, what's your story?"

Taking his time, using the menu as a reason to delay the response, the agent tried to decide whether he wanted to play cat and mouse with detective Maxine Nichols or not. He found her intriguing and did not want to put her on the defense. Before he could decide to play it cool with her, better to gain her trust than toy with her just because of her good looks, the server appeared at the side of the table - an unsuspecting rescue from having to provide a response for now.

"What can I get the two of you to drink today?" she asked.

Wells nodded indicating to Max to answer first, and she turned to the waitress. "I'll have a Diet Coke," she answered, distracted briefly by the pierced eyelid on the pretty server. *What a shame,* she thought, wondering why beautiful young women felt compelled to put pins through their faces.

"I'll have an iced tea," Wells said, looking at the girl. "And I think we're ready to order." He didn't want to waste time. He wanted to get to the victim's home. With little time to work this case he needed to come up with a profile and fast.

"Go right ahead, then. I can take your order now."

"Okay," Max started, ordering a veggie burger and fries. Wells followed suit.

Once the food arrived, Max pushed up the sleeves of her long-sleeved, police-issued LAPD shirt and reached for the ketchup sitting at the edge of the table next to the salt and pepper. Applying an ample portion of ketchup to the burger and on her plate next to her fries, she looked over at Wells and toasted him, raising her sandwich in cheers towards him.

"*Bon appétit!*" she said, smiling.

Wells added some ketchup to his plate as well and nodded back in appreciation of the gesture. Catching the scent of seasoning, he suddenly realized how hungry he really was, and took a nice-sized bite out of the burger. He looked across the table at Max and noted that she was deep in thought. He took the opportunity to observe her noticing how her full lips seemed to kiss off every bite of fry. Not wanting to stare, he looked back down at his meal, and began eating as he realized just how stunning she really was.

Max knew he had been watching her. After chewing through three or four bites of her veggie burger, she dropped the sandwich back onto her plate and took a sip of her Diet Coke. "So?" she asked with a lopsided grin.

"So?"

"So, I believe I asked you, what's your story?"

"Oh, *that* so."

"Do you always avoid questions like this?" Her green eyes sparkled across the table mischievously.

"No, not usually, you seem to be bringing that out in me," he offered, teasing her. "I guess there's not a lot to say. My father was a cop, and you probably can guess the rest from there. Runs in the genes, I suppose. Grew up listening to his stories about chasing the bad guys and it seemed like the right thing to do. I graduated high school, went to college and studied forensics, then applied to the FBI academy right after graduation. Completed training at the academy and the natural place for me, given the forensics training was profiling. I love and hate it, if you know what I mean. How 'bout you? What's your story?" He leaned back, feeling pretty good that he'd just lobbed a question right back at her.

Max studied him for a few seconds, thinking. She *did* know what he meant, probably all too well. "Me? Not much to tell either, probably more of a rebellious story than following in the family footsteps. No cops on my side. Actually doctors, both parents. So, when I told them I'd applied to the police academy, they were, well, not so happy. I think they pictured me in children's medicine or something, and that's so far from who or what I wanted, it's like they never really knew me."

Biting into another fry, chewing slowly and swallowing, she raised her gaze up to his blue eyes. "Married, kids?" She had already noticed that he wasn't sporting a wedding ring, though it didn't hurt to ask. She'd seen him watching her on a few occasions, though this had happened a lot throughout her life, and with most men she seldom gave it much thought. This man was making her somehow feel more aware.

"No, not me. You?"

"Ha, no way, not ready for anything like that. Why haven't you? You seem like the marrying kind to me."

"Guess I haven't met the right woman. I know that sounds cliché, but it's true. Oh, and the job makes it rough – travel, crazy hours, at the drop of a dime, I'm off to somewhere else for another horrible crime. Not a lot of women want to share those end-of-day stories, much less have them wrapped around their children." He paused for a moment, as if wondering if what he just said was true.

"Your dad did it though, right? You turned out okay."

"He did, it's true, but the marriage didn't survive it. Parents divorced when I was twelve, had every other weekend with the old man."

"So it made you cautious about marriage. Natural, I guess," she acknowledged, finishing the last bite of her sandwich and sucking a drop of ketchup off her right index finger. Taking a napkin from the dispenser, she delicately wiped her hands and wiped a crumb from her lips. Then, taking another long draw on what remained of her Diet Coke; she pulled out some bills from her back pocket and plopped them down on the table. "It's on me. You ready to roll? Crime scene is waitin'."

Wells enjoyed watching Max clean herself up, as he sucked down the last of his tea. He thanked her for lunch and followed her out the door.

Walking back out into the sunshine, the pair were caught by the smell of salty air and the cool ocean breeze. They headed back up the block to where they'd parked the car and climbed in, with Max telling Wells to head down the street and then pull out onto the Coast Highway. The day was gorgeous, and people were enjoying the beach in a variety of ways – surfing, beach volleyball, jogging, and walks on the sand. Seagulls swayed over their heads in unison with a colorful kite here and there. Traffic was typical – stop and go at each of the lights, cars whipping in and out of the driveways of the homes crammed along the road, purchased by people eager to have front-row seats to the ocean view. Wells took in all of these observations waiting for the next set of instructions from Max who rode next to him seemingly doing the same.

They drove in silence for a while, and then Max directed him to turn right onto Mulholland Drive.

Here the road became more interesting, curving upward with sharp twists and turns. Wells imagined it would be quite a fun drive in the appropriate sports car. He forced the thoughts of the two of them driving along with the top down enjoying the day and was grateful when Max interrupted him five minutes into the climb up the mountain side, pointing through the windshield.

"Just ahead on the right is Camp Shalom. It's a retreat where organizations can have team-building challenges or have weeklong camping events – everything from horseback riding to ropes courses. Past that about a mile there is a big tree on the left. We'll pull off there and then hike in about 100 yards."

Wells nodded, noting the iron name over the entrance as they passed the camp. The area was devoid of traffic. There were rock cliffs and undergrowth all around, but there was no sign of human life or homes – no mailboxes or driveways indicating any homes sitting away from the road. It was the perfect place to leave bodies. This revelation made his stomach churn a little, the burger feeling heavy now. No matter how many crimes scenes he covered, he always had the same feeling.

25

"Pull over here," Max said, directing him to the tree and the small turnout on the opposite side of the road.

Signaling to the left and feeling a little silly about it, since there was no one on either side of the road to acknowledge the indicator, he pulled across the yellow lines and rested the car under the tree. Putting the car in park, he released his safety belt and pulled on the car handle. Max was already outside the vehicle and heading into the underbrush, so he followed quickly behind her. He certainly didn't want to get left behind up here.

"He dumped them out here, just down this incline and in the cluster of trees. No reason for anyone to ever find them, I suppose, if it wasn't for a couple of kids sneaking out from the camp to fool around. They stumbled on the site and about shit themselves. It was just after midnight when I got the call. Crime team unearthed all six of the bodies before dawn – shallow graves just deep enough to keep most of the animals away. Rain had unearthed a hand and the kid, male, tripped over it, fell down, flipped on the flashlight to see what the hell had grabbed him, and got the surprise of his life." Max paused for a moment as she took a glance at Wells, giving him a moment to take in his surroundings. Their eyes met and he nodded for her to continue. "I had hoped that we would get a break, given the number of bodies and the fact that they were all intact, but there was no DNA on any of them. They'd been fully cleaned up, clothes lying beside them in the grave. They were all still wearing their jewelry. One of them, victim number three, Jason Sampson, still had on his Rolex. The bleach had ruined it, of course, so we have a pretty solid time of death on him. It's pretty clear that robbery isn't the motive."

As she talked, Max continued to hike into the brush, dodging the brambles careful not to flip the branches back into Wells' face as she went. Suddenly, though, she came to a halt.

"Right here," she said, sweeping her arm in a semi-circle. "Laid out in a row, neatly placed very close to each other."

"Any signs of remorse when you found them? Hesitation marks in the cuts?" Wells asked. He already knew the answer but felt he had to ask. If he'd overlooked something in the photos, this was the time to know about it.

She shook her head. "None, they were neat. Nothing to indicate that he'd loved them or had regrets," Max said knowing he would understand.

Wells nodded, looking around and going over the facts in his head. If the un-sub had felt bad about what he did, the victims would have been covered in blankets, or lying with their arms crossed over the chests, or had their eyelids closed. There would have been something that showed the killer had cared about their modesty or feelings.

"We know he spent some time with each of them, but there was no sign of sexual assault on any of them. This guy is pissed, inflicting a tremendous amount of pain, but I can't figure out what he's so angry about."

Wells was already heading to the car. "Okay, let's move on to the first victim's grab point and home. Then I want to drive by each of the others. In the order they happened." Wells hoped something about these facts would help confirm his preliminary thoughts and needed to be sure he had not missed anything in the case photos.

Joining him on the climb back out of the brush, Max briefly paused when she reached the car. She took one final glance around always hoping something here would speak to her. Opening the passenger car door she climbed in and buckled up. "Head on up Mulholland. First victim, Kelly Tompkins, lived in Calabasas. We'll go by her home. Then I'll show you the last place she was seen, which is where we believe he grabbed her."

Wells followed the curves of the road, feeling the engine pull a bit as they climbed higher before starting the drop back down into the valley. He'd heard of the fires up in these areas, and took in the thickness of the dry underbrush. That kind of stuff would no doubt fuel a fire very quickly, he thought. That led him to the next logical point, and he wondered if they would have found the bodies at all if there'd been a fire before the discovery.

Maybe that was the un-sub's hope. No bodies, less chance of being caught.

After considering the possibility for a second, though, he discounted it as too unpredictable. More likely, the un-sub didn't expect anyone to stumble into the brush on the hillside for any reason and felt safe placing the bodies there. They were never intended to be discovered. Still, though, it made it seem like the un-sub had some knowledge of the place. He filed that thought away and turned his attention back to the road in front of him.

With Max instructing, Wells wound the rental through a neighborhood until she asked him to pull over. He saw a large two-story home, adorned with a cactus garden wrapping around the front porch and up the side of the driveway, which led to a two-car garage. He guessed it to be about 3,000 square feet and imagined that the price tag for that kind of place in California was probably above a half a million dollars. She'd been well off, though he wasn't sure that had anything to do with her death.

On the house, the now-sagging crime scene tape was still attached to the front door. Obviously, no one was staying here at the moment. He remembered that the victim was married with two children. Her husband was an executive at some firm in Los Angeles and had been in Dallas on a business trip during the disappearance. His alibi was good, and he had been eliminated as a suspect.

Wells heard a dog barking next door and quickly determined that this was definitely *not* the grab site. The homes were too close together and too close to the street. There were dogs barking and children playing, and this particular house was too far down the road with signs indicating a security system to be a good spot. The un-sub couldn't have snagged her without someone seeing it happen. And according to the file, there hadn't been any sign of break-in or any reason to believe the un-sub had ever been in the home.

He continued past the home. There was no need to stop or go inside – he already knew there was nothing to see.

"Okay, next stop, Starbucks," Max said with a big smile, showing off her perfectly straight, white teeth. "Coffee sounds good, and we believe that's the grab spot. Kill two birds with one stone, eh?"

Wells returned the smile. Considering the types of detectives he'd worked with before, he was glad to find Max as casual as she was. A guy could definitely get a rougher deal. Wells navigated the rental onto Ventura Highway and followed her directions once again, spotting the familiar Starbucks logo up on the left in a strip mall next to the Albertson's grocery store. Going back over the case file in his head, he remembered that Kelly had last been seen at about 10 am at this location. He pulled up in front of the Starbuck's; in much the same way Kelly might have done the day she went missing. The parking lot was expansive and empty at this time of day – few vehicles and fewer potential witnesses.

Max was once again out of the car nearly before it could stop. Wells followed, and they headed into the coffee shop, where they were greeted by the barista.

The young man behind the counter was most likely a college student, based on his age and hairstyle. Max ordered a tall vanilla latte and turned to Wells with inquiring eyes, asking silently what he wanted to drink.

"Tall Pike, please," he said, slowly turning his gaze to the area around him. It was a typical Starbuck's, complete with coffees, cups, and pastries for purchase. The tables were aligned perfectly for the student or executive to drop in and log onto the wireless service. So what was so special about this place that their un-sub had decided to nab his first victim here?

Handing the kid a credit card, Wells flashed his badge and asked, "On a typical week day, how many people come through here around 10 am?" He'd already seen that there was only one person in the coffee shop now, a kid hammering away at a laptop in the farthest corner from the door.

"It depends," the barista answered, a little taken back by the credentials flashed in front of him. "But by then, most people have come through. It can be pretty quiet at that time, maybe one or two people in here at a time. The morning rush really dies off after nine o'clock," he finished, handing the Pike to Wells and turning to finish up the latte. Putting the lid on the cup and adding the cup sleeve he asked, "Do you need your receipt?"

"Yes, thanks. Oh, and one more thing, do you usually work the morning shift?" Wells added.

"I do, every day except for Friday and Saturday."

Wells knew it was unlikely that the un-sub as skilled as the one they were searching for would make simple mistakes, but he needed to see if anyone stood out. "Have you ever seen someone in here that was different, didn't fit in or stood out in some way?"

"This is about that woman, right?" The kid waited for a response, and when Wells didn't answer, rushed on. "Lots of people stand out, but mostly the students. You know crazy hair, clothes, and piercings. Everyone else that comes in usually wear business clothes. No one ever did anything that made me like freak out or anything. But I've already told the cops all that."

Taking the receipt, Wells thanked him and picked up his coffee. Max turned with him from the counter, but then suddenly swung back around to the kid.

"Is there anyone who always came in here then suddenly stopped?"

The kid thought for a second, then shook his head. "Not that I can think of."

Max thanked him and carrying her Latte in her right hand proceeded back out to the car. It was now four o'clock and the sun was starting to fade. Wells didn't expect to get much from this interview, but he was still disappointed.

"Next we head to Encino. Vic number two, Danny Alonzo, was snagged from outside his apartment. Least that's what we think. It was late at night, and he was returning from his night job. No one saw or heard anything. He left his job and dropped a co-worker off at his apartment before arriving home. We know he made it, because his car was in the drive, keys still in the ignition."

From there, the process was the same with each of the following stops – Max leading Wells through the order of events; showing him each of the locations where the victims had lived or were last seen. They returned to the LAPD building just after 8 pm, stepping out of the car and heading toward the building. Wells stretched his long legs and followed Max up the steps. It was dark now, and the night air was crisp with the ocean's cool edge that can only be felt in Southern California. In the distance, a siren rang out just as the doors to the building snapped shut, locking out the sound and the night air.

"What's next?" Max asked, heading for the coffee pot on the table at the back of the office.

"I'd like to take the files with me this evening, if that's okay. With any luck, I'll have a profile for you in the morning." Wells studied Max, wondering if she was going to deny him access to the files. He didn't know why she would, but people got funny ideas in their heads, becoming territorial especially when the FBI came in on a case.

Max regarded him for a minute, and then nodded, conceding that he could have the files overnight. "What time do you want to meet back up in the morning?" she asked.

Wells smiled, grateful for the time with the files to gather his thoughts and the idea that she trusted him enough to allow it, "Eight o'clock work for you?"

"Yep. Well, I guess that's it for tonight, then."

"It is, but tomorrow we'll have some direction. Remember, this is my specialty." He grinned, picked up the files, and then looked at Max. "You need a ride home or anything? It's pretty cool out there tonight, and you rode in on your bike."

Max tossed her hair back and laughed. "I ride that bike in every day, unless it is raining really hard. Thanks for the offer, but I'll be fine." Grabbing up her jacket and helmet, she tossed back the last of the cup of coffee she'd poured, crinkling her nose at the taste. "Eight o'clock sharp, then."

"Yep," he said. They turned and walked silently out into the night, each heading to their respective modes of transportation. Wells watched as Max headed to her motorcycle and a twinge of concern began to mount for her. As the primary investigator for a serial killer case and a beautiful young woman, his chest pulled just a bit at the idea that the killer might target her as a victim.

Leaving the parking lot he followed the directions to his hotel and pulled into the Hilton Garden Inn parking lot where he had reservations. He hadn't checked in yet. It had been too early – he'd gone right to the police department to talk to them. Popping the trunk, he collected his overnight and laptop bags, looping the laptop bag strap over the roller bag he pulled it through the parking lot into the hotel lobby. He'd traveled a lot, lately, and this was becoming routine.

With the case and the events of the day still rolling through his mind he was a bit distracted when he was instantly greeted by the woman behind the counter.

"Good evening sir, do you have a reservation?" she asked, looking up over the reading glasses sitting on the tip of her nose, her wispy grey hair swept back in a bun.

He pulled his thoughts out of the memories of the burial site and smiled, "Yes I do, last name is Wells," he replied handing her his driver's license and FBI-issued credit card.

She looked at the computer and clicked a couple buttons. "I see your reservation here, Mr. Wells. Staying for two nights?"

"That's correct."

After typing in the computer for a few moments, she said, "Okay, you're all set," and slid the room keys to him in an envelope. "You're on the third floor, and here are two complimentary bottles of water for you to enjoy during your stay. Breakfast is served from 6:00 am to 10:00 am right over there in the Americana Grille."

Wells thanked her, tucked the water bottles into the pocket of his bag, and headed left of the reception area to the elevators, pushing the up arrow. Riding the elevator up to the third floor, he exited and was guided by the sign posted on the wall indicating that room 311 was to the right. He slid the room key into the key guide, a green light flashed identifying his key, the door clicked, and then he was in. Looking around the room he noted it was the same as every other hotel room he had stayed in recently.

Dropping his laptop bag onto the bed, he reached to flip on the light. He would only be in town for two days, but he quickly unpacked the items from his overnight bag, filling the closet with his things. As he entered the bathroom to lay out his toiletries he washed his hands, leaning down to rinse his face to wake himself up for the long night of reading.

And it was going to be a long night. He needed to go over every file again, to ensure that the profile was accurate. He couldn't afford to overlook any details. Having an accurate profile could be the difference between a closed case and a cold case, for Detective Max Nichols and the city of Los Angeles. This case was already starting to turn cold, as the killer's pattern looked like it had changed. The killing spree had been fast, with numerous murders in a very short span of time, and now it appeared to have suddenly stopped. Why? He hadn't put his finger on it yet, but he had a theory. With any luck, his work tonight would confirm his suspicions.

Chapter Five

After leaving the beauty college, Jack returned to his home to complete the application. He knew it was critical that he get the details correct. He wanted to make sure that there were no mistakes. Leading this new life included remembering certain aspects like a new social security number. He needed to keep it all straight. The name was the easiest part – he'd gotten to pick that – but the rest had to be provided, and newly memorized, while attempting to forget the ones he'd used for the previous thirty-five years of his life.

At six o'clock, he settled down at the kitchen table and began the tedious process of completing the paperwork. An hour later he realized that he was hungry. Jack understood the importance of keeping his strength and nutrition up. For a moment he remembered a time not very long ago, in a land with the sea nearby where none of that mattered. For a time he allowed himself to lose focus on such matters. More recently, of course, he'd found a new purpose in life. Remaining fit was important to him again. He needed to be strong and healthy to ensure he was worthy of his new life. Smiling, he rose and began to prepare a chicken breast, applying rosemary, salt, and lemon, and placing it in the oven to cook.

Next he began working on a salad. As he was cutting the lettuce into small pieces, the glint from the edge of the knife caught his eye. He paused, his mind flitting to Benz. Recognizing the feeling in his stomach, he told himself to push down the desire that had plagued him his whole life. It was too soon. The funds for his car hadn't yet been transferred, and until they were, he couldn't take care of the car salesman.

Thinking for a moment about what it would be like when he *could* take care of Benz, and the feeling he got from those thoughts, made him grow warm on the inside. Struggling to return his focus to the preparation of his meal, he decided a glass of wine would complement the food nicely. Reaching into the wine rack next to the pantry, he retrieved a wine glass from the cupboard and poured a glass of Pinot Noir. The red of the wine returned his thoughts to Benz and the others.

"You don't need to. There are other ways," he heard a small voice saying.

"I know," he said out loud, without even realizing. Then the light sound of the chicken sizzling in the oven forced his thoughts back to cooking.

After finishing his meal and straightening the kitchen, Jack settled back at the table with his second glass of wine and began studying the papers, double checking everything he'd written, and comparing each number and date to the driver's license he carried with the name Thomas Jennings on it. Pleased that the forms were accurate, he returned the documents to the folder Mandy had given him and set it on the counter next to his car keys. He'd be ready to leave in the morning, to meet her and complete the process.

Heading back to the master bedroom, Jack caught a glimpse of himself in the mirror, still wearing the pink tank top and white dress shirt. He thought he looked ridiculous and believable all at once. The clothes themselves made him want a shower, and he began stripping out of them. Tomorrow would be a big day. There were things he needed to prepare, and it would take some time to get everything in order before he started. He needed supplies, and the preparation had to be perfect.

Most importantly, he had to stay safe. If he got caught, they'd never be together again.

The shower felt good on his skin. It soothed him and made him feel cleansed of the person he was going to become. The person he had been living as most of the day. Thomas. Not that he had any issues with homosexual men. In fact, he could really care less about any of that. He believed in science, and how people lived their lives had never impacted him. He only cared what people would think of *him*. And Thomas would make people think of him exactly the way he needed them to.

This new persona would most certainly divert attention away from any questions. And that was the important part.

Before settling down into his bed to flip mindlessly through whatever was on the news, he decided that he would go down into the basement and survey the area again. Pulling on a T-shirt and the jeans he'd worn earlier, he left the bedroom and walked back through the house. Opening the basement door, he thought of the way he would conceal the entrance. It would be simple to confuse people about what was here. Basements were fairly rare in Oklahoma, so no one would think there was a basement at all, if he built the cover out properly. By the time anyone figured it out, he would be gone, and he would have his life returned to him.

When he opened the door, the basement felt dank, cool even. He figured that was good, and smiled slightly. Using a fictitious name, he had shipped some things to the house and those items were stored in the basement. Nearly everything was in his new identity now, allowing the trail from his past life to essentially stop in California.

In fact, he thought that finding Jack Tyler in Oklahoma and associating him with any of the things that he'd done in California would be nearly impossible. He was careful, always careful. His meticulous care forced him to plan ahead. He had most of the medical supplies he would need. He had practiced the procedure again and again. His medical background afforded him the sources he needed to secure the necessary supplies. He thought his plan would work exactly the way he envisioned. He merely needed to complete the basement and everything would be ready.

He could purchase the rest of what he needed for preparing the basement from any home improvement store. As a boy, he'd spent many summers helping his father and grandfather around the house, and those painful years had taught him many capabilities. He would use his basic carpentry skills to prepare the room for the restoration. It wouldn't take him long.

Looking around, he considered the various aspects of his plan, making sure that everything still made sense to him. The main room in the basement maintained the look of a small family room. A sofa pulled out into a bed against the wall to the right of the stairs, and a floor lamp sat next to the sofa. In the far corner was a walk-in freezer, which Jack had purchased when he first moved in. Because many Oklahoma residents had a heavy interest in hunting, it was common for people to have large freezers in their homes for storing meat. No one had asked any questions. The freezer settled tightly into the corner, measuring 6 feet high by 48 inches wide and 6 feet deep. He remembered special ordering it from Sears, and how narrowly it had made it through the double-door basement entry and down the steps. Despite the struggle to get it through the door and installed, it was perfect for what he intended to use it.

There were a few miscellaneous paint cans in the corner, and a small flat-screen TV mounted on the wall near the sofa. The only other furniture was a small kitchen-style table with two chairs. In the room to the left of the stairs was the utility room, which included the washer and dryer, hot water heater, and furnace. That entire section was bare of any flooring. The back room, which had been used for canning by the previous owner, was smaller. It would be perfect for lining with washable wall panels. There was already a sink in the room and plumbing out through the floor. In the middle of the room sat a canning table, previously used for preparing fruits and vegetables, approximately 6 feet long and 3 feet wide. He would have bought something similar if it wasn't already there. The table was made of stainless steel, and therefore it fit perfectly into the plan. It glistened with a shine, nearly as pristine as any operating room he'd ever used.

His mind flashed quickly through the numerous operations he had conducted, briefly reflecting on the feeling of cutting into a human body. Being a highly skilled, happily married, and successful surgeon had afforded him a good lifestyle, and it had kept the dark side at bay. But then …

"Jack? Jack, what are you doing?" He heard the voice in his head, and suddenly he was just a boy again, twelve years old and standing in the woods behind his father's home. The dead cat was still warm in his hands. The sound of her voice startled him, as he had been so focused on what he was doing, the feeling of the warm blood washing over his fingers, the knife shining in his fist.

"Hope! What are you … I'm, I'm sorry." Suddenly tears streamed down his cheeks. He felt afraid – afraid of getting caught, afraid of Hope telling his parents. But mostly he was afraid of Hope being mad at him.

"Jack, why?" Hope looked from him to the cat and back again. The look on her face showed her confusion, hers eyes big and starting to fill with tears.

"I … I …" The tears continued to flow. Jack dropped the cat and fell to his knees beside it, turning away from the cat and turning his back to Hope, not being able to stand the look on her face. He squeezed his eyes shut and the tears washed down his cheeks.

"Jack?" she said as she slowly approached him. Looking down at the cat, she turned her head from it and focused on her friend, her best friend, the boy she had known and shared every waking moment with for as long as she could remember. None of this made sense. Had he done that horrible thing to the cat? Had he found the cat this way? "Answer me, Jack. What happened?"

"Hope, go away!" he shouted at her, pulling away, turning further from her eyes, those beautiful eyes, the eyes that knew everything about him, everything, except for this.

"No, Jack, I won't go."

"Hope, go, please go. I can't, I can't do this …"

"Can't do what, Jack? I want to know what you did or why you did this. Tell me and we can fix it together." Hope held her ground, pleading with the broken and sobbing boy on the ground.

Suddenly he felt that there might be a chance. She wasn't running away. She said they could fix it together. How? Why? Could she mean it? Was it a trick? She had never tried to trick him before. Well, at least not over anything important. They were always tricking each other over silly things, but never in a mean way.

"I can't help it. It just happens to me," he stammered, stealing a glance her way.

"Jack, what do you mean it just happens? What happens?"

"I mean, I have these feelings and I can't stop them. The only thing that makes them go away is doing … is doing *that,*" he said, his eyes darting to the cat lying on the ground in a matted heap of fur and blood. The intestines were hanging out of a gaping wound in the middle of its stomach, its eyes bulging from the head.

Hope looked down at the cat and then quickly averted her eyes. "Jack, I can help you. You don't have to do this. Not if you don't want to. There has to be another way. We'll find it together, and no one will have to know."

The tears beginning to subside, then, and Jack looked quickly up at Hope's face. Her eyes caught his before he dropped them to the ground in front of him again.

"How?" he asked softly.

"I don't know yet, but we'll figure it out. Come on, Jack, let's go. We'll clean you up and then figure it out."

Getting to his feet, Jack kept his eyes on the ground in front of him. He felt weak, his hands and knees shaking, and then he felt his body shudder. Suddenly he was trembling all over, barely able to control his body. Hope kept walking beside him, saying nothing until they reached the creek. Jack struggled to pull himself together and gain control of his trembling legs.

"Wash off your hands, Jack."

Without questioning what she said, he did as she asked, watching the blood wash away from his hands, downstream with the cold spring water.

Jack looked around, realizing he was still standing in the middle of the basement. The memories had come in a flood, and were bittersweet. Hope had taught him how to control his dark side. Together, they had built a plan and stuck to it, and it had worked. It had worked for a long time, and things were perfect. Being a surgeon had helped him. Until that day. The day of the terrible accident, and now he needed to focus on gaining his life back. Doing just that, he forced himself to look around the room one final time.

Deciding he was well prepared, he climbed back up the steps and closed the basement door behind him. Suddenly, he realized how tired he was. The memories had exhausted him, and now he could think of little more than getting to bed. Heading to the master bedroom, he stripped off his clothes, dropping them into the hamper inside the closet. Falling into bed without even turning on the TV, he fell further into a fitful sleep, his dreams filled with images that flitted through haunting faces of past victims, operating rooms, and the many successful surgeries, thankful loved ones, necessary body parts, sunny days during a happy time in California, gay men, and images of his beautiful Hope.

He woke feeling nostalgic and determined, and headed off to the shower to prepare for his day. For the next several months, maybe even up to a year, his lifestyle would make a drastic change. But he figured he'd already gone through the most difficult time. This should be easy by comparison. Reflecting on the past year, he thought that anything would seem easy. In that year, he'd gone from being a well-respected surgeon in Beverly Hills, a loving husband and father, to a widowed, angry killer. He had been forced through loss back to the tormented and broken twelve year old boy. Well not any more.

He could make the transition from that to a gay single man in a snap.

Forcing down the thoughts about how he got here, he let the shower cleanse him, shampoo and soap washing down his muscular body and into the drain. Jack allowed himself to imagine that the cleansing of his body was rinsing away the thoughts, forcing the memories back out of his mind and pushing the dark feelings away. Those feelings were starting to press down on him, making his skin nearly itch with the need he could never truly explain or deny, and he was glad to find some relief. The operating room had given him an outlet, but that was no longer part of his life, and the feelings were getting harder to control.

"Focus, Jack," he said out loud, almost startling himself. "Thomas," he restated, and smiled. His stomach growled reminding him it was time to get the day started with a healthy breakfast.

After again carefully choosing from his newly purchased wardrobe, Jack dressed and headed to the kitchen, where he whipped himself up a veggie omelet and washed it down with a Veranda Starbuck's coffee, made in the Keurig that occupied a space on the counter next to the refrigerator. Finishing up, he cleared the dishes and took a final look around ensuring the kitchen was immaculate. Returning to the bedroom, he stood observing himself in the mirror. Stunning, he thought, and collected his jacket remembering that the weather report yesterday had called for light rain. Once again, he returned back to the kitchen where he grabbed the folder with the completed application and snapped up his keys. He found himself almost chuckling at the thought of going to cosmetology school, but it was necessary, as this was how he'd meet the right kind of donors. The plan required up-close exposure to a variety of women. This program and new profession would ensure he had lots of variety.

Backing out of the garage into the daylight, he squinted. It was still early, only nine o'clock, but he wanted to get the application in to ensure he could get into the next class. He also had much to do. He wanted to get started today and needed to get the supplies for preparing the basement.

As he headed out past the Casino and read the neon sign, he noted that Tuesday was ladies night. For a brief moment, he thought this could also be a possible solution, but quickly discounted the idea, realizing that the women at the casino would never do. Gambling was often tied to smoking and drinking – behaviors that his Hope would never have indulged in.

Continuing through town, he found he was pulling into the Clary Sage parking lot with little recollection of how he'd gotten there. This made him a bit nervous, but he shrugged it off, getting out of the Toyota and heading into the lobby to find Mandy behind the counter as she'd said she would be. Her smile was immediate and genuine when she looked up and saw him approaching.

"Thomas, great to see you," she said.

"I've filled out the application, and I'm so excited. I can't wait to get started." He returned her smile, sliding the folder across the counter to her. "I think I have it all filled out correctly, including the financial aid parts."

"Well, I can look it over and call you if there are any issues, but it should be fine," she offered with confidence. "We're so excited to have you joining us here at Clary, and I know you'll love our program. Once we get your approval, I'll call to confirm your start date and time, okay?"

"Oh, girl, I know I'm going to love it here," Jack gushed, batting his eyes slightly and dropping his wrist, once again acting the role of Thomas. "If there's anything I need to do, just let me know. My cell number is on the application and that's the easiest way to reach me."

"Great, Thomas, don't worry about anything. I'll be in touch real soon," she replied, smiling.

He waved good bye and tossed a smile over his shoulder, then headed back out to his car, consciously applying just a little sway in his hips. Mandy watched him go smiling then shrugged and picked up his folder and started looking over the pages and keying them into the computer program to complete the application and enrollment process.

Jack climbed back into his car and headed down Sheridan to 41st street cutting the car up toward Home Depot, checking off the mentally prepared list of things he would need to get started. With only one week before his classes would start, he needed to get the majority of the building done on the basement quickly. When he started school, he'd be spending his time studying for his exams, and wouldn't have time to do any building. It was important that he pass his exams with flying colors, so that he could find work in his new trade quickly, without any unnecessary delays.

He also knew instinctively that he would not be able to control the dark impulses much longer. Staying focused on the end result was critical to ensuring he did not make any mistakes, there was no room for error if he was ever to have his life back.

Entering the home improvement store, he grabbed one of the flat bed carts with the vertical metal bars providing separations for large long building materials. Heading directly to the building materials aisle, pushing the flatbed along, and listening to the front wheel wobble as he walked, he began looking up and down the aisles for bath panels. Cutting through a few aisles, he finally found what he was looking for and, after thinking about the color, he chose pure white panels. He had previously measured the canning room and had determined that twelve 4x8 panels would allow him to completely cover the walls and ceiling. And make for easy cleaning. He counted out twelve and loaded them onto the cart.

He also loaded up two sheets of plywood. Next, he gathered cases of bathroom caulk and construction adhesive. He grabbed two large rolls of duct tape, some rope, a circular and jig saw, a drill, and a hammer. He couldn't decide if he would need nails, so being unsure he put a box of ten penny and a box of small finishing nails on the cart too. Heading to the paint department he selected a gallon of off white interior that would match his kitchen, a gallon of acrylic outdoor deck paint and several large rolls of plastic drop cloth. He proceeded on to the hardware department, seeking out some heavy duty concrete bolts for securing the stainless steel table to the floor. Originally, he had thought it was not really necessary, but decided, better safe than sorry.

With each item he laid on the cart, he grew more excited. By the time he was ready to check out, he was nearly unable to focus. When the clerk asked him if he'd found everything, he pulled himself out of his excitement and felt his heart rate slowing back down. He nodded to her and laid his small items out on the counter for her to scan.

Then he noticed that the clerk was looking at him a bit funny, and realized how this must look. He had to remember that he was posing now as an obviously gay man. He smiled with a hint of girlishness at her. Seeming to have her suspicions answered, she giggled a little and continued to complete the transaction, accepting his cash and providing him his change. A few moments later, he was pulling the cart up next to the SUV. He would now get the chance to try out the folding seats and use the back area. Loading in the panels which barely fit, he was forced to load them at a slant from ceiling to floor across the back. He nestled all the other items in under and around them. Next, he took the rope and opened the package, securing the panels in as they would have to ride hanging out the back about a foot for the short trip across town.

Once certain that he had everything secured properly, Jack pushed the cart to the cart return area across the parking lot. After checking his load once more, he opened the door and entered the vehicle.

Inside, he sighed, knowing that the feelings surging inside him were going to get stronger and stronger. He would have to do something soon. It had already been over a month since he'd last given in to the need, and without his medical career and Hope by his side, there was only one way to satisfy the darkness inside. It was important that he fight this as long as possible. He also realized that losing control would put everything else at risk, and that he would never allow. Better to satisfy the craving than let it get out of control.

Chapter Six

Agent Wells had studied the information in every file until the wee hours of the morning. He'd spent his time marking the individual facts about each victim, location, and the order in which the bodies were laid out at the dump site. He'd then taken all of that information and related the aspects within the different situations. There weren't many factors that stood out, really, but he had completed the process. At about 4:00 am he sat back, looking at what he had.

Then, nodding to himself in a manner of gaining his own agreement for the profile he'd developed, he gathered all the gruesome photos and case contents, and put them back into their respective folders.

Looking over towards the nightstand next to the bed, he saw that the digital clock read 4:15, and yawned, thinking he could get two hours of shut eye before heading back to meet Max and deliver the profile. She would have her hands full with this one; there was no doubt in his mind. Slipping out of his clothes and sliding in between the cool sheets, he set the alarm on his phone for 6:30 and clicked off the lamp. Sleep came quickly, but behind his eyelids were images of gaping wounds and blood, so much so, that in his dreams he imagined the coppery smell.

The fitful scenes were blurred with pictures of a motorcycle-riding seductress engaging him in passionate lovemaking. His mind was drawn between the two scenes, the murderous images seemingly pulling him back in every time he began to allow himself the freedom to be seduced.

Then the alarm went off, and Wells glanced around, trying to understand where he was. It took a moment for him to get his bearings, but then he hit the clock for a seven-minute snooze, turned flat on his stomach, and went back to dozing. When the alarm sounded again, he clicked the off switch and snapped on the light swinging his feet over the side of the bed and onto the floor. For a brief moment, he thought of all the other feet that had hit the floor on this hotel room. Immediately resisting where his mind headed with that line of thinking he stood up stretching his long, muscular legs, crossed the room and pulled out the clothes he had packed for the day. After showering, which felt amazingly refreshing, he dressed and then finished the preparation for the day with a final review of the files he had left sitting on the desk across the room. Packing everything back into his briefcase, he scanned the clock. It read 7:07. Just enough time to grab something from the complimentary breakfast. Grabbing the hotel key, car keys, shouldering his gun holster and picking up his briefcase, he exited the room and proceeded to the elevators. He could already smell the savory scent of coffee and bacon.

After enjoying the omelet the cook proudly prepared and downing three, much needed cups of coffee, Wells headed out into the morning light. The California sun was up, but there was a light chill in the air, causing him to shudder slightly as he clicked the remote to open the car and place his briefcase inside. He glanced at the palm trees that lined the parking lot and gave himself a moment to think about how nice it would be to live here. Then he pushed the thought away. He'd never been a dreamer and now certainly wasn't the time to start.

When Wells arrived at the LAPD station, he noticed that the sleek motorcycle Max had arrived on just yesterday was already sitting in the space. He wondered if she'd had as restless a night as he had, and smiled slightly at the memory of a fitful two hours of sleep that had been filled with ugly images, washed away by visions of that seductress on the motorcycle.

"Stop it," he muttered under his breath, realizing that Max was that seductress.

Inside the doors, the guard at the desk nodded his approval for Wells to go on in. Apparently, seeing him with Chief Harding and Detective Nichols yesterday had been enough to give him free rein, at least for now. Heading to where they'd spent the day working yesterday, he found Max standing at the coffee machine, and felt a slight sense of deja vu.

"Good morning," he said, walking up to her.

She jumped, spilling a bit of coffee out onto the table in front of her. "Jesus, Wells, didn't your mother tell you not to sneak up on people?" she snapped.

"Oh, sorry, I thought you heard me walking up," he apologized.

Mopping up the mess, she shot him a look. "No, I didn't, and damn it you startled me."

He watched, amused, as she cleaned up the coffee and refilled the cup. After stirring in both cream and sweetener, she stomped back to the desk where they'd spent half the day yesterday. Filling his own cup up, he followed her, noting to himself that she obviously wasn't a morning person. He set his briefcase on the table, opened it, and pulled the files out, laying them down in front of her.

She settled down into her chair, her demeanor indicating that she'd shed the frustration from the earlier coffee incident. "So how was your night?" she asked, eying the files. "Did you make any progress on our un-sub?"

"Yes, I'm ready to present you with a profile."

"Great, mind giving me a preview before we get with the chief?"

Wells looked at her and nodded in agreement at the recommendation, "Sure. After looking through the individual details on each case, it's obvious that each of the victims are random attacks. There's absolutely nothing in common with any of them, not a single connection. Their shopping, friends, texting, and phone habits are different. The obvious things we would expect to be present in terms of economic, race, gender, or social equities are all missing. The only connection is the manner in which the victims are eviscerated, and the very careful precision with which the incisions were made. The clean wound tracks were most telling to me. There was something there that I couldn't put my hands on at first, and in my initial assessment I kept feeling like I was missing something. I finally decided that I was probably wrong. I'd assumed that the clean wounds were about remorse, or possibly had been cleaned as a part of the process during the cleanup of the kill site. I had basically considered that the body was treated as just a component of the location, and therefore cleaned as a result. Since we haven't been able to see any of the actual locations where the murders took place, this is still a question, but I personally believe that the cleaning of the body is very intentional. It would seem impossible for that level of precision to happen in each case without intent. This brought me back to remorse, but the suffering each victim endured continued to leave me unsettled. I then realized that it's *more* than just intentional. Those wounds were intentionally cleaned as part of the ritual or act, not out of remorse, but out of requirement. There is an absolute need for perfection." Wells stopped as Max took in what he'd stated so far.

When she nodded, he continued. "I believe our un-sub is a white male, between thirty and forty years old. He's meticulous, and this leads me to believe that he is, or at least was, high functioning, likely a professional. Possibly in the medical industry, maybe even a doctor or vet. There's a precision to the incisions that an unskilled person wouldn't be able to execute, especially given the fact that each of the incisions were delivered perimortem, and there were no signs of sedatives or painkillers in the blood stream of our victims." He paused, swallowing at what he was about to say. Max already knew it, of course, but it didn't make it any prettier.

"The victims would have been struggling, yet the wounds are perfect. This means he's talented and enjoyed the process of killing his victims. He has no remorse and is driven to get inside the victims. There's no sexual motivation. He's an absolute narcissist, and his needs, goals, and plan are all that matter. Given the fact that no trace evidence was left at any of the scenes, he's been doing this for a while, and either has periods of inactivity, or he moves on to new hunting grounds. These victims are most certainly *not* his first kills. Even with the first victim, the wounds showed no hesitation. That doesn't happen, and with this level of skilled execution, I think he's had a lot of practice. He's strong, remains in good physical health, and is easily accepted in the mainstream. There is likely some trigger that set him off on this specific spree. Find what that is, and you'll find your guy." He paused again before continuing with a final thought. "I'm concerned, though, that your un-sub has already moved on."

Max had been sitting watching Wells as he delivered all of this information. With the last line she raised her eye brows. "Why do you believe he's moved on?"

"He was progressing, with shorter time between his kills, and now he's off his cycle. If you look at the timeline, he was getting progressively quicker and quicker. Less time was elapsing between kills. He never went backwards, taking more time between kills. But now more time has elapsed since the last two kills. To be more specific, I counted the number of days between the missing person's reports for each of our victims and the estimated time of death to gain the time between kills. He was previously escalating. I believe this means he's stopped or moved on. He could have been picked up for some other crime, but I doubt it. If he stuck to his timeline, he should have taken another victim three weeks ago. Given the fact that we discovered his dump site, I think you'll have to work off the cases you have until he kills again, and we have no idea when that might be. Nor do we know *where* that might be, or where he might seek to dispose of them. He killed successfully for quite a while without being detected. I suspect finding him again will be a challenge."

Max's disappointment showed on her face. "So we've gone cold," she said with a certain level of frustration in her tone.

"I can't say for sure, but I'm afraid that is a possibility." He hated telling her this knowing she was eager to find the un-sub, and they both knew solving a cold case was much less likely.

She thought for a moment, and then grinned. "*Or* I can go looking for people in the medical profession that recently left the area, or have suffered some major event – divorce, death, things like that. Maybe I can get a list together."

Wells watched as Max displayed a new level of energy, smiling to himself. "Shall we go tell the chief?"

Shrugging Max stood up. "May as well go get it over with. He's going to be thrilled."

Chapter Seven

Getting back to the house Jack backed the SUV into the open garage about half way and then unloaded his supplies against the far wall. The basement did not have an outside entrance which was ideal for providing cover, but not for getting supplies through the basement doors. Jack remained unworried as they had delivered the freezer and gotten it down there so he knew it could be done. He made numerous trips slowly working everything through the narrow doors and down into the basement. Looking around he took in his payload including the medical and taxidermy tanning supplies. His eyes scanned over the bottles of bleach he had been purchasing each time he went to the grocery store. He had decided to buy a bottle per week rather than buying several at one time. He now had eight of them. Perfect. Heading back upstairs he reached for a Coke Zero from inside the fridge and guzzled some of the bubbly drink down. Then he headed back to the bedroom to change into some work clothes.

Once he had on a pair of work jeans and a long-sleeved t-shirt, he headed back downstairs to start the makeover on his new surgical room. Pulling out an extension cord, a carpenter's pencil, and tape measure, he opened the jig saw box and installed the smooth-edged blade, perfect for making clean cuts through the bath paneling. Measuring the first wall and then marking the panel accordingly, he worked away at installing the panels onto the walls, fixing them into place using the adhesive. Normally, he would have trimmed off the edges with a baseboard, but he didn't want the boards overlapping anywhere. He needed to be able to hose the walls and floors down, and know for certain he hadn't missed any areas.

Hours must have passed without Jack realizing, because the sound of his stomach growling broke through the work noises. It was the first time he actually looked around, and when he did, he realized that he had most of the panels cut and fixed to the walls. There was only one more bottom panel remaining. He had worked from the ceiling down, making sure everything flowed top to bottom for easy rinsing. He still needed to apply the caulk, but decided that could wait for another day, and headed up out of the basement after admiring his handy work one last time. *Oh yes, this was going to be good*, he thought. This was the perfect place to complete his work. He felt his stomach tighten; not much longer now, and he would be reunited with Hope.

When he got upstairs, he took a look at the clock on the oven and was surprised that it said 8:33. Where had the day gone? He didn't feel like cooking a big meal, and fixed himself a pre-made salad instead, with a few raw vegetables and some cheese. He made a conscious note to remember to eat a little better tomorrow, as he needed his strength. He also needed to get some real exercise tomorrow. He liked to stay in shape, and had been letting himself slip lately. He had a lot to do over the coming months, and he wanted to be at the top of his game for Hope. He couldn't let her down. Not this time.

Tomorrow he would pick up the cashier's check for the sale of the car and deposit the funds under his new identity, so that no one could trace a relationship from his old identity to his new. Money wasn't really an issue, of course, as he had plenty of money from the sale of his home in California. Besides that, moving from California and the type of lifestyle he'd led there as a prominent surgeon, and relocating to Oklahoma meant he had a lot more money than he reasonably needed here. He'd moved the funds around over the last several weeks, cutting the connection with his previous identity. He had researched and spent a good deal of time learning how to manage accounts off shore in the Caymans. Once the car transaction was complete, Jack's identity would simply cease to exist. There would not be a single paper trail leading to him in Oklahoma. He'd made sure of that. He didn't think anyone was looking for him, but if they were, he didn't think they'd ever find him here. Dr. Jack Tyler had simply disappeared.

Finishing off his salad, he suddenly realized that he was very tired, and headed into the bathroom to shower off the adhesive smells, sawdust, and dirt. When he was done, he settled into his boxers, slid between the sheets, and clicked on the TV, flipping through channels until he found the news. He sat replaying his day with nothing really capturing his attention until they started a story about a serial rapist sexually torturing women across the city.

He was repulsed by this. What kind of man took sex from women? He could picture the man sneaking in through windows or doors, though, and he felt a stirring in his own groin. But his excitement wasn't sexual in nature. The stirring he felt came from imagining himself taking one of those women and bringing her here to be with him, feeling inside her body as the life in the organs began slipping away. But he'd never have sex with any of them. That would be cheating.

When he started paying attention again, the story had ended and the newscast had moved on to the weather. The report said it would be windy tomorrow, but nothing remarkable; no tornado warnings or anything that would disturb his plans. Before nodding off, he wondered when he would hear from Mandy about his first day of class. He hoped it was soon.

Chapter Eight

"Well, damn it," Chief Harding shouted, slamming his big fist down on his cluttered desk. "You mean to tell me that this bastard has beaten us?"

"Sir, with all due respect I think we can still get him," Max stated with more conviction than she actually felt.

"Chief Harding, I think it's worth it to apply a couple of resources to check out the medical angle. While it might be a long shot, it's still your best chance at finding this guy. I'm officially here until tomorrow, and I'd like to offer my help until I leave," Wells added.

"I don't like it at all; Nichols, but I'll give you the support of our forensics database analyst for one week. Then you're off this case and onto an active one. If Wells is right, we're wasting our time, and I can't afford to have detectives working cold cases." the chief finally answered.

Max nodded, knowing not to push the offer. One week; that meant she had to work fast. If she could uncover any leads at all against the profile Wells had provided, she might be able to get Harding to let her stay on the case. Without any leads, though, she knew for sure that this was a cold case. And if that happened, it would be moved out of her department. Max had certainly worked many cases, but for some reason this one was important to her. Usually there was so much more to go on, at least a minor trace of DNA, but with this one the killing was methodical and the burial site told Max there was something different about this case. She couldn't shake these feelings and because of them she felt compelled to see it through to an arrest.

"Don't make me regret this, Nichols," Harding boomed at her, waving his hand and dismissing the two from his office.

After leaving the office they preceded down the hall until they were out of hearing range, "Well, that went really well," Max said.

Wells found her demeanor to be more sarcastic after dealing with the chief. The man was gruff and barely gave opportunity for either of them to speak. "He's just being realistic," he stated trying to defuse the situation a bit

"I know, and that means I have to work fast."

"Well, let's get after it," Wells said, slapping his hands together. "I'm all yours for the next day. Where do we start?"

Max led Wells down the hall and onto the elevator. They went up two floors, where they found a young man, apparently rocking out to some good tunes through ear buds properly poked into each ear. As they approached, he unplugged his right ear and raised his right hand as if asking them to stop.

"Oh no you don't, Nichols," he said to Max before she'd said a word, "You're not coming up here batting those big green eyes at me and thinking I'm going to stop, drop, and roll like I always do. I've got my orders, and that's not going to work this time." He shook his head, but Max smiled.

"Aw, come on Bobby," she started. Wells watched her obvious eye batting while she continued as if she hadn't heard him. "This time it is different. This time I have the chief's support. I've got one week, and I need you to work your data magic."

"Man, here we go. Okay, what do you need?" Bobby offered, surrendering easily.

Max grinned and gave him that *don't pull my chain* look. "First we need to see a list of any medical licenses that *haven't* been renewed or were suspended in the last year, including veterinarians. Keep it to Los Angeles County to start with. We can narrow our search after we see what this pulls up. We also want to research medical professionals who've gone through a divorce or loss of an immediate family member. If we can find people who're on both lists, that narrows our search right there."

The young man bounced as he started pounding the keyboard in front of him, still bobbing to the music in his left ear. "You got it, Detective, give me a few hours. I'll let you know what I find as soon as it's available." He popped the ear bud back into his other ear, dismissing them, and went to work.

Max looked at Wells. "What do you think the list will net?"

"It may be quite long, honestly, and we'll have to really narrow it down. Look for people who live closer to the grab or dump site. If we get lucky and there's crossover to both lists, we could have something really solid to work with. Once we have that list, I can forward it over to the FBI and have the names run through our database. I'll check for any federal crimes, just to see if there's anything else we might have overlooked."

Max nodded. "Bobby said it'll take him at least an hour, want to grab lunch?" she asked, looking at her watch. She was surprised to see that it was already 12:30, but that made it a good time to grab a bite to eat.

"Sure, lead the way."

They headed back down the elevator and out to the parking lot, where Wells had parked in visitor parking near the front of the building. The sun was shining and the spring air felt nice and warm. Wells sucked in the warmth and raised his face to the sun, taking it all in, while Max watched him, enjoying the fact that he truly seemed to be soaking the air, breeze, and sunshine into his tall, muscular frame. As much as she hated to admit it, she enjoyed his company, and his story yesterday had made her want to relate to him, though it seemed they'd come up a bit differently. His hair was shining in the sun now, and the dark curls that just barely swept the nape of his neck moved softly with the breeze. She found herself wanting to wind her fingers into those curls, and felt herself blushing at the thought.

Agent Wells drove through downtown, passing City Hall as Max directed him to Engine Co No.28 – a downtown favorite of hers that offered American dishes, including a special spicy fry recipe. The ride in the car on the way over there was quiet; there was an obvious attraction in the air that neither of them could deny, though neither wanted to talk about it either. The silence was only broken by Max directing Wells on each required turn. Each took quick sideways glances at the other when they felt it safe to do so without being noticed. But neither said anything.

Once in the restaurant and seated in a comfortable booth, Wells broke the silence, "What's on your mind, Detective?"

Surprised by the directness, Max felt off of her game; she was used to being the one in control. She paused for a moment, and then decided to talk about the case first.

"I'm trying to get my head around why our un-sub would leave. It seems to me that if there's a trigger to start his killing spree, there must be a trigger to stop."

"It could be the discovery of the dump site," Wells offered.

"Maybe, but my gut says there's more to it than that. I'm sure we're missing something here, it's just a matter of figuring out what it is."

Silence wrapped around them again. The server approached, a big strapping man that looked less like a server and more like he could have been a firefighter on a real engine. After taking their orders, he disappeared, reappearing almost immediately with their drinks. Once they were alone again, Wells eyed the beautiful detective across from him and continued the conversation.

"I don't believe that's what you were actually thinking, though it *is* a good thought."

Max huffed. "Really, Mr. Smarty Pants, and when did you get to be a clairvoyant?"

"Okay, maybe not. Well, let's talk about something else then. Yesterday you told me that your parents were disappointed in your career choice. How do they feel about it now?"

Studying him closely, the detective wondered where this was leading and how much she would share with him. He was already making her feel things she hadn't felt for a long time, and she had no idea why. They'd only spent a day together, so she was chalking it up to raw physical chemistry and convincing herself that she shouldn't allow sexual attraction to get in the way of reason. That meant giving him the safe, careful answer.

"My parents are okay with it. I think they may even be a little proud, but it took a major crime to shift their thoughts."

"How so?"

"Two years ago I was on a child abduction case. After a really difficult search, we recovered the child. A child everyone thought for sure was dead." Listening intently Wells recalled his time on the flight to California. He had studied her profile and a brief case history on the plane, and knew there was more to the case than she was offering. She'd nearly died in the recovery of that child. He'd read it carefully, taking in every part of the case, fascinated that she'd given that much to the case. Of course the file hadn't said that she was female. Everything in the file had led him to believe that Detective M. Nichols was a male. He should have pulled full name and photo. He would not make that mistake on any case in the future. It was always important to know as much going into a situation as possible, and he had failed to do that this time.

"Impressive. Sounds like a great outcome."

"Yeah, we were all pretty excited. Handing that boy back to his mother was worth everything we went through trying to find him. Getting a death penalty conviction for the kidnapper was icing on the cake."

Agent Wells started to respond, but the waiter appeared with their food, setting it down in front of them, the aroma reaching up and teasing his senses. He knew it was due to lack of sleep, but he felt like he was starving. This always seemed to happen as if his body naturally knew it needed more fuel.

"Wow, this looks fantastic." He nodded to the heap of meatloaf and spicy fries on the plate in front of him, then glanced at her plate. "And so does yours," he laughed, looking at the matching plate sitting in front of her. He hadn't noticed it before, but they'd ordered the same thing.

Max gave him a flirtatious, approving smile, and before she realized it, her eyes had locked with his in a rich, blue, green reflection of mutual attraction and lust. Breaking the gaze, she looked around the restaurant. "Cool place, huh?"

Wells grinned, realizing that for just a moment he'd rattled her strong resolve. His eyes followed her gaze around the packed restaurant, where nearly every table was loaded down with a variety of city and business workers from the nearby buildings.

"Yes very cool. It is all very…," he paused slightly, hoping to draw her gaze back to him, "…interesting. Especially the people."

Looking again into his eyes, Max realized they needed to stop this one way or another. They were never going to get any work done otherwise. So in her typical fashion of absolute directness, and before she could stop her mouth, she blurted out, "Agent Wells, what's happening here?"

Wells was taken by surprise, not used to a woman addressing something so directly. He took a bite of the savory meal, buying some time to think of the appropriate answer. He matched her gaze, which hadn't wavered since she asked the question.

"I'm not sure, Detective Nichols," he said, playing on the formality in which she'd asked the question. "I can only say that I'm here on professional business, and have nearly concluded what I was sent to do, but I always enjoy the excitement of a new case and helping in the possible apprehension of a serial killer. But in this case ..." He paused, taking a drink of his iced tea. "I can also say that I'm enjoying this case for other reasons as well. I know that I'll be disappointed when I return to Washington and I find myself hoping for other opportunities to see you." Leaning back, he waited to see what she would say.

"Wells, this is ridiculous. We've known each other for barely thirty-six hours," she recanted almost chastising him as if his assessment were not mutual.

"I know that, Max. But you asked, and I can only tell you how I'm feeling and what my thoughts have been. And frankly, I can see in your face and eyes that you feel the same way."

"I ... I ... I don't know what I feel. Look, let's try to just stay focused on the case. You leave tomorrow, and we'll probably never see each other again."

"I know." Wells acknowledged that fact, his eyes dropping to his food.

They continued eating their meals in silence, both enjoying the food less now. When neither of them was able to clear their plate of food, Wells paid the bill and led her back out into the sunlight. The day was truly beautiful, and for a minute they stood on the sidewalk looking at one another. After a moment, a smile crept up on each of their faces. Max considered his comment, *"find myself hoping that I'll have other opportunities to see you."* Her stomach fluttered at those words, and she fought to not allow them to control her.

Back at the headquarters, they took the elevator back up to see what Bobby had discovered. When they arrived on the second floor, he greeted them with a smile, filled with extra-large white teeth.

"Well, my favorite and most beautiful detective returns," he tossed out, making Wells laugh out loud. "I have some interesting data for you right here on this thumb drive. Let me show you." Popping the thumb drive into the computer USB slot, he once again started hammering away at the keys of his computer. "Okay, here's the deal. There are a *lot* of doctors in Los Angeles County," he said dragging out the word lot. "I sorted the data first by active and by city. There are several tabs on the files for you to parse through and manipulate. The next tab contains all of the inactive licenses. I included the date the license expired, was suspended, or was revoked. Tab three includes some info on malpractice suits. I threw that in since it might mean something. I separated out nurses, vets, techs, and hospital workers. I did *not* include in my search janitors or housekeeping." He paused for a moment, waiting for them to get the joke, and then sighed at the silence. "Even without those, it's a very big number, but I figured with the city reference I allowed you to narrow those down if you want to focus in on certain areas."

He looked between the two of them, then continued, "Using the same list, I also included the information you wanted for recent losses of immediate family members." Finally, he handed the flash drive over. "I hope it's what you want."

"It's perfect, Bobby," Max said. Then, looking at Wells, she shrugged. "Looks like a long night ahead."

"Indeed it does, so let's get started," he quipped.

Thanking Bobby for the thumb drive, Max and Wells returned to the first floor, planning to set back up in the room they'd used the day before. As they walked through the station, a few fellow officers gave out their hoots and hollers to Max and sideways glances at Wells, as if sizing him up. Wells did not appreciate the behavior, but he noticed that Max dished it right back. He also observed that she was obviously well liked, recognizing that the teasing was only offered to those who fit in, and she clearly did. He expected that the kidnapping case she had spoken of earlier helped solidify her place on the team. She had gone to great lengths and put herself at risk to save that little boy, but she had done so in a manner that followed protocol and reduced risk for others. That part set her apart from your run of the mill detective. This woman had Hollywood beauty, sex appeal and stones. All of these attributes made it incredibly difficult to get her off his mind.

After putting on a pot of coffee, Max took the files on the drive and emailed them over to Wells so they could each work the files separately, which would allow them to work more quickly. Pulling up the first file, Max took note of the fact that there were over two thousand physicians alone. The number was daunting when she considered all the other medical professionals and veterinarians. It seemed that they'd be looking for a needle in the haystack.

A second pretty alarming finding was that the divorce rate in the medical profession was very high, with around fifty percent of the names marked as divorced, some of them twice. They would definitely have to break the data into more sub groups.

"Let's do this to start with," she suggested. "Focus on removing all the females and put them onto a separate tab. We'll only look at them if it feels like we're not getting anywhere with the males. Then break the men down to those divorced within the last year, and cross reference to see if anyone from *that* list is on the list of expired or suspended licenses. You work on the males with license issues and I'll work on the males with relationship issues. Then we can compare our files. Deal?"

Wells was scanning the data as she talked. "Deal," he said, nodding in agreement. He was already starting to parse through the data, setting up filters so that he could sort out the males versus females.

It took some time, but eventually they had the list down to a total of sixteen hundred. They filtered that by divorced and unmarried, and brought it down even further to just over a thousand. The file with males, who had suspended, revoked, or non-renewed licenses took them to just under three hundred. Now they had some data to compare.

Max got up to refill her coffee and grabbed Wells' cup as well, offering to refill his too. He looked up. It was the first time they'd paused in nearly three hours. They were now ready to really get into some data, and it was a good time to take a break.

"Thanks," he said, accepting her offer. He caught her eye briefly and felt the slightest increase in his heart rate, recognizing that familiar feeling from his dreams the night before.

She returned a moment later, setting the coffees down on the table and leaning over his shoulder to see the file he was working. He now had the data lined up to compare license numbers as the single point of reference. He decided to run a pivot table against the two fields and see if he got a count in each one, and their eyebrows went up when they saw the data showed a total of nine matches for recent divorces and licenses that were no longer valid for whatever reason. Looking through the list, they noted one was a chiropractor, and decided to drop him off the list for now.

Eight remained on the list, none of which matched up to recent family losses or malpractice suits.

Still, they decided to follow the same process for all the other medical professions, to get a complete list of people in the medical profession, who could have the skills required to commit the murders. Starting back in, they found this data even more challenging as the gender was not listed in every case. Given the profile was a male un-sub they would want to separate out the males from females. They agreed to separate out those that they could not identify in the data quickly and realized that if they needed to, they would simply have to go through it later one by one.

They were halfway through the process when Chief Harding came through the door, taking up the whole frame. "What are we learning Nichols? Any luck with data being a guide?" His gruff voice and scowl displayed his frustration, which obviously hadn't subsided since hearing the news that the killer had likely moved on.

"We're narrowing in on a few people to look at, sir. Our focus right now is on medical professionals with recent losses, malpractice suits, or other life events that might be triggers to have set him off on the spree," she answered quickly.

"And how is *that* coming along?" he barked, looking between Max and Wells.

Wells jumped in at that point. "Slow, but our goal is to have some solid leads for Detective Nichols by the end of the day."

"Good," the chief barked. "Nichols, you've got one week. Find the bastard."

Before Max could reply, the doorway was empty, the chief having moved on.

Wells noted the wrinkle on her brow and said, "Hey, it's a long shot, but we're going to give it our best."

Max looked up, leaned back, and stretched, thinking. Glancing over Wells' head, she saw that the clock on the wall showed 7:30. "Let's take a break; I need a change of scenery. Oh, and what time is your flight in the morning?"

Wells studied her for a minute. "A change of scenery, eh? Okay, how about this? Let's move this effort to my hotel." Before she could say anything, he held up his hands and offered an explanation. "Look, there's room service, plenty of room to work on these files, and we get out of here. That way we can work right up to my 8:45 am departure time."

As he was saying all of this, he was trying to convince himself that capitalizing on the extra time and the luxury of room service was all he had in mind. He finally decided that whatever else he had on his mind didn't matter, as they actually *had* to keep working. And they needed food. Convincing himself of that, he further concluded that his idea was a practical suggestion, nothing more.

Max was about to protest, but then stopped herself. "Okay, Wells, but no funny business," she said, giving him a look that said 'don't you dare,' while wagging her index finger at him.

"I promise." Wells smiled, making an X with his right index finger across his heart. "I'll drop you back by here to get your bike on the way to the airport."

Max began gathering up the files. Wells cleared away the cups and pushed the chairs against the metal table. She joined Wells as they headed towards the front door. Stepping out into the night, the air was refreshing after being in one place for the past six hours. Max felt the stiffness in her body and observed Wells stretching his back, apparently working the soreness out. As they climbed into the car, they started talking about the eight physicians on the narrowed-down list. There were two that had stood out most, as their offices or homes were in closer proximity to the dump site. One was in Woodland Hills, the other from Malibu. Either of those could have easily driven up from the freeway or Pacific Coast Highway to dump the bodies.

"You know, I think we should look at the make and model of their vehicles, as well as their family history. The un-sub will have had a vehicle that could transport a body. It's weak, but it could help narrow the search. Plus, family history may tell us something."

Wells glanced over as he continued to navigate the car towards his hotel, but agreed with the thought. "Worth a look. Why don't you call Bobby and have him run them. In fact, have him run all of them while he's at it."

Max was already dialing Bobby on her cell phone. She spoke into the phone, describing the added data she wanted, waited a moment, and then thanked him, saying something about him being a doll. Then the call ended.

"He said he should have it in about an hour. He'll email it over as soon as he does," she told Wells.

Pulling into the hotel parking lot, Wells found a space that allowed him to park close to the door. They walked together into the hotel lobby and headed past the front desk while nodding a greeting back to the hotel receptionist. At the end of the hall on the right was the elevator, and Wells punched the button to take them up. Once in front of the room, Wells scanned his key card and opened the door, standing back to allow Max to enter first.

Walking in, Max looked around the room and suddenly realized that they were alone in a room with a bed. Heading over to the desk, intentionally ignoring the bed, she set her computer bag down and started setting up. Wells presented her with the room service book and turned the page to the menu.

"I say we order a variety of stuff we can snack on, and a fresh pot of coffee," Max said, looking over the menu.

"Sounds great, go ahead and order." Wells was already unpacking his laptop bag, ready to get back to work.

After ordering a variety of appetizers and the coffee, Max hung up the phone and sat down at the desk. Pulling back up the files, she began pouring over the data again. Wells joined her on the opposite side of the desk, and both worked in silence until a knock at the door brought them up out of the data. Wells went to the door and led a young man in pushing a cart displaying several platters with warming lids on them. The smell of cheese poppers and coffee immediately filled the room. By now it was 8:30 pm, and Max realized how hungry she really was. Lunch seemed long ago and neither of them had finished their meal after the sensitive conversation.

Setting the food onto the counter where the in-room coffee maker sat they each filled a plate with a few items and stood for a minute marveling at the view outside the window. As Max turned back towards the desk, Wells took her plate from her and set it on the desk. Her eyes raised up to meet his, and as he stood looking down at her, he could not resist the temptation of the thoughts that had been floating through his conscious and sub-conscious mind, wrapping her in his arms he drew her to his chest. Before she could collect herself, he was pressing a kiss onto her mouth. The feel of his lips and his hands on her lower back took her breath away. She pushed against his chest, but he held his grip until she relaxed into the kiss. Max responded to the gentleness, then, and the kiss turned passionate as she felt her lips part to accept the soft sweep of his tongue. She wrapped her arms around his neck and drew him in closer, enjoying the strength of his arms and his firm body against her own.

Finally pulling back, Wells looked into her eyes again and smiled at her beauty. Max returned the smile, but just as Wells leaned down to kiss her again, his cell phone rang, the face displaying FBI HEADQUARTERS. He picked up the phone, grimacing.

"Agent Wells here," he said quietly.

Max listened to the one-sided conversation as Wells recanted what they had thus far discovered, apparently bringing his director up to speed. She heard him say, "I'll see you tomorrow afternoon," ending the call and turning to face her.

Before he could say anything she said, "We should get back to work."

There was an air in the room as they settled back into their chairs, but neither spoke of what had just happened. Each choosing instead to begin the tedious process of sorting out the data the way they had agreed. They continued to nibble on the appetizers, occasionally sneaking glances at each other. At ten o'clock, they had more data to merge and compare. This time, the list they got was much longer, including over seventy people as suspects.

Sighing, Max pushed back from the desk.

Wells sensed her frustration. She was facing a daunting task of having to work through a huge list of suspects in less than one week if she was going to gain her boss's approval and keep the case active.

"So, let's prioritize the most likely un-sub first, using everything we know about our guy. That way when you start working the leads, your chances are better."

Continuing on, Wells outlined the profile again and focused in on the triggers that might start a vicious spree. "He's angry, literally ripping these people apart, but meticulous in his process and precise with his cuts. Talented even. He also cleans up afterwards, leaving no trace of evidence, making him an organized and methodical killer. So he's rational. But something set him off and something else made him stop, or I'm totally wrong about the timeline being meaningful."

Feeling energized by Wells' input, Max started reprocessing some of the data. "I think doctors, or more specifically surgeons, would be our most likely candidates. If you think methodically, they have to have a lot of training, due to the nature of their jobs, and the precision of the incisions seems to point that way. I would think vets next, for the same reasons, followed by surgical assistants and vet techs."

Wells was nodding in agreement, rising from his chair and leaning over her shoulder as she worked. He could smell her hair and her skin, which smelled faintly of vanilla. Every time she moved, his senses were assaulted with her fragrance. It was intoxicating, but he forced himself to concentrate on what she was saying. They had work to do, after all.

After several different manipulations of the data, Max remembered that Bobby was going to be sending over a file. Checking her email, she saw that he'd already done so. Pulling the email up, she began comparing some of the names on her list. Nearly all of the surgeons had either a sports car or a SUV. Some had both. The list became less specific as she drilled further down, using the logic they'd discussed.

Wells had sat back down. After two hours of working on this he pulled his chair up beside her, and they leaned back in their chairs, staring at the computer screen. They had a new list now. It was prioritized according to profession, geographical proximity, and possible triggers, and was sorted from 1 to 112. There were, of course, more if these didn't pan out, but this was the starting point. Max would have to work through each one of these, hopefully finding something that helped her identify her un-sub. It was a start, and more information than she'd had that morning.

Wells and Max looked at each other and smiled. For the first time today Max felt like there was a possible solution to finding the killer. Their eyes locked, and the kiss from earlier seemingly still burned her lips.

Standing up, Wells poured two fresh cups of coffee and handed one to Max. Their hands touched briefly, and she felt a fluttering in her stomach. Thanking him, she took it and drank the warm liquid. It was now almost one o'clock in the morning, and she was beat. Tomorrow was going to be another long day if she wanted to find this guy. Setting her coffee aside, she looked up at Wells, she knew she should leave now, but she was not able to pull her eyes away from his.

"Not much more we can do tonight. I guess I should go and let you get a couple hours of sleep."

"Max, we left your motorcycle at headquarters," he reminded her, smiling.

"Oh, damn, I'd totally forgotten that. I'll just call for a cab."

He shook his head. "Look, stay here with me. I'll sleep on the sofa, and you can have the bed. We'll both get some rest, and then I'll drop you off in the morning." He meant what he was saying, but after the kiss they had shared earlier, he wasn't sure he could live up to his words. His nostrils were still filled with the smell of her hair, which had not left his senses from earlier.

She shook her head back. "I really don't think that's a good idea. I really should go," she said, starting to gather up her laptop.

Moving around behind her, Wells took her hands from the computer bag and turned her to face him. "Stay with me. I want more time with you." He pulled her in to him and began kissing her this time more deeply, more passionately.

Resisting at first, she tried to pull herself away, but found that she couldn't stop the desire that was welling up inside. Her body was responding to his touches, his kiss, and she found herself pulling him in closer. His hands gently drifted over her body, stopping and pressing on her lower back to connect their bodies completely. She could feel his passion pressing against her, and this sent an electric charge through her entire body. She heard a soft moan, and then realized it was coming from her. Her lips parted, and she returned the probing kisses. His hands came up into her hair and gently caressed her neck.

Leaning back, he looked deep into her eyes, seeing the desire they shared. He began unbuttoning her blouse and slowly moved her to the bed, laying her down gently and sliding his warm, muscular body against hers. He enjoyed the contrast in her femininity and incredibly toned body. Slowly they removed each other's clothing, and after he produced a condom from his wallet, they spent the next couple of hours engaged in sensual lovemaking. At first, their connection was timid, but it became erotic and finally settled into gentle and tender caresses and kisses, as they repeatedly brought each other up and over the edge.

At about four o'clock, exhausted from their hours of research and passion, they began to doze, their arms and legs intertwined.

Six o'clock came all too soon. Wells propped himself up on one arm to gaze down at Max, taking in her beauty. Her hair was tossed, and a wavy lock swept across her brow. Pushing it back with one finger, Wells gently kissed her lips and then unwrapped himself from her and slid out of the bed.

She woke as he pulled away. "Where are you going?" she whispered.

"Shower."

"Um, may I join you?"

"I'd love that."

Slipping from the covers and wrapping a sheet around her body, she followed him into the shower. They spent a few minutes taking in the beauty of each other's bodies in the light of the bathroom. After lathering each other in playful fun, they rinsed and helped towel each other down.

"No fair, you actually have clean clothes to put on," she complained at him, gathering up the clothes she had come in.

Getting dressed in silence, they each packed away their work and belongings and prepared to leave the room. Then they stood facing each other, just inside the room door. Wells started to say something, but Max placed her finger over his lips and kissed him gently.

"I know the game and so do you," she whispered.

Wells knew she was right but hated the idea that he might never see her again. They each grabbed a bagel from the hotel breakfast area and headed out into the day. The air was crisp outside; the morning sun had not yet taken the chill off. Max hugged her body as if to lock out the morning cold as they drove back to the headquarters where her motorcycle was parked. There was a moment of joint silence before she leaned over and gave him a quick kiss on the cheek. He felt the warmth of her lips and knew he wanted much more, but could not for the life of him picture how to work that out. Feeling frustrated with the circumstances, he looked down at her, taking in her green eyes and trying to read what she was feeling.

"Will you let me know if you catch your guy?" Wells asked, studying her face.

"Sure thing. Take care, Agent Mark Wells." Max got out of the car, pulled her motorcycle jacket tight, strapped the laptop bag to the motorcycle seat, and pulled on her helmet. As she slid her leg over the bike, she waved her fingers at Wells in farewell. Then she rolled the bike away from the parking strip, and fired the starter button. With a quick tap of the gear peg, she pulled away and tore out of the parking lot.

Wells sat staring out the windshield and watched her go, not wanting to accept the fact that he might not ever see her again. Finally, he put the car back in drive and pulled away from the Los Angeles Headquarters, on his way to LAX to catch his flight back to Washington D.C.

Chapter Nine

It had been two days since Jack submitted his application to Mandy. He'd spent his time on the renovations to the basement, trying not to focus on the dark feelings that were burning inside him or the anticipation of the phone call saying he was accepted to the program and could start next week.

This morning he'd been working on the caulking, wanting to make sure he had the seal perfect. Looking around, he was pleased with his work. No room for error. It had to be 100 percent washable, but he thought he'd nailed it. He'd always prided himself in running a very sanitary operating room, and this couldn't be any different. Perfection was to be achieved, nothing but the best for Hope.

He was so absorbed in his work that he barely heard the phone ringing. When he did, he answered, careful not to get any caulking on it.

"Thomas?" a voice on the other line asked.

"Yes, this is Thomas," he replied, throwing in just a hint of flirtatious lisp.

"Hi, it's Mandy from Clary Sage, and I have great news for you."

"Oh, girl I can't wait, Please tell me," he said, grinning. He'd started to worry about this, and was glad to hear from her.

"Well, we have you all approved and set up to start the accelerated classes next Monday. Your instructor's name is Melody. You'll love her. She's the best. Also, we have your financial aid all approved, so you'll have some more papers to sign on the first day. But all the new students go through that information during orientation. There's nothing for you to do right now. Just be here at eight o'clock Monday morning, okay?"

"It sounds perfect. I'll see you Monday. Thanks for all of your help, Mandy." Jack hung up the phone, and a smile crept up on his lips. This was going to be way too easy. The only thing he had to do was ace the class. With his acceptance in the program, he would have the means to a variety of women, allowing him to choose the perfect mate. Now all he had to do was get the rest of his identity scrubbed, so that every aspect of his life could be lived as Thomas.

He'd completed all the financial transfers from the sale of his convertible, making sure the paper trail on Jack died in Los Angeles and couldn't be traced to Thomas. But he did have one last piece of unfinished business. There was something he *must* do.

Tonight, he would do it tonight.

"Hello, can you tell me if your salesman Benz is working today?" Jack clung to his cell phone, waiting anxiously for the receptionist on the line to answer.

"One moment please …Yes, he'll be here until seven o'clock tonight, and he works tomorrow too," she finally said.

"Oh perfect, thank you." Jack clicked off the line. *Perfect,* he thought as he descended the basement steps. Checking his watch, he saw that it was now 5:30. All he needed to do was make sure the basement was all set.

The room was complete, and everything was ready. The caulk he'd purchased was supposed to set in thirty minutes, and it had been four hours since he had finished the application. Checking to make sure that it was dry, he applied a light spray of water to it and wiped it away. The caulk stayed in place – definitely dry. He proceeded to thoroughly scrub his hands, making sure there were no remnants of caulk on his skin or under his nails. He definitely did not want to leave any trace evidence where he was headed.

Moving out of what had once been the canning room, now converted to his new surgical room; he walked across the floor over to the supplies in the opposite corner and took a look at the items on the built-in shelves. Everything was perfectly arranged and labeled. Lifting the amber-colored bottle marked Chloroform; he drew out 5cc into a syringe – enough of the chemical to induce sleep for at least an hour – and dropped it into the tube, then capped it. He pulled surgical gloves from an open box, also on the shelf. Tucking the gloves into his pocket, he headed back up the basement stairs.

In the kitchen, Jack flipped on the light and headed down the hallway, turning on the lights as he went. In the bedroom, he laid the gloves and syringe on the nightstand while he pulled on tight-fitting jeans, work boots, and a tight, long-sleeved shirt, remiss of any buttons or snaps. You could never be too careful; he would never wear anything with items that could be pulled off. He wasn't expecting a struggle, but he had to be especially mindful of that sort of thing now. Double checking himself in the mirror, he pulled on a jacket, picked up the syringe and gloves from the nightstand, and put them in his pocket.

He headed back through the house, turning the lights back out as he went, and collected his keys from the counter. Once he was in the garage, he walked around to the back of the SUV and opened the hatch, and then crossed the garage to the workbench, where he'd placed the rolls of plastic sheeting and several rolls of duct tape. Taking a roll of each and a carpenter's knife to the back of the SUV, he carefully rolled a strip of plastic out to the carpet, where the seats were folded down flat. He cut the sheet just large enough to cover the floor and halfway up the walls of the storage area. He then used duct tape to hold the sheet in place.

Finally satisfied that he had the area covered, he closed the hatch and returned the plastic and knife to the workbench, putting the duct tape in a small satchel stored behind the seat. The satchel contained his surgical instruments as well – scalpel, blade, forceps, speculum, stethoscope, and scissors. Having them in his car meant that he was prepared for anything that might happen. He had similar instruments and more in his operating room.

With everything set he climbed his long frame into the driver's seat and hit the button on the garage door opener mounted on the visor. Remembering something, he climbed back out of the SUV and went back to the trunk area again. Lifting the hatch he reached inside and slid the interior lights to the off position, closed the hatch, and went back and got back inside. By the time he was backing out of the driveway, it was already 6:15. It would take him twenty minutes to get across town and find a place adjacent to the dealership where he could watch and wait. But tonight he'd be able to relieve the darkness inside him, and that alone was calming. Tonight would give him what he needed to control his urges until he was out of school and could begin the restoration of his life.

The anticipation of the hunt was almost as exhilarating as the kill. The radio was playing some familiar tune, though he couldn't quite recall who sang it. Even so, he found himself humming along as he drove. He headed down Memorial Avenue and stopped as lights changed, tapping the steering wheel as he drove. Pulling into a strip mall across from the car lot, he pulled through until he was facing the dealership in a way that allowed him to see the entrance doors. Hoping he would be able to see from his parking spot, he wondered if employees left through those doors or if there was some parking in the rear of the building specifically for employees. He sat tall in his seat now and watched eagerly, waiting for Benz to complete his work day.

Jack's eyes barely blinked. Like an animal waiting on its prey, he held his vigil. Thirty minutes into his watch, he saw a man starting across the parking lot and recognized the slight limp of the car salesman. Immediately alert, he turned the key in the ignition and backed out of the parking space, idling in the strip mall exit and preparing to drop in behind Benz as he left the dealership. After a moment, a white, two-door Mercedes appeared at the dealer entrance, making a right out of the lot and heading north on Memorial. Jack pulled out into the opposite lane of the white car and followed, staying two cars back. The white car made it easy to follow, especially with the dealer plate on the rear.

Continuing to keep the car within view, but back far enough to avoid recognition, Jack watched as the car signaled the intention of getting onto the ramp for the Broken Arrow Expressway heading east. Sliding over to the right lane, Jack followed the Mercedes onto the ramp, remaining a car behind. Benz continued on to the Elm Street exit and followed the ramp off to the right coming to a stop at the light. Jack exited too, but changed lanes to avoid sitting right behind or beside the salesman.

When the light changed and the traffic went forward, Jack laid back slightly, allowing some distance to grow between the two cars. Benz moved over into the left lane, pulling in front of Jack and going through the light at Washington Street. Jack got lucky and caught the light just as it was turning yellow, then eased off the accelerator slightly to keep pace with the Mercedes. The turn signal indicated that Benz would be turning left at the next street. Jack carefully peered through the windshield and saw that the street sign read W. Toledo Street.

Not wanting to lose him, Jack followed cautiously into the neighborhood, watching closely as the car disappeared around the curve at the end of the street. Edging on very slowly, Jack caught the car turning right again onto another street. He didn't make the same turn, afraid that he might look suspicious, but drove on past, narrowing his eyes to see where the car had gone.

He smiled when he realized the street was a dead end. Perfect. Nowhere to run. Continuing to the end of the block, he turned the SUV around in the last driveway and pulled forward, slowly approaching the street Benz had turned on. Down the street, he saw the car pull into the house at the end and enter the garage. The garage door was just closing.

Knowing from the conversation they'd shared at the car dealership that Benz lived alone, Jack decided that he could drive to the house without really being noticed. After all, it was best to catch the man off guard, before he was settled in. Jack pulled into the driveway, then reached behind the seat and pulled his black medical bag forward. He opened his satchel to remove several items: a rag, rubber gloves, scalpel, and shoe booties. He slipped the booties on over his shoes, then pulled on the rubber gloves and slid the scalpel into his back pocket. Folding the rag into a perfect square, Jack depressed the plunger on the syringe, saturating the rag with Chloroform. Last, he grabbed the roll of duct tape and stuffed it into his jacket pocket.

Exiting the car, he walked up to the door and knocked. A moment later, he heard the door lock disengage, and saw a surprised Benz opening the door. Before Benz could speak, Jack forced the rag over the salesman's mouth, pushed him through the doorway, and kicked the door closed behind him, while looping his arm around Benz from the back and pulling the stunned man's back tight against his chest. The car salesman was so surprised he didn't even have a chance to put up a fight. Jack held him tightly and let the Chloroform do its work.

Benz grabbed momentarily at the arms that held him. He fought against the chemical, and Jack knew he was feeling the burn in his throat, as he watched the man's face indicate the panic that was setting in and the desire to stop what was happening. But as the drug took over and as he began to lose consciousness, the last word he managed to mouth to Jack was "Why?"

Jack let the man slump to the floor. Looking around the home, he took in the modest furniture, few pictures on the walls, and immaculate kitchen. The home was neat as a pin. Jack approved of Benz's single and simple lifestyle, with no wife and the children all grown, off living their lives. Benz had been doing this right. That wouldn't help the man in any way now, but Jack did have respect for a man who understood how to keep it simple.

Cautiously pulling back the curtain, Jack peered out to see that the street was quiet. After ensuring the street was clear and all was quiet outside, he looked around the room. There was a giant clock with a barn and landscape painted on it, hanging over the living room couch. It read fifteen minutes to eight. Most people should be home from work and safely in their houses, but he would still need to be cautious. Jack took a few minutes to explore his surroundings. Only the living room light was on, which was perfect – people would assume that Benz was settled in for the night. Jack never brought anything with him that wasn't completely necessary, but sometimes, like now, he wished he had something to conceal his victim. He usually grabbed people in the dark, off the street or from an open area. It was rare for him to go inside someone's home. He really did not like it, as there was a chance of being seen or leaving behind evidence. In this case, though, he didn't have much choice. Coming into Benz's home without any supplies was necessary. He would have to improvise with items from within the home.

Noticing an area rug under the coffee table, Jack decided he could remove Benz in this. Of course, the easiest thing would be to just kill him here, but he really wanted to try the surgery room in the basement. He also wanted some time. He knew he had to make this one last until he finished his training at the school, as he had to remain focused on school and not allow the darkness to cause him to lose that focus. The school was the means to his goal, and there was no room for error. It was important that he keep the dark feelings at bay for just a little while. It wouldn't be too long now before he could begin reclaiming his life.

Deciding the rug was perfect; he slid the coffee table away and placed it next to the opposite wall. He then rolled Benz onto the edge of the long side of the rug. The Chloroform would last a while longer, but he reached into his jacket pocket and retrieved the duct tape. No use taking chances. Holding Benz's hands together, Jack applied the tape in tight loops, and then did the same with his feet. He then made two loops around Benz's head, covering his mouth, careful not to cover his nose. Rolling the rug into a tight tube with Benz securely inside, Jack applied the duct tape around each end then moved the table back in front of the couch. Looking down, he saw that there was a slight hint of where the rug had been. Shrugging to himself, he decided it didn't really matter, as there would be no indication of when the rug had been removed. Benz would simply disappear, and no one would know why.

Hitting the button on his key remote to open the hatch on the SUV, Jack took another peek out the front window. It was solidly dark out now – safe to get going, time to get Benz out of the house and into the vehicle. At approximately 160 pounds, Benz wasn't a real challenge for Jack. He intentionally maintained his health and worked out regularly, so that he could handle any situation. Lifting Benz up inside the rug, he took a moment to balance the weight properly, and then pushed open the front door with his foot quickly before exiting the home. Jack stepped carefully down the two steps on the front porch and lifted the rolled rug into the back of his SUV, pushing it in diagonally with the tip of the rug pushing slightly between the two front seats. Closing the hatch, Jack returned to the home, took a quick look around and ensured he had the duct tape and rag in his pocket. Before leaving the house, he locked the front door and pulled it closed behind him.

Entering the car, he slid off the gloves and shoe booties, putting them back into his satchel, and then backed out of the driveway, heading down the street and only turning his headlights on when he was about to turn onto the next street. Jack worked his way back down Elm and onto the Broken Arrow Expressway, opting to head west. The turnpike would be a little faster, but he hadn't purchased a pass and didn't want to stop at any toll booths or have the cameras at the toll stations record his movements.

Driving cautiously, Jack was on high alert as he drove, keeping his speed limit right at or under the posted roadway signs. He navigated his way back on to Highway 169 and then took the ramp to Highway 412 heading him home. It only took him twenty-four minutes to get home. He hit the remote control garage door opener. He pulled in, waiting for the door to close behind him before getting out of the SUV. Opening the hatch first, Jack went into the house, turning on the lights and opening the basement door so that he could carry the rug easily down into the basement.

Then he returned for his cargo. When he had the rug safely in the basement, he laid it down on the floor of the main room. Carefully removing the scalpel from his back pocket, he cut the tape from around the ends and rolled it open. For a moment he thought Benz might be dead from being confined in the rug, but then he saw the reflexive movement of his eyelids. He was still alive, thank goodness.

Lifting the man up, he carried him into the operating room and laid him on the surgical table. Then he pulled his stethoscope from the wall, where it hung with the other tools of his trade. Listening to the heart rate of the man, he confirmed that Benz was still unconscious enough for prepping. Using the scissors from the tray, Jack proceeded to cut away Benz's clothing and the duct tape he'd applied to his hands and feet. He then secured him to the table, using clear plastic zip ties through rings that had been applied to the underneath of the table. Jack wasn't sure what the rings were actually for. He'd assumed they were for hanging vegetables for drying. But he knew exactly what he would use them for now, and that was really all that mattered.

Once Benz was secured to the table, and all his clothing removed, Jack covered the lower half of his body with a disposable hospital operating sheet, leaving the man exposed from the waist up. Looking around, satisfied that things were as they should be, Jack walked back upstairs to shut the car and make sure the house was completely secured. He didn't want to be interrupted. Closing the hatch to the SUV, Jack retrieved his keys from the ignition and then headed back inside, clicking off the garage lights and pulling the entry door shut behind him. He then went around the home checking all windows and doors. *You can never be too careful*, he thought to himself.

Once he was certain the entire house was safely prepared, it was time to return to the basement. The pain he'd felt for the last few days was slowly being replaced with excitement. Before descending the steps, Jack pulled the door closed behind him. Soon he would need to build out the faux wall in front of this entrance to keep it hidden. For now he was alone, and it didn't matter. All that mattered was Benz on his table and the fact that the Chloroform should be wearing off.

✳✳✳

As Jack entered the room, Benz, who was just starting to awaken, blinked in an effort to clear the fogginess from his head and eyes. His head was killing him, and he could not figure out why his arms and legs would not move. Jack leaned over him, "Hello Benz. Did you have a nice nap?"

Benz blinking furiously now as recognition started to seep into his mind and he remembered the handsome man wanting to exchange his Mercedes for a far inferior vehicle. Recognition soon began to shift to fear as he started to recall through the dull, throbbing in his head this man, *what was his name…*, Jack, standing outside on his porch. Beyond answering the door he could remember nothing else. Shifting his eyes around him he saw the overhead lights and the stark white walls oddly paneled in what appeared similar to bathtub wallboards. Realizing he was strapped down to something, he tried to pull free, but was unable to move. Trying to speak, he struggled with the soreness in his throat and the tape over his mouth.

✳✳✳

"Benz, no need to worry with small talk, we just have fate now. Just know we were brought together by circumstances. It really is nothing more or less, I assure you." Jack had moved over to the corner of the room, where a shelf held neatly folded operating scrubs, booties, and scrub caps. Jack proceeded to disrobe and change into a set of operating scrubs, complete with a scrub cap covering his hair. He pulled booties on over his shoes. Returning to the surgical table, he pulled forward a rolling surgical tray and stood admiring the shiny tools, which he'd laid out perfectly. Finally, choosing a number 5 scalpel from the tray, he leaned down over Benz.

By now, Jack was no longer concerned with the panic in Benz's eyes or the manner in which he struggled to speak. He was merely focused on the task at hand. Embracing the darkness far outweighed any compassion he might have felt for the man who had shared the story of losing his wife.

Even as a child, Jack had enjoyed taking life while the victim squirmed for its freedom. Unlike many killers, Jack's needs weren't sexually motivated in any way, nor was it about the act of inflicting pain. Jack cut people because he had to. Doing it while they were alive, alert, and awake meant that the blood would still be coursing through their veins, and this was the part that fascinated him most. Then, once the blood all ran out, the heart would stop. At that moment, he would feel a twinge of remorse. Fleeting and sudden, then over.

But never enough to stop.

For a moment, he reflected on that day when Hope had found him with the cat, how she had promised they would find a way together. And they had, but that had been taken from him. Not for long, he thought firmly. He would soon have that back. It all would start on Monday with getting through school. Then he could find Hope and have his life returned to him. Everything would be good again.

Jack returned his thoughts to the man in front of him, leaning over as Benz watched in horror, struggling against the zip ties holding him down on the table. Without thinking about it, Jack took the scalpel and made a long incision from the top of the man's chest to just above his pelvis, straight down the middle, and right through the hard core of his navel. Benz writhed against the pain and the restraints, screaming, as the blood began to ooze out of the wound.

Jack wanted to do it now. But he fought the urge to reach deep into his body and touch all of those parts, knowing that if he did, it would then be over and he would once again have the darkness hovering around him. In fact, he thought, he showed the most restraint he'd ever allowed himself. Instead of reaching in, he reached out to the tray, selected the sutures, and slowly began sewing Benz back up. Benz had fought hard and now watched in horror as each stitch was applied to his chest. Once Benz's body was back intact, Jack inserted an IV drip with saline and antibiotics into Benz's left arm.

Benz would survive this round, and Jack could do this a few times before he needed to finish the deed.

Taking a few minutes, Jack cleaned the surgical tools meticulously, and scrubbed his hands, then returned the tools to the tray in perfect order again. Feeling slightly relieved of the pain inside, he peeled off the gloves and stripped out of the scrubs discarding them into a laundry basket. He collected the rest of his clothing, ready to return to the real world. Double-checking the IV and Benz's pulse, though shock had rendered the man unconscious, satisfied that he would live, Jack headed back upstairs. He was exhausted and hungry as the euphoria slowly cleared from his mind.

Deciding it was too late to eat a heavy meal; Jack selected a can of soup from the cupboard. He committed to eating healthier tomorrow, before he could spend any more time with Benz, but this would do for now. Pouring the soup into a bowl he popped the creamy broth into the microwave and tossed the can in the trash can under the sink. Suddenly feeling chilled and remembering he was naked, Jack walked through the dining area and down the hall to his bedroom. Pulling on workout pants and a t-shirt, he heard the microwave sound that his soup was ready, and he returned to the kitchen.

Jack carefully removed the soup from the microwave. Setting it on the counter next to the sink, he poured himself a glass of water. Carrying both items to the dining room table, he sat down facing the front windows. The curtains were drawn closed, blocking the view of the woods beyond his driveway. He liked that view and enjoyed the wildlife that could be seen frequently playing in the trees or foraging for pecans. When he was a boy he would have had to hunt them, but he no longer needed animals. These days he could just enjoy the beauty they possessed on the outside. Besides he already knew what they possessed on the inside.

He finished his soup and looked around the room, anticipating a time when he would share this place with Hope. Granted, the house was nothing like the lavish home they'd owned in California, but Hope had always told him that as long as they were together, it really didn't matter where they lived. And he believed her. Full and relaxed, he collected the bowl and glass and walked over to the sink to wash them out. The clock on the stove read 11:33. Yawning, Jack turned out the lights and headed to bed.

***

Benz woke and shivered uncontrollably from the pain, blood loss, and exposure. Looking down, he saw that he had no more than a paper sheet covering him. His arms and legs ached from the inability to move, and the zip ties tore into his flesh. He felt like he couldn't fully breathe either, with the duct tape still covering his mouth. It was dark in the room, and even though Benz's eyes had long ago adjusted to the darkness, he desperately looked around the room hoping for some way to escape. He worked through the pain in his head trying to understand why he was here. *That man, what was his name?* He tried to remember once again through the haze in his head. He had sold him a car. Why was he doing this to him? Terrified he struggled to understand that he was strapped to the table. He couldn't move, and there was no escape. He fought to stay awake, but found himself drifting in and out of consciousness.

Chapter Ten

Max rode home through the cool morning air, the force of the wind against the motorcycle waking her up. Thoughts of the night with Wells flooded her mind as she whipped in between cars down the palm tree lined streets. Arriving home she pulled into the drive of her California style bungalow and grabbed her things, pulling the bagel from her pocket she nibbled on it as she entered her home and walked down the hallway to her bedroom.

She stripped out of her clothes and pulled on her thick terrycloth robe. She then slipped into bed and pulled the blankets up around her shoulders. Sleep took her immediately, but her dreams were torn between images of strong hands roaming over all the right places on her body, blue eyes that seemed capable of knowing her every thought, and bodies buried in shallow graves, split open down the middle, with their insides hanging out.

She was ripped from her dreams when her phone rang. Looking over, she saw it was the chief. She needed to brief him on the progress she and Wells had made the night before, but she wasn't quite ready to, and rolled over to look at the clock instead. She'd been asleep two hours, and it was time to get moving. As she made her way to the shower and climbed in, she found that she had only one thought on her mind - it was time to get to find this killer.

Out of the shower, teeth brushed, she ran her brush through her long wavy locks and quickly dressed, passed through the hall adorned with family photos, and entered the open kitchen, putting on a pot of coffee. Retrieving her laptop from near the front door, she set it on the kitchen table and let the computer boot up while she got a cup of coffee. Then she settled down at the kitchen table, ready to start going through the possible suspects. As she pulled up the computer files, she pressed callback on her cell phone, ready to return the chief's call.

He wasn't in a good mood. "Nichols, where the hell are you and what have you found?"

"Good morning to you too, Chief," she replied with a bit of sarcasm in her voice. "I've got a lot, actually. We have the files narrowed down to the most likely suspects, and I'm starting to work through them now."

"Is Wells still with you?"

"No, sir, he left a couple of hours ago."

"Well, keep me posted."

"I –" Before she could respond the call had dropped. The chief had hung up on her.

Sighing, Max returned her attention to her laptop. Starting with the list of surgeons, she found the first name in the LAPD database. She needed to map these out, so that she could go and talk to these people one at a time. Pulling out the first twenty names, she began the tedious process of mapping the last-known work and home addresses. For a brief moment, her mind drifted, wishing Wells was here to help her with interviewing these people, but she pulled herself back into focus. She didn't have time to allow her thoughts to drift to the night before, or the man responsible. She had a killer to catch.

After a little over an hour, Max had her list mapped out, and she knew who she wanted to call first. She sent the information to the printer in her bedroom, and hoped that her guy was on the short list of most likely suspects. Then, before heading back to the bedroom to change into real clothes, she sent an email over to Bobby, letting him know that she was going to interview these people. You could never be too careful, and since she was going out on her own, she wanted someone else to know where she was. Taking a quick pass at her now dry hair with the brush, she quickly applied some mascara and then pulled on shoes. Moving down the hall again she walked through the living room to the entry way stand and collected her keys and her gun holster belt, checking the 9mm Glock; and slid the belt over her shoulder. Leaving behind the helmet, this was a job that required her car. She grabbed up the list from the printer and exited the house through the kitchen into the connected garage, hitting the garage door opener button mounted on the wall.

She climbed into the leather seat inserting the key into the ignition listening to the low rumble of the Honda Civic. Engaging the clutch and dropping the gear in to reverse, Max backed the car out of the garage into the sun and down the driveway past her motorcycle.

The first person on the list was a Dr. Henry Solomon. The good old doc had gotten a divorce just before the killings started and had a malpractice complaint against him, though it had been settled out of court. Also putting him at the top of the list was the fact that he worked and lived near the dump site in Chatsworth canyon. Either the divorce or the malpractice complaint could have been enough to trigger him, sending him into the killing spree. Having both made him the top pick. Max worked her way out to the Ventura Highway. It was almost noon now, and stopping by his office might be the best shot of actually talking to him. Visiting him at his office might also be enough to throw him off, if he had anything to hide.

Thirty minutes later, she pulled into the parking lot of the medical center where Dr. Solomon practiced medicine. When she got into the building, Max glanced over the directory and found Dr. Solomon's office on the second floor. The elevator was just at the end of the hall. Max entered the car and selected the floor. As she exited, she saw the sign on the opposite wall that indicated suite 204 was to the left. As she entered the office, she removed her badge from her gun belt and walked up to the counter. Flashing her credentials, she asked the red haired, thirty-something, woman behind the counter if she could speak with the doctor.

The woman's eyebrows rose immediately when she saw the badge. She looked up at Max and then back to the badge again. "Umm, okay, one moment please. He's with a patient." Getting up from behind the counter, the woman disappeared down the hall. A few minutes later she returned and said, "He'll see you in about five minutes. He's just finishing up."

"Thanks." Max proceeded to look around the waiting room, curious about the doctor himself. The place was tastefully decorated in modern décor, with local contemporary paintings adorning the walls. Everything was clean and colorful, the tables layered with magazines including *Time, Parenting,* and the *Local Scene.* As Max stared at a painting on the wall, the door opened beside the patient check-in counter and the redhead asked Max to follow her.

She stopped in a consultation office and before closing the door and leaving Max alone in the room said, "The doctor will be right with you."

Moments later, the door opened to reveal a man wearing scrubs. He was slightly grey at the temples and wore small round glasses. He stood about six feet tall and was in good shape. Max immediately assessed his physical capability of committing the crimes for which she was about to question him. Deciding that he would be more than capable, she extended her hand and introduced herself.

"Detective Max Nichols, Dr. Solomon. I was hoping to ask you some questions."

"Of course, but what is this regarding?" he replied with a bit of irritation in his voice.

"I'm investigating a series of murders that happened over the past several months, and was hoping you could help me," Max offered, studying his reaction to the statement.

He looked a bit shocked, "I'm sorry, I guess I don't understand. Murders? How is it that I might be able to help with something like that?"

"I understand you recently underwent a divorce." Max intended to press on him to see if she could get a rise out of him.

"Yes, but what does that have to do with your case?"

"Is your wife still in the area?"

"Yes. Look, Officer, I'm more than willing to help, but I would like to understand what all of this has to do with me and my ex-wife."

Max ignored his demands for answers and continued, "I also understand that at about the same time, you settled a malpractice case for a fairly substantial amount of money."

The doctor was becoming increasingly irritated, "Yes, I did! Officer, I'm sorry, but I'm not sure what you're implying or what all this is about. I don't think I like your line of questions."

Max acknowledged that she had raised his blood pressure just a bit. That was exactly what she was hoping for. Now she wanted to see if she could get him to say something special.

"It's Detective," she stated, correcting the fact that he had attempted to minimize her. "That's a lot of pressure for one person to handle all at one time. Would you agree, Doctor?"

"Yes, but nothing a few months in the Bahamas didn't correct," he snapped.

"You took a trip? When was that specifically?"

The doctor looked like he was thinking for a second. "I left just after my divorce. I needed some time, so I bought a sailboat in Nassau and spent two months sailing around the islands. I returned to work a month ago. My patients needed me, and with the alimony and malpractice payout, I needed the money."

"Can anyone confirm the time you were away?" Max pressed on.

"Yes, my staff, my lawyer, and I have all of the expenses, including the boat purchase."

Max paused. If the doctor was really out of the country, it wasn't possible for him to be the killer. "Would it be okay with you if I validated your timeline with your receptionist before leaving?"

"Yes, one second I will have her come speak with you."

Max waited only a moment before the doctor returned with the receptionist.

The doctor handed her a folder, "My expenses from the trip. Janice can give you whatever else you might need. I have a patient," after accepting Max's card he left the room.

Max asked the receptionist about the doctor's travel timeline and confirmed he could not have been the killer. Handing the receptionist her card, "Please thank the Doctor, for his time. If I have any further questions, I'll be in touch." The receptionist took the card and shook her head as she led Max out of the room, obviously confused by the whole exchange.

Max rode the elevator down and exited the building, heading back into the sunshine, frustrated and grateful all at once. At least she could check this guy off the list completely. She knew some would be a lot tougher. She was already thinking about the next person on the list – a doctor who had lost his mother. Knowing the loss of the mother/son relationship had led to plenty of serial killer sprees in the past, especially if there was any abuse during childhood, Max was hopeful that the next visit would indicate something. Pulling out of the parking lot, she worked her way back to the Ventura Highway.

Doctor Jackson Dailey was further out from the dump site, but still close enough to be reasonable. His office was closer than his home, and again it made sense, given the time of day, to go there first. Though none of the victims had any connections to each other, Max wondered if one of the people of interest had used their exposure to patients as a means to hunt their victims. She made a note to try to tie this together later. She pulled into the next medical building parking lot, amused that it was somewhat similar to the last one and thinking that her next few days would be filled with sterile hallways, waiting rooms littered with magazines, and elevator rides with boring music piped into the speakers.

Dr. Dailey's waiting room was much busier than the last one, and Max wondered if this had anything to do with the malpractice suit Dr. Solomon had settled. Los Angeles County was huge, but small at the same time. Word of a doctor making errors definitely got around. Not that it mattered; she'd already crossed Dr. Solomon off the list and could let him go.

Following the same drill, she produced her credentials at the window, and the two receptionists shared a glance, the blonde one informing Max that the doctor was booked with appointments today. Max smiled and replied that it would be important for him to make time, so that she didn't have to take him downtown with her. This tactic usually worked, and it did this time as well. The dark-haired receptionist, named Becky based on her name tag, left briefly and returned, inviting Max to come through the door and into the back office. She led Max to a patient room, and the doctor appeared immediately, extending his hand.

"Dr. Dailey," he said in an introduction of himself. "I understand you need to speak with me. Is there something wrong, Officer? My wife and kids are fine, right?"

Accepting his grasp and realizing the doctor had assumed there must be a personal emergency involving his family; Max quickly put him at ease. "I'm sorry to have caused you concern for your family. They're fine, I'm sure. I'm Detective Max Nichols, and I'm actually here on official police business. I'd like to ask you some questions. It shouldn't take too long."

Max spent the next few minutes walking through similar questions with Dr. Dailey. In this case, the man had buried his mother and then taken his father into his home to care for him. He seemed genuinely focused on his family. His mother had been ill for a long time and unresponsive for nearly a year. Eventually she'd required extensive care. Max didn't see any indications that this man was her killer. He had offered his surgery schedules freely, and given that his surgeries often started very early in the morning, she was hoping to count him off the list by tying his hospital schedule to dates and times when the victims had gone missing. If he was in surgery when even one of the victims disappeared, there was no way he could have committed the crime. She was certain that there was only one killer, and if he didn't commit one of the crimes, then he hadn't committed any of the crimes. She left the meeting feeling confident that she could cross him off the list.

Returning to the car, Max pulled out the list of dates for the disappearances and quickly compared them to Dr. Dailey's operating schedule. He'd been in surgery on two of the dates and times when victims were last seen. As she suspected, then, Dr. Daily wasn't the killer.

Moving down the list, she identified the next name, and then pulled out of the parking lot feeling signs of hunger and frustration. She decided to pull through Jack in the Box to get a couple of tacos and an iced tea before heading to the next interview.

Chapter Eleven

Jack had slept peacefully for the first time in weeks, and it felt good to be rested. Keeping his promise from the night before to have a healthy meal and work out before visiting Benz downstairs, Jack went into the guest room just opposite the master, which he'd setup as a gym, complete with leg press, free weights, a tread mill, and boxing bag. After a full hour of working out, he hit the shower. His muscles felt good, his mind was clear. Pulling on sweats and a t-shirt, he headed to the kitchen, where he prepared himself a vegetable omelet, wheat toast, and a cup of black coffee. Clearing his plate, he took a moment to enjoy the feeling; this was the best he'd felt in weeks. Having Benz downstairs was enjoyable, but knowing that he was close to bringing Hope back was the real reason for his light heart.

Jack finished cleaning up the kitchen, then took a few measurements of the basement doorway, drawing out a plan of how to make the basement entrance appear to be a pantry. There were two good things about this plan. One, it protected him from discovery if or when he had any guests, and given that his social life was about to become enhanced, this possibility was more likely. He also knew Hope was certain to love the extra storage for food items. Before he started though, he needed to go to Home Depot to buy the necessary supplies.

And before he did that, he wanted to spend a little more time with his current guest.

Heading down the concrete stairway into the basement, he wondered how Benz had done overnight. He considered whether he would need to give him any nutrients through his IV, and decided that unfortunately, with school starting in just a few days, he wouldn't be able to keep the salesman around that long. This made him feel slightly sad, but he knew it was the way it had to be for now. Pushing down those feelings, he entered the surgical room and found Benz awake. Checking the IV and discovering it empty, he removed the bag and replaced it with a full one.

Seeing Jack enter the room, Benz immediately started to struggle against the restraints. Jack could see he was weaker now, his teeth chattering from the cold and loss of blood. Fear cloaked his eyes as Jack entered the room, which seemed to escalate the chatter and tremble even more. Trying to plead and beg for mercy came out as mere noises, gurgles and grunts, the duct tape restricting any means of forming words.

Jack went through the ritual of applying his surgical scrubs, gloves, and booties, then stood over Benz looking at him, checking his wounds and deciding what to do next. Considering the amount of time he had remaining between now and the first day of school, Jack was deciding how long he could keep Benz here before he had to dispose of him. In the end, he decided that he couldn't think about that now; today it was about enjoying the time he had left.

Rolling the surgical tray closer to the table, Jack selected the suture removers, and one by one, pulled out the stitches he'd applied the night before. Benz struggled hard, but Jack ignored his thrusts, muffled screams and grunts, remaining focused on the process and his own personal needs. Some minor healing had already begun, keeping the wound from immediately falling open. Jack returned the suture removers to the tray and picked up the same scalpel he'd used the night before. Looking at Benz, he saw the fear rising as Benz realized Jack was about to cut him again. The panic rose, and the salesman writhed on the table to no avail. Moving slowly, Jack carefully reopened the wound in the man's torso.

This time, Jack spent a little more time sliding his hand into the opening and feeling the pumping, slippery organs inside. The excitement rose in his chest. He felt Benz resisting the pain and crying out under the duct tape. Before long the man passed out from the pain. Blood flowed from the wound, pooling around Benz's body on the table. Jack was careful not to allow too much blood loss, knowing if he did that Benz would die tonight. He wasn't ready for that to happen.

Slipping his hand back out of the wound, he cleansed the area with a saline and antibiotic solution, then carefully began the process of sewing up the wound again. Benz remained in an unconscious state as Jack went about cleaning up and putting everything back exactly as it had been. He'd always been an excellent surgeon with careful organizational skills, and this was no different. He'd managed a tight operating room, displaying top surgical skills as one of the best in his field. The canning room was no different; he managed it in the same careful fashion, maybe even more so, as he had to keep the level of bacteria and evidence as minimal as possible.

He checked the IV again and made a mental note of when he'd need to change it out. Considering for a moment the advantage of buying a baby monitor to allow him to hear his captive from upstairs, he quickly discounted the idea as too risky. If anyone was visiting, there was a chance they might hear noises coming from the basement, and that wasn't acceptable. Besides, after Benz, he wouldn't be holding anyone for a long period of time. He wouldn't need them to remain alive for very long. After taking what he needed he would discard them quickly.

Disposing his scrubs into the laundry bin and thoroughly cleansing himself of any possible blood, he dried off and put his sweats and t-shirt back on, then headed back upstairs. He would make the run to Home Depot and begin the work on the pantry. He must get that finished before starting school. Upstairs again, he carefully closed the basement door and then pulled on a light jacket from the closet near the front door. He slid on his tennis shoes and headed out to the garage with the list of supplies and sketch he'd made earlier.

Jack spent the rest of the week continuing to spend quality time with Benz in the basement, each time getting a little more invasive, opening the wounds, exploring a little deeper into the organs inside Benz's body, then stitching him back up until the next time. Benz was weaker with each experience, despite the continued administration of IV fluids. His body now was ravaged with fever likely due to infection in the wound that was time and again opened and closed with each of Jack's visits. Jack noticed that Benz no longer struggled or fought against the assaults to his body. Benz's eyes indicated defeat; he had given up on surviving and now simply waited for the day when the painful invasions would end.

When not in the basement, Jack worked on the pantry design, enjoying the physical demands of the job. The pantry was almost finished and he was scheduled to start school on Monday, just three days from now. Having already planned where he would dispose of Benz, he'd decided that he wanted to do it on a weekday rather than a weekend, to minimize the chance of hunters stumbling upon him. He knew he needed to end his time with Benz, and while this revelation made him a bit anxious, he had to move on. And the decision was getting him that much closer to having Hope back in his life. Tonight would be the night to finish the task. Once Benz was gone, he would focus entirely on his school. He hoped that his time with Benz would be enough to hold his desires at bay until he could start building his life with Hope once again.

He only needed to add the trim to the pantry, which was now the perfect cover for the basement entrance, opening from the left side and swinging outward to permit entry to the concrete stairwell, with the hinges hidden. He'd built in shelves that would appropriately house various sizes of cans and boxes, and even put one on the bottom that would accommodate larger kitchen appliances. He knew Hope would enjoy this, as he remembered her complaining about this in the first house they'd owned in California. The memory brought a smile to his lips. Standing back and looking at his work, he was proud of how this had turned out. The trim he'd purchased matched the cabinets in the kitchen, which would provide further cover to any visiting eyes. Feeling good about the work, he decided it was time. The sun was about to set, which meant if he got started now, he would have some time with Benz before he had to drive him out of town.

When Jack first moved to Tulsa, he'd spent time with a realtor, and each house's surroundings were an important part of his decision. He looked at the surroundings near the homes, assessing rural land that showed the most potential for the disposal of unnecessary parts. He was very pleased to see how quickly one could get outside the city and into a rural area. Tulsa was fairly spread out, and all the surrounding areas offered thick trees and heavy underbrush – perfect places for his needs. Jack remembered reading of Tulsa when he was a boy in one of his medical magazines. He had always pictured what it would be like here, so moving here had made perfect sense. On one house-hunting trip, the realtor had taken him east of Tulsa to a small rural community called Inola. They had gone down a road called Lock and Dam, and Jack had seen several adjacent roads winding off into the trees, thick with weeds and brambles, proving they were hardly ever used. Jack remembered thinking this was the right place – a small town where nothing ever happened. No one would ever think to look for bodies buried out there.

Of course, the realtor had no idea that Jack was more focused on the surroundings than the three-bedroom ranch style they'd gone out to view. He had committed the drive to memory and could clearly picture each turn in his mind. As the sun set he would be ready to take that drive again.

It was nearly dark outside now. He needed to get started, so he wouldn't be rushed. This was his last time with Benz, and it needed to carry him for a while. But, before he could spend that quality time, he first needed to prepare everything for transporting Benz. There couldn't be any signs of ever having a body in his car. Every step of the process required thinking ahead. Jack had no way of knowing if the police would ever look in his vehicle, but he needed to know that his tracks were covered well enough that he would always have enough time to leave if necessary. Opening the pantry, he entered the basement, closing the door behind him and heading to the surgery room. Pulling out sheets of plastic, he carefully laid them onto the floor in the main room just outside the surgery room. He set the duct tape onto the tray of the rolling surgical stand and looked down at Benz.

The man was nearly gone. Despite the IV, he hadn't eaten in days, and had been slowly fading away. The repeated attacks on his body had made him shut down emotionally. His eyes were now devoid of any recognition, all hope had left his body, and no longer did he seem to respond to the visits from Jack at all. Benz was, for all intents and purposes, already dead. Jack knew Benz realized he was going to die and had likely already resigned himself to that idea. He probably even welcomed the fact and wished it would come sooner. Jack's daily visits, where he repeatedly opened up the salesman's body and slid his hands inside, then sewed the man up, had delivered pain no one should ever endure. In the days prior, Benz could be heard quietly praying for the pain to end. Jack had assured him that he would only die when he allowed it.

Jack knew what Benz must have thought throughout the last few days, and at this point, giving the man peace was the natural next step. Leaning over Benz, he whispered, "Thank you for providing me a few days of satisfaction. I know the feeling is not mutual, but you see, the pain you had to endure has given me great pleasure, and for that I am grateful to you. Benz, it will be over soon. I can't keep you here any longer. Tonight, you'll be free." For a brief moment, he saw relief, maybe even gratitude in the man's face. Turning, he put on a full set of surgical scrubs. Picking up the suture remover, he removed the sutures from Benz's body for the last time, and then used the scalpel to open him up again. This time he used the tissue scissors to cut the tissue of Benz's abdomen in two circular shapes on either side of the original incision. Once the organs were exposed Jack reached his gloved hands deep into the cavity of Benz's body and eagerly felt inside. One by one he touched each of the vital organs caressing them, in complete awe of the significance of each function. He gently squeezed the heart, feeling each beat, a euphoric feeling coming over him as it slowly stopped pumping. He watched as the blood slowed until there was nothing flowing. Benz had struggled but died as the blood flowed out of his body, and his heart stopped while Jack held it in his hands.

Jack leaned back, his own heart racing while Benz's stopped, as if his heart had taken on the pace for both. Forcing his breathing to slow and trying to regain control, he took out the stethoscope and listened for a pulse in Benz's neck, satisfied that the man was now dead. Using the surgical scissors, he cut the ties that had held Benz captive to the table since being brought here days ago. Disposing of the ties in the waste can, Jack began carefully washing down the body, removing any possible evidence, the bloody water swirling down the drain in the floor under the stainless table. He finished with a bleach bath, washing the body and table again and again until the water flowed clear down the drain, and the areas around the wounds had been bleached clean to the point of being nearly absent of any blood. Finally, he poured an ample amount of bleach down the drain, to make sure that there were no signs of Benz ever having been there.

Now Jack lifted the man from the table and lowered him onto the plastic on the floor, wrapping the body tight in the plastic wrap, and securing the ends with duct tape. Confident that the body was secure in the wrap, Jack lifted the bundle up onto its end and then onto his shoulder so that he could carry it up the stairs and out to the SUV.

Once in the garage, Jack laid the roll on the floor of the SUV, confident that the plastic would hold the body still. He pulled a tarp off of the shelf over the workbench and spread it over the plastic roll, concealing the body as a precaution. He didn't think anyone would look in the back of his car, but if they did they'd see only the tarp.

Going back into the house, Jack checked the time. He'd spent more time with Benz than he realized, and it was now nearly eleven o'clock. This was perfect. It was getting late, and most people would be settled in for the night. He would need to drive very carefully; at this time of night, the police would be looking for people who had been drinking. Before making that trip, he had to go one more time into the basement. He gathered all of Benz's clothes and placed them in a plastic bag. Back upstairs, he grabbed a bottle of water and his keys, returned to the garage, slid a shovel under the tarp next to the bag of clothes, and was ready to go.

Backing out of the garage, Jack headed east onto Highway 412. Setting the cruise control at exactly 65, he drove for fifteen minutes before seeing the sign for Inola. Tuning right at the Fiesta Mart about an eighth of a mile before the exit ramp that led to the small town, he passed the Dollar General on the left and liquor store on the right, just as he remembered, then continued down the Lock and Dam road out into the darkness, leaving the lights behind him. Driving three more miles into the night, he saw a road off to the right that had grass nearly growing over the path. No cars had passed him in the last two miles, and the houses had gotten farther apart. This was the place. Jack turned the SUV down the unpaved road and killed the headlights. Working his way slowly down the path, he found himself appropriately concealed in the trees and pulled the car off the road.

Before stepping out of the car, he slid on gloves and surgical booties. Retrieving a flashlight from the glove box, he popped the trunk hatch and retrieved the shovel from under the tarp. Then he began working his way out into the woods, using the flashlight to help guide his way. Most people would look for the path easiest to travel, but Jack wanted the most difficult path – the least likely for anyone else to travel. As he got further into the thicket, he found a small opening that looked like a site where deer may have been bedding for the night. Pulling back some of the brambles, he began digging up under the brush there, preparing the final resting spot for Benz.

The soil was soft due to the recent rains, and after about thirty minutes, sweat beading on his forehead despite the cool air, Jack decided that the hole was deep enough. Returning to the vehicle, he pulled the plastic roll, with Benz inside, out of the car and hoisted it up onto his shoulder, retrieving the bag of clothes with his left hand, while balancing the body with his right. He carried both back into the woods, carefully watching his footing so as not to slip.

When he arrived back at the opening, he laid the body face up in the hole with the clothes beside it. Then he filled in the hole and pulled the brambles back over the disturbed dirt. Finally he assessed the area with the flashlight, ensuring that everything looked natural and undisturbed. Returning to the car, he placed his gloves and booties in the satchel and slowly pulled the SUV back down the dirt road. Looking both ways and seeing no sign of any cars, Jack flipped on his headlights and pulled out onto Lock and Dam Road, heading back out to the highway.

He felt both peace and sudden fear as he headed towards the city lights, seeing Tulsa coming back into view. Having Benz over the past few days had kept his demons at bay, and that made him feel peaceful. The fear wasn't of being detected, but rather driven by the fact that he knew he'd have to contain the darkness by himself for several weeks. He knew this would be a struggle, and he hoped that focusing on getting his license to provide manicure and pedicures would be enough to keep his mind off of his needs. *"Focus on the plan Jack"*, he silently told himself.

He spent the weekend finishing up the pantry trim, cleaning his car inside and out, giving a second bleach bath to the surgery room, and making sure that everything in the house was perfect for Hope. He went to the grocery store and shopped for canned and boxed goods to fill out the pantry shelves, giving them the perfect look of a stocked kitchen. He grabbed two more bottles of bleach ensuring that he kept that supply stocked. He even bought a blender, bread machine, and food processor to put on the bottom shelf. He spent Sunday evening preparing his wardrobe for the week and his transformation to Thomas – the persona he would have to retain throughout the next several weeks.

On Monday morning, the alarm went off early. Jack got out of bed eagerly; ready to begin the journey that would bring his beloved Hope back to him. After a quick work out and hot shower, Jack dressed in a colorful button-down shirt and jeans. He spiked his hair slightly with gel, and intentionally applied a little too much cologne. Giving himself an approving look in the mirror, he walked down the hall through the living area and into the kitchen to have a healthy breakfast. Downing his coffee, he cleaned up and then checked the time. He would be a few minutes early to school, showing the appropriate amount of first-day excitement.

Arriving at the school, he was greeted and led to the classroom, where the first hour of class was spent on introductions, an overview of the course curriculum, and school policy. When all eyes in the class turned to Jack, he introduced himself as Thomas, offering a general background of having grown up in several places throughout the United States. Thomas was the only male in the room besides a small Asian man, whose family owned a nail salon inside a local grocery. He was not all too surprised by the demographics of the group and was pleased with the arrangement.

Before the day was out, Jack was already forging friendships with some of his classmates. The charisma that he'd always had would ensure that Thomas was a big hit, just like Jack had always been. Settling into this new persona, he thought that things were going just as planned.

Chapter Twelve

Max had spent four days interviewing the surgeons on the list, and so far nothing had popped. Everyone either had a very strong alibi or just didn't meet the profile Wells had outlined. Max knew she was running out of time. The chief was losing his patience with her, and had started telling her they needed her on the latest big case. Someone was driving down the highways shooting passengers on city buses, and they needed as many men – and women – as they could get on finding that killer or killers. She couldn't stand the thought of being pulled from working her current case. She really needed a break but couldn't afford to stop working. It would most certainly mean the chief would pull her, and this killer would get away with killing six people – something she was not willing to accept. Taking a deep breath, she forced herself to continue on.

The next name on the list was a Dr. Jack Tyler. It was about nine o'clock in the morning and she thought she would head to the hospital where he conducted most of his surgeries. Dr. Tyler was Doctor of Internal Medicine and Cardiology, often performing emergency splenectomies, appendectomies, gallstone removals, and heart surgeries. Through the process of interviewing now more than twenty people, she'd learned that most of the surgeries were conducted early in the morning. She was hoping to catch him just following a surgery.

Reading over the notes she'd taken, she saw that Dr. Tyler had lost his wife and four-year-old daughter in a car accident, a certain tragedy that anyone would find devastating. She wasn't even sure how *she* would handle such a horrible loss. Arriving at the hospital, she parked and entered through the main entrance, then approached the information desk, asking the volunteer behind the counter about Dr. Tyler while displaying her credentials.

The elderly woman seemed a little rattled by the display of the badge, but she quickly recovered and called security to help the detective.

A security officer arrived a few moments later. "Hello, Detective, may I help you?"

Max glanced up at the tall, dark-haired man and nodded. "I'm looking for a Dr. Jack Tyler. My records indicate that he's a cardiac surgeon at this hospital."

Shaking his head, the security officer, whose name tag read D. Reynolds, said, "Now that's a real tragedy. A real talent, that man. He received the Patient's Choice Award two years in a row, had everything going for him. Last year, Dr. Tyler lost his wife and child in a car accident. Took a leave of absence and hasn't come back. I'm not sure where you'd find him. Last I heard, he wasn't doing well. Then again, after a loss like that I don't know who would be."

Her gut churned with excitement, and she thought she might finally be on to something. Thanking the security officer, she headed back out to the parking lot. Once inside the car, she checked the address in her file for Dr. Jack Tyler's residence. Peeling out of the parking lot, she headed in that direction.

As she pulled onto the street, her excitement dropped. The house had a 'sold' sign on the front lawn, right in front of the lavish home that the Tyler family had shared – a beautiful Tudor style house, right out of the 20th century, with a sweeping, curved driveway. The house appeared to be unoccupied, though, and Max quickly jotted down the real estate agent's phone number. Maybe the agent would be able to tell her where Dr. Jack Tyler was living now. Dialing the number on her cell, Max connected with the real estate office

"Coldwell Bankers, how may I direct your call?"

"Yes, I'd like to speak with Janet Brinkley please."

"One moment please."

As Max waited she thought, *"Where are you, Jack? Are you my guy? Did you kill six people and bury them up in the canyon, Jack?"* Max heard a brief pause, followed by some soft music, and then a new voice on the line. "Good morning, this is Janet."

"Good morning, Ms. Brinkley, my name is Maxine Nichols. I'm a detective with the Los Angeles Police Department, and I have some questions for you regarding the sale of the home of Dr. Tyler."

"Detective? Oh, um, yes, how may I help you?"

"Can you tell me how long ago you closed on that home?"

"Yes, the final closing was about a month ago."

Max's heart sped up. That would match roughly with the last murder. "Did you help the seller, Dr. Tyler, buy another home locally?"

"No, I'm afraid not. Dr. Tyler was really suffering from the loss of his family and said he wasn't prepared to buy another home."

"Do you have any idea where Dr. Tyler is living now?"

"No, he never gave me any forwarding contact information. When he's ready, I hope he'll contact me to purchase a new home. He definitely needs the tax write-off."

"I understand. One more question, can you tell me how the funds for the proceeds from the sale were handled?"

"I'm sorry but I can't give out that kind of information".

"I know this is unusual, but I really need to contact Dr. Tyler, you don't have to tell me specifics. I can get a warrant and bring you downtown for questioning, require you to provide copies of all of your sales contracts, I really don't want to do *all* of that," Max stated in her most sympathetic voice.

"Well, ummm... they were transferred to his Bank of America account."

"Great, Janet, thank you. You've been very helpful."

"May I ask what this is regarding?"

"I'm afraid it is a police matter. Thank you, Ms. Brinkley." Max disconnected the call without giving the woman a chance to ask any more questions.

After disconnecting the call, she hit speed dial to contact the chief. When the chief picked up, she could barely contain the excitement.

"Chief, I may have found something. I have a doctor who lost his wife and child in a tragic accident. He's off the grid, sold his home about a month ago and seems to have disappeared. I'm going to have Bobby do a trace on his phone, bank accounts, and credit cards, to see what I come up with."

"Good work, Nichols. Keep me posted on what Bobby finds." The call disconnected without another word, and Max shook her head. That was all the recognition she was going to get until she actually found him, evidently.

She bit her lip and called Bobby, wanting to get on this lead before it went cold. "Hey Bobby, it's Max."

"Max, I know that sugary voice anywhere. How's your doctor search going?"

"Well, that's why I'm calling. I may have something, but I need you to run some more info for me on a Dr. Jack Tyler. He's an internist specializing in cardiac surgery. Credit cards, banks, the works – focus on recent activities and any purchases around the dates of the crimes. Plus any activity that might indicate where the good doctor is *now*."

"You got it, my detective beauty. I'll email you as soon as I have something."

Max checked her watch and decided she had time to run and get a cup of much-needed coffee while she waited. For the first time in days, she was excited that this case might have some hope. Pulling back out of the neighborhood, she headed to the closest Starbucks – one of the swanky ones you found in expensive neighborhoods.

That thought brought another with it – one of the vics was last seen at a Starbucks. She wondered whether Dr. Jack Tyler was a frequent Starbucks patron. Thinking she might be on to something, she picked up her cell phone again.

"Bobby, I need one more thing. A photo of the Tyler, can you send it now?"

"Sure, Max darling, anything for you. It's hitting your email now."

Max checked her phone and saw the mail flag blinking. "Thanks, Bobby, you're the best."

Max headed into the Starbucks, opening the email and downloading the photo attachment. She glanced down and saw that the doctor was polished and handsome. *Very* handsome. Dark hair and light blue eyes, charming looking actually. Not exactly the monster one would think capable of killing six people by cutting them right down the middle, peeling back pieces of skin from their abdomen, and cleaning them with ample amounts of bleach.

Still, it was worth a try. Approaching the counter, she ordered a Venti Pike with room for cream. Once she had the drink, she showed her credentials and asked the young black woman –

who had her nose oddly pierced through the middle – if she recognized the picture.

The barista took the cell phone and looked at it for a moment. "Oh, yeah, I've seen him in here before, but not for a while. He used to come in here almost every day. He was an early bird, always came in real early."

"What was he like?"

"He was good, seemed real, you know. Like kind – gentle almost. I know he was a doctor, 'cuz he would come in here with his scrubs on sometimes. Always ordered a Venti Pike, black. His name was Jack. I know, because we write the names on the cups. Is he okay? I heard about the family. It was on the news, and I haven't seen him since."

"I'm not sure. I was hoping to talk to him. Thanks for your time." Picking up her cup, Max headed over to add some cream and sweetener. Then she headed back out to her car, hoping Bobby would have some information for her. But he hadn't sent her anything, and she decided to head home to get her laptop booted up.

Pulling into her drive and then into the garage, she gathered up the papers scattered around the passenger seat and headed into the house, dropping the keys and her holster onto the stand next to her helmet. Immediately powering on her computer, she waited for the wireless to connect and then opened her LAPD email account. She noticed right away that she had new mail from Bobby.

"Thank goodness," she murmured. The sooner she got into this, the quicker she could find this guy.

Diving right in, she pulled open the bank statements first. The accounts were lucrative, and showed all the normal activity – utilities, random purchases, and mortgage payments up until about a year ago. Then the accounts got sporadic, the balances dipping. Most of the monthly bills were on automatic payment, so those seemed to continue, but the normal payroll direct deposits stopped. The credit card purchases charged directly to the checking account suddenly changed from high-class eateries to fast food purchases and liquor stores. Jack Tyler was obviously hurting, and his accounts showed it.

Then a large sum was deposited – over $1 million in proceeds from the sale of the home. Then suddenly, the bank account was closed with no paper trail of where the funds had gone. How could one move more than $1 million with no paper trail? Max sat back, frustrated. Now she was sure this was her guy. He'd fallen apart for a while and now was off the grid. It matched the profile, and the timeline was right. But where had he gone? What was he up to now?

And how could she find him?

Opening up the file regarding background information, she found no living relatives. The wife, Hope, and the daughter Faith had perished in an accident involving a semi on the 405 freeway. The truck driver had fallen asleep and crossed into their lane, flipping the car and crushing down on it, killing the mother and child instantly. Dr. Tyler's mother and father had both died years before, and he'd been an only child. Hope's parents had also both passed. Hope's sister Mindy Prescott appeared to be living in Arizona with a husband and two kids, and reaching her might be the only way to learn more about Jack Tyler. Max thought about calling the sister, but if Jack was her guy and he was living nearby, he could be tipped off. Deciding she needed to drive over to Arizona, a quick calculation said that she could be there by evening. Maybe he had relocated near Hope's sister.

At that point, Max picked up the phone and called the chief again. "Chief, this is our guy, but he's in the wind. I want to make a run over to Arizona and talk to the sister-in-law. She's the only living relative. Bank accounts are closed, and house has been sold. Wife and daughter dead. He went into a drunken stupor for a while after the accident. I think he must have killed our six vics, and I don't know what he's up to now. But we have to find him before he kills someone else."

The phone line was silent for a minute while the chief took this in. Finally, he broke the silence. "Roll with it, Nichols, but I think you need to take someone with you in case our guy is over there. You start showing up there asking questions; it could be risky if he's in the area. Take Officer Cortez, I'll let her know. She'll be ready to depart in forty-five." Then the line went dead again.

Filled with the first sign of hope in a while that she might catch this guy, Max packed up her laptop, stuffed some clothes and toiletries into an overnight bag, grabbed her Glock and keys, and headed off to the headquarters to pick up her partner for the trip. She wasn't sure she loved the idea of taking someone with her, but she had to admit the chief was right. She needed to be careful. Trading out her personal car for a Crown Victoria police-issued vehicle, she logged the mileage per protocol and went to find her road mate. Inside the building, she went to the second floor and found Cortez ready to roll, with a bag tossed over her shoulder.

Lorraine Cortez was a thin, Hispanic woman with sharp features and beautiful, clear, olive skin. She'd earned a reputation as a serious cop who wouldn't take any crap from the guys, despite her looks. Max had never worked with her, but she respected her just the same. Only a couple of years on the job, Cortez had collared her share of perps and pulled down a kingpin from the east side drug ring in an undercover sting. She seemed to be the real deal.

The woman threw her head back in a tough nod as Max walked in. "Heard we're going on a trip. What've we got?"

"Possible murder suspect, the six dead bodies found in the Malibu canyon. I have a potential lead, road trip to Arizona to talk to the sister-in-law, only living relative."

"Okay, I'm ready. You can fill me in on the way."

"Deal, let's go."

The trip to Arizona was mostly uneventful. Max and Cortez had gotten acquainted with each other, sharing their stories of how they each joined the police academy and why they'd wanted to. Cortez had described growing up in the hood, how she was sick of the violence, and had vowed to help put a stop to it. She'd seen a lot in her young life. At just twenty-four she'd lost two cousins and a brother in gang war. Her own mother was an addict, and her dad was long gone. It had been a rough road, but somehow, through perseverance, she'd managed to come out on the good side. After graduating the academy, she'd work as a beat cop for a while and then grabbed the opportunity to go undercover on a drug raid – a dangerous role she'd navigated very well. Her work had netted the shake down of one of the biggest meth dealers in East Los Angeles and gave Cortez a name in the precinct and a likely promotion to detective soon. Max shared her story too as they continued to drive, making their way out of Los Angeles and out into the desert.

The six-hour drive over to Phoenix had them pulling into town just after dark. They decided to check into a hotel and then go by the sister-in-law's house, thinking they would arrive before eight o'clock, when the family would be home. Finding a Hampton Inn, they booked two non-smoking rooms on the second floor and rode the elevator up to drop their bags in their respective rooms. Meeting back at the car just moments later, Max noted the time was a little after seven thirty. Cortez navigated on her iPhone as Max drove through the city streets. About twenty minutes later, they were pulling up in front of a Spanish-style stucco home, with a cactus garden lining the walkway up to the front door.

The two women exchanged a glance and then nodded at each other indicating their individual readiness before exiting the car. It was possible Dr. Jack Tyler was inside this home, and they needed to be prepared. Max unclipped her Glock in her holster, with Cortez following suit. Approaching the house, the women stood on either side of the door as Max rang the bell. After a few moments, the porch light came on and the door swung open, offering a beautiful, blonde-haired, blue-eyed woman, standing about 5'5". She gazed out at them with a questioning smile.

Max did a double take. Bobby had sent photos of Jack Tyler's wife, and this woman could have easily been her twin. There was no doubt they were looking at Hope's sister.

Displaying her badge, Max started, "Good evening, Mrs. Prescott, sorry to bother you so late. I'm Detective Max Nichols, and this is Officer Lorraine Cortez. We were hoping we could ask you a few questions regarding Dr. Jack Tyler."

The woman at the door appeared shocked for a moment, looking from one woman to the other. "Jack? Is he okay?"

"I am not sure, ma'am. That's why we're here. We're hoping you can help us fill in some blanks," Max replied, feeling both relieved and disappointed that the man they were seeking wasn't at this particular home.

Backing away from the door and gesturing for them to come in, the woman said, "I'm not sure I understand, but please come in."

As they entered, they were overtaken with the smell of homemade bread and something that smelled like meatloaf. Max suddenly realized she was very hungry, and that she'd barely eaten all day.

Then a man suddenly appeared from what Max assumed was the hallway, interrupting her thoughts. "Honey? Oh, I thought I heard someone at the door," he said.

"Paul, these ladies are from the LAPD, and they're asking questions about Jack."

The man looked surprised. "Jack, really?"

Max reintroduced herself and Officer Cortez to Paul, and then accepted the offer of a seat on the couch. She'd learned over the years that sitting could help put people at ease, and she really needed these people at ease. Feeling very certain they were alone, except for perhaps the kids down the hall, Max opened the dialogue.

"Mr. and Mrs. Prescott, thank you for talking with us. First, let me say how sorry we are about the loss of your sister and niece. We are investigating a series of crimes in California, and we were hoping you could tell us where Jack is living now. "

Mrs. Prescott looked at her husband and shrugged. "Please, call us Paul and Mindy. As for Jack, we haven't seen him in a while. After the accident he wasn't doing so well. We tried to help, even tried to get him to come and stay with us for a while, but he wouldn't have anything to do with it."

"How long have you known Jack?"

"Gosh, I've known Jack my whole life," Mindy replied. "We grew up next door to each other. Hope and Jack were friends since they were very young. Jack was always at our house. Our parents were friends, played cards together, that kind of stuff. But his dad was gone a lot, traveled with his job. Hope started dating Jack as young as seventh or eighth grade. They got really tight one summer and just never separated after that. Always having a really … interesting bond."

Max noticed that the woman shuddered when she said interesting, and narrowed her eyes. "When you say 'interesting,' what does that mean?"

"Oh, I don't know. Jack was a charmer, handsome and sweet, but for me there was always something strange about him. I never really understood my sister's fascination."

Max and Cortez exchanged a glance, and Mindy continued.

"I don't know what it was, but I know my sister loved him. And there's no doubt that he loved her. He made a wonderful life for her. They were very happy, especially after Faith came."

Max nodded, then went back to something Mindy had said. "You said Jack was always at your house as kids. Did you or your sister spend much time at *his* house?"

"I wasn't over there as much as he was at ours. Hope spent a lot of time over there, but I think they spent that time in the woods rather than in the house."

"Were there any issues with his family life? Were his parents stable?"

"I always wondered about his mom. We never talked about her much, and it seemed like she might drink a lot when his dad was gone."

"I see. And when was the last time you saw your brother-in-law?"

"It's been a few months, now. He started drinking and took a leave of absence from work. Things got really dark for him then, and as much as I hate to say this, I didn't want my children around him. Not when he was like that."

"When you say he got dark, how do you mean?"

"He was acting strangely, not just with the drinking, but with something else. He seemed … I don't know, sneaky, not wanting anyone in his home. I assumed it was because he wasn't taking care of the house. One day I went to his home, he told me to go away and just leave him alone. I didn't know how to help him, so I honored his wishes and left."

Max took a deep breath, but made up her mind. Mindy had obviously noticed some strange behavior in her brother-in-law, and Max didn't think the woman would be opposed to answering a more personal question. "Mindy, what can you tell us about Jack's history? Did you ever know of Jack hurting anyone or did you ever have reason to think that Jack was capable of hurting anyone?"

Surprised by the question, Mindy looked at her husband before answering. "I don't know. Like I said, Jack was always a little off to me. Everyone else was so taken by him. Too much so for me, I guess. I never thought he was as genuine as other people did, but could he hurt someone? I don't know the answer to that. I know he never hurt my sister. He was loving and kind to her. He was a little strange as a boy, spending hours in the woods alone. He had very few friends until high school, except for Hope, but she talked him into joining the football team and he got stronger, gained more friends and developed socially. His good looks always carried him, and the girls loved him. But I don't think he ever dated anyone besides Hope. One summer, when they were about twelve, Hope started pushing him to read everything he could on medicine and sciences. By the time he was a freshman in college, there was no doubt that he was headed to medical school, with Hope as his biggest cheerleader. She was constantly telling him that he could do it, and he did. Right out of college he went to Stanford medical school on an academic scholarship. His grades were off the charts. Hope went with him and helped him work through everything. They were married as soon as he started his residency."

"Okay, this has been very helpful, Mindy. Just one more question. Do you have any idea where Jack would go? He's sold the house and hasn't returned to work at the hospital."

"I'm not really sure. He grew up in California, but there isn't any family left there. So, I really don't know. Without Hope I'm not sure what Jack would do."

Max handed her a business card. "I'd like to thank you for taking time this evening, and again, I'm sorry for the late intrusion." Both Max and Cortez stood to leave.

"Detective, is Jack in some sort of trouble?"

"I'm sorry, we don't really know. He's disappeared, and it's all a bit mysterious. We'd like to talk with him and know that he's okay. If you happen to hear from him, please let us know."

"I will." Mindy and Paul led the officers to the door, holding hands to comfort each other.

Thanking the couple they heard the door close behind them. Once outside, Cortez gave Max a knowing look. "This is your guy, Max. Now we just have to find him."

"I think you're right." Climbing back into the car, Max looked over at her temporary partner and added, "But first things first. I'm starving, and that house smelled great. Let's eat."

Cortez flashed her beautiful, white smile. "Not going to get any complaints from me," she answered.

They Googled restaurants, and quickly found an Italian pizzeria nearby. When they arrived, they rushed in, took in the garlic aroma, shared a glance, and grinned in mutual approval. Max asked for a private table, wanting to talk about the case without the other patrons overhearing them. Though it was after nine o'clock, the restaurant was still pretty busy. Max took this as good a sign at a chance for great food. After all, people didn't crowd into a restaurant with bad food.

After ordering some pasta, garlic knots, Caesar salads, and glasses of red wine, the women tore into the food, savoring the bread and wine first. Cortez washed down a bite of bread with a swish of wine, then opened the conversation.

"So this Jack has some secrets. Did you see the way Mindy shuddered when she said there was something off about him?"

"I sure did. I wonder what secrets Jack had as a boy that she couldn't put her finger on. I also thought it was interesting that she talked about him spending hours in the woods. What was he doing out there? And then she kept saying things that indicated a turning point. That 'one' summer, suddenly Hope was pushing him. If he had these tendencies as a boy, Hope may have found out and then pushed him to turn his desire to hurt things into helping. If he liked cutting things, it would make sense for her to push him into med school."

Cortez thought about this for a moment as she tore off another piece of bread. Just as she was about to say something, though, the rest of their food arrived. They each received a creamy dish of penne pasta with sun-dried tomatoes, capers, and artichoke hearts, and it smelled delicious. As the server walked away, Cortez spoke again.

"Do you think someone who has the urge to kill can control his feelings in that way? Would it be *safe* for him to be a surgeon, or could he just flip one day and start killing his patients? Seems like that might be a bit of a stretch."

"I know, I know," Max agreed, shaking her head her thick locks swaying with the motion. "Something about the fact that there was a change that one summer," making air quotes with her fingers, "is really bothering me."

"What about another road trip? We could head up to Ojai where they all grew up. Maybe we could take a look out in those woods. I know it's been a long time, but maybe there's some special place that was Jack's killing ground back then. It's a long shot, but it might be worth a try. Could be some neighbors around there that still remember him, and they could tell us if there was anything weird going on. Missing pets, that kind of thing. That's usually where these guys start."

Max liked the way Cortez thought. "You might be onto something with that. Maybe Hope caught him and decided to help him. We don't have enough for a subpoena, but if we could get the new owners of his old house to let us stomp around out there, we might stumble onto something. We have to find him before he kills again!"

By the time they finished up their meals, they had agreed they would get up early to grab a quick breakfast, so they could be on the road to Ojai by seven o'clock. Even with the early start, they would not get there until after three o'clock with stops, not leaving them much time to go through the woods. They would have to hurry, so they would have enough daylight to explore Jack's playground if offered the chance to do so. Bidding each other good night in the hall of the hotel, they went off to their separate rooms to settle in for some rest.

When she got into her room, Max called the chief and gave him an update before changing into a pair of men's boxers and a t-shirt. Once she was in the bed, she settled back against the pillows and laid there for a moment thinking of Wells. She was enjoying Cortez's company, but wishing that Wells was crawling in bed with her, remembering the warmth of his skillful hands on her body. Forcing those thoughts from her mind, she chalked them up as silly. After all, they'd only spent one night together, and he lived across the country. She had considered calling him when she got the lead on Jack Tyler, like he had asked her to, but she decided it would only delay the inevitable. They lived worlds and jobs apart and there was no way a long distance relationship could work out. She punched her pillow and allowed her mind to settle down into images of Jack Tyler as a boy in the woods. That was far more important than missing Wells. She had a case to solve, after all. Slowly, she dozed off to sleep.

Morning came too soon, Max quickly showered then packed her sleeping clothes, ran a brush through her long hair, dabbed on makeup and decided she looked good enough. Collecting her things she took one last glance around the room, ensuring she had not left anything behind. Cortez was already in the breakfast lounge, and looked fresh as well. Her big brown eyes connected with Max as she dropped her bags next to the table.

"How'd you sleep?" Cortez inquired.

"Good morning. I slept hotel good, how about you?" Max replied with a slightly tilted smile.

"Good, once I got settled. I couldn't stop thinking about Jack Tyler, though. We need to know a little more about his parents. Usually there's some abuse or something that sets off these behaviors. Do we know anything about that?"

"We don't. Although Mindy said the dad traveled a lot and the mom was home alone, possibly drinking. There could have been some abuse from his mom, or Jack may have had some abandonment issues with his dad, if he was rarely there."

Cortez nodded, thinking. "That may be what set him off as a boy, and if you're right about Hope knowing and helping him, that would explain the bond between them. Maybe she knew he was abused, felt sorry for him, and decided to help."

Max considered what Cortez was saying. She believed they were on the right track, convinced this was the right guy. Now, she just had to find him and prove it before he struck again.

"He *will* kill again. With Hope gone, and the fact that he's not working at the hospital, which has been his vehicle to channel his desires, he won't be able to help himself. All the controls they built have been taken away. The question is... how or why did he suddenly stop, since we know he was escalating? What changed?"

"Maybe he found another woman to replace Hope. If a new woman is creating enough of a distraction right now, it might be enough to keep him from killing anyone else. Or maybe he stopped only because his kill site was discovered."

Max shook her head. "I don't think so. Mindy said he'd never dated anyone besides Hope. This is a girl he'd known since he was born, practically. I doubt he'd be able to settle for anyone else, or keep it together socially. As for the kill site, he was already off his pattern when we found it. I think he'd already stopped. I think he's just moved on. I think he's still killing, but now he's somewhere else."

On that note, the women grabbed an extra cup of coffee for the road, tossed their room keys on the counter in the lobby, thanked the hotel clerk, and left. They had to find this guy's story – and him – before he killed again.

After fueling the Crown Vic, they were on their way, discussing the case throughout the trip back to California. Max had emailed Bobby, requesting the childhood address for Jack Tyler. Bobby sent the information back right away. Cortez resumed the role of navigator, giving Max the directions from her phone.

By two o'clock they were pulling into the small, quaint town of Ojai, the streets lined with unique eclectic shops. This was a beautiful little town, and Max had always loved it, often coming up here on her days off just to enjoy the tranquil, peaceful setting. There was a place called Boccalli's on the outside of town – a restaurant that sat in a beautiful location, and was a hot spot where bikers of all sorts stopped on weekend rides through the beautiful mountains. She particularly loved that you could sit and eat outside under the trees. During the summer months the place was always busy – a definite favorite for local and weekend visitors. Max could imagine growing up in this beautiful little town and wondered of the life Jack had here.

As they drove through town, she pictured Jack as a boy, walking along these streets, going to these places. The car followed the winding road further north. As they continued climbing up the road, the terrain began to change, and soon they were in a mountainous area, driving through a thick forest of tall trees. Max assumed they must be getting close and began looking for addresses. Finding a mailbox at the end of a driveway with the number they were looking for, Max slowed the vehicle down and pulled into the winding drive. Orange trees, not yet in bloom, lined the driveway that led to a large home with a Mediterranean flare made of Mexican stucco. They wound up the drive and arrived at the house, which sat nestled against a brace of trees that led deep into the hillside. Within those trees was the likely childhood playground for Jack and Hope. Max could see why a boy would want to play out there. The beautiful foliage looked like the kind of place you would hike and climb for hours. The area was truly beautiful, and the trees would provide any child the perfect playground, with room for imagination and mystery. And privacy, if the child so desired.

In fact, she thought, it was the perfect place to practice killing. There were plenty of places to hide. The trees draped low, and in some areas were thick almost appearing elusive. Any number of animals certainly lived in those trees and no doubt, when darkness set in, coyotes would be heard howling as they raced after their prey.

Pulling around the circular driveway to stop just in front of the walkway that led to the door, she saw that the house looked deserted. A garage was attached to the two-story home, which had beautiful flowers lining the walkway and surrounding the house in planters. But there weren't any cars around. Someone had a green thumb, at least, and had spent a number of hours loving this flower garden. Walking up the path, Cortez rapped on the door using the ornate door knocker, and waited. After a few moments, the big door swung inward and a small, elderly woman who must have peaked seventy stood peering at the two officers through small silver-framed glasses and the lines on her face.

"Good afternoon, ma'am, I'm Detective Max Nichols, and this is Officer Lorraine Cortez. We were hoping to ask you a few questions," Max said, pitching her voice to a softer tone.

The woman smiled at them, pushing the wrinkles on her face up around her eyes. Her silvery hair shone in the afternoon sunshine. "Well, hello," she offered. "I don't believe I've ever seen two more lovely policemen in my life."

Max and Cortez each pushed back a laugh at the comment – policemen, really? "Thank you, ma'am, could we come in for a moment?"

"Oh, dear where are my manners?" The woman stepped away from the door and let them in. "May I offer you some lemonade?"

Max graciously accepted the offer for the cool drink. They'd been driving for a long time, and giving them lemonade would set this old woman at ease. "Yes, that would be lovely, Mrs…?"

"Please, call me Vivian. I'm no longer married. My husband passed more than a decade ago," the woman said, cutting Max off and offering her guests to take a seat in the living room, before heading off to the kitchen to get the drinks.

As they waited, Max and Cortez checked out their surroundings. The home was nicely decorated with what looked like expensive antiques. There was ornate woodwork around the ceiling and a beautiful mahogany mantel over the fireplace at one end of the room, while at the opposite end a large bay window allowed a view to the backyard. Off in the distance, Max could see the woods. The carpet was a dark paisley design that looked quite expensive. Jack's father had been in software sales in the early days of the Internet boom, Max remembered, and by the looks of the home, he must have done well.

Then Vivian returned carrying a pitcher of lemonade and three glasses filled with ice cubes. Setting the tray on the coffee table, Vivian poured the lemonade and handed a glass to each of the women, then settled into a winged back chair opposite them and smiled.

"Now, to what do I owe the pleasure of this visit? I don't get many visitors these days." A look of sadness passed briefly across her crystal blue eyes. Max gulped, she hated the idea of this woman being all alone, and it made her question her own life. *Would she end up alone like Vivian?* Returning her thoughts to the woman across from her, Max continued, "We're curious about a family that lived in this home years ago – the Tyler's. Did you know them?"

"Oh yes, the Tyler's. We bought this home when Mrs. Tyler passed away. Mr. Tyler was already gone. Jack was the only one still around, and he'd become a successful doctor down in Los Angles. He didn't have any interest in moving back up here. We'd always admired the home, so when the opportunity presented itself, my husband couldn't resist."

Max could hardly contain her excitement. "So you knew this family?"

"Yes, we had lived about a mile from here for years. This is a small community, everyone knows everyone. As a teenager, my daughter babysat for Jack when he was a little boy."

Max contemplated this. She was talking to someone who knew Jack fairly well. "Really, what can you tell us about the Tyler's? She asked hoping to gain more insight to the type of boy Jack was and possibly how he was raised. Any insight into Jack might help lead her to where he was now.

"Well, they were a bit of a strange family, what with the husband gone so often. I never quite understood the arrangement. Mrs. Tyler, Janice, was a beautiful woman, but she was alone far too much. I suppose it only stood to reason that she would find ways to get through the long, lonely stretches when her husband was out of town."

"Oh and how would she do that?" Cortez asked her voice tense with suspicion.

"Well, there were rumors. Mind you, I didn't pay too much attention to those. But there were always suggestions that she had some male suitors coming around when the mister was out of town. People said that some of them weren't very nice, and I always worried for little Jack."

Finding the opening she was hoping for, Max jumped on it. "And what kind of boy was Jack?" she asked.

"He was a dear little boy. A little on the softer side most times, gentle with my daughter, and kind, but there were times where he seemed … different."

"Different? In what way?" Max probed further as her mind processed her thoughts. *Now she was getting somewhere. Hope's sister Mindy had said similar things. How different was Jack exactly?*

"I can't really say, other than … well, at times, it seemed like he was lost inside his own head."

"Vivian, we were told that Jack spent a lot of time in the woods behind this house. Have you or did your husband spend much time in the woods?"

"My husband did a bit. He liked to walk along the stream and enjoy the wildlife, but I never spent any time out there. I focused my time in the gardens. I know there's a play house off in the woods that Jack used to play in when he was a boy. Both he and his friend Hope, who he later married, went out there to play for hours. My daughter really enjoyed babysitting for him because he was always off exploring somewhere. They were only about

116

four or five years apart in age, and she never had to do much to entertain him. Not like kids today, who never want to get outdoors, what with all of the electronics and such."

"Vivian, would you mind if we took a walk out to that play house? We'd like to see where Jack played when he was a boy."

"Oh, dear ... what is it you're looking for? Is Jack okay? Has something happened to him?"

Thinking it might play out better with this woman to be subtle, Max offered, "Jack's missing. He wasn't doing very well after Hope and their daughter Faith died, and now he's disappeared. We're trying to find him, and knowing a little more about his boyhood might help us figure out where he would go."

Vivian shook her head in despair. "I heard about the accident, a real tragedy. Those two were so in love. They were inseparable as kids, all the way through high school. I don't know what you might find out there, or even if that play house is still standing, but you're welcome to go take a look. It sits out about 200 yards or so into the thickest part of the trees, just north of the creek."

Standing up, Cortez placed her drink – now empty – back on the tray. "This is very helpful, Vivian. It's not very likely that anything out there *will* help us find Jack, but it's worth a look."

Max followed suit, placing her glass back on the tray as well. Thanking Vivian for the drinks, saying they would let themselves out, Max and Cortez walked quickly through the room and back out into the sunlight, heading past the garden and into the tree line. They walked through the trees single file, with Max taking the lead, and could hear the rustle of the breeze and soon the trickle of the creek Vivian had spoken of. Before long, Max caught a glimpse of what appeared to be a small building, nearly overgrown with brush. That had to be it.

"Cortez, look up ahead," she muttered.

Cortez peered into the distance and caught sight of the building as well. "Looks like we found our play house."

The women approached the building cautiously. They didn't have anything with them to help them clear the way, but they joined forces in pulling away the brambles that had nearly overtaken the building. After a few minutes of tugging and tearing at the vines, weeds, and brush, they'd pulled back enough of the bramble to expose the small door. Max couldn't help but think that they were looking at something right out of a Huckleberry Finn novel. A dream play house for most boys. They bent to pull on the door and got it open after a few tugs.

"Have I told you I hate spiders?" Max asked Cortez, who looked like she was none too pleased about the small, dark building. She pulled out two sets of small, dark gloves, and handed one pair to Cortez.

Cortez looked at her curiously

"Always got to be prepared," Max explained.

Ducking into the small door frame, Max stepped into the main room of the play house. It was nearly empty, except for a small beanbag that had seen better days, with tiny holes bitten in it from mice. The once white, and now graying, beans spilled out over a toy gun and a soiled, tattered cot that sagged in the middle. Cortez ducked in behind Max, hesitating a moment while her eyes adjusted to the darkness. Max watched as Cortez took in the surroundings, carefully avoiding the spider webs that swept between the corners. Something scuttled across Max's shoe and down into a hole in the floor board, causing her to shudder and suppress a scream.

While Max was wiping away spider webs, Cortez shook her head at her partner, but continued to look around, climbing up a built-in set of stairs that led to a small loft at the far end of the little building.

Standing on the fourth step, poking her head up to peer into the loft, Cortez saw that the area was empty except for a small stack of magazines and a rusty old Swiss Army knife that had long been abandoned.

Collecting the knife and the magazines, Cortez lowered herself back down to the main floor. There was a page folded back in the magazine that really caught her interest.

"Max, check this out." She handed the magazine over, pointing to the page in question. "He studied this page a lot, based on the obvious wear."

Max took the magazine and looked over the page Cortez had flipped open, her eyebrows raised. The magazine article was about the proper procedure of conducting a heart transplant, and the pictures were detailed close-ups of each step in the process.

One photo was of particular interest to Max – the photo showing the initial incision, straight down the abdomen. Exactly like the six victims.

"Cortez, this is our boy," she said quietly. "Now we have to find him."

Continuing to look around, Max thought for a moment about the rodent that had scurried through the floor board, and wondered what else might be hidden under the boards of this little house. Kneeling down, ignoring the thoughts of spiders or worse, she pushed on the ends of the boards, trying to see if any seemed particularly loose. At one end of the building, she found a board that was different than the others.

She looked around for something to use on the board, and grinned when Cortez leaned over her shoulder and offered her the Swiss Army knife. Taking the knife, Max pried on the board until it gave way. When she pulled it to the side, she could see down to the ground below the playhouse. Under the floor board, barely visible through the leaves and dirt, was a metal box.

Holding her breath, Max reached down and pulled the box out of the hole, setting it on the floor of the play house. She sat staring at the box and anticipation grew of what might be inside. She was hopeful and yet almost afraid of what she might find. There was a small padlock holding the box closed. One swipe with the knife opened the hasp, and the lock dropped off. Max gave Cortez a questioning look, then reached to remove the lid.

Inside the box was a deck of playing cards, some rubber gloves, a knife that was much bigger than the one Max had used to pry the lock open, a change of clothes that were now moth eaten and appeared to be those of a young boy, and a series of small, random bones. None of the bones were large enough to be human. They also didn't belong to a single animal, given that there were three unique sets of jaw bones.

"His trophies from his early days of killing," Max breathed out. They'd definitely found their man. Now she would just have to prove it.

She reached in to pull out a small folded paper that looked like a letter, and opened it. The words were too faded to completely discern what the letter had said, though she could make out a signature from Hope. Reaching into the small side pocket on her gun holster, she fished out an extra-large evidence bag, and carefully placed the box with all of its contents, magazines, and Swiss Army knife into the bag, sealing it with adhesive evidence tape.

"I think we have enough here to have reasonable suspicion that Jack Tyler committed our murders," she said. "Now we have to find him."

Stepping back out of the play house, the women both furiously brushed at their hair and clothes, stripping away any webs and leaves.

"This place gives me the creeps. Let's get out of here," Cortez offered first.

"No arguments here," Max replied, quickly making her way back through the brush the way they had come. Then she stopped. Out of the corner of her eye, she'd seen what appeared to be something carefully carved into a tree. She jetted off the path they'd forged on their way into the playhouse to get a closer look, and motioned for Cortez to follow her. They stopped, staring, in front of the tree.

Before them, carved into the wood, were the words, 'We can do it together. I promise.' A heart circled the words, and under the heart were two letters – J and H. The initials had a unique look, as if each had been carved by a separate hand. Jack and Hope had made their solemn vow right here in the woods, where it all began.

"Hope definitely knew Jack had a problem, then," Max said. That confirmed her suspicions.

"She must have been helping him," Cortez agreed. "Maybe trying to fix him."

Max nodded. She'd convinced Jack to make medicine the vehicle for channeling the impulses to kill. As a surgeon, Jack could cut people open and touch their organs without it being a bad thing. If his impulse didn't require killing, but was a fascination with the internal organs, then the doctor gig was the perfect outlet. Hope and Jack had found a way to keep him from hurting animals, and ultimately people.

"And when Hope died, the outlet was damaged, and ultimately the channel was closed. He slipped right back into his old ways, no longer denying his impulses, and there was no one there to stop him. Only now he was an experienced surgeon, capable of much worse things than a little boy practicing on animals," Max said, concluding her thoughts out loud.

Cortez let out a low whistle as she read the carving in the tree. Pulling out her cell phone, she snapped a photo of it, and they returned to their path and exited the tree line with the evidence bag in tow. Max went back up to Vivian's door and tapped lightly.

The silver-haired woman returned to the door, smiling. "Well, how was your adventure?"

"We found a couple of items that we think might be useful," Max replied, holding up the bag. "I was hoping we could take these with us to have our analyst look over them. There may be something in here that'll help us figure out where to look for Jack. Once we're done with them, we can return them to you."

"Oh I don't care what's in that old building. If you think it'll help you find Jack, please take what you need. I don't need them returned. I've never even seen anything out there."

"Thank you, Vivian, this has been very helpful," Max said, offering her a business card. "If you think of anything Jack may have said that might indicate where he would go one day, please call me right away."

"I will. I sure hope you find him soon. He must be lost without his family."

Max thanked her one more time and then waved good-bye, heading back to the car where Cortez waited. As they left Ojai and headed back towards Los Angeles, Max grew more anxious about their findings. They were definitely onto something and it was only a matter of time before they caught up to Dr. Jack Tyler.

Getting back to police headquarters after seven o'clock, Max and Cortez went directly to talk to the chief. After walking him through everything they knew, and the fact that they needed forensics to try to recover the letter, they grew quiet. He leaned back in his chair, forming a steeple under his chin with his thick fingers.

"Good work. Get that letter down to forensics, along with the knife. Let's find out if there's any blood on that blade, and if so, what kind. I'll let you keep working this for a couple more days, and if you can get a lead on your guy, we'll make this case active again. If we can't get a lead on him, we'll have to wait until he strikes again. My guess is that our guy can't just stop, and as soon as he kills again – no matter where he is – we might be able to pick up on the lead. Get Bobby to load this up on the national database. If he strikes somewhere else, hopefully we'll hear about it. Cortez, you stay on the case with Nichols."

"Yes, sir," Cortez responded, excited to keep working the case.

"Thank you, sir," Max stated, suppressing her emotions as she turned to leave.

The women left the office and stopped outside, the door closing behind them. Max let out a big sigh. "Well, we bought some more time. Let's get these in and see if anything in here tells us where our boy went. While forensics is trying to recover the letter and run blood analysis on the knife, we can go through the magazines to see if there's anything else in there. Maybe we'll get lucky and find a specific story about a special place. Jack might have been harboring some childhood dream of moving to some other state." Cortez nodded to Max as they headed down the corridor to the forensics department.

The forensics lab was led by an unusual man named Porter, with bushy eyebrows and unorthodox ways for getting things done. Despite the oddities, Max really respected him. He ran a tight ship, and she'd built a relationship with him over the years. He knew she didn't ask for unnecessary favors, so when she came knocking on his door he was generally willing to help. After first complaining about short staff and heavy workloads, of course.

Today would prove no different. He fussed at her for a few minutes, then picked up the phone and called in two of his forensics specialists, giving them sharp directions to drop what they were doing and see if they could find anything useful on the items Max had brought in for review. They would study the bones and give some insight into what animals they had belonged to, how they had died – if that was possible to figure out – whether their blood was on the knife, and, of course what the letter had once said.

Having not eaten since the breakfast at the hotel, Cortez and Max headed down to Engine Co. No.28 to get something for dinner. When they entered the building, the smells and memories wafted over Max as she remembered the last time she had been here, it was with Wells. At that time they barely knew each other, but it was here that those first hints of attraction had developed. All heads turned as the two attractive women entered the restaurant. People stared as the hostess led the women to their table. Max was further tortured by her memories as they were seated at the same table where Max and Wells had shared lunch.

Cortez noticed a shift in Max's mood and wondered what had just happened. Cautious not to pry, she let it slide by not asking what was up. A few minutes after ordering Max seemed to be back to normal, starting to talk about their last two days. After tearing through their food and paying the bill, the officers decided to meet back at headquarters at eight o'clock in the morning to see what the lab had come up with and then spend some time working the magazines. Returning to the parking lot, they said their good-byes and headed for their respective vehicles.

Chapter Thirteen

Jack had been enjoying school. He was making friends, and with his attention so focused on studying, he rarely felt the darkness nagging at him. The instructor was fantastic, and he had made fast friends with her. They had fun days where they did silly things and often were pulled in by the stylist to practice on each other. Jack had never had so many people fondling with his hair, hands or feet in his life. He had been uncomfortable at first but quickly accepted it as a necessity.

Leaving school each day, he would return home, eat, workout and hit the books making sure that when it came time to test he was well prepared. Each night he would fall into bed exhausted, and his mind would run through the random clients that came in to have their nails done by the students at discount prices. So far no one specific had caught his eye, but he knew all he had to do was remain patient. She was out there. He knew it, and it was only a matter of time. His job for the moment was to remain focused on completing school.

Chapter Fourteen

The next morning, Max got up early, not having been to the gym in several days, and in desperate need of a workout. After over an hour of aggressive boxing and free weights, she hit the locker room for a shower before meeting up with Cortez. She grabbed a large cup of coffee on the way in, and entered the room where she and Wells had worked the case together over a week earlier. Cortez was already settling in at the table.

"Hey, good morning," Max greeted her. "Ready to go see what the lab has for us?"

"You know it," Cortez replied, grabbing her own coffee off the table and following Max to the lab.

Approaching Porter, Max smiled, trying to tame him before he started in on his usual tirade. But he shook his head warningly.

"Nichols, it's too soon for anything yet. This is Los Angeles. Do you know how many crimes happen every day?"

"I know Porter, I know, but I also know you can work magic sometimes. You can't blame a girl for trying." Max batted her long eyelashes and flashed a huge smile full of beautiful white teeth at the grumpy, old man.

"Yeah, I know what you're up to Nichols," Porter said, wagging his finger at her. "Come on; let's go see what we have." He waved for her and Cortez to follow him into the lab. Approaching one of the two lab techs, Porter nearly shouted, "John, what do we have on the knife and bones?"

The man jumped, but grinned when he saw Max. "Yes sir, I actually do have a few things for you. The bones are from at least three different animals – two cats and a squirrel. There could be more, but it'll take a bit of time to sort through them. Looks like at least one of the cats and the squirrel was killed with some sort of knife. There's sharp scarring on some of the bones. My initial analysis suggests they were cut down through the abdomen with the knife, going deep enough to strike some of the breast and rib bones and cause the scarring. More time with the bones and I'll be able to confirm this. Maybe even match the scarring to the knife. I've also identified that there was animal blood on the blade and down inside the hinge. I confirmed the blood is a combination of feline and rodent, which is consistent with the bones."

"Can you check for prints on that knife? We might be able to match to our suspect," Max said quickly. If they could prove without a doubt that it was Jack killing those animals, it would strengthen her case.

"I'll see if there are any prints to lift, sure. Give me until tomorrow to do that part." Obviously done with his report, he turned back to his work station.

Porter then shouted out to the other lab tech, "Jose, where are we on the letter?"

The young Hispanic male appeared with the letter vacuum sealed in a plastic bag. The writing on the letter was now obvious, and Max flexed her hands. He'd obviously done something to the letter to lift the ink to the surface. That meant they'd get to see what Hope had written him. Obviously something important enough to keep.

"Here you go, sir. I was able to get most of the writing to appear. There are a couple of spots that are too damaged to repair, but I made you copies of what I have. I can try to do some more work on the missing elements, but I think you can figure out what the message is from what I have so far." The tech handed Max a copy of the letter in a file folder.

Looking at the techs and Porter, she grinned. "You guys are the best. Call me if you come up with prints before tomorrow morning, otherwise, we'll see you then." Max accepted the folder, glancing at Cortez, and the women rushed out the door.

Back up in the meeting room, Max opened the file folder and took out the copy of the letter. It appeared to be written by a young person, with a few words spelled wrong, and read:

Jack,

I know you are scared. I am too but I know together we can be stronger. I wont let you down. I have an idea on what we need to do. You will have to promise me that you will listen to me and fight hard to stay with the plan. One day we will be together and you will be special. We can use the play house to study and prepare. _____e will go away together and live happily ever after just like in the farie tales. I believe in you and us and will always love you like you always love me. We have to keep this secret. No one else can ever know. I brought you some books today. You need to start to study these and let the

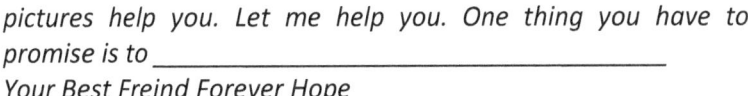

pictures help you. Let me help you. One thing you have to
promise is to _____
Your Best Freind Forever Hope

The blanks in the letter were areas where the damage had been too great, but the overall message was clear. Hope had known Jack had a problem, and she'd vowed as a young girl to help him.

Max and Cortez looked at each other across the table, Cortez speaking first. "You nailed it. Hope *did* know. There's no real evidence here, but knowing about the animal bones and Jack going off the deep end after her death, this guy is absolutely our killer."

Max nodded, but still wondered about one line in particular. *What had Hope asked Jack to promise her? What exactly was the plan he had to stick to? Was it that he wouldn't kill anymore, or that he would keep it only to animals, never hurting a person? How could all of this help lead her to the where Jack was now?* Max feared these answers might never be known, unless Jack would answer them one day, and she needed to find him before he *did* kill again. Max wondered what had happened that drove Jack to kill, she pictured these two young kids trying to work through something as challenging as containing the urges to kill and a tight feeling formed in her chest.

Sighing, she turned to the next problem. "Well we still don't know where he's gone. Let's read these magazines page for page, see if there's an indication of where ole' Jacky boy may have gone. These might be our only chance of getting a lead on where he is. With his bank accounts closed, no family connections, and quitting his job, we don't have any place to look for him. And I don't want to have to wait until he starts dumping bodies again." Max picked up the magazine with the photos of the heart surgery and started flipping through it. Obviously, Jack had spent a lot of time studying this particular magazine. Maybe the answers lay here.

Cortez picked up another magazine. Starting with the cover, she read line for line from cover to cover. After two hours, Max threw down the magazine she had been reading through, frustrated. Nothing was jumping out at her. It was like she was looking for a needle in a haystack. Cortez too showed her frustration, leaning back in her chair shaking her head.

"I have no idea what I'm looking for. Why couldn't this guy have underlined the next location in here?" Cortez scoffed, somewhat joking.

Max laughed at her frustrated humor. "I know. I was hoping this would be easy. Let's get some fresh coffee and dive back in. I need some air and a walk. My ass is numb from sitting in that hard chair." Standing and stretching her thin, muscular frame, Cortez joined her, walking out of the meeting room and down the hall. Two officers were heading their way, including a tall black male Max recognized as Officer James Wilson, and a Hispanic man that Max didn't know.

"Yo, Cortez, hear you made the big time working a multiple with a girl dick," Wilson cat called after them.

Cortez shut him down. "Don't be jealous, just because Max here has one and you don't." The women laughed all the way out the door, while the Hispanic male patted Wilson on the back and said, "You just got told."

The women shook their heads at the ridiculous ways of some of the male officers. Part of the hazard of being a female cop was standing up to such interactions. Walking up the street to a coffee house frequented by the whole force, Max soaked in the sunshine, though the air was still brisk. She was ready for summer, preferring warmer temperatures. It felt nice for a moment to shed the case and the demons that came with trying to constantly think like a killer. Cortez fell in line beside her, also enjoying being outside and stretching her legs. They walked in silence to the coffee house, both churning through their own thoughts. After ordering their drinks, they pulled up stools in the window booth that faced the street and looked out at the people passing them.

"If there aren't any leads in those magazines, where do we look next?" Cortez finally asked.

"I don't know," Max admitted, shrugging. "We're out of leads until he either strikes again uses a credit card, or some other financial tie, or we get a tip. Adding his profile and the specifics of how he kills to the national database will help us if he lands somewhere else and kills there. Hopefully, other precincts will be looking for similar crimes. I can do the same once a week or so, but I hate that we may be waiting for him to kill someone else before we know where he's gone. That means we're not doing our job."

Cortez looked out the window, her eyes shining with the sunshine, her sharp features tense, deep in thought. Suddenly she stood up, saying, "Well then we better find something in those magazines. Let's go figure out what we're missing."

Max smiled at her enthusiasm, grateful for the help and motivation. "Okay, let's do this."

They walked back to the headquarters with a rejuvenated energy, their heads cleared by the fresh air and coffee.

When they got back into the meeting room, Cortez said, "I have an idea, let's write down every city in those magazines. Just make a list and catalog the associated page numbers. At least we'll see if there's some sort of theme. Then we can look at any stories that cover that theme." Stopping, she looked to see what Max thought of the idea.

"I like it. Let's do it. I didn't really understand those articles anyway. At least this way I feel like we have a strategic approach."

They spent the next several hours listing every city in the seven magazines, noting duplicates, and then noting the publication dates and page numbers. When they were done, Max looked up at the clock on the wall and was shocked to see it was already seven o'clock. Where had the day gone? They had a long list, but there were some cities listed more often than others. Los Angeles was listed the most times, followed by New York City, Phoenix, then Miami, and then on to cities with smaller populations, like Baton Rouge and Tulsa.

"I think with this list we can contact the local authorities and see if any recent crimes match our case. We can also go onto the database and look for possible matches, narrowing in on these areas. He was a kid and would have been open to suggestion. It makes sense that he would have gotten his idea to move from something he'd read when he was young. It's going to take days if not weeks to let everyone know and go through the database. I hope the chief lets us stay focused on this. My gut tells me our guy is either here in the city, still waiting to strike again, or has moved to one of these places. He studied these magazines for years, dreaming of these places. I think we'll find him in one of these cities. The question is which one, and how?"

Chapter Fifteen

Jack had spent the past two months deep in his books, studying and learning the proper techniques for giving manicures and pedicures, applying nails in the various hottest styles – French tips, half-moon, two-tones, and pink and white – all coined as nail art. He had worked on the relationships with his fellow classmates, most of who were female, and had pulled off the perfect impersonation of a gay man. The girls were constantly trying to hook him up with a male friend of theirs, though he'd always decline, saying he didn't have time for a relationship. On several occasions they'd all gone out for drinks after school, sharing stories about their clients. He was fitting in well, just like he'd hoped.

He was getting practical experience, through his training, and was becoming very confident this had been the right decision. Working on the clients he had seen a lot of woman, and he could sense that with more exposure he would be able to find the perfect one. He just had to keep looking. Jack had always applied himself and had a level of dedication unusual for most people – a skill Hope had helped him develop. In this case, the dedication was in his desire. Or rather … not desire, but the *need* to have Hope with him again. There simply wasn't room for lack of focus, not if he was going to accomplish his goal. With that in mind, even the darkness had been manageable. He'd absorbed himself in the nail school activities and friendships so deeply that he'd hardly thought of his internal need. It certainly wasn't gone, but for now he had to stay focused on the goal. And that was enough to keep the need buried.

Melody had proven to be a perfect instructor and a good friend, promising Jack – as Thomas – that she would help him find work as soon as he graduated. He had professed a strong financial burden and said that he needed to get to work quickly. None of that was true, of course, as Jack had ample means, but no one could ever know that. No, his desire to get working quickly was for a much different and more urgent matter. He soon would have his life back. He was going to put the pieces back together. She was out there. The perfect fit; he just knew it. Completing his classes had just gotten him that much closer to finding her.

The time had flown by, and he would be graduating tomorrow. It was hard to believe that he'd met the 600 hours of study required in the state of Oklahoma. The only thing left was taking the exams to get his license, and securing a place – or ideally two – where he could apply his new training. He'd already scheduled his exam date in Oklahoma City, where the Oklahoma State Board of Cosmetology was located. It wouldn't be long now until he found her and brought her home.

The next day, Jack showed up ready for his graduation. This was a true turning point in his life, and he was taking it seriously. He'd dressed for the occasion and the part. Everyone had decided that after the graduation ceremonies, they'd go to dinner and then to Club Majestic for a night of dancing. Jack had never been a good dancer, so he spent the last couple of weeks in between studying, watching videos in the evenings of gay men in various gay clubs throughout the world. This had helped him prepare for both the evening of dancing and also how to behave in such a setting. He'd even gone out one night by himself, to a male club called Maverick's, just to get a feel for the environment and to watch how the men interacted with each other. He couldn't afford to blow his cover now. He was way too close for that.

Jack was enjoying the graduation celebration. The school had provided cap and gowns, and they had laid out a red carpet and a platform for each student to walk up and accept their diplomas. Some of the students had brought their family members, and Jack spent time being introduced to several of his classmates, significant others.

The week before, the whole class had worked on the evening plans, and they had agreed to meet at the Olive Garden to have dinner. The drinks had started flowing there with everyone having a glass of red wine with dinner. The festivities were wildly fun. Jack was relaxed, enjoying the time with the students he had grown close to over the past couple of months. Everyone was in good spirits, telling favorite class stories, until it was time to head to the club. Jack had avoided riding with anyone, saying he might get lucky tonight, to which everyone had laughed. He met up with the group outside the club after circling the block a couple of times looking for a parking space, finally finding one a block away just past an alley in front of an old abandoned brick warehouse.

After paying the cover charge and receiving a stamp on their wrists, everyone went in, with Melody wrapping her arm inside Jack's. Jack really enjoyed her high energy and infectious smile. He considered her a friend and liked her company. Of course not in any romantic way, that would be disloyal, but spending time with her was pleasurable and had made the time go by faster. They approached the bar and ordered their drinks, the music pumping and the bass so loud it seemed to vibrate inside his chest. Jack bounced along to the beat, trying to look natural. It wasn't long before he was approached by a younger man, probably in his early twenties. The kid started flirting with him, making his interest apparent, and Jack had his first challenge. All he had to do, of course, was flash that beautiful smile – the one that made just about anyone fall in love with him.

It worked like magic. Within minutes the handsome and well-built, though small, young man with sandy brown hair and blue eyes, was swooning over Jack.

Melody flashed her bright smile and winked at Jack, leaving him to flirt as she was pulled onto the dance floor by a few of the other girls.

Jack tossed back his drink and ordered another, allowing the liquid to loosen him up. Before long the young man, who had introduced himself as Gary, pulled Jack out onto the dance floor. Jack was able to successfully carry the beat, while displaying some suggestive moves. Unfortunately, this only further interested Gary, and the younger man moved closer to him. In response, Jack could feel the familiar darkness rising up inside him, and gulped. If he wasn't careful, Gary was going to get lucky tonight. He just didn't realize how.

Jack offered to buy Gary a couple more drinks, pretending that he too was drinking more, but he actually only ordered Coke for himself. The music was so loud when he placed the order Gary couldn't hear. Jack wanted to have his wits about him from here on out. The dancing and drinks flowed as fluently as the music. Jack and Gary continued to dance wildly with Melody and the girls, the group randomly dancing together in playful abandon. It was getting late, as was evidenced by the packed dance floor with sweaty, intoxicated patrons.

Gary was hinting at leaving together, which met with Jack's thoughts perfectly. As Jack led Gary out the door, he flashed Melody a smile and held a thumb and finger to his ear, indicating that he would call her. Melody laughed, giving him the thumbs up as she watched the men disappear out the door.

Outside, the night air felt good on Jack's sweaty body. Gary was clinging to his hand as they headed down the street, away from the sound of the pumping music into the darkness. When they got further down the street, Jack invited Gary to come home with him. He knew the younger man would accept and wasn't surprised when he did.

The men rounded the corner and passed the alleyway where Jack had parked. He unlocked the doors to his SUV and watched Gary climb into the passenger seat. Then he opened the back door and reached into his lab bag where he had a syringe of Chloroform and a rag carefully tucked away. There was no time to apply gloves, so he depressed the syringe into the rag, dropping the syringe back into the bag pocket. Closing the door and looking to be sure no one was around, Jack climbed in behind the steering wheel and leaned over as if he was going to kiss Gary. His companion was completely compliant, but instead of Jack's lips coming into contact with the young man's mouth, it was the chemical-soaked rag that stole his breath away.

Jack held Gary back against the seat, watching as Gary struggled against the rag for a few moments and then slumped against the window. Jack propped him up and leaned his head back in the seat, to make it look like he was just settled back against the head rest. Once he was confident his sleepy passenger looked natural to anyone outside, Jack pulled the SUV out and headed towards the highway entrance and home. Jack felt excitement surge in him as the darkness swelled at the opportunity that had so naturally presented. His mind raced as he considered the risks. This was not how it was supposed to be, yet Gary had made it so...*easy.*

Carefully watching for any signs of police while making sure he maintained his speed, Jack felt the excitement growing inside him. This was an unexpected treasure, and while it wasn't in his plans, it had played out so naturally that he couldn't pass it up.

This would be the last time before Hope came home, and he could return to his normal life. He knew Hope would understand. She always had in the past, and there was no reason to think this time would be any different.

As he drove, Jack considered the consequences of his spontaneity. People had seen him with Gary, but they hadn't talked to anyone other than his classmates. He'd been careful not to tell anyone that his name was Thomas, he had paid cash for everything, and he didn't plan to go back to this club any time soon. Gary had told him he was new to town, and didn't really know anyone in Tulsa. This information seemed to minimize the risk, as it was unlikely that anyone would report Gary missing for the time being.

Jack wondered suddenly what it might be like if anyone *did* report him missing. There had been a newscast on Benz missing two days after Jack had taken him from his home. The police report had said he'd last been seen leaving work and then disappeared from his home. It had gone on to say that there was no sign of forced entry and no sign of a struggle. At the time of the report, Benz was still zip tied to Jack's table in the basement. He had watched the report, but he had not felt any specific need to hurry. He was certain no one would trace Benz to him. He had immediately determined there was no need to change course and had fully enjoyed Benz. However, he recognized that he would need to move faster with Gary, since he had just been seen with him.

Gary had said that he had just started working as a waiter two days ago. He had spoken about not yet having made any friends at work, and that this had been his first night out to the club. Even with no friends or family in the area, there was a chance that an employer might report him missing. But even if they did, would the police spend much time on a missing man who had just moved into the area? He didn't think the employer would even report an employee missing. Waiters and waitresses came and went. Jack decided that given the short employment, the employer would most likely think the new employee was unreliable, and had simply quit without giving any notice. His thought process gave him comfort.

It wasn't even worth worrying about, really. Smiling to himself, he concluded that he was safe and could proceed. The excitement of his decision welled up inside him, causing his heart to race just a little bit faster.

When he arrived home, Jack pulled into the garage and quickly went into the house and opened up the pantry door, exposing the basement stairwell. Returning to the garage, he opened the passenger door and pulled Gary out, lifting his sagging body up onto his shoulder. The young man had a small frame, but was muscular, and Jack struggled with getting him balanced properly as he navigated the stairwell. He accidentally knocked Gary's head against the wall on the way down. Gary responded mildly with a groan, but between the chloroform and the alcohol, he nodded back out.

In the surgery room, Jack disrobed Gary and placed his nude body on the stainless steel table, which Benz had previously occupied. He thought about it for a moment but decided that he couldn't afford to keep Gary. A disappointment, but he really couldn't risk it. Additionally, he decided he would need to be especially cautious; with Gary being a gay man, there could potentially be other risks. Though not likely, Gary could be positive for HIV. He would need to be extra cautious with any blood contact. Putting on his surgical clothing and gloves, Jack carefully zipped tied Gary to the table.

Gary was beginning to wake up, and at first he smiled at the sight of Jack standing over him. As his vision slowly cleared, though, he became aware of the fact that he couldn't move his arms or legs, and that he was in a very strange place. Jack hadn't yet placed duct tape over his mouth, and Gary struggled to speak, swallowing hard in an effort to wash away the drugs in his system.

"Thomas, what are you doing?" he gasped.

Ignoring the question, Jack pulled the rolling surgical tray toward him.

Gary's eyes searched the room wildly. His eyes fixed when they saw the scalpels and various tools on the tray. He began to struggle against the zip ties, screaming, "Noooooo! What are you doing, Thomas?"

Jack didn't enjoy hurting people, really. It was the touching of life and the witness of death that he required. He didn't like hearing Gary's pleas. He grabbed the roll of duct tape off the shelf and applied a six-inch strip over Gary's mouth, quieting the frantic man. Then, selecting the scalpel off of the tray, Jack made a perfect slice, opening Gary right down the middle just like he had Benz. Gary thrashed about on the table against the pain and restraints. His eyes bulged from his head and he cried out unintelligible pleas through the duct tape. Blood poured out, and Jack's heart raced as he watched the flow. Choosing the retractor from the tray next, Jack used the tool to separate the incision, allowing him access to the tissue and organs inside Gary's chest and abdomen.

By the time Jack had the retractor in place, Gary had passed out from the pain, but Jack hadn't even noticed. He was fixated on placing his hands inside Gary's body. With Benz, he had to resist going too far at once, as he wanted to keep Benz alive. But this time there was no need for personal restraint. Gary would be dead soon, and Jack could do what he wanted. He took the rib spreader and used it to push Gary's ribs apart, allowing him a complete view and access to all of Gary's organs. The feeling of euphoria rolled over him as he carefully explored the now-dead body on his table.

Jack was enjoying his time with Gary so much that he lost track of time, and when he next looked up, he realized it was nearly four o'clock in the morning. Deciding he had to move Gary quickly, he began the process of cleaning up and prepping the SUV for transporting Gary out to the Lock and Dam road. Since no one had stumbled onto Benz, Jack thought he had the perfect place to dispose of Gary as well.

When Jack arrived at Lock and Dam, he found the area much as he had before – no one around. The townspeople of Inola were sleeping tight in their beds. Retrieving the flashlight and shovel, Jack made his way out into the woods, finding his way to Benz's resting place from memory. Soon he was in the familiar clearing and began digging under the brush and trees near where he had buried Benz. Once he'd dug deep enough, he returned to the SUV and lifted Gary out in the standard plastic roll. He carried Gary through the woods and deposited him and his clothes into the hole, just like he'd done with Benz and the others in California. Next, he carefully replaced the soil, making sure the body was

139

fully covered. While he was there, he fanned the flashlight over the entire area, looking to see if anything had been disturbed by humans or animals. But everything seemed to be in order. No one had discovered the site.

Satisfied, Jack returned to the car, loaded the shovel and flashlight, then climbed into the driver's seat to make his way back home.

Jack awoke to banging on the door, followed by the doorbell ringing. Not used to having visitors, he'd never even heard the doorbell ring before, and it took a moment for his mind to recognize that there was someone at the door. His night had been long, and he'd fallen into bed quite exhausted. Shaking off the fog, he climbed out of bed and pulled on some pants before navigating his way down the hall. Going through a mental checklist, he thought that he'd left everything in proper order after returning from Inola just a few hours earlier. It was safe to have someone in the house.

He thought.

As he approached the door, he saw Melody standing on his front porch. She'd been here once before when he hosted a study group, but he hadn't expected her to show up unexpectedly.

Opening the door and smiling, he greeted her, "Girl, don't you know when a guy has to sleep?"

"Good morning, lover boy. Is your guy still here?" she giggled, looking around the house.

"I'm not that kind of guy, really! How dare you," Jack teased back as he led her into the kitchen area.

"Okay, I really am sorry to barge in," she said as she settled into a seat at the dining room table. "But I have some great news and couldn't wait to tell you."

"Really, do tell."

"Well, I have a friend who owns two salons in Tulsa, one out on 191st and the other in mid-town. She's looking for someone to work both locations. I immediately thought of you because you were saying you needed a lot of hours, and I think this will give you those hours without having to deal with two different manager styles."

"OMG, this *is* fantastic news," Jack exclaimed with flair.

"I thought you'd be happy. I want to set up an appointment with you and her tomorrow. Will that work for you? Then if you hit it off and she hires you, you can start setting up and work under her license as an apprentice until your exam in a week."

"This just sounds too wonderful," Jack said, beaming at her. "Have you eaten? All this good news is making me hungry."

"Sure, you want to go get something? IHOP is just down the street, isn't it?"

"It is. Just let me grab a shirt and some shoes. I'll be right back, honey." Jack sashayed out of the room and down the hall to dress quickly and add some gel to his hair. He hoped she wasn't wandering around his home, and his heart thumped at the thought. What if she found something? What if he'd forgotten to close the pantry?

He rushed back to the kitchen to find Melody still sitting at the table, enjoying the view. His mind settled then, and he grabbed his keys.

"Okay, I'll drive. My car is behind your garage door," she offered, standing.

"You're a doll. Shall we?" He waved his arm toward the door in a sweeping motion, inviting her out the door.

Melody had grilled Jack during breakfast about his date the night before, but he dodged the questions, saying he wasn't a kiss-and-tell kind of guy. Melody had accepted it as a good enough answer, and the conversation turned to the possibility of him working for her friend. She had placed a call and set up a meeting for Jack the next morning. He was very excited, and had chatted about it nonstop for the rest of the meal. Then breakfast had ended, and Melody had dropped Jack back off, waving good-bye.

He went inside and immediately went down to the basement to verify that he'd appropriately cleaned up the night before. Things looked to be in perfect order, but he didn't trust his state of mind after his time with Gary. He went through the process of cleaning it again, bleaching every nook and cranny. Once he was satisfied with his work, he walked back upstairs to shower and settle in, awaiting his interview in the morning. He spent some time selecting his clothing for the occasion. He had a ten o'clock meeting with the owner, at the midtown location. The 191st Street shop was a bit of a drive from Catoosa, but in a way this was really good. He knew police looked at patterns, and considered location heavily in an investigation. Working at salons that were far apart and one that was far from his home was a good strategy.

The morning came, and Jack followed the usual routines, readying himself for his interview. He wondered if the salon owner, Samantha, would ask him to perform any specific manicuring demonstrations to show ability to do the job. He wasn't worried though. He knew he was ready, and this seemed like a better option than having to answer fake questions. Either way, he knew he could do it.

Pulling up in front of the address Melody had given to him, he saw a bright red sign over the door for The Beehive. There was a contemporary drawing in the sign, depicting a woman with chiseled features and a big beehive hairstyle. *Clever,* Jack thought to himself, considering the contrast between the 60s and contemporary. The windows had writing in big white letters, displaying the various services provided, which included manicures and pedicures.

Jack took a deep breath and headed into the salon, the door chiming as he entered. A tall, brightly dressed woman came from a back room, while two other women gave pedicures to patrons seated in the recliner chairs with bubbling water at their feet. The salon was tasteful and clean. Jack approved of the layout and could picture himself working here.

When the woman approached, he introduced himself. "Good morning, my name is Thomas; I have an appointment with Samantha."

An infectious smile broke across her face. "I'm Samantha. Good morning, nice to meet you, Thomas. Come on back here to my office where we can chat."

The next forty-five minutes were spent discussing Jack's recent graduation, station rent fees, and the how money was shared for the services offered. Samantha talked about the flow of traffic between the two salons. The 191st Street location had much better foot traffic, while this location had more repeat business and people on a fixed income. Jack figured he would get a good cross-mix of the population, which was exactly what he needed. He wasn't interested in social status. He *was* interested in specific attributes, and finding those was all that mattered to him. So this would work out perfectly.

By the end of the interview, Samantha was charmed by Jack. He'd used his smile and charisma to draw her in. He left the shop with a set of keys to each location and an assigned work station, which he was free to start setting up right away. She'd given him a work schedule that split him between the two locations. Samantha had sent him to the 191st Street location to meet the other salon workers. She told him to go ahead and set up there as well, as soon as he had time. He had gone directly over to the other location and after meeting everyone, he'd spent an hour hanging out with the girls that worked there, making sure he would fit in. Feeling very comfortable with everyone he had bid his farewell telling them he would see them soon.

After leaving the second shop, he called Melody on his cell and thanked her profusely. Things were coming together so smoothly. Doors were opening and setting the plan in perfect motion.

Chapter Sixteen

Max and Cortez had spent two weeks working the magazine leads before the chief pulled back their hours. The man now named The Freeway Killer by the media had ramped up his activity, and more innocent people had been killed while absentmindedly riding the buses across Los Angeles, innocently reading a book, listening to music, or working emails. The mayor was all over the case, and the six unsolved murders had gone cold. The media and city focus had been replaced by this active killer. The chief said – in no uncertain terms – that Max and Cortez needed to get on the Freeway Killer case and quit working the cold leads.

Before being pulled back, however, they'd successfully transferred the details of the case into the national police database and contacted over fifty local precincts, inquiring about any similar activity. While they'd come up empty handed. Max still had hopes that she'd get the call one day, telling her that they'd found a match in another city somewhere in the United States, and Dr. Jack Tyler had been located. This wish came with a dread, as it would likely mean another body or bodies had been found. Ideally, they would get something that could really link this guy. Then they could use the media to help find him.

To Max's frustration, they hadn't been able to run any news reports with the doctor's photograph, linking him to the crimes even as a person of interest. They didn't have any solid connection of Jack Tyler to the murders. Max had suggested they put his photo out as a missing person, but no one had officially reported him missing, and there was no crime in leaving of your own free will.

Both Max and Cortez were frustrated with the lack of leads, and had been forced to settle back into their normal routines and assigned cases. They saw each other in the headquarters, but were currently working on different assignments. Each missed the partnership. Max had recommended Cortez for the detective's exam. She wanted to see Cortez apply next time it was offered, and had told the chief that Cortez had natural instincts, and with the success of the drug case had a proven track record. Her skills were certain to be an asset to the team. Max had offered to mentor

Cortez as needed to help her pass the detectives exam. The thought of mentoring Cortez made Max think of Wells. Not that she and Wells had been on uneven footing, but she admired his skills as a profiler and found it very interesting.

Max thought of Wells often and considered calling him on occasion, but she always resisted the urge to do so. Given the distance between Los Angeles and Washington D.C., she considered the pursuit of the relationship fruitless. The idea of a long-distance relationship was ridiculous in her line of work. Still, though, she couldn't help but wonder if Wells thought of her, or if she'd just been a one-night conquest. The night had seemed so natural, though … She'd been with other men, but this had been different. Very different. Even different from the man she'd nearly married – her college romance. They'd been comfortable together, sure, but they'd grown to that point over time, not fit perfectly from the moment they met.

Any time her mind went to thoughts of Wells, she would force herself back into work.

✷✷✷

Back in D.C., Wells was working his own cases. There was a stack of files piled up in front of him that required profile reports, but his mind often drifted to the long locks of auburn hair and the full lips that had kissed him with an incredible passion. He would frequently caution himself to not allow those thoughts to lock him in, as he couldn't envision how their paths could really cross again. Max was in love with her job, and if he was truthful with himself, so was he.

He had spent some time working the list of leads on the un-sub that Max was looking for, in his spare time. He had not had much time to spend on it, but he had parsed through it a few times and as he narrowed down the list he emailed his thoughts to the chief. He wasn't even sure if Max got them and he'd secretly hoped the information would have sparked her to call or email back. On a few occasions, he had called Max then hung up when he had gotten her voicemail, never leaving a message.

Considering calling again, he stared at the phone for a moment and decided against it, returning his thoughts to his files.

Chapter Seventeen

Jack had started working for Samantha, and forced himself to settle into his role as gay manicurist. The girls he worked with loved him, swept in by his natural charm. At the 191st Street location, he shared the time with Vietnamese sisters Ly and Anh, and their three cousins Cam, Kim, and Hong, who also worked the midtown location. They spent hours chattering and giggling. Jack couldn't understand them when they spoke in their native language but watching them was always fun, and occasionally they would work at teaching him certain words or phrases. The sisters loved the playful disposition he displayed and teased him mercilessly - he enjoyed their company. It was a pleasant atmosphere, and he was gaining the experience he needed. He'd taken his exam in Oklahoma City, traveling there with a couple of his classmates. He was still awaiting his exam results, which he should be receiving any day now. He felt confident that he'd done well, as the tester had given him good cues, and he hadn't had any issues during the test.

Now, with his shift having just started, Jack was standing at the front counter when a beautiful young woman walked in. Jack's heart nearly stopped when she looked at him and smiled, her beautiful blue eyes sparkling. *Oh*, he thought, *they're perfect*. He couldn't believe his good fortune. He tried not to show his eagerness to help her when she asked if she could get a pink fill. Instead, he greeted her with a warm smile and casually led her across the salon, offering her a seat. Settling her into his nail station, he put on his face mask, using it as a bit of a cover to observe her without much notice. He began making small talk with her, sneaking peeks whenever he could to get a glance at those eyes. They were the perfect shade, and had those little flecks of grey. *Yes, this was right.*

After carefully removing the previous nail cover, filling her nails, then applying the pink polishing crème, he gave her nails a final buff to make them shine, and led her back to the wash station. She dried her hands then proceeded back to the front of the store. At the checkout counter, the young woman handed him a credit card, giving Jack a chance to ask for her ID. She handed him her driver's license. While waiting for the credit card to process, he carefully memorized the address. He hoped it was current. Smiling, he handed it back, thanking her stealing a final look at those eyes. His heart fluttered.

When he finished up his shift, Jack returned home to get some supplies. First, he restocked his doctor's bag in the car with a fresh syringe and rag. Next, he lined the trunk with plastic, *just in case*. He wasn't going to risk everything he'd dreamed of and planned for by taking shortcuts. He would check out her house tonight and then decide how to proceed, based on what happened.

Once it was dark, he headed out to the address, navigating the SUV through neighborhoods until he came upon the right house. He would have to wait, as he knew nothing about this woman, other than that her name was Angela. He didn't know if she lived alone, but in looking at the house and knowing how striking she was, he doubted it.

After a while, he saw a car pull into the drive, and a man got out and entered the house. Jack thought that this was probably her husband. Realizing the husband would offer a challenge he did not want to take, he began thinking back to their conversation and other options. He remembered that she'd said she liked to jog in the park. He'd passed a park just a block earlier, and wondered now if that was the park she'd meant. He watched the house as long as he dared, not wanting to be seen sitting on the street for too long. Deciding the occupants were settled in for the night, he started up the car as he contemplated his next steps. He didn't have to work until noon the next day, so he thought he would come by here in the morning to see if he could catch her heading out for a jog. Pulling away he pictured those beautiful eyes looking at him. He could hardly wait to see them again.

Jack returned home slightly disappointed. He wanted so badly to begin the process. But he knew he had to be careful, or the whole plan would be ruined. And he'd never be with Hope again. Wanting so desperately for her to come home, he forced himself to calm down and focus, deciding this time could be well spent preparing rather than remaining disappointed with the evenings events. He pulled back the pantry door, opening up the stairs to the basement and descending into the darkness, flipping on the light at the bottom of the steps.

The room had slowly taken on more of a medicinal smell. Specialists said that smell was the strongest sense in terms of association for memories, and for him, the familiar smells of alcohol, bleach, and the coppery remnants of blood comforted him and made him feel safe. From those smells, he could imagine the smell of Hope's hair – the shampoo she'd used that hinted of jasmine and lavender. The memory made him want to buy some the next time he was at the grocery, and he made a mental note to do so. He wanted her to have everything she needed when she returned.

Going into the corner of the main room, Jack dug around, looking for a box of canning jars that had been left behind. Finding what he was looking for, he pulled out two of the smaller jars and found their matching lids and seals. Taking the jars into the surgery room, he set them on the table next to the sink and applied a small amount of bleach to each, then carefully scrubbed them until they shined. He soaked the seals and worked away any food residue until these too were in perfect shape. He carefully rinsed out the bleach and then applied alcohol to each jar swirling it around to ensure it washed away any leftover bleach. Finally, he thoroughly dried each jar, and then filled them with a mixture of 50 percent alcohol and 50 percent formalin. Sealing the lids tightly, he viewed the fluid in the jars and gingerly placed them on the shelf over the sink, next to the chloroform and other chemicals he had for his work.

That should do nicely, he thought as he scrubbed his hands meticulously, cleaning every nail on both hands with a small brush as if he was preparing for a surgery. Satisfied that he'd set things up perfectly, he returned to the main floor to prepare something for dinner. He made sure to close the pantry door behind him. After finishing up his dinner and cleaning up, he headed to the bedroom.

Jack could hardly sleep in his anticipation of the morning. Waiting wasn't something he had ever enjoyed, though working with Hope had helped him master the ability to control his impulses, making them work for him rather than them driving him to do things he would regret. Taking a quick shower, he was up and leaving the house very early. He couldn't be sure what time Angela – *was that her name?* – would go running. He knew that some people ran very early in the morning, and she might be one of them. He could only hope that she would show up to jog, and that he would see her easily in the dark. He decided to wait closer to the park and avoid the possibility of being seen sitting on the street.

The park was small, and there weren't many trees, making it easier for him to find a spot where he could see the street from the angle which she would most likely come. He wished he had some coffee, but had resisted the idea, not wanting to challenge his bladder. He needed to be able to wait as long as necessary. The location he'd chosen in the park also gave him a good view of the street to see any drivers in oncoming cars. Should she be leaving her home in a vehicle, he might be able to see her in the car, then he would be able to follow her. Excitement filled him, but he forced the tingling to settle as he waited and watched. After waiting nearly two hours, he finally decided that he'd been wrong. She wasn't a morning runner after all, or she'd decided not to run this morning. He'd have to come back tomorrow, and the next day, until he worked out her schedule.

He knew exactly what to do. After all, he'd done it many times in California.

Jack spent three days watching the park and the house. He'd followed a car one morning, but realized it must be a neighbor after the woman stopped at the local market and got out to go inside. This morning he was sitting in his usual spot, where he had a view of both the street and the park. He'd started to become frustrated with the whole thing, but had been physically tempering these emotions, forcing himself to remain patient, when suddenly he sat straight upright. A slender woman came running into the park, heading down the path just east of him, into the stretch of trees that dropped down by the creek. He was certain it was her. The path would wrap around and come back up in front of his car, unless the woman turned around, but the park loop was only about a mile around. He was pretty sure most people would complete the loop.

He had intentionally nestled his car just at the end of the tree line, before the expanse of the park opened to picnic tables, swings, and slides. This spot provided some cover, while still allowing visibility to the street and park entrance. It was perfect.

150

His pulse began to race as he waited for the woman to come into view on the path. He found himself nearly holding his breath as he waited, until he finally saw a bobbing movement on the path. Pulling on gloves and removing the syringe he'd prepared days earlier, he sat with his eyes fixed and ready. It was early, and still a little before full daylight. The sun had started to rise, but the park was still cloaked in a darkness that lingered, especially in the forested areas. Jack was counting on that darkness to cover him as he grabbed her and got her inside the vehicle.

A few more moments passed, and Jack could see her approaching. Popping the trunk latch, he stepped out of the car and hid himself perfectly behind a tree, right at the edge of the path. He would be able to see her from here, and as soon as he was certain this was the woman from the salon, he'd grab her and be able to look into those eyes… *Hope's eyes.*

The woman rounded the last bend and was on the final incline, heading right towards him. He could see her clearly now and there was no doubt that this was her. Depressing the syringe into the rag from his pocket, he waited until she ran passed him. Then, stepping out from behind the tree, he cleared his throat, causing her to stop at the sound, startled. Just as she started to turn to see who or what had made the noise, Jack looped his arm around her neck and pressed the rag over her face, pulling her back against his chest. She fought against him for a few moments and then went slack in his arms as the chemical entered her body.

Jack laid the woman out in the back of the SUV and covered her with the tarp he'd loaded three days earlier. Once she was secure in the back, he shut the trunk door. Resisting the temptation of looking into her eyes, he quickly hurried into the driver's seat, reminding himself that there would be ample time for that soon. He pulled out of the park gate just as the sun was peeking over the horizon. As he drove, he removed the gloves, shoving them deep into his pocket while paying close attention to the posted speed limits. Arriving at his home, he pulled into the garage and quickly closed the door behind him. Opening the trunk door he pulled the tarp aside and lifted the woman out and cradled her body as he entered the house, delicately balancing her as he opened the pantry and the secret door that would allow him entrance into the basement. The excitement inside him surged as he realized that his plan was finally coming together. He was almost euphoric as he laid the woman on the metal table.

Removing her clothing, he zip tied her to the metal table in the same manner as his prior guests. Today, though, his mission was quite different. He would wait for her to awaken, as he needed to see those eyes one more time to be sure. If they weren't perfect, he would still have some fun with her, *BUT* if they were perfect...

While he waited in an effort to temper the excitement in his chest, he got himself ready by pulling on his surgical gear. Just as he was preparing the instrument table with the required tools for the task, the woman started stirring. She let out a few moans as the effects of the chloroform began to wear off, followed by attempts to raise her hands, most likely in an effort to rub her head, as chloroform was known to leave the patient with a wildly painful headache. When she found that she couldn't lift her hands, she fought harder to wake up, thrashing her head about. Fear was no doubt setting in.

Jack leaned over her, lowered his mouth next to her ear, and softly asked her to calm down. Her eyes opened, and recognition slowly settled on her face, followed by a look of fear and puzzlement as she tried to understand what was happening. All Jack saw were her eyes, though, and could think of little else. *They were perfect, beautiful, a perfect match.* Moving to the shelves behind him, he pulled a portable light off the top shelf and carefully mounted it to the instrument tray, plugged it in and pulled it over the woman's face. He leaned in and looked closely at the exact shape and color of her irises and pupils. Once again, he felt the excitement surge through him. Hope, he was looking into Hope's eyes! He thought he would never get to see those beautiful eyes looking back at him again, but there they were.

The woman was awake enough now that she was starting to cry and attempting to scream. Not wanting to hear any of her questions or screams, he tore off a strip of duct tape and secured it over her mouth, immediately silencing her to muted and muffled moans. She stared at him, and he intentionally blocked out all parts of her face except for her eyes. She was crying, and he didn't like that; didn't want Hope's eyes crying. He attempted to soothe her, talking gently, telling her not to worry – that soon they would be together and she would never need to cry again.

As he continued to try to calm the woman, he lifted the round, closed-blade speculum off the instrument tray and inserted it into her right eye, forcing the lids to remain open. The woman's back arched upward as she thrashed against the pain. He had only removed an eye as a surgeon once before, when he was a resident doctor in the ER. He clearly remembered the experience and just like on that day, his mind flashed to a time in the woods behind his parent's house when he'd done this to a cat. He'd been about ten, and vividly recalled spending time looking at the series of five or six muscles and how they had seemingly wrapped deeply in the back of the head. He had finished the act by slicing into the eyeballs and remembered being fascinated by the lens, which had reminded him of the shape and size of an M&M candy. He remembered that for a brief moment he'd been tempted to taste it, but had resisted the urge. Instead he had spent some time simply enjoying the jelly-like substance inside the eyeball.

He wouldn't be cutting the eyeball open this time though. This time the eyes were perfect whole. Drawing his thoughts back to the present, he returned to the shelves behind him and retrieved the two canning jars. Setting the jars onto the tray next to his scalpel, he removed the lid from the one on the right, carefully applying a prescription label and with a pen marked the jar 'Hope Right.'

Jack had carefully prepared for the type of tools he might need. Before moving to Oklahoma he had purchased some specialty tools that he felt might be required in executing his plan.

Jack lifted an evisceration scoop, which was the perfect tool for completely removing the eye from the socket. The tool was normally used for Endophthalmitis – a very painful disease, usually caused by fungi and bacteria. As Jack leaned in over the woman again with the scoop in his right hand, she screamed through the tape on her mouth thrashing her head back and forth. Jack realized he needed to contain her head, to avoid damaging the eyes during the surgical process. Retrieving the duct tape, he applied a strip across her forehead and around the entire table binding her head in place to the table. Now, with the woman contained, and the attempts to move her head restricted, though her pain and terror showed on the features in her face, he could begin the procedure. She continued to buck against the restraints, and her

153

muffled screams continued. Jack became oblivious to her reactions or the torture he was injecting and carefully used the scoop to extract the eye from the socket, passing through the speculum. He then took the scalpel and cut the muscles and optic nerve that were keeping the eye from completely falling from the socket. Once the eye was free, Jack studied and admired its beauty, then gently lowered it into the solution of formaldehyde and alcohol.

The woman had writhed through most of the extraction, and as shock took over her feet twitched at the end of the table. Jack noticed them only momentarily before removing the speculum from the right eye and inserting it into the left eye, forcing the left lids open. He repeated the procedure on the left eye exactly the way he had on the right eye and at some point during the procedure, the woman's feet stopped moving. She'd completely lost consciousness.

Now with two jars properly labeled as 'Hope Right' and 'Hope Left,' Jack double checked the seal on each to make sure the eyes were stored safely. He stood in front of the shelf, staring into the jars, with Hope's eyes staring back at him. His heart raced as he stared into the beauty of his wife's eyes. They were so perfect. He then looked back at the woman on the table and stifled his excitement at the next steps. He needed to finish this. Jack found himself explaining to the eyes that he was only doing these things to bring them together again, at which time he would be able to return to the medical profession, once again stopping the darkness from controlling him. After finishing his explanation, he watched momentarily nervous, waiting until he was certain Hope's eyes had given him approval to finish his task. Returning a loving nod to the eyes facing him from inside the respective jars, he smiled before turning back to the table where the woman lay unconscious, two gaping holes where her eyes used to be.

The woman's breathing was labored; she remained unconscious. But the removal of her eyes alone wouldn't kill her. She could easily live like this, but that was never the plan. Even though nothing else about this woman was a match to Hope and all he wanted from her was her eyes, there was far too much risk to even consider allowing her to survive. Besides, Jack had a need that must be fed. This woman had donated her eyes, yet there was so much more she could offer. So much more she could do for Jack.

Returning his attention to the surgical tray, he lifted the scalpel and made his signature incision down the center of her torso, then used a sternal saw to cut right through the sternum. Next, he inserted the retractor to push open the chest. As he dug his hands deep into the cavity, he couldn't help but think that Hope was watching him. She had watched him only once before, the day when they were kids so long ago. He was glad this time, for he didn't need to feel ashamed of what she was seeing. She knew, and she accepted him as he was. Hope had saved him all those years ago, and it was being with her that would save him again. The thought of this gave him a warm sense of pleasure. He'd nearly forgotten what it felt like to feel pleasure, but today he was happy. This really was going to work.

Jack spent time touching and feeling inside the woman even after her heart stopped pumping blood to the other organs. Suddenly he became aware of the time and realized he needed to finish up here, as he would need to go to work soon. He couldn't mess up his job, not with it being the source for completing his plans.

Jack carefully cleaned up the surgical tools with the same precision he'd used during every surgery he'd ever performed as a highly recognized surgeon. He then washed down the woman's body, cleansing it fully with bleach to make sure there was nothing on the body that could be traced to him. Satisfied, he turned his attention to the room and washed the walls and floor, making sure everything rinsed to the drain in the center of the floor. Then, taking his scrubs off, he deposited them into the laundry and realized he had three pairs in there now. Those were evidence, and he needed to handle that. He stuffed them into the washer with bleach and detergent.

Heading upstairs in the nude, he went straight to the shower, glancing at the alarm clock on the nightstand as he passed. He had enough time to shower and get something to eat. He'd have to deal with the disposal of the body tonight after it got late and it was safe to do so. On the way home from work, he thought, he'd fill his SUV up with gas. That way he could go straight out to Lock and Dam Road without having to make any stops along the way.

After his shower, Jack dressed quickly and prepared a smoothie and some toast for breakfast. He was famished from his morning, but had little time for anything else. After finishing up his toast, he went back into the basement to take one more look into Hope's eyes, telling them he would be home soon. He pulled the basement door shut, and sealed the basement with the pantry. Then he headed out for the day at the salon. He whistled as he drove feeling especially light hearted today.

Jack disposed of the ravaged, eyeless body just after midnight. He'd carefully assessed the area out at Lock and Dam and was pleased to see that nothing had been disturbed. He had paid special attention to the road heading into the area, checking to see if there had been any recent travel, and then, noting nothing out of the ordinary, he returned home, feeling confident that there would be plenty of time to complete his plans without being disturbed. He just had to wait it out until the right opportunity presented itself again.

Over the next two weeks, Jack spent his time carefully observing his clients at the two salons, though he didn't find any likely donors. His disappointment was starting to overcome him when a woman entered the midtown salon, where he was scheduled to work until four o'clock. He watched as she asked for a pedicure and was led to the back and seated in one of the pedicure chairs. He'd just started applying a full set of nails on a repeat client that had come in a few minutes earlier, and almost forgot where he was as he stared at the woman. Trying to avoid notice, he soaked in the shape of her frame and the graceful way she moved through the room. Her hair was the wrong color and her eyes, well, those didn't matter. But her posture, the way she moved... Without even standing near her, he was positive that her height was exactly right. Oh, she was perfect!

Careful to not pay too much attention to her, Jack put on his Thomas persona, flamboyantly laughing and joking with his client. He knew keeping up this façade was imperative; if anyone came around asking about a missing woman, he needed to be the last person they would suspect. He tried to focus, but he couldn't help stealing occasional peeks at her as he held his client's hand, using a purple brush to dust off the fingernail powder. He kept it together for long enough to apply a new set of beautiful, red, shiny fingernails, then moved his client over to place her nails under the nail dryer, setting the dryer timer to five minutes.

He rushed back to his seat, glancing at the woman again. She was nearly done, and his shift was over. He busied himself tidying up while keeping an eye on the woman. He needed to get over there and stand next to her before she left. To his delight, he'd just finished cleaning up his station when the woman stood up, thanking Anh for the pedicure and handing her some money. He worked his way to the front of the salon, finished up by straightening all of the nail polish in the stand near the front of the door. He stalled for a bit, taking the payment from his client, telling her to come back again and then said his good-byes to his co-workers before strolling out the door.

Just outside, he stalled again, pretending to be texting someone as he waited for the beautiful woman to exit. She came out the salon door moments later, passing him as she headed towards her car. He was parked beyond her, at the back of the lot where most of the employees parked, giving him an opportunity to pass her. As he walked after her, he carefully observed her, forcing down the excitement. He assessed her height to be a perfect 5'4". A perfect fit.

Finally walking past her, he said, "Honey your nails look lovey," overly emphasizing the gay male attributes he had so successfully adopted.

"Oh, thank you," she replied, looking down at her feet before opening her car door.

"See you next time." He waved and headed to his SUV. He sat in his vehicle long enough for her to pull out. Then, carefully staying back, he followed her out of the parking lot and out into the street, allowing the few cars moving down the street to separate them. He paid close attention to her car. It was a Silver Camry, with a license plate holder that read 'Indian Nation.' He recited the license plate number to himself over and over, wanting to remember it in case he lost her.

For a moment the sun got in his eyes and he thought he *had* lost her, but then he saw the car turn left. He quickly navigated the SUV into the left lane, almost missing the opportunity to make the turn when a red pickup slid in between them. In the end, the truck provided the perfect cover as she got on the highway, heading for Owasso.

The car continued travelling towards Owasso. Jack remained behind the vehicle intentionally staying in a different lane allowing a car or two in between. Road construction nearly separated them as they wound through cones and narrowed roads near the Tulsa International Airport. They travelled for several minutes, before he saw the red turn signal. She was going to exit at 89th. She must live in Owasso, he decided.

The car got off the freeway and made a couple turns, heading into a modest neighborhood with smaller, single-story, ranch-style homes. She pulled into the driveway at the first part of the curve – one of the smaller homes on the street, the roof was a rusty brown shingle, a white barn-style cross-stitch over the front entry, and a corral-looking front porch. The entry was remiss of any flowers, and the grass was still brown from the winter frosts.

Jack drove past before she exited her vehicle and continued on down the street. As he checked out the neighborhood, he noticed some sort of industrial building backed up to the housing addition. That might give him access to the back yard without being noticed, which would be ideal. He decided to take a look around on the next block to see what was there as well. Wrapping around, he saw that he could enter the parking lot to the industrial building from the parking lot of the pharmacy. Following the parking lot around, he saw that he could pull all the way through to the back of the building to come up just behind the backyard fences for the houses on the other side.

This was perfect. The only concern now was whether or not this woman lived alone. The house showed some signs of disrepair, which could mean that there was no man around. Or it could just mean their financial resources were limited. Not knowing who all might reside inside the home, he would need to proceed cautiously. Jack decided that given the time of day and the fact that it was still daylight, the best choice was to wait until later. For now, he'd drive across town to put some distance between himself and the area, so that no one would associate him with having been in the area on this particular day. After driving for 10 minutes, he pulled into a restaurant parking lot having deciding that it was likely going to be a long night, and he should get some dinner.

After allowing himself plenty of leisure time with the meal, he finished up and then called Melody to check in. It was important to keep up the charade that was supporting his plan.

"Hey girl, I haven't talked to you in at least a week. How the hell are you doing?"

"Thomas, honey, how's my favorite graduate doing?" Melody replied.

"I'm good. I still can't thank you enough for connecting me with the salon. I love it, and am perfecting my fabulous skills every day," Jack replied with an intentional lisp.

"Oh, that's so great to hear. I miss seeing you every day. We need to get together for lunch or something soon, or another girls' night out. What happened to the guy you met at the club? Have you heard from him?"

"Girls' night sounds fantastic, but of course I'll settle for lunch with you anytime. As for the boy, no. I think he had a boyfriend, actually. Besides, you know me. I'm not ready to settle down with just one cowboy." Jack laughed at his own words.

"Well I'm going to find you a man. I promise. We'll get you to settle down one day, just have to find you the right one," Melody teased.

"Okay, well when you pick him out let me know. Give me a call to let me know your schedule, so we can make a plan. I know you're a busy woman."

"Okay, let's try to get together next weekend, maybe round up a few of the other girls too. Miss you, Thomas, mu-wah," she said, blowing him a pretend kiss through the phone.

"Miss you too, dear. Talk to you soon, kisses." The call disconnected, and Jack smiled to himself. He actually enjoyed Melody and would truly miss her, but once he had Hope home with him, there would be no reason to carry on the façade.

It was now fully dark outside and approaching nine o'clock. That meant it was time to try to gain access to the woman's backyard from over the industrial fence. He headed back towards the house. The first thing he had to do was try to figure out whether this woman lived alone. If she did, it would certainly make things easier. Otherwise, he would have to follow her for a while until an opportunity presented itself. If that happened, he needed to get close enough to get her into his SUV without anyone seeing him. He'd done it several times in California and was confident he could do it again. Through the excitement of finding her, he really was hoping he could get into the house tonight.

He already had everything he would need if she was alone. Turning back onto 89th East Avenue, he pulled into the parking lot of the pharmacy and headed to the back of the industrial building. There were no cars in the parking lot, and the lights were now all off, with the exception of a few parking lot lights and exterior lights near the entrance that appeared to work on motion sensors. He turned his headlights off to conceal his car and reduce the chance of anyone seeing him pull around to the back. Then he followed the fence line along the curve of the street, trying to align to the house. He pulled his car in behind the dumpster to provide some additional concealment, and pulled a syringe, rag, and a small Swiss Army knife – a childhood favorite – from his medical bag, tucking them into his jacket pocket. He slipped on gloves, hair cover, and booties, then got out of the car.

He walked over to the fence, checking the homes on the other side through the slats in the boards, until he identified the smaller brown house with cross fencing trim over the back sliding glass door. He recognized that as a perfect match to the front of the house. This was the place. He pulled himself up over the back of the fence, just far enough to look into the yard for dog houses or toys – indications of pets or children, which could get in the way. He saw neither. The backyard had similar disrepair as the front, further providing hope that there was no man living here. There were weeds on the edges, and it looked like no one had trimmed the grass all summer. There were no flower pots or anything showing that the woman gave any specific TLC to the yard either. It seemed almost sad to him, that the graceful creature he'd observed at the salon had no one appreciating her. It pleased him to think that it wouldn't remain like that for much longer.

Feeling fairly safe that he could drop down into the backyard, Jack swung his body up onto the fence and slid down into the yard, dropping low to the ground. He stayed still for a few moments, hearing a dog barking a few houses away. Once the barking stopped and the dog had settled down, he thought it was okay to move closer. As he approached the house, he slid along the side fence and then hid behind the only tree in the yard, which was nestled up close to the back patio. He could see a single light on in the back of the home, casting a small glow out onto the yard on the opposite side. He assumed the light was coming from a bedroom, which meant she was likely still awake. He would have to be careful, not wanting her to hear him. Continuing to slide along the side of the house, he approached the window, knowing he couldn't be seen by anyone on the inside with the lights on. He peered through a small slit in the curtain and saw the woman lying on the bed, apparently watching TV, based on the flashes of light flickering across the walls and ceiling.

Careful not to make any noise, he tried to look around the rest of the room, seeking any indication of who else might be in the room or home. The rest of the house was dark, except for a small glow through the sliding back door, possibly from an oven clock or some other appliance in the kitchen. As he took in the contents of the room, he noticed that the closet door was open and he could see clothes on the inside. Peering more intently at the items in the closet, he saw shoes and dresses. Nothing that obviously belonged to a man. He looked at the items on the dresser and saw a small, delicate jewelry box atop a lacy dresser runner and a few other items, none of which were masculine. Next he focused his attention on the nightstand. He noticed that there was only one. *Interesting,* he thought, as he realized that this was the ultimate indication that she was sleeping alone. An ideal situation.

He had one final task, and that was to try and check out the other bedroom. He was pretty sure by the size of this home that it was only a two-bedroom, so he began to work his way down the side yard along the house to the next window. This one was a single window, and he could barely see into the room. The mini-blinds that covered the window were just barely turned open. There was a small nightlight in the hallway, providing just enough illumination to give him a view of the room once his eyes adjusted. He saw what looked like a queen-sized bed with a comforter designed with some kind of flower that he couldn't quite make out. The bed was empty, though, and there were no pictures or toys to indicate that the room was occupied. Very sparsely decorated, it looked as if this room was rarely used.

Jack thought for a moment and decided that it was safe to proceed. He was going to get lucky tonight, if he could find a way in. Testing the window for this guest room, he found it locked. Returning along the house to the back again, the way he'd come, he went to the sliding glass door. He gave it a nudge and realized it was locked, but not very well. He could slide a knife up in between the door frame and the wall and lift the latch. Reaching into his pocket, he pulled the Swiss Army knife out and flipped it open. Sliding the knife in between the frame and the door, he began working. It took him a few minutes, but he heard a click as the hasp sprung free from the latch.

Resisting a smile, he slid the door open just enough to slip through and closed it again. He was in. Allowing his eyes a moment to adjust to the darkness of the room, he decided that the best thing to do was find a place to hide and wait. The woman was in bed – a good sign that she would be turning in early. He wouldn't have to wait much longer. Thinking the guest room would give him a place to stay while listening for her to settle down for the night, he slid through the small dining area, past the kitchen and down the hall to the left. The guest room door was a few feet from the master bedroom. Here he would have to be especially careful, since the master door was open. Sliding slowly past the picture mounted on the wall in the hallway, he waited until the TV went to commercial and the volume seemed to increase, and then slid into the guest room. Holding his breath, he prepared himself in case she had sensed someone in the house and came looking. He waited with the syringe in his hand, ready to depress it into the rag if needed, but heard nothing. He checked the time on his watch and saw that it read 9:45. He hoped when the news came on, she would turn out the lights and doze off. He waited patiently, listening for the show to end.

The TV show ended; she'd been watching *The Mentalist*. Jack had recognized the storyline, having watched it on occasion. He liked to watch some of the cop shows, only his motivation was different than hers. He liked to watch and learn what not to do. Now the news started, and he heard movement. The woman got out of bed and came out of the bedroom, heading off down the hall. Jack stayed in the shadows of the guest room, watching the kitchen light come on and hearing a cupboard open and close, then the sound of water. The light turned back off then, and she came back towards the master bedroom, carrying a glass of water. Even in the near darkness, Jack could see her perfection. It was amazing. He was in awe for a moment, nearly forgetting why he was here. Focusing, he listened and heard the sink water running, and assumed she was brushing her teeth. Then light footsteps on the carpet, blankets moving, and the TV went off, followed by the lights going out. She had turned in for the night.

Jack waited another half an hour. The house was silent, and he could hear every move, listening as she pulled her covers tight around her and turned in her bed. He waited several minutes after he heard light breathing and knew it was time.

Stepping out of the shadows, he pulled the syringe from his pocket and depressed the plunger into the rag. Entering the master bedroom, he approached the bed, where he could see through the darkness a slight lump under the covers. As he got closer, moving silently across the carpeted floor, he could see her head resting on the pillow facing the opposite direction. Leaning over her, he pushed the rag over her mouth and in one quick move splayed his body out over hers, pressing her into the bed and immobilizing her with his weight. Her petite body had no chance against his strong, long frame. Struggling against the pressure Jack felt her losing control as she fought against the weight on top of her. Moments passed with the rag crushing against her mouth and nose. He felt her trying to avoid taking any breaths until she could no longer resist, and gasped for air succumbing to the burn of chemical in her nostril and throat. Next, her head would begin to ache. She stared into the face of the man through the darkness. Her eyes registered a vague familiarity as she looked into her attackers eyes, but before she could completely pull the recognition together into words the darkness took her and her body went limp then still.

Jack waited a few more seconds, making sure that she had a good amount of Chloroform in her system for the thirty to forty minute drive ahead of them. Now that he had her contained, he took a moment to consider how he would get her into his vehicle. It was too risky to take her out the front. The driveways were all short, with the houses set close to the road. Someone would very likely see them. He wondered whether he could slide her over the fence, dropping her gently over onto the ground, and felt certain that he could do so without hurting her. As he thought this through, one thing became clear: he didn't want to cause her any bruising. Her body needed to remain the flawless perfection it was. He decided he'd wrap her in one of the blankets for extra precaution, then dispose of it in the dumpster before leaving.

Rolling her in the comforter from the bed, he carried her out to the back patio and laid her on the concrete while he closed the sliding glass door. He took a moment to listen for any noises and look around for any lights that had turned on or other changes that may have taken place. All he saw or heard was the quiet.

The night was clear with a few stars in the sky and a light breeze that felt refreshing. The stars shining reminded Jack of days when he and Hope would stay out late, lying under the stars telling stories to one another. He looked down at the blanket roll at his feet and smiled; they would have nights like those again. Picking the blanket up, he stayed in the shadows as he made his way to the fence at the back of the yard. He checked the parking lot for any motion, cars or indications that anyone had come along while he was inside the home, but saw nothing out of the ordinary and lifted the blanketed woman up and over the fence. The woman couldn't be more than 110 pounds, and though she was knocked out cold, the blanket made her easier to handle. He lifted her up, gently not wanting to harm her.

Once she was on top of the fence, he carefully allowed the roll to slide to the other side. He let go, and heard the bundle connect softly with the ground. Hoisting himself up after her, he took one more, quick look around before pushing himself up and over the fence, landing next to the slumped woman. The blanket had slid off and her head dangled forward, evidence of her unconscious state. Wrapping her quickly, he lifted her and headed to his SUV, where he opened the back hatch, slid her in onto the plastic, and pulled the tarp out from under the cargo door to cover her quickly. With her body safely on the plastic, he took the blanket and threw it in the dumpster, totally aware that he must open and close the lid quietly. He hurried back to the vehicle, backing away from the building. Removing the gloves and hair cover, he stuffed them into his pocket as he pulled around through the parking lot. He waited to turn on the headlights until he was closer to the exit, then made his way to the highway heading towards home.

Back at the house, Jack carried the woman into the basement, realizing now that he didn't even know her name. Absent mindedly shrugging to himself, he realized that it really didn't matter. He went about securing her to the table without her waking up, and took a few minutes to prepare her properly. He'd already stripped her of all clothing, taking his time while she still was in a deep sleep to examine all aspects of her body. It was nearly perfect. The only issues being that her hands and feet were way too large, and her hair coloring wasn't right. She also had a large nose, and the positioning of her features was too broad.

Well, details, he thought. The torso was perfect, as were her breasts, nice flat belly, and the pubic region and legs were really a perfect match. Before securing her to the table, he'd rolled her over and examined the arch of her back and buttocks. Yes, this would all work. He had forced himself not to become sexually aroused. This woman wasn't actually Hope. Not *yet*... He had to be careful. He was dedicated and wouldn't allow anything to test his loyalties.

Preparing the items needed, Jack set to work in the room. He paused for a moment as she stirred briefly, to take in the beauty of her slender torso. His eyes paused momentarily, on her breasts and the perfect nipples, puckered against the cool air. Taking a deep breath, he continued on. *Not yet,* he chided himself. He had work to do first. With the tray set, all he had to do was wait until she awakened before he could begin. It was true that he really didn't need her to be awake, but he enjoyed it so much more that way. Then, not wanting to listen to her if she got upset, he decided to go ahead and apply duct tape to her mouth. She stirred again.

✳✳✳

Feeling very heavy she tried to pull herself awake, but something seemed to be pulling her back into a restless sleep. Thoughts of hands and darkness entered her mind, but they seemed far away. And then fear set in as she again tried to force her eyelids to open. She could see light and someone. Her head pounded as she tried to think about what was happening right now. Trying to roll over and sit up, she felt as if someone was pulling her back down. Fighting the urge to allow herself to return to sleep and let her headache settle, she forced her eyes open again and as the blur cleared she saw a man standing over her. Suddenly realizing it was a doctor, she felt relief, she must have been in an accident. The hospital, that was where she was, of course, but what happened? Had she been in an accident? Letting her eyes adjust, she shivered from the cold. Focusing on the doctor, he was tall, and handsome, and he had on surgical scrubs and gloves. Had she had surgery? Looking about the room, she saw the light and tray. Lowering her eyes she suddenly realized she was completely naked on the table. Why would she be naked? Looking back at the doctor she was going to ask, but then suddenly she realized she had seen this man before. The parking lot somewhere, *where was it*? She could see her feet at the end of the table, toes. *The salon*! She had seen this man in the parking lot at the salon, but that did not make any sense. He worked at the salon, he wasn't a doctor. At that moment the fear welled up inside her and she struggled to get up. Her hands and feet were bound with something, and when she tried to demand what he was doing she realized she could not speak. There was something covering her mouth. Any sounds she made came out garbled and unintelligible through the tape.

✳✳✳

With the woman fully awake now, Jack decided he could begin. He had taken extra precaution and applied two strips of duct tape across her calves and thighs, and across her forearms, ensuring she would be unable to move against the procedure he was about to perform. He tried to calm her, telling her not to worry, and that it wouldn't be long. She didn't seem all that interested in listening, though, and continued to struggle against the tape and zip ties, so he didn't waste any more time on conversation. As he picked up his bone saw, her eyes grew wide with terror, and like the others she screamed under the tape covering her mouth. Her eyes followed him straining to see what he was about to do as he moved the light to the end of the table. Her body went completely taunt as he made a quick incision with the scalpel at about two inches above the ankle bone, in a complete

166

circle around her leg. Then he took the bone saw and began to saw through the tendons and muscle.

After a few good thrusts back and forth, he came to bone and pushed and pulled as if taking a limb off of a small tree. Jack was so focused on the precision of his work that he barely noticed the woman writhing in agony as he cut through her leg. Once the foot and ankle fell free, he set to work on the left ankle, adjusting the light so he could see, and making sure he was precise in cutting at the same place and at the same angle as the other leg. Blood from the severed limbs spurted and poured off the end of the table onto the floor, pooling around Jack's feet, his surgical booties absorbing the crimson puddle.

By the time Jack moved to her hands, the woman had passed out from the pain and blood. She would likely bleed out before he was finished, he realized. That was okay, though, as this time he wouldn't be reaching inside to touch the wonderful organs. This time he would preserve and keep the beautiful parts needed. Following the same process, Jack removed both hands and stood back, admiring his work. The woman was dead now, having lost nearly all of her blood through the wounds. In the final moments, one of her arms had caused an arterial spray on the wall. Clean up would take some time, but first he had some work to do to preserve the torso and legs.

Jack had fervently studied the effects of body preservation, and while no single science seemed to preserve a body forever in its pliable state. He had found through some experimentation that with the combination of cryonics, embalming and taxidermy he could preserve a body for a very long time. After several experiments on animal carcasses, he had a cat that was still in good shape for – now – well over six months. He had attempted the process several times in the past and hadn't been successful, but he had finally happened upon a formula that worked well. The animal looked as good as any prize mounted on a wall, but it was still somewhat pliable, like a living creature. It was truly amazing.

He had to keep the specimen in a cold, dry place, of course, but had kept it out with him for several hours during the week, to test the effects of the elements. So far there were only minor signs of decay, but to Jack it was perfection. Storing the torso of the woman in the walk-in freezer would preserve it until he could finish his work. He had not performed this on a human, but there was no reason to expect it would work any less favorably. Excitement filled him.

Taking special care, he wrapped the torso in cloth similar to what the ancient Egyptians had used for mummification, and stored the body carefully in the freeze for now. Double checking the temperature, he placed his hand lovingly on the door before turning to collect the hands and feet, which he threw into an oversize baggie, sealing it shut. He then began the process of cleaning up. Spraying everything carefully, he washed the blood off of the walls and pushed the pools of blood towards the drain with the water pressure. Once the majority of the room was washed down, he applied a heavy application of bleach, scrubbing and swabbing all the areas. Carefully, he cleaned and polished every tool, using a surgical scrub brush to get into every crevice. He cleaned for hours until the room sparkled and his sinuses burned from the smell of the chemicals. Satisfied, he removed all of his surgical clothing and threw it in the laundry, then hosed his own body down with bleach to ensure that all possible blood was washed away.

He dropped the baggie with the hands and feet onto the shelf in the freezer, at the far end from the body, and decided that he could wait to dispose of these later. No need to make a special trip to Lock and Dam just for those. Besides, he was tired and thirsty. Checking the clock, he saw that he'd been busy for hours. It was nearly four o'clock in the morning – no wonder he was tired. Heading up the stairs and closing the basement door, he entered the kitchen. Grabbing a bottle of water from the refrigerator, he went to shower. Even though he had bleached himself, he now needed to feel clean - shower clean - not surgical clean. Refreshed after his shower, he dropped into bed not even bothering to pull on any clothes, only taking time to set his alarm for work. The covers and pillows enveloped him as he dropped into a hard despite short sleep.

Chapter Eighteen

Jack had visited the freezer several times over the past two weeks. He hadn't opened the freezer not wanting to risk any damage to the body, but just being near it comforted him. Now he was standing over another woman. *Oh*, it had taken time, but he'd finally found the right fit, while giving a manicure and pedicure to this woman. He'd hardly been able to contain his excitement when he saw the size of her hands and feet. Even the fingers and toes were perfectly shaped. And the veins in her hands were exposed just right, running down her wrists and across the back of her hands down to her fingers.

He'd struggled to focus on the manicure at the time, as he filed her nails down, dust from her layered over his hands and up his arms. The excitement of having the flesh from such perfection layering over him was nearly all consuming. He knew he'd finally found the right match to the rest of the body in his freezer, and had ultimately followed her for several days, keeping a careful distance, and making sure never to be seen. She was married, and it had been difficult to find her alone in a place that was safe enough to get close without being seen. Finally, though, he'd caught her just before closing outside of a small dry cleaning shop in Catoosa, ironically, and conveniently very near his home. She'd dropped off her clothing in the small strip mall after the other nearby businesses were already closed, leaving no one else in the parking lot. As she came out, obviously having retrieved some clothes which she carried by the hanger, the shop worker flipped the closed sign around, and waved good-bye. She walked to the back of her vehicle and opened the trunk to put her clothes inside. After assessing the shops for any signs of video surveillance, Jack had sped up behind her and pulled her into the SUV, drugging her. The trunk lid on her car had conveniently blocked them from view.

He closed the trunk of her car careful to not leave any prints and then pulled away before anyone had passed by. It would be a while before anyone questioned the car parked in front of the shop; by then it would be too late.

Now she was lying on his table fighting, cussing and swearing through the tape on her mouth, and writhing against the zip ties to no avail. This one had some spunk. While amusing, it caused him no real concern. She wasn't going anywhere. Not today. Not ever.

Following the same procedure he'd performed just a couple of weeks before, Jack carefully removed her feet and hands, in precisely the same order. At first, the pain had caused her to fight hard against the restrains, forcing him to work very carefully to keep each incision and amputation precise, but otherwise things had gone perfectly. Like the woman before her, she too had calmed sometime before the first hand was removed, the artery in the wrist spurting the final pumps of blood loss that brought on death.

Quickly, not being able to resist the temptation of seeing and feeling the organs inside her body, he took the sternal saw and cut down the middle of her torso, breaking through the breast bone and ribs. She was already dead, though, and he found the experience a little underwhelming. He always got more gratification in being able to feel the organs as they stopped beating or pumping. He truly loved the feeling of holding life and yet experiencing the death, but he had more important things to focus on today and therefore moved on quickly.

He spent little time with her, not wanting to leave the recently removed hands and feet unattended for too long. He needed to get to them soon, and he moved quickly preparing them. After wrapping them, he gently placed the wrapped package into the freezer, right next to the body. He resisted the desire to look at the body, and closed the door quickly, ensuring that it didn't remain open for too long. It was important to preserve the ideal temperature inside. He also took the baggie of unacceptable parts out of the freezer, and laid it on the shelf near the door.

Next he meticulously cleaned the body, just as he always did, using bleach to remove any possible trace evidence. He then wrapped the body of his latest victim in plastic, preparing her for disposal. Her name had been Lily. She was a nice enough lady despite her feisty demeanor, but she was now serving a much greater good. She would be a part of greatness beyond anything she'd ever dreamed. She may not have realized the greatness she had been rewarded, but he certainly did. Stripping off his surgical scrubs, gloves and booties, he washed himself and the body thoroughly with bleach. After drying her, he lifted the body and carried her, minus her feet and hands, to the car, laying her out in the back and covering her with the tarp. He prepared everything for the trip to the Lock and Dam Road.

As he entered the bedroom his cell phone rang, startling him. Looking at the display, he saw Melody's name, and then, hesitating for a moment, he clicked the answer button.

"Hey girl, what's shakin'?"

"Thomas, I have been meaning to call you. Hey, what do you think about going out and shaking our money makers on Saturday night? Some of the gang and a couple of the newbies in the class are talking about it. It should be a blast."

"Sure, just let me know the game plan. I'm in," Jack replied, throwing in a bit of a lisp.

"I'll get all the details, but we're thinking of Club Majestic again. The music is pumping. Probably just all meet up somewhere. I'll call you tomorrow and let you know the 411," she chirped.

"Sounds wonderful, love you! Ciao." Jack hung up the phone, then took a deep breath and laid the phone back down so he could get dressed. It was getting late, after ten o'clock. He needed to gather his tools and head out to dispose of the body.

Jack returned from the Lock and Dam Road after taking the woman's body out and digging a hole next to the others. He'd deposited her, along with the hands and feet of the other woman, and both sets of clothes, all into the same grave. After carefully covering the grave and taking a surveillance of the area to make sure nothing appeared to have been disturbed, he'd returned home to begin the most important part of the work. Restoring the pieces … pulling the parts together to make everything right once again.

Taking the torso and legs from the freezer, he laid the body out onto the table and began carefully stitching the new, more appropriate sized feet onto the stumps where he'd removed the others. The work was tedious, but he wouldn't accept anything short of perfection. And he was willing to take his time. He worked with expert precision, using the most expensive sutures, made from polyester. They were non-absorbent and had good tensile strength, capable of holding the knots well while slipping through the tissue with ease. He wanted to make sure everything aligned and looked as natural as possible. Though it was unnecessary as he could have

171

clipped them, he carefully reattached all the ligaments and muscles.

He had been working for hours when he finally had the hands and feet sewn into their proper positions on the body. He lifted and bent each foot and hand, admiring the way they flexed. He could see the graceful abilities each held. His heart fluttered for a moment as he admired the body in its entirety. It was getting close but things weren't right yet. The hair coloring and facial features were wrong. Suddenly he knew what he had to do to correct those. It was late, and this would have to wait until the timing was right. But he would continue to focus on the plan. He knew the right one was out there he just had to find her.

For now, he would leave things as they were. He cautiously covered the body in the cloth, wrapping every part with a tenderness and love. The feeling was overwhelming and one he had missed terribly. After completely reapplying the cloth, he put the body back into the freezer, being ever so gentle as he laid her flat on the shelf inside. Double checking the temperature, he gently closed the door. He had been working for hours and had totally lost track of time. It was the middle of the night.

Chapter Nineteen

Max had been working long hours on the Freeway Killer case. They had some strong leads now and were narrowing in on a suspect. During her off time, she had created an investigation room at her house to work the Dr. Jack Tyler case on her own. She hadn't told the chief of her off-hours endeavors, but she couldn't let those people lay cold for years without any explanation as to why they had been killed. She'd removed everything from the wall in her living room, and the wall was now covered with a sheet pinned up near the ceiling and filled with the pictures of each victim, the places of their abductions, homes, and the autopsy photos. She'd pinned the sheet so that she could pull it down quickly if she needed to, for any unexpected guests. So far it hadn't been an issue. No one had come around, and she studied it frequently.

Every hour of free time she continued to work the case. At least once a week, she checked VICAP and NCIC for any related crimes or trends in missing person's reports that might match her case. Her instincts told her that Jack Tyler would kill again. It was just a matter of when, and if he would do so in a single location or if he was out traveling the world, killing people in other countries. So far nothing had turned up. The number of missing people was, sadly, too large for her to track every single one. He could kill a person on the other side of the nation and bury the body in a random spot, and it might never be tied to her case. There would have to be a pattern of missing people, or victims found with identifying markers and buried in shallow graves in a remote area for it to be tied to and match her case. She silently questioned, *"Would this actually happen, and how would she feel about it when it did?"* Not able to answer the question she continued to study the sheet covering her wall each time she had a chance.

She sat on her living room sofa stared at the wall and sipped on a glass of red wine, and found herself wishing a body would turn up somewhere. It was the only thing that would give this case an opportunity to draw to a close. She knew in her heart that Dr. Jack Tyler was the killer. But he'd seemingly completely vanished, and until he turned up again, she wouldn't get any further. After a moment, she chastised herself for even thinking such a thing. Forcing herself to stop thinking that she hoped for that exact thing to happen, she returned her thoughts to the wall.

Her eyes moved to the lists that she had complied over the weeks since she and Cortez were taken off the case. She mentally checked through the commonalities in all of the murders. He'd used bleach to clean each victim, leaving no trace evidence. There had been no sexual assaults, and no specific victim type, with both males and females found. Each victim had been savagely opened and explored with the precision of a medical professional. All wounds had been applied perimortem, with the victims being split open while still alive. Their organs had been explored until pain and trauma brought on death. The amount of suffering was immense, unfathomable, *"How could a person do this to another? Where are you Jack Tyler?"* she silently asked.

Her eyes then travelled to the lists of cities she and Cortez had made from the medical magazines young Jack had spent endless hours studying. Max was certain that Jack had absorbed each and every word. But that didn't answer the biggest question.

"Where are you now, Dr. Tyler?" she asked out loud before taking another sip of her wine, allowing the red liquid to swirl in her mouth and ravish her taste buds before she swallowed it.

Getting up from the sofa, she walked into the kitchen and poured the rest of the wine into her glass, emptying the bottle she'd been nursing over the past few days. She put the bottle into the recycle bin, then glanced at her watch and sighed at the time. She hadn't been able to sleep over the past few weeks, between the Freeway Killer and thinking about the six bodies – no, not bodies, *people* – who had lost their lives for what appeared to be no reason. Suddenly realizing she was exhausted, she looked at the clock. It was past midnight now, and six o'clock would come soon. Deciding she needed to at least try to get some sleep, she headed off to the bedroom, only to lay awake for a long while unable to get the images of Jack out of her mind.

Max found herself watching the clock until nearly two before falling into a fitful sleep full of fast cars racing up to buses, cities racing past her, one after the other, and a man with dark hair and blue eyes leaning near enough that she could almost see him clearly…Jack always eluding her. He always faded away before she could make him out.

The radio alarm sounded way too early, and Max rolled over and hit the snooze button longing for a few minutes of thought free sleep. After the third time, she finally pulled herself out of the bed, stretching her small, muscular frame as she headed into the bathroom. *Another day,* she thought to herself.

Maybe today would be the day she caught the bad guy.

Chapter Twenty

Jack had been patiently waiting for the day the perfect girl crossed his path. He hadn't seen her yet, but he had a sense that it would be soon. He was able to remain patient simply because he knew what was waiting for him at home. There was a calm feeling inside him that he hadn't felt for a very long time. There were times when anxiousness would start to grow. When that happened he would sit quietly near the freezer in the basement and a unique calmness would quickly overcome any impatience he felt.

While he waited, he passed his time working. He'd enjoyed another night out with his old classmates and a few new people from the most recent class. Everyone had danced, drank and laughed a ton. He'd been careful not to allow any men to approach him in the same way Gary had, though. He was too close to having his life back in order to risk it on a spontaneous moment of self-gratification, and an easy victim would have been too tempting. A few men had asked him to dance, and he had indulged them briefly, then cut it off, saying he was out with his "girls" for the night. This had worked, allowing him to enjoy his time in the role of Thomas, letting off some steam and getting some good exercise in on the dance floor. He'd returned home late and had fallen asleep on the couch next to the freezer in the basement.

Now he had the next two days off from work and was looking forward to working out and having some free time, though he knew that each day delayed his quest, stalling his ability to finish the plan. He made some coffee and gathered the newspaper up while flipping on the TV to check out the local news. Over the past few weeks, there had been stories on each of his victims, as local missing people. Most were brief, and so far there had been nothing connecting any of them together. No bodies found, so the people were all just single missing person reports, and nothing more. He had been pleased with this, knowing he still had plenty of time to finish his plan.

He was shocked when he removed the rubber band from the newspaper and folded the paper open to the front page to find a spread with a photo of three of his victims. Benz, Angela and the last woman, Lily, were all staring back at him from the front page of the *Tulsa World* under the caption, "Have You Seen Me?"

Jack's heart rate increased as he read and re-read the article, his mind racing with the potential consequences of the victims being lined up together. Reading it for the fourth time, he noticed there was no mention of Gary, which he considered good, and also attributed to the fact that Gary had been new to the area. Nor was there any mention of the woman from Owasso. He'd never known her name, and since she was from a different town he quickly assumed that the police hadn't made any connection. Deciding that the missing connections were good, not all of his victims had been connected, this detail had to add some difficulty to any investigation.

Jack carefully scanned the page, then went back and re-read every detail several times. So far, the police had no leads and had been unable to make any connection between the missing people. Jack smiled, as he knew they'd never get what they were searching for. The people hadn't known each other, and there was no repeat behavior to track. As he continued to read, trying to find any other important information, a news cast came on the TV asking the same question as the paper.

Jack's head jerked up at the news anchor's voice. It was smooth, soothing actually, and he suddenly realized he'd never really paid attention to her. He listened intently as she reported that police were asking for any information on the disappearance of these three people, pointing to the photos behind her, which matched the newspaper article identically. She continued on, saying police were trying to determine if there was any connection between the missing people, but that none had been identified. Then she gave a phone number – the tip line to provide any information. Jack suddenly realized that he'd been holding his breath, but that it was only partially because of the news report. The other reason was because of the woman staring back at him from the TV screen.

She ended her news report with, "Jessica Jenkins, reporting live Channel 2 News."

Jack mumbled under his breath, "Reporting live," and scowled when the station broke away from the newscast and moved off the woman. He wanted to see more of her. Her face was flawless, the shape familiar. He waited as patiently as possible until the commercials had ended and the news returned, only to be further disappointed when they went to weather, leaving him waiting even longer. He sat mesmerized, he was anxious and excited waiting for her to return. Finally, there she was in front of him again. He grabbed the remote control and hit the button, engaging the DVR to record. Now he would be able to watch her any time he wanted to and he would be able to study her closely. As the cameras zoomed in on her face, he made sure the record button in the top corner was blinking. After several minutes he clicked the DVR button again, stopping the recording. He then selected the recording he'd just made and played it back, watching intently with the remote aimed directly at the TV, waiting for the perfect spot. Then, just as the camera zoomed in, he clicked the pause button, allowing her face to nearly fill the whole screen.

Jack got up and went over to the television, kneeling down to look at the frozen image on the screen very closely – her fully formed lips, hair the perfect color of natural blonde, her small nose that tipped up ever so slightly at the end, and the way her head tilted to the left when she smiled … even her perfect white teeth fit. Her complexion was flawless, and had that honey warm look that tanned easily in the summer. The smile drew Jack back, reminding him of when Hope got her braces, and how shy she was at first, demanding that he not tease her. He'd thought she was beautiful even with the braces, and never once did he tease her. He also remembered the day she got those braces taken off, and how it had nearly made him stop breathing; her teeth were suddenly perfectly straight, the white gleaming against her golden skin. On that day, he saw the most beautiful creature on earth, and today she was back on his TV screen, staring back at him.

He suddenly realized that his two days off from work at the salon were a sign. A miracle really, because they'd shown him where she was. Now all he had to do was find her and bring her home.

Chapter Twenty-One

It was just before dawn, and the two hunters had parked their truck along Lock and Dam Road. They were dressed in their full camo gear, guns propped against their arms, with barrels pointed safely at the ground, heading down the dirt path that led out into the brush and trees. The brothers had never hunted here before. But they didn't see any signs that warded them off, and thought it looked as good a site as any. Deer season would end soon, and time was running out to stock the freezer. Avid hunters, the two had hunted all over the Rogers County area. Denny, the older brother, had already gotten his deer for the year but had agreed to help his younger brother David try to nail one more before time ran out. Neither of the young men were natural killers; they hunted only for food. Both men had kids to feed, after all, and deer season was as good an opportunity as any to stock the family up on good meat, jerky and the likes for the cost of ammo and a hunting license. Each year, they went out and took down one deer each, enjoying the meat during the rest of the year. Today they hoped to meet that goal of stocking the freezer and began the walk down the road looking for the perfect place.

Part of hunting was a trust in the silence between the brothers. They used hand signals to communicate, not wanting to scare off their prey. A few hundred yards down the road, they found a small opening that led to a clearing, and decided to start there. Finding themselves in the middle of the clearing, David pointed to an area that looked like deer may be bedding down here at times. They both noticed a bulk of brambles and thick underbrush that grew up and around some of the trees and nodded in agreement that they could wait inside that thicket without being detected, Denny signaling with a flip of his index finger to go under the brush and David nodding his acknowledgement. As David worked his way in, his foot dropped into the soft soil causing him to swear under his breath. He pulled his boot out shaking off the dirt then took another step forward. Denny was laughing at him, holding back the sounds and grabbing his gut, showing his amusement at David's plight. The brothers continued to push their way into the brush with David continuing to lead the way, lifting and ducking under branches and brambles, careful to not allow their clothes or guns to get snagged. As David got further into the thicket his other foot dropped into the soft soil this time seemingly landing on something hard. Once again, he cursed, thinking they should have continued on until they found a tree they could settle up into.

Denny laughed out loud this time as he watched his brother struggle in the soil, "Bro, what is up with you this morning?" he inquired, keeping his voice low.

As David pulled his boot up out of the soil, something caught his eye through the early morning darkness. It was… plastic or metal? "Man this place… there is something in here," he responded.

Reaching down, he grabbed the item which was now lying next to his soiled boot, lifting it up to his face to get a better look. It was a baggie with something inside, but what it was he was not sure. It looked like someone had left their food out here or something. He first wondered if another hunter had been here recently. Maybe someone had attempted to lure some animal or had brought some bait out here for fishing down at the creek, which he knew was about a quarter of a mile further down the dirt path. Letting his eyes settle on the dirty bag. He squinted to get an even better look, while trying to hush his brother who was behind him prodding him to keep going. He held the bag up between their two faces peering through the dirty plastic. An eerie recognition came over the brothers at exactly the same time, seeing the finger nails and toes of the severed hands and feet that were the contents of the bag.

"What the hell?" David shrieked, dropping the bag.

The two young hunters began quickly backing out of the thicket. David's hands were shaking as his foot again dropped into the soil. He was struggling with calming his stomach. Losing the battle, he bent over just outside the brambles and threw up the eggs and bacon he had eaten before leaving the house with Denny.

Denny was already reaching for his cell phone.

"911, what's your emergency?" asked the dispatcher.

"Yes, um, my brother and I are hunting out at Lock and Dam Road, and we found … we found a plastic baggie, and … well, ma'am it has body parts in it," he said, swallowing heavily.

"Sir, did you say body parts?"

182

"Yes, ma'am, it looks like hands and feet."

"What's your name, sir?"

"My name is Denny. Denny Parker. I'm with my brother David."

"Okay, Denny, please stay on the line while I dispatch an officer out to your location."

"Yes, ma'am."

Denny held on the line listening as the dispatcher continued to speak with him telling him when she had made contact with someone, and that they were on the way. She had asked him a few more questions, including if they were both okay. He could tell she was merely trying to keep him calm and on the line while they waited. He looked over and saw David had taken a seat on a log a bit away from the thicket where the baggie now lay. He tried to focus on the questions the dispatcher was asking him as he worried about his brother. In the distance he could hear a siren getting louder as it got closer, and felt a sense of relief as the sound grew closer.

Denny told the dispatcher the police had arrived and disconnected the call, putting his phone back in his camo vest. David was looking a bit better now and rose as the lone officer approached. More sirens could be heard in the background, and soon fire and rescue were also on the scene.

Inola has a strong volunteer fire department, like most of the small towns scattered all over Oklahoma. Within minutes several volunteers were standing around. The officer, a young man probably not much older than David, with a name tag clipped to his chest shirt pocket that read D. Metz, worked his way into the thicket.

Pulling out an evidence bag, the officer lifted the baggie with a leather-gloved hand and dropped it in. Coming back out of the thicket, officer Metz held the baggie up to take a look at it and nodded his head in realization that in fact these did appear to be partial human remains. He had never seen anything like this before. Having graduated from the Academy just two years earlier, working in Inola, he usually only handled drunk driving, a few domestic disturbance calls usually by the same drunk drivers and traffic offenses. Pulling his radio mouthpiece off of his shoulder strap he depressed the button and spoke the words for his boss to come on the line and then outlined what had happened. The local police chief responded that he was en route and had already contacted Rogers County Sheriff.

Over the next hour, more officers arrived and cordoned off the area with yellow crime scene tape. Denny and David went with an officer to the police station, where they were questioned for details and then released. The Investigation Division of Rogers County took over the scene, and began a search for any other body parts. Leading the investigation Detective Adair was a tall black man, skin so dark it nearly glistened, taking on a hint of blue. He sported a Mr. "T" Mohawk making him stand out. He was a serious man and was careful to not run on too much speculation, but he was working on the possibility of the rest of the body being somewhere in the area. The Sheriff barked out orders to the team to pair up and search through carefully, warning them about destroying possible evidence, and instructed them to go slowly. Another detective and a crime scene analyst were assigned to the area of the thicket where the baggie had been found. Adair had been informed that the brothers who had discovered the baggie containing the hands and feet had mentioned their boots sinking into the dirt, and his instincts told him they were on the right track. The detectives working the thicket soon called out to Adair, showing him the soft soil and indication of recent activity. Instructing them to get shovels from the fire and rescue team, they returned to begin carefully sifting through the soft soil removing it gently. After several minutes the analyst held up his hand and called out, "got something!"

Standing over the shoulder of the young man, Detective Adair watched as more soil was removed. What appeared to be a body, wrapped tightly in plastic and bound at the top and bottom with gray duct tape was revealed. Together they lifted the plastic roll out of the dirt and laid it out on a tarp that had been rolled onto the ground behind them by one of the fire and rescue team members. The CSI took several photos before beginning to remove the plastic, gently cutting through with a box cutter. Pulling back the plastic revealed the partially decayed body of a young male.

"Damn it all to hell," Detective Adair said out loud as he reached for his phone to call the coroner to get over to the scene ASAP. The hands and feet had been clearly female.

The team continued to dig which revealed more bodies. After spending nearly twelve hours out at Lock and Dam a total of five bodies had been recovered, two males and three females. Each body had been carefully placed on the tarp on the ground and photos had been taken. Detective Adair contacted the FBI and asked them to come in, indicating they had a potential serial killer. He was connected with Agent Mark Wells and began explaining the situation in Oklahoma, multiple bodies buried in a remote area just outside of town. Wells got a tingling in his stomach as he imagined the area. Requesting photos to be sent to his phone immediately, he began wondering if this could be the same un-sub as the one in California that he had worked with Max on. He couldn't help himself for hoping so.

After receiving the photos Wells pulled together a group of agents to meet him in the conference room. Projecting the photos, he began to deliver the details he had so far. After answering any questions the team had and instructing them to be prepared to depart in two hours, Wells concluded the briefing and returned to his office. Clicking open his contact list on his cell phone, he scrolled down to Max Nichols's name. Standing there for a while, he considered his next move before hitting the green phone key. With a nagging in his stomach he reconsidered, clicking end before the call had connected. He scrolled to Chief Harding's name, deciding that he must follow protocol.

Chapter Twenty-Two

Max was sitting in her living room, looking at the murder board on her wall again. Cortez had come over to work with her, and they were half celebrating. They'd apprehended the Freeway Killer at last. It was nice to just relax for a minute, but they knew they had work to do. Max had spent the last two hours catching Cortez up on her work over the past several weeks – how she'd continued to work through the cities where Dr. Jack Tyler might strike next.

Max sat waiting for a reaction from Cortez not sure if she would approve of the continued quest to find Jack Tyler. She relaxed when Cortez said, "Well, I am impressed."

They still agreed that Jack had either moved to another state or, he was responsible for more of the current missing persons that piled up each day in LA. Max had set up a notification tracker in the database to advise her of any crimes that matched the criteria of these victims, but nothing had hit yet. She'd also taken all of the cities and prioritized them by common aspects, such as terrain. She was looking for places that had areas where he might hide or get lost. As she'd continued to study the list of cities compiled from the magazines they had recovered from Jack's playhouse, she'd slowly rearranged the order according to which was a most likely new location for Jack. She'd moved three cities up on the list because the location offered close proximity to a city, but also had quick access to rural areas that would serve well for disposing of bodies.

The cities that had made the final list were Phoenix, Tulsa and Albuquerque. On a map of the USA, she had placed red circles around each of those and now shared her rationale with Cortez. Phoenix was a big city surrounded by desert. Tulsa was a mid-sized city surrounded by rural farm land, and Albuquerque was another mid-sized city surrounded by mountain and desert. They were ideal for Jack's activities. Narrowing it down without more to go on, though, was going to be tough. And knowing which city they *thought* he'd gone to didn't get them very far. Not until he did something wrong.

They talked about the possible cities, snacked on cheese and crackers and drank wine, enjoying the evening.

Cortez took a moment to explain, "I am grateful that you trusted me with this," waving her hand toward the wall of evidence. "I learned a lot working with you and personally haven't stopped thinking about Tyler either."

As they continued to discuss the case, and aspects of the job, and the male officers that gave them a hard time, across the room, Max's laptop sat on the kitchen counter, the email box flashed new incoming mail. As she enjoyed another glass of wine, she remained unaware that she had a notification from the database of a recent discovery that matched the search criteria she had entered, just outside Tulsa, OK in a town called Inola.

Max and Cortez continued to talk, looking through the case files for any new clue. Anything they'd missed. Maybe there was something that they'd overlooked. Suddenly a cell phone rang, and they both reached for their own.

Max gave Cortez that "It's mine" look as she hit the answer button, not taking the time to look at the caller ID. "Detective Nichols" she said into the phone.

"Nichols!" the chief nearly shouted into her ear. "Sorry to bother you. I know we just ran back-to-back shifts for weeks, but I got a call from our FEEB friend, and you might be interested." Max sat up. He was referring to the nickname local police often called FBI agents. She was definitely interested now. "Remember Agent Wells? He has a serial in Oklahoma that looks like it might match your dump site serial. Round up Cortez, I want the two of you to fly to Tulsa tonight. Wells specifically asked for your assistance on the case."

Max was stunned. This was the break she'd been waiting for. She stood, and was pacing back and forth now, with Cortez staring. Her mind raced. Jack was at it again, somewhere near Tulsa. Tulsa was one of the top three. Her eyes darted to the wall and the three red circles. She was right, her instincts were right. As this all settled on her, she realized the chief had said *Agent Wells.* Her heart raced, and she realized as she listened to the chief bark out orders to her that she had been holding her breath. Glancing at Cortez, she decided there wasn't any reason for the chief to not know that Cortez was with her, but Max had not acknowledged that Cortez was sitting in her living room, it just kept things clearer without him asking questions.

Finding her voice and calming her thoughts, "I'll find Cortez, sir. What do we know?"

"Not much. Five bodies, some of the work looks to be a match, but he's evolved. He's amputated limbs on one of the bodies. They're just starting the investigation. The bodies were just discovered there about fourteen hours ago. Wells will meet you and Cortez there. Now go nail that bastard!"

"I'll do everything I can, Chief," Max replied, her heart racing.

"Keep me posted every step of the way," he finished. Then, as usual, the line cut off and he was gone.

Cortez looked at Max. "What the hell was that all about?"

"You won't believe this," Max replied as she walked over to the murder board on her living room wall. She picked up the red pen and circled TULSA three times. "I was working with Agent Wells of the FBI on this case before you and I got paired on it. He came in for a couple of days, helped with the profile and some of the research. The chief just got a call from him and they've discovered more bodies. And guess where they are?" Not waiting for Cortez to answer, she continued, "In a small town just outside of Tulsa." She tapped the word TULSA again with the pen, then turned back to Cortez.

"Let's go. We're heading to Tulsa, first flight out. Go home, get some clothes packed, and bring your laptop and service weapon. Be sure you're carrying your LEOFA License", referring to the license *Law Enforcement Officer Flying Armed* that allowed officers entrance onto an airplane with a weapon under certain circumstances. "I'll pick you up in an hour."

Cortez looked shocked, "Max this is…" her voice fading off, quickly standing and grabbing her keys, she headed out the door without saying a word.

Max knew what she would have said. This was an interstate case. A case to build a detective's shield on, a chance not many got offered.

Chapter Twenty-Three

Jack immediately performed a people search for Jessica Jenkins. He couldn't get her address but did locate a phone number. He decided to try something, and dialed the number. When the woman answered, he almost couldn't talk, already certain he was speaking with her directly.

"May I speak to Jessica Jenkins, please?"

"This is Jessica."

"Ms. Jenkins, I'm terribly sorry to do this, but my name is Thomas and, well, I'm with Rainbow Florist, and we have a delivery for you. I would normally never call the recipient, but unfortunately we've attempted to contact the sender without any reply for over twenty-four hours. I'd really like to get your delivery to you, but the address we have leads to an empty lot."

She laughed, sounding delighted. "I don't know who would be sending me anything, but you can deliver them to my home. My address is 1619 W. Apache in Jenks."

Jack bit his lip. "Oh, well I see the problem here now. We have 1916, and that address doesn't exist. Again, I'm so sorry for having to ask you and potentially ruin the element of surprise, but we'll get these out right away."

Jessica thanked him and said good-bye, and Jack sat back, hardly able to breathe. He stared at the address he'd written on the paper in front of him. He was so close.

Without realizing it, Jack had been sitting staring at that address for a really long time. When he finally did realize it, he turned on the TV, hoping to catch the news and potentially see Jessica Jenkins live again. As he waited, a breaking news report flashed across the bottom of the screen, and the station icon flew in from the left, leading into the news report.

In the new screen, a male anchor with a receding hairline sat at a desk with a stack of papers in front of him. "We're sorry to interrupt your regular programming, but we come to you this evening from Inola, Oklahoma, where local authorities have made a grisly discovery. Details are still coming in, but according to sources, several bodies have been discovered in shallow graves just off Lock and Dam Road, west of the city limits."

Jack felt his body go cold, and he barely heard the rest of the report. They'd found the bodies. And if they for some reason compared this to the cases in LA …

His mind immediately went to the options he'd previously laid out: he could leave now and finish the plan elsewhere, or he could fly to the Cayman Islands and disappear. He'd spent a few weeks setting up an International Business Corporation to host his offshore account for a fictitious company, giving him access to his money at any time, and complete privacy protection. He had several identities ready, two of which had been associated with the offshore account. He could quickly assume either of them if he needed to disappear again. He could get out of the country and become a completely different person.

But he needed to have Jessica before he could move on. She was perfect, and what were the chances of finding anyone else like that? He couldn't… *wouldn't* leave without her. *No!...* He would not let Hope down this time. He would be there for her, and he would not get caught. He would *not* fail. He would simply need to work fast. With that thought, a sudden realization set in – he didn't have much time. Returning his focus to the TV, he saw photos of police swarming over the area out at Lock and Dam. Yellow crime scene tape marked off the road around the clearing, where the deer slept at night and Jack had laid his victims to rest. He watched with a sense of urgent anticipation at the scenes wishing they would pan in closer so he could see more details. He felt anxious and eager at the same time, feeling somewhat conflicted by the excitement of knowing they had found his special spot. Those feelings quickly passed and turned to anger. Why did they have to find it so soon? He just needed a little more time. His eyes remained fixed on the TV as the report continued.

In the background, the anchor continued on. "So far, the police have no leads on who may have committed these horrible acts of violence. Now we'll return to your regular programming." The camera panned back, and there sat Jessica Jenkins, looking as beautiful as ever.

Jack knew what he had to do. Pulling his laptop up, he looked for more information on Jessica Jenkins, performing searches on her name and Tulsa, Oklahoma. He scrolled through the search results returned to him by Internet Explorer and saw one that looked promising – the link to her online biography. Clicking the webpage open, he found a story detailing her life, including where she was born, where she went to school, and now where she worked. He scanned the details of the page and leaned back when the he came to the end. No mention of a husband or children; Jessica Jenkins was single, and would therefore likely live alone. Smiling, he started to formulate his plan. First he needed to go see where she lived, so he could determine what options he had. Looking at the clock, he decided he could do that right now.

Chapter Twenty-Four

Max and Cortez waited at the airport for the next flight to Tulsa for over an hour, with Max pacing up and down in front of the boarding gate. They'd spent nearly forty-five minutes going through special security checks to get clearance to board the plane with their service weapons. Their weapons were checked since they weren't actually transporting a prisoner, but they would be able to retrieve them immediately upon deplaning. It had taken a lot longer than Max liked, and that further delayed their trip.

In the end, the only flight they could get had a connection, with a two-hour layover in Dallas before their final leg to Tulsa. After retrieving their service weapons at gate security, Max turned to Cortez.

"We'd better eat while we can. Who knows when we'll get a chance once we get to Oklahoma."

"Not going to get an argument from me," replied Cortez, as she followed Max through the terminal in search of food.

It was getting late, but most of the restaurants were still open. After wandering down the terminal for a little while, they selected Friday's. Asking for Cortez to order her a coffee, Max excused herself to go to the rest room before sitting down. Looking at herself in the mirror, she silently made herself two promises: one, to catch Dr. Jack Tyler and two, not to be distracted by Agent Wells. Running her hands through her thick, wavy mane, she took a final look at herself in the mirror before heading back to the table, where Cortez sat with menus and drinks in front of her. During the meal they discussed everything the chief had told Max on the phone. Max pulled up her laptop, logged onto the airport Wi-Fi, and downloaded all the crime scene photos the chief had forwarded to her while they were inflight. They looked through each one carefully and recognized the grisly similarities to the dump site in Malibu.

After finishing their meals and paying the server, they headed to the gate, where the status displayed on schedule and boarding in thirty minutes. They approached the boarding gate counter and once again checked their service revolvers, receiving gate check tags. While they waited they sat in silence each running the case through her head and picturing what they would be facing when they arrived in Oklahoma. The Chief had arranged for a car and a local officer to meet them at the airport to escort them to the crime scene. After boarding the plane, they settled in anxious to be on the ground in Tulsa.

The pilot announced the upcoming landing, and the wheels dropped, making a loud noise when they engaged. Looking out the window, Max saw that it was late now, and the city was lit up with lights that spread out and slowly diminished into the night the further you looked past the city. She wondered where Inola was out in that darkness. She knew it was reported as east of Tulsa, but she couldn't identify from which direction they were approaching the airport. The landing was a single, quick and smooth bounce onto the tarmac before the brakes pushed them forward against their seatbelts. Grabbing their bags from the overhead storage and laptops from beneath their seats, they anxiously waited to deplane. After collecting their service revolvers they moved through the airport. Max flipped open her cell phone, restoring the service, and dialed the contact number Chief Harding had emailed her while they were in flight. Speaking for a moment into the phone as they continued to walk through the airport past the baggage claim to the airport exit, she turned to Cortez, "Our escort is waiting at the rental car area."

After getting the car and meeting up with Officer Parker, a young man who could not be more than twenty-five and who had been assigned to escort them out to Inola. They departed the airport and headed onto the highway, following the dark blue car marked Rogers County Sheriff in bold white letters down either side. They drove for about a half an hour, with Max and Cortez trying to get their bearings in the night. Passing the Hard Rock Casino, Cortez called out the possibility of trying their luck at the slots or craps tables after catching and arresting Tyler. They laughed an artificial laughter that helped to mask the tension that mounted the closer they got to their destination. Turning off the highway, they drove into the darkness with the sheriff's vehicle seemingly the only other source of light and life. Max clocked the trip as just over five miles from the main highway before they pulled off behind other police vehicles. There were lights set up, but it appeared the investigators were packing it in for the night. These people had been working the scene since early the prior morning, looking for any evidence that could possibly be found. It was now just after midnight and the air was cold. Officer Parker led the two women up to Detective Adair and introduced them.

"Welcome to Oklahoma, Detective Nichols, Officer Cortez," he said as he shook each of their hands. "I'm sorry we're meeting under these circumstances."

"Thank you, nice to meet you too, Detective. The feeling is mutual," Max responded, accepting Adair's strong grip. "Let's just get to the scene. If you could walk us through how the bodies were found, that would be great."

Detective Adair spent the next thirty minutes covering the burial site, showing exactly where the bodies were discovered and explaining how the hunters came upon the body parts. After answering their questions, he offered to take them over to where the local team and the FBI agents had set up their operation. They agreed, hopping into the car, and after just a few minutes they found themselves in the small town of Inola. It was obvious that the local residents had been tucked in for hours, evident by the absence of any glimmering lights in the windows of the small homes that lined the street. Arriving at the City Hall building, Max observed it included a small court room that had been turned into temporary Investigation Headquarters. As they entered the building, they saw that the investigating officers had covered one entire wall with photographs and lined the room with tables. One person was standing in front of the room, giving a rundown of each of the photos.

Max felt her stomach drop when she realized the person was Wells.

"We thought we had four bodies, but we actually have a partial fifth body," Wells was explaining as he pointed to a photo of two hands and two feet in what appeared to be a kitchen storage baggie. "These hands and feet match each other, but they don't match any of the bodies we have."

Pausing when he saw Max and Cortez enter the room, Wells stared for a moment before returning to his explanation. "While we have a body where the hands and feet are missing, these," he tapped the photo, "do not *match* that body. This means there's another body that we have yet to discover." Stopping again, Wells turned his attention to Max and Cortez. "Ladies and gentlemen, I've asked for some additional help from California, and I see that they've joined us. This is Detective Maxine Nichols and Officer Cortez. I personally worked with Detective Nichols on a case that had some very similar characteristics. We have reason to believe that the un-sub may be the same person here as in that case."

Everyone turned and looked at the two uniquely stunning women, and Detective Adair immediately asked, "What makes you think these two cases are related?"

"Max, uh Detective Nichols, do you have your case files with you? If you could share your victims' photos, place them up here along with these please," Wells answered, pointing to the murder board.

Max glanced at Cortez as she rested her laptop bag on the table in front of them and began removing the case files she'd brought with her. She walked up next to Wells, avoiding any eye contact with him as she felt his gaze on her. She struggled to keep her emotions off of him and his presence, which seemed to fill the entire room. She began taping the photos to the wall under the photos Wells had just been talking about. She lined the victim photos up in the order in which they were killed, and as she was taping them up, she began describing the case known facts.

"We have a total of six victims. There was no sexual assault on any of the victims. They were all buried together – though in individual graves – in a remote area in the Malibu canyon, just north of Los Angeles. The victims' clothing was placed in the graves with their bodies. The victims were both male and female, and each was killed after an incision was cut down their torso, cutting completely through the sternum. The incision was executed with a high level of skill and allowed the killer to have access to the internal organs while the victims were still alive. The organs were touched … massaged perimortem. None of the victims were given anything for pain, and there's no doubt that they all suffered greatly, ultimately dying from the trauma and blood loss. Each body was precisely cleaned with bleach postmortem."

A young, pretty, black woman raised her hand. "Agent James," she said, indicating her name. "Were any of the bodies mutilated by the severing of body parts?"

"No, that does appear to be a deviation, but everything else fits. We also have reason to believe that our suspect might have relocated to this exact area. Our case went cold, but after weeks of investigation we believe the killer is a well-known surgeon from the Los Angeles area, named Dr. Jack Tyler. He may have relocated to one of several locations. The Tulsa area is in the top three of our list."

"How did you identify Tulsa as a possibility?" Agent James asked.

"We believed the precision of the incisions required a level of skill that only someone with medical training could have executed. On that theory, we identified several medical professions and began narrowing down that list, specifically looking for someone who had an event that triggered them and set them off. Dr. Jack Tyler suffered a loss – a trauma he didn't recover from and ultimately disappeared. When we investigated his past, including his childhood home, we discovered his childhood trophies – animal carcasses and some medical magazines that had been lovingly studied."

Max added some more photos to the board – pictures of the items they'd discovered in Jack's play house. "We created a list of cities from within those magazines. Tulsa was on the list, but more importantly we felt it met the profile of possible locations, having the flexibility and convenience of city life, along with quick access to a rural area as a possible dump site."

As Max talked, Cortez taped Dr. Jack Tyler's photo on the wall next to all the others. Tapping the photo, she said, "We believe this is your suspect, but we also assume that he's using a new identity. Like your case, there was no physical evidence to directly link Tyler to any of our bodies. He's a person of interest, and we really want to speak with him. But we do *not* have enough to put him at any scene, and therefore have not put out an all-points bulletin to bring him in for questioning. We need something to tie him to these bodies, any of these bodies," Cortez said, motioning her hand to the photos on the board.

Wells, who had been quiet and stood back while they shared their theory, stepped forward now. "Ladies and gentlemen, our first order of business is to find the other body. If we find her, maybe we find our guy. There are certainly enough similarities between these two crimes to consider the possibility that the unsub is the same. If so, he may be escalating, which led to the severing of the hands and feet. Or there might be another reason for his change in MO. Understanding what he's doing with the remaining body might lead us straight to him." The room, filled with local, federal and out-of-state officers fell quiet as they all took in the information.

"We'll know in the morning whether the bodies here in Oklahoma had any sexual assault, or if the killer used bleach to clean the bodies. Those two things would certainly tie this case together with the case in California. The Chief Medical Examiner's office has committed to getting us preliminary results by morning. Full autopsy results won't be available for a few days, possibly even weeks. We've asked for immediate identification against missing person reports, and we hope to have these very soon as well. Once we have them, we'll focus our efforts around how the victims spent their last days and hours, to try to find any connection between them. For now, it's nearly two-thirty in the morning, and I'd suggest we all get some rest. Tomorrow is going to be a busy day. Let's reassemble at eight o'clock, right here."

At that, everyone began to slowly pack up and depart the room. Soon, only Detective Adair, Agent Wells, Agent James, Max and Cortez remained. Wells offered to lead Max and Cortez to the nearest hotel, which was back in Catoosa near the casino they'd passed on their way out to Inola. Max consciously tried to not allow anything she was feeling show to Cortez, but she caught Cortez watching her as she hesitated to accept Wells offer. Max hoped that Cortez would chalk it up to her desire to stay and keep working to track Tyler and hoped Cortez would not ask any questions.

Max hadn't thought about Wells being in the same hotel, and she instantly reacted to the thought of it. Her stomach dropped and she felt her pulse quicken. She needed to focus only on the case, but his presence was hard to ignore. She caught him watching her occasionally and somehow felt exposed and warm under his watchful eye. She wondered *why* he watched her. Was he feeling the same things? Was he hoping for a repeat one night stand? Chiding herself as having a childish reaction to seeing Wells again, she accepted the offer and followed Cortez, James and Wells out the door into the night.

Chapter Twenty-Five

Just before the ten o'clock news was about to start, Jack headed over to the address he'd written down for Jessica Jenkins. Knowing that she would be on the news at ten, he thought that this was the best opportunity to get into her home. Once he was in, he'd wait for her to return from the news station, then take her.

And then, of course, he could finish the plan. As long as he got her quickly enough. Time was critical now. He couldn't spend days following her around; tonight had to be the night. Before leaving, he had ensured he had everything ready, double checking his stock. Confident he was set he made the trip across town into Jenks, a more elite town which literally connected to Tulsa.

Once Jack got to the house, he drove by, scoping out the neighborhood and checking to see where he could park. He also looked for a way to enter the home. The neighborhood was nice, and the homes were placed a good distance away from each other, each with a good acre for a yard. Jessica's home was mostly made of brick – a two-story with nice landscaping, despite the time of year. Obviously a landscaper cared for the yard, as Jack was fairly certain that Jessica's schedule didn't allow for her to keep the yard this nice.

He decided to park the vehicle a block over, to keep it from being seen on her street for any longer than necessary. He walked down the street, paying careful attention to neighbors, dogs and the street lights as he walked. The air was brisk, and he felt chilled under his light jacket. Maybe it was the air, or maybe it was the excitement that was mounting. He wasn't sure but he welcomed the fresh air. When he got to her house, he took a quick look around, then slipped on his gloves and slid up the side yard. Trying the back gate and finding it open, he pushed in, ducking into the back yard. Once inside, Jack laid his back flat up against the brick wall of the house, certain he'd gotten in undetected, and continued sliding down the side of the house through the back yard. He checked the two windows he passed to see if either showed any indication of a security system or happened to be unlocked. Neither had a sensor, and there hadn't been any signs in the front yard about a deterrent for a potential burglar. Continuing to move around the parameter he made his way to the opposite side.

Jack noted a garage door that allowed access into the back yard and appeared to enter the house from the attached garage. He smiled to himself, as this was the perfect entry. He was prepared to take the door knob apart with his pocket knife, but found, to his surprise, that the door was unlocked, giving him immediate entry into the garage. As he'd hoped, there was another door that led from the garage into the house. Slipping on the booties and hair cover, he opened the door and found himself inside a mud room, followed by a laundry room and kitchen. He turned the other way and found a hallway, where he thought he could wait until he heard the garage door opening. Then, he found a doorway, and stood perfectly still; with a determined resolve uncommon to most people.

It wasn't long before he heard the sound of the garage door opening, a car entering and the door closing as the car engine was killed. Pulling the syringe and rag from his pocket, he depressed the plunger, depositing the chemical into the rag, and slipped back into the mud room just behind the door. He heard the car door close and the sound of high-heeled footsteps approaching and, as the door opened, stepped quickly behind the anchorwoman, wrapping his arm around her neck and slipped the rag over her nose and mouth. Her purse and keys hit the floor as her arms flailed up in an effort to push him away, but he knew it was useless.

***

A terror she had never felt before filled Jessica as she fought and kicked her legs backwards, but his arms were strong, and his was grasp tight around her face. She felt her arms and legs going numb, and as if her vision and hearing were slowly being taken from her. She continued to try and fight against the sweet, yet pungent odor filling her mouth and nose and the grip on her body. It was only moments before she knew she was losing. Unable to gain control of the grip on her, she slowly faded away.

***

Her body fell limp, and he gently lowered her onto the ground. Grabbing up her keys he returned to the garage and climbed into her car discovering the garage door opener mounted on the visor. Opening the door and exiting with the car, he lowered the garage door and drove over to the next block. Parking her car behind his SUV, he changed vehicles after grabbing the garage door opener from the visor. He pulled his car into the garage using the opener and closed the door behind him. Spreading the plastic out in the back of the SUV, he re-entered the house and lifted Jessica Jenkins up and carried her outside to the garage. For a moment he studied her face as he laid her down in the back of the vehicle. *Beautiful*, he thought. He covered her unconscious body with the tarp after carefully securing her hands and feet with duct tape. He opened the garage door and backed out watching the door close as he drove away into the night, his heart racing.

***

Jack arrived home quickly, pulling the SUV into the garage. He popped open the rear hatch to lift Jessica out and carry her down into the basement. With familiar precision, he removed her clothing and strapped her to the stainless steel table, then carefully prepared her for surgery. With an amazing amount of excitement, he realized that this would be his last surgery. There was work following this surgery, of course, to perfect everything so that Hope could come home. But this was the final step.

And this time he had to make a change. As much as he enjoyed the lack of sedation in his patients, he didn't want this beautiful face crying. It was important that she was at peace during this process, and she needed to stay hydrated. Connecting an IV drip to her hand, he administered both a saline and a twilight sedative. Then, after waiting the appropriate amount of time, he began preparing his surgical tools. Realizing he was missing something, he climbed the stairs and went to his room, where he had a wig head that he'd gotten during his classes at Clary Sage. He'd nearly forgotten about it, but decided it would be perfect to assist him during the procedure.

Returning to the basement, he began the procedure. Taking his scalpel, he made incisions at the neck and then parted her hair and made an incision along the part. Working methodically, he made the fewest number of incisions necessary, ensuring that he minimized the damage. Once he was done, he slowly pulled back at the incisions, peeling the beautiful face and hair away from the victim and snipping away at the arteries that supplied blood, nerves and underlying fat to separate it from the body. He put the face and hair onto the wig head temporarily, for safe keeping, and turned back to the woman.

To his delight, Jessica was still alive. Her breathing was labored, but she was alive. He removed the IV from her arm, as it had served its purpose – to prevent her from crying on that beautiful face – he took his time to enjoy her before she died, oblivious to the grotesque, bloody mess where her face had once been.

Opening her up as he had the others, he stuck his hands into the cavity, feeling the life leave her body. His time with her was short, as the trauma from the removal of her face and scalp had caused too much blood loss, but at least his needs had been satisfied. For now. He cut the zip ties holding her body to the surgical table, then washed her down before laying the dead body out on the a roll of plastic and dropping the remote control for her garage alongside her, ultimately sealing her away with duct tape.

After hosing down the table and cleaning it of all signs of Jessica Jenkins, Jack went to the freezer and gingerly lifted the body from the storage, bringing it into the surgical room and gently laying it on the table where Jessica Jenkins had been just moments before. Beginning again, he followed the same process and removed the face on the body from the freezer. When the work was completed, he slowly lifted the face from the wig head and fit it onto the head of the body, replacing the face he had just removed. Once it was aligned, he used the underlying fat from Jessica Jenkins' face to shape the cheeks and nose. When it was finally set to his satisfaction, he began stitching the incisions closed.

He had worked tirelessly. It had taken hours to make the changes to the perfection Jack demanded, but he'd wanted only the best for Hope. When he completed the procedure, he stood back, looking at his work and at how beautiful she looked. She was perfect – her hair, nose, chin and cheekbones perfect now. She looked just the way he remembered her. As his eyes travelled down her body, he felt an excitement he hadn't felt in over a year. He could now prepare the final steps in the restoration.

With the face in place, it was time to apply the final pieces. To fully restore his beloved Hope, he needed to add the window to the beautiful spirit she'd been. Looking over at the shelf, he turned and collected the two Mason jars with the beautiful eyes in them. He'd been waiting to truly be able to enjoy gazing into these eyes, and now was the time. He cautiously removed them, one at a time, and worked to insert them into the eye sockets of the face he'd just built. He worked steadily, making sure to properly stitch the rubber band-like muscles so that the eyes would work the way they should.

Jack applied his combined taxidermy/embalming method of tanning to restore and preserve the look so that Hope's face and body would be perfect, preserving the body while keeping the supple feel of real skin, and the ability to overcome some of the issues with rigor in a deceased person. He worked for hours, laboring over his creation to get the look and feel that he required. He would, of course, still have to follow the storage process, keeping the body cold most of the time. This saddened him slightly. But it was the only way, and he was grateful for the opportunity to have Hope back with him, even if there were minor sacrifices to be made. The process was long and tiring as he worked focused on precision.

Exhausted from his work, Jack finally put the body in the freezer before thoroughly cleaning up in the room. He then loaded Jessica's faceless body into the SUV for disposal, along with the unsuitable face, nerve and fat scraps. He couldn't go to the Lock and Dam Road, but he really didn't care any longer about the police finding the body. He knew they could not track the body to him, and besides he had what he needed now.

Deciding that heading anywhere in the direction of Inola was out of the question, he headed towards Keystone Dam, figuring there were plenty of places he could drop a body around the lake. He drove until he found an outlet on the east side of the dam that was free of any people, boats on the lake, or cars in sight. After disposing the body in the water behind a thick layer of brush and tossing the extra parts out into the lake, pretty certain the fish would take care of those quickly, he worked his way back to the SUV and then home, exhausted from the night's events.

Jack had fallen into a deep sleep as soon as he returned home and had awakened with a start, dreams of police coming as he and Hope ran off into the distance. Shaking off the dream, the images soon fading into the back of his mind, he smiled to himself. While running may be exactly what he and Hope would do, he had plans right now. Getting up and stretching his long muscular body, he pulled on a pair of jeans and then tugged a t-shirt over his head. Bare feet padding down the hall to the kitchen, he pulled a bowl out of the oak cupboard and dumped Raisin Bran in, followed by milk, and ate greedily. As he made a pot of coffee, immediately enjoying the aroma from the coffee beans, he tried to remember if he'd eaten the day before or not, but finally shrugged. It really didn't matter. He finished the bowl of cereal just as the coffee chimed readiness. He opened the cupboard again and pulled out his favorite cup, which said 'World's Best Daddy.' It made his chest ache every time he used it, but he would never throw it away, as it reminded him of Faith, making him feel as if she were still part of his life. Filling the cup full of the freshly brewed drink, he turned toward the pantry and let himself into the basement.

When he opened the freezer he stared in amazement, then lifted the body out and carried her to the surgical room. He laid her gently on the table, then returned upstairs to the master bedroom, where he opened the other closet and stood staring for a long moment at the clothes. Deciding today needed to be a celebration; he selected a dark blue dress that was simple, but elegant. He pulled out a pair of heels in a satin that matched the blue of the dress, and then went to the bathroom, gingerly carrying the items, to pull out the makeup kit. Next, he went to the shower and retrieved the shampoo and conditioner, then grabbed the blow dryer that was under the sink and the brush from the drawer. Hands full, he headed back downstairs to the basement, hanging the dress on a nail in the wall and setting the shoes on the table under the shelves.

He pulled out the adjustable hose that he'd used to wash down the room and guided it over the body with a tenderness that he only had for Hope. He bathed the body and washed the hair, being especially careful not to get too much water around the incision areas. After rinsing the body, he went out to the main room for a towel, and then proceeded to carefully dry the body and hair. Taking the blow dryer and brush, he slowly dried her hair, styling it with a part in the middle, exactly the way Hope always liked to wear it. Pulling a small can of hair spray from the makeup bag, he sprayed just enough hairspray to hold the hair in place.

With her hair styled, he began to dress her, carefully pulling the dress down over her hair so as not to mess it up, then rolling her gently to the side so he could zip the dress along the back. Next, he pulled the dress down over her hips and then laid her back on the table, moving down to her feet, where he carefully slid the shoes on. His heart raced as he slipped the first foot in and realized it was a perfect fit. This was almost his own version of the children's story Cinderella, he thought, smiling at the beauty lying before him. Returning to her head, he slowly and methodically applied makeup – first the light base that Hope always wore, followed by mascara and lipstick in the perfect shade of pink. Hope was a natural beauty, not requiring much makeup at all.

Once he had the makeup perfectly applied, he lifted her from the table and carried her out to the main room, seating her on the sofa and gingerly manipulating her into a seated position, propping her up with a pillow behind her back. Looking at her carefully, he realized that something was missing, and raced back up the stairs, taking them two at a time. He quickly gathered what he needed and returned to her, pulling out the diamond necklace and putting it around her neck.

As he leaned in, he resisted the desire to kiss her, telling himself that it wasn't time yet. He wanted everything to be perfect first, just like it had been… *before*. He placed the matching bracelet on her right wrist, seeing that it covered the sutures perfectly, and finally, with his heart beating nearly out of his chest, placed her wedding and engagement rings on her left ring finger, whispering under his breath, "With this ring I thee wed." As the wedding set slipped over her knuckle into place, he leaned in and ever so gently placed his lips over hers.

Without even realizing it, the tears began pouring down his face. They were tears of joy, relief and love. He had missed her terribly and looking at her now renewed his belief that he could have his entire life back just as it had been. Jack leaned back and looked at Hope, who was as beautiful as ever, her eyes shining back at him with love. He ignored the jagged incisions around her scalp and hands, and the fact that her head sat a little lopsided. To him she was perfect. He decided he could afford some time with her before heading into work for the day, and settled onto the couch next to her, wrapping her in his arms.

After an hour of sitting and holding onto Hope, Jack tore himself away from her, knowing that he would need to put her away for the day. It saddened him, but he promised himself to be grateful, knowing that she would be there waiting for him when he returned from work. He moved one of the chairs from the table into the freezer and then carried her over and gently seated her in the chair, allowing the shelves to prop her up. Then he kissed her lips tenderly.

"I love you, Hope. I've always loved you," he vowed, before tenderly touching her face with his hand. Turning to close the door behind him, he whispered, "Rest darling, and I'll see you when I get home tonight."

Once back upstairs, he turned on the TV to see what was going on with the investigation of the bodies he'd buried out on Lock and Dam Road, or whether there was anything about Jessica Jenkins that he needed to worry about. He knew deep inside that it was only a matter of time before the police made the connections, and he needed to leave before that moment came. There was little he needed to take with him, other than Hope, and he'd already figured all of that out. Today he would quit his job, giving notice at work so that he could focus on getting out of Oklahoma safely if he needed to. After all, he didn't need the money. Deciding he had better check the news first, he settled into his chair and flipped on the TV.

The news only briefly touched on the bodies in Inola, but it was filled with concerns for the missing anchorwoman Jessica Jenkins. The Tulsa Police Department and the Oklahoma Bureau of Investigations were working closely with the Rogers County Sheriff's Department and the FBI, the reporter said, trying to determine if there was any connection between her disappearance and the recent murders.

Yes, he decided, it was time to leave. He'd envisioned having more time with Hope before having to separate again, but he knew it was for the best, and in the long run they would be together forever. Turning on his computer and opening up the desk drawer, he looked through the various identities he had and selected a passport in the name of Jackson Phillips. Putting it to the side, he logged onto the Internet and searched for tickets to the Caymans, leaving within two days.

After securing a ticket which, unfortunately, had a layover in Houston, he searched for cold storage rentals in the Fayetteville, Arkansas area. Finding a place that had commercial cold storage, he called and spoke to a woman, making sure the space was acceptable. Using a credit card in the name of Jackson Phillips, he placed a deposit on a storage unit that was 9 feet high by 4 feet wide and 7 feet deep. He explained to the woman that he would be in the next day to pay for the next three months, at which point she had explained that he would be granted a passcode to the privacy entrance for twenty-four hour access. With that setup Jack went through a mental list of his plans, making sure he had not forgotten any small details.

Jack leaned back from the computer, thinking through the details. After a few moments, he decided everything was in place. The drive to Fayetteville was less than two hours long and with the proper provisions Hope should be able to make the trip easily. He knew she was fragile, so he would need to take even better care of her now than he had when they were in California. He would never let anything happen to her again. Never again would anyone be allowed close enough to harm her. No one would ever be able to take her from him again.

Feeling good that his plans were secured, he headed off to the shower and to work for the last time.

Chapter Twenty-Six

When the team arrived at the hotel, Max and Cortez had checked in, saying good-night to Wells and Agent James. But Cortez must have caught a glimpse of something off in Max as they rode the elevator, causing her to ask, "What is up with you?"

Max was startled by the question. "What are you talking about?" she joked, throwing on a petulant look and working hard to not show how she was feeling. The truth was she was loaded with emotion. Between her desire to find Jack Tyler and Mark Wells being in her presence, she was struggling to keep it all together

"Um, just ever since we got here you seem off your game. What's up?"

"Oh nothing, I must be just tired. I promise to be on my game in the morning."

"Yeah, okay, I understand," Cortez threw back at her.

The elevator doors opened then to reveal Agent Wells standing there with an ice bucket in his hand. Max stood back as Cortez, stepped out pulling her suitcase behind her.

Looking back and seeing Max and Wells both frozen in their spots, Cortez asked, "Are you coming or what?"

Max realized she'd just been standing there staring, and now the doors were about to close on her. "Or what," she muttered. "I'll see you at seven o'clock downstairs, Cortez."

Cortez gave a confused look. She glanced between her partner and Agent Wells, then shrugged and waved her hand, "Okaaaaay, seven it is."

As Cortez rounded the corner, Wells stepped forward, grabbing the elevator doors as they tried to close, and allowed Max to step out.

"Max, how have you been?" he asked.

"Mark Wells. I'm good, though I'd rather not be chasing a serial killer in Oklahoma," Max replied, not sure what to do or say to him, and again chastising herself for immediately admiring his strong jaw, muscular shoulders and good looks.

She watched as Wells took her all in. She wasn't sure if he realized he had done the top-to-bottom gaze. *What was he thinking?* Her hair was tossed from the wind making it fuller with the waves flowing past her shoulders and circling her face. Her light green eyes looked at him with a certain resistance.

"Max, I wanted to call you like a hundred times, and just didn't know what to do or how to make it work," he offered her with his hands splayed out to his sides.

"It's okay, Mark. I understand, and I know what you mean. Look, I'm tired. It's been a long day, and tomorrow's coming soon. We have a case to focus on, and I really don't want any distractions from catching this guy."

With a deflated look on his face, Wells nodded and pushed the button for the elevator, raising the ice bucket in salute. "I'll see you at seven, Max. Sleep well."

"You too," Max replied as she pulled her suitcase away and turned the corner, following the arrows indicating her room was to the left.

As he waited for the elevator car to return to the floor, Wells watched her until she turned the corner. When the doors opened he stepped into the elevator and pushed the button to the floor below, cursing under his breath at his inability to handle the situation with Max better. His inability to pull her in and make her understand that she was all he thought about besides work and the number of times he reached for the phone to call her was more than he could even admit to himself. Exiting the elevator and wandering down the hall to the ice machine, he decided when this case was over that he and Max Nichols would have a much needed talk. Scooping the ice into the bucket, he smiled at the thought.

Max slid the hotel room key into the door and watched the green light illuminate. She then pushed the door open and flipped on the lights. Seeing Mark Wells was something she'd pictured a million times, but then when she was standing there in front of him she couldn't muster anything more than *"see you in the morning"*. Sighing, she dropped her laptop bag onto the desk and unpacked her clothes quickly into the drawers, and then spread her toiletries out onto a hand towel on the counter in the bathroom. Tired, she slid out of her clothes and pulled a tank top over her head, and slipped into a pair of men's boxers, drew back the covers, set the alarm on her cell phone, and crawled into the bed.

Unable to sleep, all she could think about was Wells and Jack. She lay staring up at the ceiling trying to decide what she was to do with her feelings for Wells. She could not deny seeing him and being near him had filled her with emotions she thought were under control. She kept trying to convince herself that all they had was two days and a single passion filled night, but that one night had amounted to more than she had felt any other time. The problem was she had no reason to believe it meant anything to Mark. His eyes drew her in. Every time he looked at her it was as if he were pulling at her. *Why?* She would have to figure out what he wanted from her, but the case had priority now. Finding Jack was the single most important thing she could do right now. For all she knew, he was still killing people. She had to stop him and she had to do it soon. Her mind flitted between the beauty of Agent Mark Wells, the darkness of Dr. Jack Tyler, and photos of dead, bodies as she drifted off to sleep.

The alarm went off in what seemed like ten minutes. Max threw the covers off, rubbed her hands over her face, and slipped out of the bed. Deciding not to consider what might possibly be on the floor, she went into the bathroom in her bare feet, turned on the shower and looked forward to the steam of hot water. After her shower she headed back out into the main room and pulled her clothes from the drawer when she heard a phone ring in the room next door. Though she was initially annoyed at the paper thin walls in hotels, she stopped suddenly when she heard his voice.

Wells was on the other side of the wall. He'd been sleeping right next door all night. Running her fingers through her thick hair, she cursed under her breath and returned to the bathroom where she finished getting ready, thinking maybe a cold shower would have been more appropriate.

Showered and refreshed, Max collected her laptop and files. She stepped out of her room she was stopped in her tracks as Wells exited the room next door to her. They headed to the elevator after making the obligatory good morning statements to each other, and as they approached the elevator they found Cortez already entering the elevator car. She stuck her hand out, stopping the doors from closing, and invited them to join her for the ride down. They entered the elevator, saying good morning to her, and then stood silently for the rest of the ride.

Exiting when the doors opened, Cortez and Max headed off to the coffee station. "Okay, for real, what am I missing?" Cortez asked when they were alone.

"It's a long story. Just let it go, Cortez," Max warned not wanting to share something she herself barely understood or had yet figured out the proper place for it.

Throwing her hands up in compliance, Cortez poured her coffee and walked away to set it down on a table.

Soon the other agents filled the breakfast room, spreading out at the tables and milling about the room, devouring a variety of items from coffee cake to the hot egg and sausage sandwiches in the warmer. Wells had selected a seat at another table but could not keep his eyes from drifting over to the table where Max and Cortez sat. After thirty minutes, he stood up, signaling that it was time to go. Everyone gathered up their coffee cups and equipment as if on cue and began heading to the cars outside to make the twenty minute drive back to Inola.

Arriving back to the City Hall in Inola, the team immediately began to assemble and work out the case files. Wells took charge, along with Detective Adair, addressed the group.

"Good morning, everyone. We have a lot of work to do. If we're going to find our un-sub, we need to see if there's any way to connect our victims. Let's review what we know at this point. This morning we received the preliminary results from the coroner. We have the identities of all of our victims. There was no sexual assault, and each victim was cleaned with bleach. This definitely makes a very close similarity to the murders in California. We believe he'll have a fairly specific hunting ground. We need to look at anything that might tie any these victims together. One more thing – we do not believe there will be any connection between the California victims and the Oklahoma victims. There is no reason to believe any of the victims are related in any other way than having come across the path of our un-sub."

"Sir," Agent James asked, "why not just put Tyler's photo out as a person of interest and flush him out, bring him in?"

"We're afraid he'll run. If Tyler is our guy, and we do believe he is, then we know he's assumed another identity. He's a man of significant financial means, and we have no reason to believe that he won't immediately assume yet another identity, leaving the area to move on and kill elsewhere. We're prepared to put his photo out there if we can't tie something together quickly, but we'd rather do this ourselves. Tyler is smart. He has a sadistic side, but he's not a sexual sadist. He also has narcissistic tendencies, hence becoming a surgeon, and this has manifested into somewhat of a God complex, allowing him to justify his need to cut people. Basically, he is a narcissist who manifested into a surgeon. He will protect his image." Wells paused, letting everyone soak in the information. "Okay, we also have another issue. We have a missing anchorwoman, Jessica Jenkins. We believe we're looking for her still alive. We don't know if her disappearance is related, but if it is, we need to work quickly to narrow our leads. There is plenty of work to do and one of these details is going to tell us how to find Tyler and possible Jessica Jenkins."

No one said a word, though assignments were handed out. Detective Adair agreed to take on the difficult task of notifying the next of kin for each of the victims. Agent James was sent with him to help conduct the interviews with the families.

Meanwhile, Max and Cortez were asked to start pulling as much information as they could about each of the victims. Max first printed out photos of each victim, numbering them in the order of reported death, based on the coroner's report. She added their ages as she went – Victim #1, Benjamin "Benz" Callen, 60; Victim #2, Gary Collins, 31; Victim #3, Angela Perkins, 28; Victim # 4, Sylvia Franklin, 28 (hands and feet only); Victim #5, Lilith "Lily" Nathan, 32 (missing hands and feet) – and applied them to the murder board, assigning their names to each and aligning them to the photos from the burial site out on Lock and Dam Road.

As she applied the last photo, she stood back, looking at the total visual devastation Tyler had caused across two states. Max and Cortez agreed that they would begin working on the female victims first. Max was troubled by the photos. Something was niggling at her, and she could not let it go.

Suddenly, it dawned on her. "Wells, I think I know what he's doing," she offered with an energy she hadn't felt in a while.

"What have you got Nichols?" Wells asked as all eyes in the room turned to her.

"I think he's making a body from the others. The missing eyes," she said as she pointed to the photos both dead, and alive, of Angela Perkins. Continuing on, she said, "The severed hands and feet." She pointed to the photos of Lily Nathan. "We have various other body parts missing or present. I think … I think he's rebuilding his wife."

The room was silent for a moment as everyone soaked this statement in. All eyes were on Max and the photos as she pointed to each. Heads started to nod as the others began to make the connection Max was exploring.

"What about the male victims? How do they fit in?"

"I'm not sure. I admit that part doesn't fit." Her eyes dropped in disappointment that those victims did not match with her theory. "But, I still think I am right," she said standing her ground. "Hope was his world. Without her, he crumbled. His narcissistic personality will somehow believe he is capable of *restoring* her."

Cortez jumped in before anyone else could say anything. "Maybe they simply got in the way, or maybe he couldn't control his urges, and those were just thrill kills, keeping him in balance while he worked at restoring his wife. We know he's been killing since he was a child, though being a surgeon seemed to keep it at bay. But the loss of his wife Hope and daughter Faith was the trigger that set him off – without Hope, he wasn't able to keep from killing. I think Max is right. He may believe that if he can restore Hope, he can control his urges and have his life back again. He just thinks he has to … rebuild her. It's sick, but it makes a certain kind of sense."

Wells walked up and said, "Max, can you pull up a picture of his wife and get every detail you can about her? If this is true, we need to work very fast, as he may be getting close to finishing his project. And once he's done, he'll disappear again."

From the DMV records, Max pulled up a photo of Hope Tyler, who had been a vibrant-looking woman with interesting eyes and small features. Establishing a connection to the local printing device through her print settings, Max sent the photo to the printer and rushed to retrieve it, placing it up on the murder board next to the victims. Max began working to find the similarities. She began pulling up the driver's licenses for the other victims, starting with Angela Perkins. Max noted that the eye coloring matched that of Hope. Next, she pulled up the driver's license for Sylvia Franklin and compared height and weight. There was a nearly identical match. Sharing what she discovered, she wrote those comparisons on the murder board under each victim. Then, glancing over at Wells as she printed Hope's name under her photo, she noticed a flicker in his eyes, showing that he approved of her assessment of what potentially was driving Dr. Jack Tyler. This made her feel good. She felt the connection to him in that moment. She smiled at him briefly, acknowledging that she had noticed before she returned her attention to the files.

Settling back in behind her laptop, she began digging into the personal history of the first victim. Cortez helped her, and together they worked diligently, separate, yet together, comparing names of friends, work history, and married with kids or not. After a few hours, though, they'd found nothing that would connect the female victims together. The women didn't have anything in common. Stopping for a moment, they both grabbed coffee and then immediately jumped back into the information, this time attacking financial records and credit card purchases. If they could connect these women in some way, they may be able to narrow Jack's hunting grounds, and if they could do that, they could close in on him.

While Max and Cortez worked with the team back at City Hall, Detective Adair and Agent James had gone to the home of Benz's daughter. After notifying her that her father had been found and immediately dashing her hopes that he would be found alive they had spent another thirty minutes asking her if he had mentioned any unusual people or new friends in his life. She could not recall anything unusual and spoke of his pride as a car salesmen working for the local Mercedes dealer. After asking if there was anyone they could call for her, they had left her to deal with her grief and the need to make funeral arrangements.

Leaving there they worked their way through the families of the victims. Agent James had proven to be an effective partner and had superior interviewing skills, making any family member she was addressing feel very comfortable. After two more interviews, they stumbled onto a coincidence. Two of the women within days of their disappearance, had appointments to have either a manicure or pedicure. Not sure if this was an important finding or not, Agent James called it in to Agent Wells.

Wells hung up the phone, his eyes excited, as Max looked up at him. "We have a report from Agent James and Detective Adair," he said intently. Everyone's eyes turned to him, and the room, which had been a buzz as everyone worked against the clock, fell silent. "Agent James just reported that two of our victims had recent appointments to have their nails done," he said, pointing to two photos on the board. "Angela Perkins and Sylvia Franklin. We don't know where these appointments were, as neither family knew the name of the salon, but this is the first lead we have had that could potentially connect any of these victims. Let's see if we can find where these women went to have those services. It might just tell us where they went after that."

Max and Cortez were already digging through credit card purchases and now, with a specific purchase type, they had a renewed energy about their efforts.

"We're working that angle and will shift our focus to those specific types of charges," Max offered. Wells nodded, telling them to do it as quickly as they could. For a moment their eyes locked before Max returned to the records.

After looking through the purchases on the credit cards for a connection, Max found a purchase on Angela Perkins' activity for a location called the Beehive. Immediately opening up a Google search engine, she looked up the name in Tulsa, Oklahoma, and found two different locations, both indicating that they were salons providing beauty services including manicure and pedicure. Bingo!

Waving Wells over to her computer and showing him the credit card statement, she asked Cortez to look for any similar activity from Sylvia Franklin. But Cortez came up empty. There was no activity anywhere around the date of her disappearance for the Beehive.

"What if she paid cash?" Max offered.

Wells looked at Max and Cortez, nodding. "She could have, and it's a possible connection. Go check it out. If we can connect them to this location, then we may know where he's hunting."

Max jotted down the two addresses for the salons, printed out photos for the female victims, and grabbed up her phone and keys. "Let's go," she said to Cortez, who was already gathering the folder of names and credit card activities. As they were walking out the door there was a subtle nod between Wells and Max that Max was certain Cortez picked up on.

Once they were in the car and heading out of Inola toward the highway, Cortez dared to joke, "Okay, I know you basically told me to back off, but what's the deal between you and Clark Kent? I mean it's like there is an electric current running between the two of you."

Max sighed. "Look, let's just say we had a moment, okay?"

"Looks like the moment is still in play, girlfriend," Cortez replied.

"Yeah, well it's not." Silently, Max found hope in what Cortez said, but still did not want to share her feelings with anyone. Still trying to sort everything out and with no clue on how Mark was feeling, she really did not want to get into a big discussion.

They rode in silence, Max driving and Cortez staring out at the open country that displayed the complete contrast to Los Angeles. After a while Cortez broke the silence. "I can't believe this. It's hard to believe there is this much open land just moments outside of the city. You know, I had a cousin that had lived on a farm in Texas. I spent a few summers there. I had kinda forgotten the feeling of freedom open land offers." She continued on by telling Max of those summers, playing in the creek, running through open hay fields, and fishing off the dock. She stopped when the casino came into sight.

Pulling out the paper Max had written the addresses on, she said, "Looks like the midtown location is the closest. I think we should go there first."

Max nodded in agreement to the suggestion, and Cortez plugged the address into the navigational system on her cell phone. Max took the exit and followed each turn as Cortez called them out. Within a few minutes, they were pulling into a strip mall with cars parked in front of the variety of storefronts. Max and Cortez took in the surroundings. The parking lot was stacked three rows deep. Looking at the vehicles in the lot it appeared they were in a moderate part of town.

Entering the Beehive, both officers flashed their badges to the young Asian woman behind the counter. "My name is Detective Nichols, and this is my partner Officer Cortez. We're with the Los Angeles Police Department and are currently working a case with the local authorities and the FBI. Can you tell me who is in charge, please?"

With wide eyes, the young woman nodded and quickly scurried to the back of the salon. Looking around, Max took in the store, then gazed back out to the parking lot, trying to think what Jack Tyler would see if he was looking in and watching women from there. The salon was thick with chemical smells from hair dyes to alcohol. To Max it reminded her of a near medicinal smell. Before this recognition could fully form, she turned back around to see a small, thin and attractive Asian woman heading towards them. *This must be the manager*, she thought.

Extending her hand to the officers, the woman offered through a controlled accent, "Hello, my name is Kim. I am manager on duty. My boss Samantha not here right now. How I can help you?" Her face exhibited a look of concern and confusion.

Accepting her offer, they each shook her hand. "Kim, I'm Detective Nichols, and this is Officer Cortez. We're investigating a series of serial murders in both Los Angeles and Oklahoma, and we have reason to believe that at least two of the local victims may have visited your salon just prior to their disappearance. Could we show you some photos to see if you recognize any of the victims?"

Nodding her head with a bit of apprehension, the woman glanced down at the first photo – one of Angela Perkins. Her eyes widened as she nodded her recognition. Next, Max showed her the photos of Sylvia and Lily. Kim pointed to the photo of Lily. "She come here. This one go to our other location."

"What about this woman? Have you seen her before?" Max asked as she showed the photo of the missing anchorwoman, Jessica Jenkins.

"Oh yeah, she on Channel Two News," she quickly acknowledged.

"What about in here? Has she ever come into one of the Beehive locations?"

Kim shook her head. "No, I never see her here."

"Have you seen anyone unusual around lately, maybe a man sitting in the parking lot for too long?"

Thinking for a moment before answering, she replied, "No nothing like that."

"What about men in the salon? I assume you have male clients that come in to get a manicure?"

"We have a few males that come here, most are regulars, though, been coming a long time. The only other man is Thomas. He work here."

"What can you tell us about Thomas?" She asked thinking maybe they were onto something.

"He work both places, just like me and my cousins. He funny, but he no like girls."

Max and Cortez had exchanged a look at the offer of Thomas working both locations, but Max felt her excitement falter at the thought of him being gay. That didn't fit the profile. They could still check him out, but Max was certain their un-sub was heterosexual.

"Thank you, this is very helpful. Can you please contact your boss and let her know we're on our way to the other location, and that we'd like to speak with her too?" Kim nodded, accepting a business card from Max and agreeing to call if she saw anyone that looked suspicious.

When they left the salon, Max immediately called Wells to let him know that they had confirmation that all of the dead women were customers of one or the other of the Beehive locations. Hanging up, Max looked over at Cortez, "He's been here watching the woman from these locations. The question is what is the connection between the two locations? It would make more sense if there was only one."

"What if he hunted in two locations to throw off anyone looking?" Cortez offered. "Having a bunch of woman missing from a single location is way more likely to be noticed."

Max nodded, agreeing this seemed logical, but she still felt like they were missing something. Something was off, if she could just put her finger on it. Returning to the car Max could not shake the feeling that there was a small matter they were overlooking.

Cortez once again navigated as Max made her way back out to the highway, heading South to 191st Street, where the second Beehive salon sat. This was clearly a higher-class part of Tulsa, as the parking lot for this salon was filled with newer, high-end vehicles. Also located in a strip mall with a similar parking arrangement, it seemed someone could park their car deep in the lot and watch for specific women to exit. The variation in the locations might explain the differences in their women victims, who came from within different economic lifestyles.

This time when they entered the salon they were greeted by a tall Caucasian woman who immediately extended her hand. "Samantha, Officers. Kim called me and said you were on your way. How may I help you?"

Max immediately offered her a business card and accepted her handshake, as did Cortez. "Sorry, for the quick request to meet with you, but we're assisting in the investigation of the murders of several woman here in Oklahoma. I'd like to show you some photos that Kim acknowledged were customers of your salons. These are some of the victims, and we're looking for any connection."

Samantha nodded and looked through the photos, confirming that the victims were patrons of her salons. She showed visible signs of concern at the implication that each woman was dead. Max then showed her the photo of Jessica Jenkins, explaining that she was reported missing. Samantha said that while she knew the anchorwoman from the local news station, she wasn't a customer at either location.

Cortez jumped in then, inquiring, "Have you seen anyone around lately that may have acted strangely, perhaps showing too much interest in any of these women? A man sitting in the parking lot too long or possibly a customer that seemed overly interested in any of these women?"

Hesitating for a moment as she thought, she finally said, "I can't think of anything that jumps out, but our clients sign a registry, which would indicate any male patrons that may have been here at the same time as these women." Reaching for the notebook on the counter, she offered it to the officers. "You're welcome to take it with you if you think it could help."

"Thank you. Do you have something similar at the other location?"

"We do, and I could have it faxed to you if that would help."

"Yes, that would be very helpful." After placing a call to Wells to get the number and letting him know to expect something, while informing that they were on the way back in, Max offered Samantha the fax line for the Investigation Headquarters in Inola. She took the time to inform Wells that there was only one male employee, but that he did not fit the profile, explaining that he was openly gay. Before hanging up Wells had agreed it did not fit. Max again felt the disappointment she felt each time it seemed they were onto something it failed to pan out.

Offering their thanks for the cooperation, Max and Cortez exited back out into the Oklahoma air. The air was cool with a bitter wind, making it feel colder than the temperature would have indicated. Max hugged her coat tightly around her.

Chapter Twenty-Seven

Jack had been working at the 191st Street location when Kim called, saying some officers were on the way. His heart raced as he considered leaving now. Realizing that was too risky, it would be too obvious. So far from what he could gather from the conversation he overheard, it appeared they were just fishing. Reminding himself that he must remain calm, he'd decided to wait until he saw them in the parking lot, then went into the back room and began unpacking supplies. From here, he could hear parts of their conversation, but not be seen. He wanted to hear if they had any clues on who specifically they were looking for, and was pleased to learn that they didn't yet have a connection to him under the name of Jack or Thomas.

After the officers left, he came out of the back room and listened as Samantha told them the questions she'd been asked. Knowing the police were looking for a male client or man possibly stalking women in the parking lot, he felt comfortable that he could leave town tomorrow, before anyone realized he'd been right there under their noses. When Samantha described the situation, he'd participated in the conversation, feigning his best horrified expressions as Samantha had shared the horrible deaths of some of their favored clients. Suddenly he realized that he couldn't give notice as he'd planned; while he respected Samantha and really didn't like leaving her high and dry, he knew his sudden notice would raise suspicions. And he couldn't afford that.

He needed to get out of town, and quickly. Of course, when he didn't show up for work the next day, those same suspicions would kick in. But at least he'd be long gone. He would finish his shift, as planned, and then never return here again. By the time anyone figured out what had happened, he and Hope would be gone.

Chapter Twenty-Eight

Returning to Inola City Hall, Max and Cortez gave the others an update on their findings at the Beehive Salons. All the female deceased victims had in fact been clients at these locations. No one reported anything suspicious, and they now had the registries to see if there had been any male clients that possibly frequented on the same days as the women. Neither salon was familiar with Jessica Jenkins, and how, or if, she tied into this was anyone's guess.

Max took the registry that had been faxed over, and Cortez took the book provided by Samantha for the 191st Street location. They agreed they would note any male names in the book for thirty days prior to the disappearance of the first victim, and focus on any men that appeared more than once, or had been there the same day as the murdered women. With luck, they'd get a hit.

As the women were working their way down and compiling a list, Wells stood up and addressed the team again. "Ladies and gentlemen, I just got a call from the Tulsa Police Department. A woman's body was discovered by a fisherman, and I'm afraid it matches the physical description of Jessica Jenkins. The body's out at Keystone Dam, about thirty minutes west of the city. No positive ID yet, but I think Detective Nichols was onto something," Wells paused before continuing, gulping. "The victim's face and hair have been removed."

A quiet fell over the room as everyone sat, looking at Wells. "I've asked Detective Adair and Agent James to head out to the location. They're en route now, and will send photos of the crime scene as soon as they get there."

Max slammed her hand on the table. "Damn it!"

Wells looked at her, and it pained him to know that in some way she blamed herself for not finding Jack Tyler sooner. "Take a walk, Detective," he said to her, hoping she could see in his eyes the concern he felt inside.

She stood up kicking her chair back with her foot and walked out the door allowing it to slam behind her.

Waiting a couple of minutes, Wells followed her, walking up to her and laying his hand on her arm. "Max, there's nothing you could have done to change this. Tyler is a sick bastard."

Trying to ignore the tingling his touch gave through her clothes, she asked, "How are we going to find him, Mark?"

"We will. I promise you. We *will* get this guy. We follow the evidence, and we get our guy."

They stood facing each other for a few more moments; their eyes locked and held. Wells was the first to break the silence, never releasing the lock on her eyes. "When this is over, we need to talk."

"Mark, I don't know what there is to say, really."

"Lots, Max, there's lots to say," Wells stated before taking her by the elbow and leading her back towards the door. When they returned to the room together, Max could feel Cortez watching her has she returned to her seat and started working through the registry, again looking for connections between the two salons. Once finished, she and Cortez compared their lists of names. There were only two that repeated. Neither had gone to both locations, nor had there been any male patrons on the days any of the women had disappeared. Agreeing they should look at these men anyway, they began working through them one by one, looking at driver's license photos. If Dr. Jack Tyler was one of these men, they would have him. Deciding to collect all the male names from the registry back a full sixty days, they spent the next two hours going through the records for all men holding Oklahoma driver's licenses. They concluded none of the men were Jack Tyler under an assumed name. They had just come up empty.

Max sat back in her chair looking at the murder board, then stood up and moved Jessica Jenkins to the spot of Victim #6. When she did, the photo of Jessica Jenkins and Hope Tyler sat side by side. A chill ran up her spine at the resemblance between the two women.

"Oh my god," she murmured. "Wells," she called out, turning to stare into the room.

Cortez and Wells both came over to her and joined her standing in front of the murder board. She pointed toward the photos. "They looked almost exactly alike. I hadn't noticed it until I put their photos side by side." Wells and Cortez were both nodding, and Max continued. "What if the reason this one is different is because she was a public figure? What if he was sitting there in his Lazy Boy recliner, drinking beer, and just saw her on the ten o'clock news? His sick ass sees her and recognizes the resemblance to Hope and decides he's going to take her. That's why she was never in the salon."

"It makes sense," Wells agreed.

"He wouldn't have to find her. She was right there in front of him every single night. She was a public figure, could be easily traced and followed. He could have grabbed her from anywhere. She was the missing piece to the puzzle," Max finished.

Chapter Twenty-Nine

Jack's final shift as Thomas had ended without incident, and he had left waving good-bye to his friends and co-workers, knowing he would never see them again. He placed a final call to Melody on his way home, checking in chatting about the new students she was teaching and the possibility of a dinner next week. He knew it would never happen. It saddened him slightly to say good-bye, as she had been a good friend and a source of companionship during his time here in Oklahoma. But that time was over.

Arriving at his home in Catoosa, he immediately took two blankets from the guest room and went to the freezer, depositing them on the shelf. He'd decided that extra protection was required when transporting Hope. Wrapping her in the frozen blankets would help with transporting her to Arkansas. He would leave his SUV behind, renting a mini-van for the trip instead, so that there was no connection. The trail for Thomas would die when he abandoned the van. Once they found out about his identity as Thomas, it would lead them here, and they would find the room. Then they could trace the van, but by the time they found out where he'd gone, he would have disappeared with his new identify.

All he had to do was safely secure Hope until he could return to her.

He arranged for Enterprise to deliver a white minivan to his home at five o'clock, then he returned to the garage to move the SUV to the street. He'd park the van in the garage, where he had easy access, and then enjoyed the rest of the night. Tonight would be all about spending time with Hope, as it would be their last night together for a while. The thought of having to leave her behind, even for a short while, tugged at his heart, but he pushed those thoughts away, deciding not to let them interrupt the evening they would have together.

After the van was delivered and carefully stowed in the garage, along with a suitcase with some clothes, he printed boarding passes and then made dinner for two. He carried the beautiful plates to the small table downstairs, lit a candle in the middle of the table, and went back upstairs to retrieve two wine glasses and a bottle of wine. Once everything was perfectly laid out on the table, he opened the freezer and carried Hope, with her chair, out to sit in front of the plate and glass of wine he'd prepared for her. He offered her a gentle kiss on the cheek, ignoring the chill on his lips, then sat down opposite her at the table.

For the next hour, he told her how much he loved her and of his plans for them to be together forever. He explained why he needed to leave and compared it to one of his speaking trips when he was a surgeon. He wouldn't leave her for long, he said, devouring his meal and teasing her for eating like a bird. Hope had always had a small appetite compared to his – a trait he'd always found endearing. It seemed that some things never changed.

After pouring himself another glass of wine, he asked if she would like to join him on the sofa where they could cuddle. Of course she agreed. As he settled her onto the sofa, he brushed a lock of hair from her eyes, just like he had always done. He joined her, wrapping his arms around her shoulder and waist and drawing her close to his chest. He sat holding her, sharing his plans and recanting stories of when they were children playing in the woods together, their first kiss, their prom, and when he'd asked her to marry him.

Finally he decided it was getting late and kissed her gently, then went upstairs to get her a night gown from the dresser. It was made of beautiful white lace – the exact one she'd worn on their honeymoon. Tonight, he would make love to her the same way he had on their wedding night – gently, taking his time with her, allowing her to enjoy the moment as much as he had.

Chapter Thirty

At the Investigation Headquarters, Wells had received photographs of the body found out at Keystone Dam, and the preliminary reports, which indicated that this was in fact Jessica Jenkins, despite the missing face. The body was wearing a ring on her middle right finger, which matched a ring Jessica had been wearing the last time she was on air, and just before going missing. To him, and given Max's suggestion that Jack Tyler was somehow trying to restore the body of his wife Hope, this was enough evidence to indicate Jessica Jenkins had been taken specifically for her resemblance to Hope's face and hair color.

Wells didn't want to tell the task force of his mounting concerns – that with a face in place, the reconstruction was likely complete, which meant time was running out to find this guy before he took off again. He'd rebuilt his wife, and that probably meant he was ready to move on. They needed to move quickly. Wells was weighing the risks of putting Tyler's photos out as a person of interest, because the minute Tyler saw his own photo, he was going to run. He just wasn't sure if waiting gave them any advantages though, and his frustration was growing.

Suddenly, Max had an idea. *Benz,* she thought to herself, grabbing her files from California. "Cortez, help me look. What kind of car did Jack Tyler drive in California? We never found his vehicle."

"Mercedes, I think."

"Exactly. Benjamin Callen, they called him Benz. He worked at the Mercedes dealership. Maybe that's the connection there."

Cortez quickly pulled up the records on vehicle registrations for Dr. Jack Tyler and found a convertible Mercedes. She jotted down the VIN number and cross-referenced it to the available inventory at the Jackie Cooper dealership. "Nothing, but they could have sold it already or even traded it to another dealership."

Not hesitating, she picked up the phone and called the dealership, asking to speak with the inventory manager, looking at the clock and noting the time was nearly eight o'clock, Cortez waited for the woman who had answered to come back on the line.

After about thirty seconds, she heard, "I'm sorry, but our inventory manager has gone home for the day. Is there someone in our sales department who could help you?"

"Yes, my name is Officer Cortez. I'm with the Los Angeles Police Department and I need to speak to someone in charge please." Wells and Max stood by waiting to see what Cortez would find.

After another moment the call transferred, clicked, rang, then a voice greeted with, "Hello, my name is Steve Tatum. How may I help you, Officer?

"Mr. Tatum, I'm investigating a series of murders and am looking to see if you accepted a trade on a Mercedes convertible lately. It would be a high end vehicle over a hundred thousand. I have a specific VIN number that I need you to reference."

Cortez heard a small pause before the voice came back on the line, "Unfortunately, I don't have access to those files. Our inventory manager will be back in at nine in the morning. I could have him call you the minute he gets in. I will say, we did have a car that fits your description, but I am not sure how we moved it or what the particulars of the deal were. It was a very attractive car, I just happened to notice it wasn't here anymore."

After giving the phone number to call back on, Cortez hung up. "Damn it, I was afraid it would be too late to find out anything tonight. We'll get a phone call first thing in the morning."

Wells looked at the clock. "Let's take a break. No one has had anything to eat since breakfast. We can't do anything about the body at Keystone until we have a full confirmation, and we can't do anything about the car lead until morning. Let's go eat and get some rest, so we can get right back at it tomorrow. Our best chance to find this guy is tracking down that car and any leads the coroner might give us on the Jenkins woman."

With that, everyone started packing in their files and laptops.

"Detective Adair offered, "There's an IHOP right off of 191st Street in Catoosa, the exit at the casino. Let's go there. It's right across the highway from the hotel where you are all staying."

Max and Cortez exited the City Hall building and headed to their car. As Max was about to get into the car, Wells called out to her coming over to her side of the car. "Good work today, we're getting closer."

Max looked at his face, and for a brief moment their eyes locked. Then she turned away. "I'll see you at the IHOP."

"See you there," Wells replied with a smile before heading to his car. As he walked, his mind went back to the reflection of the beautiful green in her eyes. Jesus, she was beautiful. He knew they had a lot to talk about. Max was clearly frustrated. He was confused by her actions and found them endearing at the same time. He wanted to hold her and tell her that he had tried calling many times and hung up. Did she even care? Had she called him and done the same? There were so many questions to ask... *after they caught this guy.*

Max climbed in behind the wheel and looked over at Cortez, who had been watching the exchange between her and Wells. "I don't want to hear it," she said before Cortez could start in with a line of questioning. Cortez threw her hands up in a surrender stance at the comment and smiled at Max, who nodded at her and started the car.

They drove mostly in silence, with each of their minds processing the events of the day. Arriving at the IHOP just behind Agent Wells and his team, they parked and followed everyone inside. Max had thought she was not hungry, but the minute the doors opened and she was assaulted by the smell of bacon, she realized she was famished. The bacon smelled decadent, despite the hour of the day.

Wells told the hostess the size of the party, and they waited briefly as tables were pulled together to accommodate the group. Once seated, Max could feel Wells' eyes on her, and occasionally she dared to look at him, catching his glance. Each time their eyes met, one of them would quickly look away. The conversation was light at first, but found its way to the case and the findings the day had brought. Max felt excited and frustrated all at once, as it seemed they were getting closer to finding their perpetrator, and yet she still had no idea what name Jack was using or where to look for him. She looked forward to questioning Dr. Jack Tyler, picturing the day she would be seeing the monster face to face and wondering how it would feel trying to understand what made him tick.

Chapter Thirty-One

Jack had slept well after making love to Hope. He'd become very sad when it was time to put her back into the freezer, but she had calmed him down, her beautiful eyes assuring him that it was for the best. Everything he was doing was done for her, to ensure that they could be together forever. He was pleased that she understood, and he had fallen into a deep sleep dreaming of their life together.

When he woke, the sun was shining. Quickly waking up he'd finished packing, looking around the house for anything he thought he might need or that Hope would need once he was able to return for her. He had decorated the home thinking they would share it together, but it was just a home. And they could settle somewhere else and build a new one together. Right now the necessities and getting away together were most important.

Now he was in the shower, applying a bottle of graying hair dye. He didn't want to be recognized at the airport or storage facility, and graying out his hair was just the first step in his disguise. There was no room for errors now. Stepping out of the shower and toweling off, he looked in the mirror that hung over the sink, studying the new look. After a few minutes, he decided it was enough of a difference; no one would immediately identify him as Jack Tyler. It would take time for people to put it together, and while that was happening, he could disappear. Of course, this was assuming anyone even knew they were looking for him at all. And he still wasn't certain of that.

As he dressed he flipped on the news to see if there were any updates on how the police were progressing on his victims, including Jessica Jenkins. He wasn't surprised to see that Jessica's body had been found so quickly. Even though positive identification was pending the coroner's official report, the newscaster continued stating that the body discovered was presumed to be Jessica, based on a piece of jewelry that matched a description to one she was known to be wearing. He shrugged; it wasn't like he'd really spent much time trying to conceal it. He listened intently as the news person stated that the police were trying to determine if there was a connection between the Jessica Jenkins murder and the bodies discovered out on Lock and Dam

Road in Inola. The news reporter then asked for anyone with information to come forward, offering a phone number to call.

Jack sighed in relief. He took this to mean they had no leads at this time. Clicking off the TV, he collected a few toiletries and packed them into a small suitcase, along with some additional clothes. In a separate suitcase, he packed all of Hope's clothes, toiletries, a blow dryer, and makeup.

After packing, he went to the basement and opened the freezer, gingerly lifting Hope out and placing her on the sofa. He would need her body to soften for a few minutes so that he could lay her out in the van. The idea of having Hope ride next to him in the passenger seat was very appealing, but he knew it was too dangerous. He needed to resist the desire to have her near him in the open. He would need to lay her down to ensure she was concealed, and so that he could protect her with the cold blankets he'd put in the freezer the night before.

Next, he went into his surgical room and began collecting his supplies. He wouldn't be able to take these things with him, but he could put them into storage until he returned. He certainly didn't want to lose them. His plan was to be gone for no longer than necessary, and leaving all of this behind here in Catoosa was not a solution he could accept. He loaded the scalpels, forceps, bone saw, the miscellaneous other tools, and his suture kit into a single box. He then unscrewed the table light from the stainless steel table and placed it on top of the other items. Next, he collected the perfectly labeled drugs from the shelves, wrapping them in tissue to ensure they wouldn't get damaged or broken, and placed them into another box, along with the syringes, duct tape, and zip ties.

Taking stock of his surroundings, he thought that he had everything he needed for when he returned from his trip to the Cayman Islands. One by one, he carried the boxes upstairs and out to the garage, where he loaded them behind the driver's seat. Next, he went and got the final overnight bag and Hope's bag, bringing these out to the van as well. He stood in the garage, looking around trying to decide if there was anything out here that he would need. He ultimately determined that the answer was no. He could purchase anything out here at any hardware store when he was ready. With everything he would need carefully stored in the van, it was time to leave. Opening the back of the vehicle, he laid the tarp out flat across the carpet, folding half of it to one side.

Leaving the back of the van open, he returned to the basement and checked on Hope. He was able to gently manipulate her limbs, which meant the combination of chemicals he'd applied into and on her body was working as he desired. He retrieved the blankets from the freezer and took them up to the van, laying one out flat on top of the tarp. He then went to get Hope, and, with an intense and overwhelming tenderness he carefully carried her up the stairs and to the van. Laying her onto the tarp on her back, he slowly worked her into a flat position, then covered her with the second frozen blanket, and pulled the other half of the tarp up over her, making sure she was concealed. Last, he gently tucked the blankets and tarp around her body to ensure the blankets retained the cold for as long as possible. It was a two hour drive, and he needed to be sure that she would be safe for the entire journey.

He made one pass through the house, looking for anything that would indicate where he'd gone. Next he double checked his travel documents. He didn't want any scenes at the airport. Suddenly, remembering that he'd used the printer to print the travel documents, he returned inside to remove the printer. He wasn't sure if anything could be retrieved from this type of printer, but he also wasn't willing to take the chance. After stowing the printer on the floorboard of the passenger side of the van, he slid on his jacket so that he could turn the air-conditioner on high for the trip. It would make Hope more comfortable. Climbing in, he pulled out of the garage and down the driveway, glancing back in the rearview mirror at the house in Catoosa. He felt a momentary twinge of nostalgia but put it away and made his way to the highway, heading east to Arkansas, away from Oklahoma and the police who were no doubt hot on his trail. Or soon would be. As he drove, he promised his covered passenger that he would deliver her to safety within two hours and return for her before she could even miss him.

Chapter Thirty-Two

The team of FBI agents, detectives and officers had devoured their food and slowly dispersed from the IHOP restaurant, wandering out into the night in groups matching the cars they had come in. The table had dwindled down to Agent Wells, Agent James, Max and Cortez, who were settling up with the server. As they rose from the table, Wells indicated they would meet in the lobby at six o'clock, to hit it hard the next morning. Stepping out into the night, the air was refreshing as the aura surrounding Max and Wells was so thick it could have been cut with a knife. Seemingly pulling the air with them, they headed to their cars.

Getting into the car and starting the engine, Max could feel Cortez's eyes on her again. "What?" she snapped. "Why don't you just say whatever's on your mind and get it over with?"

"Well, now that you asked," joked Cortez, "I was wondering when you and Wells were going to deal with this thing you have between you." She made air quotes with her fingers when she said 'thing,' smirking.

Max rolled her eyes and laughed. "Thing, really?"

"Uh, yeah, really."

"Look, Cortez, that thing you're talking about never was a thing, and even if it was, it was dead a long time ago."

"Could have fooled me. Doesn't look dead to me."

Max rolled her eyes again, but deep down she knew Cortez was right. She just hoped she could get through this trip, arrest Dr. Jack Tyler, and get out of here soon before she found herself in his arms again, an action that certainly would lead to heartbreak.

Arriving back at the hotel, they found Agent James and Agent Wells standing in the lobby talking. As Max and Cortez approached, they heard Agent James say good night and turn towards the elevator. Cortez, called out to her, "Hey hold the door, I'm right behind you!" She tossed a wink to Max and darted off in the direction of the elevators, to join Agent James on the ride up to her room, leaving Max and Wells standing alone in the lobby together.

Max looked at Wells, and for a moment they just stood there and stared at each other, neither of them saying a word. Finally, Wells broke the silence.

"Well, we got a lot of ground covered today."

"Yeah, I guess so," Max replied, not feeling quite so certain.

"I know it's frustrating, but we'll get this guy."

"I hope so." Max said not quite feeling the confidence that Wells displayed.

They slowly started making their way to the elevator doors. The ride up was silent, and as the doors opened to let Wells off at their floor, he turned to her and struggled to speak. "Max, I …"

"Mark, you don't need to say or do anything."

"You don't understand."

"I think I do."

"No. What I am trying to say is …" his words trailed off.

"It's okay, Mark. Really."

"Max, it's not okay." Not being able to articulate his thoughts, he leaned in and pulled her to him to gently kiss her.

Max was surprised by the sudden move, and found herself fighting; but rather than pulling away from him, like her logic wanted her to do, her reaction to his touch was to kiss him back. His lips pressed down on hers and enveloped her in a swirl of emotion. She found her hands threading around his neck and pulling him in even closer. The passion of the kiss intensified as their bodies pressed close together, until Max caught hold of her emotions and pulled back.

Before she could say anything, Wells brushed her cheek with his hand. "That's what I wanted to say this whole time. Good night, Detective Nichols." And with that, he exited the elevator, leaving her standing there in a daze.

Realizing she was standing in the elevator alone, and that this was her floor too, Max stumbled out of the lift and headed to her room, both relieved and disappointed that Wells had already entered his own. Her head was spinning with questions. What was it Agent Mark Wells wanted from her? What did she want from *him?* Could they have these one-night stand encounters and just leave it at that? Obviously not, since they were both still thinking of each other. But could they have a long distance relationship?

Would she even be willing to, knowing how crazy both of their schedules would be? Entering her room, she quickly undressed and fell into the bed, exhausted at the thought of it all. She lay there, again her mind swirling with images of her and Wells tangled together in sheets and sweat. She fell into a deep sleep with no resolution to all of the thoughts and questions.

Chapter Thirty-Three

The morning came far too quickly for Max, and as the alarm on her cell phone went off, she opted to snooze it once before crawling out of bed. As she showered, her mind vacillated between the case and the kiss in the elevator the night before. *Awkward,* she thought to herself as she pictured meeting in the lobby downstairs. She prayed that Cortez would be slow to roll this morning, or she'd pick up on it immediately and be full of questions. Laughing to herself, she blamed Cortez for leaving her alone with Wells.

Arriving downstairs, she found that the breakfast area was crawling with people. There must have been more people checked in than the night before, and she wondered what was going on in Tulsa to draw such a crowd. Then she saw a t-shirt that gave way to the answer: 2013 National Fishing Competition, with an exaggerated drawing of a big fish snapping on a fishing line, and a man on the shore reeling it in. The shirt indicated the next three days as the dates for the big event. Max hadn't heard of this event, but there were obviously some serious fishermen and women in this room. Amused she looked across the room for anyone from the team.

Navigating her way through the crowd, she found Cortez at a table and dropped her laptop bag over the back of the chair, freeing up her hands so that she could work her way back to the coffee station. Waiting patiently behind a man with the fishing shirt on, Max glanced around the room at the crowd, then proceeded to fill a cup with the dark roast. Turning around to head back to the table, she plowed right into Wells, nearly spilling her coffee.

"Good morning," Wells said with a sly smile on his face, his blue eyes gleaming at her.

"Sorry. Good morning." Not able to say anything further, she pushed passed him, taking in the clean, fresh scent of his still-damp hair. Despite her efforts to ignore his smell, she found that she couldn't tune it out, the scent instantly taking her back to that morning in Los Angeles when they'd showered together. Her senses seemed to be on overload, and she realized there was so much she wanted to tell him. But for the moment she could not seem to speak.

Wells smiled as her long flowing hair had brushed against his arm as she passed, ever so slightly tickling him and immediately arousing his every sense. He was quickly reminded of her beauty and her seemingly lack of knowledge of the fact that, had she desired to, she could have easily been a Hollywood heartbreaker. She was a strong, assertive and intelligent woman, but none of that came from the beauty that could certainly make her hell on wheels. She was instead natural, fun and strikingly beautiful, but humble, all characteristics Wells found intoxicating.

Wells worked his way over to the group and noticed that all seats were taken except for one at the table with Max and Cortez. *Perfect*, he thought to himself. Walking up, he asked if it would be okay if he joined them.

Cortez looked up as she took a bite from an English muffin. "Looks like it was saved for you." She glanced towards Max, throwing off a big smile.

Wells slid his tall frame into the seat as he set his coffee and plate of fruit and muffins down. Max jumped up quickly and headed back to the food station, grabbing some fruit and a blueberry muffin from the bar. She returned to the table, making eye contact with Wells as she sat down, unable to ignore the statement Cortez made. Wells and Cortez were engaged in some conversation, and she found herself relieved to just sit in silence listening and eating while they talked.

As Wells and Cortez spoke, sharing ideas on Jack, eyes would drift to Max. Max smiled and tried to avoid the subtle hints by both of them in their obvious attempt to gloss over the tension that was evident at the table. Max was relieved when everyone was finishing up their meals. Everyone began to gather up their belongings preparing to head back to Inola, where they hoped new leads would deliver them something more on Dr. Jack Tyler.

Arriving at the City Hall, everyone piled out of their cars. Detective Adair and some of his team were already assembled in the make-shift investigation room, and as the others arrived and settled in at their respective tables, Wells moved to the front of the room, where the gruesome photos of the victims remained pasted to the board.

"Everyone, if we could have your attention," he started, drawing an immediate silence in the room. "I've received official word from the coroner that the body found in the lake is in fact that of Jessica Jenkins. Fingerprints provided a positive identification. We will need to conduct the official notification to the family. They've already been asking to see the body, which I strongly recommend against given the condition of the head, so we need to find a way around that."

Before Wells could continue, Detective Adair said, "My team and I will handle the notification."

"Thank you, Detective. We also need to view the tapes from the cameras at the parking lots of the two salons. The local PD will be providing the tapes to us within the hour. We'll be looking for any cars that seem to frequent the area. Run the plates on all of them. Qualify any employee vehicles that should be there. I requested a list of all employee vehicles from each of the locations in the strip malls. That information was emailed to me this morning, and I've printed out lists for you. Finally, we should have feedback from the car dealership this morning, which may confirm Detective Nichols' theory that Jack Tyler may have traded his vehicle in for another model."

Pausing for a moment to let this soak in, Wells continued, "Team, we have a lot of possible leads that can help narrow this down. Let's move quickly now. I've split the work up so that we can move faster. Nichols and Cortez, you work the car dealership angle. Then you can help with the tapes. The rest of you work the video feeds from the parking lots; anything remotely out of the ordinary report it. If you see any of our vics on those tapes, or if Jack Tyler shows up on there, report it" Wells tapped the photo of Dr. Jack Tyler that was taped on the board, with 'POI' written under it, signifying person of interest, "Report it."

Max grabbed one of the employee rosters that was circulating the room, as did Cortez. Scanning the lists, she saw Kim's name there – the Vietnamese woman they'd spoken with – as well as several women with matching last names, likely all relatives. She also saw the name of Thomas Jennings, probably the gay employee Kim had indicated worked at the salon. His name appeared on both lists. Max stared at that for a moment considering this. He was an employee at both locations, so he *should* be on both lists.

She continued to review the list, looking for anyone else that might appear on both location lists of employees. After spending thirty minutes comparing the names, though, she didn't find any other employees on both lists. Apparently none of the other businesses had any employees that worked at both strip malls. Frustration welled up as she realized that she'd yet again come up empty handed. Max had been hopeful that there would be multiple duplications on the lists of names for people who would potentially fit the profile. So far all she had was a gay male who did not fit the profile.

Cortez was still focused on the employee list when her phone rang. She answered, spoke for a moment, and gave thumbs up. Max looked at the clock to see that it was just after nine o'clock, which meant that the car dealership was keeping to their promise of getting back to them first thing in the morning. Cortez spent most of the time listening to the person on the other end, and took notes as she talked. Then thanked the person for their time and asked for a direct call back line, just in case she had any further questions. Finally she hung up and looked at Max, her eyes shining.

"Bingo! Jack Tyler traded his convertible Mercedes for a SUV, and guess who his salesman was?"

"Benz?" Max answered before Cortez could say another word.

"Yep. The car has since been sold at auction and is now proudly in, of all places, Los Angeles."

Max shook her head, shocked. Finally they'd tracked Dr. Jack Tyler to Oklahoma, had a connection between the two cities where similar crimes had been committed, and had a direct connection to one of the victims. Adrenaline raced through her veins. She waved Wells over to fill him in on their discovery.

Wells listened intently and agreed that there was now enough of a connection to get Tyler's photo out as a person of interest. "I'll work on the BOLO notification. We can line up a media conference. It's time to get the public involved. You start a trace on the vehicle he traded into. We can add that to the BOLO wire. If Jack Tyler is in this city, he's in for a surprise. We're going to find him."

He rushed off, and Max and Cortez hovered over the computer, entering the vehicle identification the dealership had given on the new vehicle. It was a silver Toyota Sequoia low profile, sufficient enough in size to hide a body, an SUV that would easily fit in anywhere. The car was still running with temporary registration tags. After a few minutes of digging, they learned that in Oklahoma the buyer was given a temporary paper license plate and required to register the vehicle within thirty days. That time had clearly elapsed, but according to Detective Adair, it wasn't uncommon for new car owners to take more than the allotted time. The car had not yet been registered, leaving blank any name association to the vehicle. The car had been bought with the cash from Jack Tyler and then never registered under any name.

Max had been hoping that if Jack had assumed an alias, this would be the lead to giving them that information, but it looked like he'd thought of that too. The vehicle had been sold to Jack Tyler, but there was no trail of Jack Tyler in Oklahoma, or anywhere for that matter. And as of this point, he hadn't yet switched to his alias. Once again, they'd hit a dead end. Max pushed back from the computer in frustration. Again, she found herself struggling with what to work next.

The tapes the local PD had promised first thing showed up late, arriving well after noon. All of the delays caused them to miss the midday news. The report would hit the six o'clock news instead, as well as the local paper the next day. This information further frustrated Max, though Wells tried to calm her through his eyes as he looked at her across the room. He locked in on her, and as their eyes connected he nodded subtle assurance to her, Max smiled back at him.

With the tapes to work on, everyone buckled down sorting through them. Agent Wells asked for one of the officers to have lunch brought in. It was likely to be a long night, and with the case starting to turn hot, he wasn't planning on stopping until they had Jack Tyler in cuffs.

Max and Cortez began going through the tapes as well, initially frustrated at the grainy picture. It was taking longer than desired due to the poor quality, and in some cases it was difficult to even determine if a person on the feed was male or female. The tapes that had been requested contained the past forty-five days of feeds from the surveillance company. The process of going through these was very slow. This was not going to be an easy task.

The food was delivered around two o'clock, and everyone stopped to grab a sandwich from the box of food and drinks. Max rubbed her eyes, already tired from straining to look at the video. With Cortez's help, she'd recorded a number of plates that they'd now cross-referenced to the employee sheets, as well as look up for owner details. This seemed somewhat fruitless to Max, as the car Jack was driving didn't have a plate at all, unless he'd stolen one. And so far, none of the vehicles recorded had been a silver Toyota. The parking lot cameras only covered about half the lot, though, picking up the store entrances and the first two rows of cars. The third row was not in the view of the video at all.

As they nibbled on their sandwiches, Max said, "Our Jack is smart. If he was hunting in those parking lots, he wouldn't park where the camera would see him. So unless he walks into the view of the camera to enter a store, we're not going to see him on these tapes."

Cortez nodded in agreement. "And if he's changed his look or comes onto the frame wearing a hoodie or a ball cap that would make it impossible for us to identify him."

"Okay, let's take a new approach then. You start looking up the plates we've collected so far, and I'll continue looking at the tapes. We can switch when the eye strain becomes too much, but let's focus on stolen plates." Cortez nodded in agreement to the plan, taking one last draw on her Diet Coke and moving back toward the computer. Max handed Cortez a report of stolen vehicles and license plates that had been earlier provided to use in her review.

Around them, everyone started settling back into the work. Max started back in on the tapes as Cortez began checking registration records for the plate numbers they'd recorded. The process was laborious and unrewarding, and before they knew it, they'd gone through an entire week of video and found nothing significant. Max looked up at the clock, and saw that it was just

252

before five o'clock. The media was starting to gather outside, preparing for the live news conference at six o'clock. Wells had a TV brought in from the adjacent police office, so they could air the statement in the room. Everyone was anxious for the report to run, and the room seemed to have a renewed buzz.

Wells walked up to Max. "I want you to join me in making the statement."

Max looked up at him in surprise. "What? Why?"

"You have the most intimate knowledge of our un-sub, and I think it's important for people to realize that we're tying this to California. I want you to assist in delivering the conference."

Max looked at Wells, their eyes locking for a moment. "Okay."

Max had participated in news reports in the past, but this was significant. Their chance to catch this guy likely hung on this report. She felt honored that Wells trusted her. They worked together to setup for the conference.

As the microphones began to appear in front of the City Hall building, Wells and Max worked preparing their statements. Wells warned Max not to engage in questions with the media. Right at six o'clock they stepped out of the office in front of the press. They had agreed on the point that the report would transition between the two of them, and they covered the facts several times, making sure they covered the details they wanted people focused on.

Wells stepped up to the podium and began. "Ladies and gentlemen, my name is Agent Wells and I'm with the FBI. This is Detective Maxine Nichols of the Los Angeles Police Department, Homicide Division. We're here tonight to ask for your help in locating this man." Wells held up a photo of Dr. Jack Tyler, facing it toward the cameras. "We believe this man has information related to the recent murders of the five people whose bodies were found out by Lock and Dam Road here in Inola, as well as that of Jessica Jenkins, discovered at Keystone Lake."

Max stepped forward as Wells stepped away from the podium and added her own piece. "We also believe that Dr. Jack Tyler, a well-known surgeon from Los Angeles, has information regarding six more murders in California. Dr. Tyler has been missing for several months, and we need your help in locating him. He was last seen driving a Silver Toyota Sequoia with Oklahoma temporary tags."

Wells stepped forward again. "Anyone with information regarding the whereabouts of Dr. Tyler should call our tip line immediately. Thank you."

Stepping away from the podium, both Max and Wells re-entered the building, declining to take any questions from the reporters, who shoved microphones in their faces and hurled questions towards them.

Wells looked at Max and smiled, "Well done."

"Yeah, whatever," she threw back at him with a bit of a grin. "Now, let the fun begin. The tips will come in claiming everything, including the sighting of Bigfoot."

"I know, but one of those crazies might just be the one that gets us our prize."

Chapter Thirty-Four

Almost immediately following the live conference, the phone tip line started ringing with all kinds of information, none of which was valuable. Several hours later, the ten o'clock news aired the conference again, and a few minutes after that Max's cell phone rang. Looking at the display, she saw a 918 area code and recognized it as a local number, though not one she'd programmed for anyone working on the investigation team. Answering the phone, she listened as the woman on the other end identified herself as Samantha, the owner from the Beehive Salons. She seemed almost frantic, and Max had to take a moment to calm her down just to understand what she was telling her.

"The man in the picture on the news, it's my employee Thomas," the woman muttered, her voice rushed.

Max paused feeling her stomach drop, "Are you sure?" She asked nearly dreading the answer. She should have trusted her instincts. She had felt she was missing something, and here it was, the gay guy right in front of her the whole time.

"Yes, I'm positive, but he's different now. I mean he's gay, and he wears a little bit of makeup and, well, he's different for sure, but I know that's him."

"Okay, my partner and I are coming to see you right away. Where can we meet?" Max struggled to keep her adrenaline from consuming her. She had moved past the fact that she should have pushed the connection with Thomas, but now she had a solid lead. A witness saying she knew Jack Tyler. They had to move quickly…*very quickly*.

"I'm at home. You can come here," she said, giving Max her home address in Broken Arrow. "Oh and Detective, he didn't report to work today."

Max hung up the phone and gathered everyone around to tell them about the call. By the time she was done, Cortez was already heading to the car. When Max started to follow her, Wells called out, "Nichols, be careful, and call us the minute you have an address on him. We'll meet you there. We all go in together. No heroics."

Max looked back at Wells, and they both paused for a brief moment before she let the door close behind her. She knew he was warning her to be safe and to stay calm. That look would carry her throughout the night. Once in the car, Max and Cortez rode to the address Samantha had provided, discussing the possibilities this new information offered. When they arrived at the address, they got out of the vehicle and approached the house, Max leading the way. Ringing the bell, she found that she could barely stand still, shuffling between feet as they waited for the door to be answered. This was the lead she'd been waiting for on this case, and she could hardly wait to follow it. Before long, the salon owner opened the door, looking stressed. She had her hair pulled back away from her face and worry shrouded her eyes. This wasn't the same confident woman they'd met the day before.

"Come in," she said, stepping away from the door.

Once they were inside, she led them into the living room, where they each took a seat on the stylish sofa and chairs. Max pulled out a file and laid out a few photos of Dr. Jack Tyler on the coffee table between them, not bothering with preliminaries.

"Is this Thomas?" she asked.

Samantha picked up the one in the middle and nodded. "Yes, it's him. Did he kill all those people?"

"We don't know that for sure, but we definitely need to speak with him right away. Do you have an address on file for him?"

Samantha hesitated for a moment, but then nodded. "Yes of course. I keep all my employee files here in my home office. Let me go pull it for you."

Max and Cortez sat in near silence as they each took in the surroundings. The house was well decorated. Samantha had an obvious decorator's flair. It had shown in her salon, and it showed here too. The furniture was modern and colorful, with pieces of glass art distributed around the walls. Everything had a curve to it, which made the room feel as if everything was flowing. Cortez nodded at Max in approval of the room, and Max smiled back at her.

Samantha returned to the room with a folder in her hand. She pulled out the application Thomas had filled out and handed it to them.

"I apologize, but this is the first time I've noticed that he only wrote in the city. Apparently he never put his street address on the application."

"Do you run any background checks?" Max asked, already knowing the answer.

"No, I never do. Most of my employees come to me through referral."

"Was Thomas a referral?"

"Yes," Samantha answered, sounding almost excited now. "My friend Melody's an instructor at the beauty college here in town. Thomas was one of her students. She raved about him."

"Would Melody know Thomas's address?"

Samantha nodded. "I think she's actually been to his home before. They're good friends. They go out dancing occasionally. You know, girls' night out."

Cortez jumped quickly to the next question. "Could we get Melody's number from you? We need to speak with her right away."

"I can call her for you. I know it's late, but under the circumstances ..." she trailed off.

"That would be very helpful," Max indicated.

Samantha pulled out her cell phone and quickly selected from the contact list, pressing send and waiting for a connection. After a couple of rings, the line obviously connected as she began to speak, asking if Melody had watched the news. She shook her head at Max and Cortez at the answer, and Max, growing impatient, motioned that she would like to speak with the other woman. Samantha told Melody that there was someone that wanted to talk with her, and handed the phone over to Max.

Taking the telephone from Samantha, Max spoke into the receiver, "Melody, I am Detective Max Nichols with the Los Angeles Police Department. We need to speak with your friend Thomas right away.

Melody started to protest. "I don't understand."

"I know this is confusing, but we don't have a lot of time. All I can tell you is that he is a person of interest in several local and out of state murders."

Max could sense Melody's sudden revelation as the words settled in.

"We need to know if you have Thomas's address. We need to speak with him right away," she finished.

"I've been there before, yes, but …, Oh hold on a second, let me see. I wrote it down somewhere the first time I went there." Max heard rustling of papers and then Melody came back on the line. "I can't find it, but it's in my GPS. I entered it in the first time I went over there. I just can't believe Thomas would have anything to do with anything like murder. He's sweet and a good friend."

Max nodded to Cortez, indicating that they had an address. "Melody, I know this is tough, but we need that address. We're on our way to your house. Don't talk to anyone before we get there, especially Jack … uh Thomas. What's your address?"

After jotting down the address, Max thanked Samantha and headed to Melody's house to pull Jack's address off of the GPS and talk with her a bit further. On the way, Max called Wells, letting him know that within the hour they would have an address for Jack.

Max drove as fast as she could to Melody's house, arriving in about twenty minutes. They pulled up in front of a modest brick home in a neighborhood of similar houses. Walking up the drive, Max and Cortez exchanged a look of both excitement and concern, fearing they might be too late. Knocking on the door, the two again waited impatiently as they heard footsteps approaching from the inside. Then the door opened, and they were greeted by an attractive woman in her mid-thirties, wearing sweat pants and a sweat shirt that advertised Oklahoma University. It appeared that she'd just pulled on the clothes, most likely due to the late hour.

Still, at least she was there and ready to give them what they needed.

Max greeted her, quickly introducing herself and Cortez, and apologized for the late hour. "We're very sorry for coming so late, but we do need to see if we can get that address from you. It's very important that we see Thomas as soon as possible."

Melody acknowledged the statement with a nod and led them to the vehicle to show them the recent history on her car's GPS system. She had already written down the address and handed it to Max. "I went there twice. Last time I was there, it was the morning after we went out dancing. Thomas had taken a man home with him that night, and I stopped by the next day. We were only there for a while and then went to get something to eat. Why do you need to talk to him?"

Max and Cortez exchanged a glance as they both made the connection that Gary was likely the man he'd taken home. "He's a person of interest in the abduction and murder of five people here in Oklahoma and six others in California."

Max watched as the color drained from Melody's face, her hand fluttering to her neck and twisting at the necklace. "Thomas is my friend. How could he know anything about those murders?"

Not answering her questions, Max continued to probe. "Do you remember the name of the man Thomas took home with him the night you went out?"

"His name was Gary. He wasn't there when I showed up in the morning, but Thomas said he'd already left."

Without confirming anything, Max continued, "We have reason to believe that Jack, or Thomas, has information about the murders, and that's exactly why we need to speak with him. When was the last time you talked to him?" Max tried to wait patiently, not wanting to push Melody too quickly yet not hardly able to wait for her responses.

Melody looked back and forth between the two women before offering, "He called me a couple of days ago and asked if we could get together soon for dinner or a night out. I mean, doesn't that prove that he has nothing to do with this? Why would he call me if he had anything to do with those people?"

"We can't be sure until we speak with him, but we believe his name is actually Dr. Jack Tyler. He's a well-known surgeon in California. Was there any behavior you thought unusual at any time?" Max asked.

"Jack? A surgeon?" The three having returned to the living room, Melody took a seat on the sofa, obviously shaken by the news. "Nothing stands out. He was a great student, got along with everyone and has been a very good friend to me, as well as a model employee for Samantha."

"I know this is unsettling, but we really need to go. Is there someone you can call to keep you company?" Max continued to try to contain her eagerness to get on the phone with Wells and get a team headed to the address, but realized she had a responsibility to ensure Melody was okay. She was clearly shaken that her trusted friend could be this person, and leaving her alone was not an option.

"I can call my sister. She lives just a few minutes away," Melody offered, still clearly shaken by the news.

Max and Cortez waited for Melody to call her sister and then offered their thanks and darted out the front door. As soon as they were on the front porch, Max pulled out her phone and called Wells. "We have an address. You won't believe this. The address is in Catoosa, less than a mile from the IHOP and our hotel. He's been right under our nose this whole time." After giving Wells the address and agreeing to meet the team in the IHOP parking lot so they could all go in together, Max started the car and turned around, heading back through Broken Arrow, pointing her car towards Catoosa.

They arrived in the IHOP parking lot in what had to be record time, and Max found Wells, Agent James, Detective Adair and his whole team, as well as the Inola Sheriff's Department waiting there. After a few minutes, they agreed to go up the driveway together and fan out across the front of the home to cut off any escape routes. Detective Adair's team would head towards the rear of the house, Wells and James would go to the front door, and Max and Cortez, along with the Inola Sheriff's team, would post along any windows and corners of the house.

If Jack Tyler was inside that home, there was no way he was getting out without walking right into a member of law enforcement.

With Wells leading the team, the row of cars headed up the same driveway that Jack must have travelled any number of times. They brought with them a large cloud of dust, which sheltered their activity from the neighbors, and pulled onto the grass surrounding the home. Then officers began exiting their vehicles and taking their respective posts. Max and Cortez walked up the drive past the SUV, peering through the windows as they passed, with guns drawn. They stopped on opposite sides of the garage entrance, their eyes on each other. Once everyone was in position, Wells and James approached the front door, knocking loudly.

"FBI, Dr. Tyler, please open the door," Wells called out.

Waiting a few seconds, Wells knocked again and tried to peer through the window in the door. There was no answer, though, and the silence from inside hinted that no one was home. Or that Jack was hiding, Max thought to herself. They would need a warrant to enter the home, and that would take time.

Detective Adair spent a few minutes on the phone, securing the warrant, and then returned to where Wells and the team anxiously waited. Max wanted to get into the home and forget the paperwork, but she knew that if there was anything inside that would connect Jack Tyler to the murders, they had to do this by the book.

"We should have the warrant within an hour," Adair said. "I have a friend who's a judge, and he'll sign it the minute it crosses his desk. Being drawn now, then it'll be taken directly for signature and brought here."

Wells nodded and gestured to everyone else, and they started moving to sweep the area on the outside. As long as they were outside the house, they might as well see what they could find, and anything in the open was fair game. A search of the trash netted nothing that connected to any of the victims. Then they discovered a burn pile, but nothing was salvageable. The garage didn't have any windows in the doors, so they weren't able to get a visual to the inside. The silver SUV Jack had traded for the Mercedes was in the driveway, but it was locked. So it too was off limits for now. They just had to wait.

An hour and a half after Detective Adair had called to request the warrant, a car appeared in the driveway with the document.

Adair accepted it with a nod and quickly read it over, then looked up. "This gives us access to the house, garage, vehicle, and any property. We're good to go. Break the door down." He nodded to the sheriff, who had pulled out a battering ram.

Within a few minutes, the doors were open, and the FBI and police were swarming the home, calling out "clear" as they entered each room. Jack Tyler was definitely not home. Max struggled not to show her disappointment as she went from room to room, trying to get a feel for the life Jack had led. He wasn't home, but this was the closest they'd been. And maybe they could find something here that would lead them to him. The home was nicely decorated and well-tended. In the master bedroom, she pulled on gloves and one by one opened the drawers and closet. Both sides of the closet seemed to be only partially filled. On the left was clothing for a man, and on the right was a woman's clothing. Max wondered if it was possible that he was living with someone. That had to be impossible, though; there was no way Jack could pull off the crimes he had with someone in his immediate life.

So why did he have a woman's clothing in his closet?

Wells entered the room as she was looking through the dresser drawers. "What'd you find?" he asked.

"Both the closet and dresser seem to be only half filled. And get this – they have a woman's clothing in them, too."

Wells looked at her with clear surprise on his face. "Maybe he had a girlfriend?"

"Melody told us he took a man home with him one night from a bar. His name was Gary. Guess we know now how that victim fit in. She never mentioned a woman being here or any girlfriend."

"Could he have had one, and she didn't know?" Wells continued, "We need to find some physical connection to Tyler. Right now we have nothing but circumstantial evidence."

Nodding, Max continued to search the room and bathroom. Finding nothing, she moved to the guest room and then to the kitchen. Searching through all of the cupboards, she found all the normal kitchen dishes and appliances. Then she opened a long cupboard next to the door that came in from the garage and found a well-stocked pantry. Something seemed off about the pantry, and she closed the doors and went out into the garage, wondering. The garage was almost bare, though, and she frowned.

Then, looking at the garage floor, she noticed two sets of tire tracks. One set was narrower than the other, and the total wheel placement front to back was different. She turned to Wells, who'd followed her.

"Mark, take a look at this," she said, pointing out the two different wheel markings.

Wells nodded. "There've been two different vehicles in here. This might explain why Jack is nowhere to be found, and the

SUV is out front. I'll get the CSI team in here to take pictures of this and see if we can get make and model off of each." He headed out to get one of the techs to come gather the evidence, and Max turned back to the garage.

It didn't take long to realize that there was nothing else interesting in here, and she started back into the house. As she did so, she noticed what appeared to be a void between the garage and kitchen that didn't make sense. Standing in the door frame to the door between the kitchen and the garage, she stared into the void, narrowing her eyes and trying to understand what she was seeing. Going back into the kitchen, she opened the pantry again. The void would be behind this pantry. Studying the stocked shelves, she turned and looked at the door frame. The distance was definitely off. Something was strange about this pantry. She began taking a few of the canned goods off of the shelves and setting them on the counter. As she was unloading one of the bigger rows, Wells approached again, looking at the pantry items on the shelf.

"Is there any reason you're unloading the kitchen shelves?"

"Yes, look at this. There's a void here. The width between here and the garage door isn't right. The pantry is too shallow to take up that much space." Max showed Wells what she was referring to by motioning between the pantry and the garage doorway. "Look at the difference between where the wall ends and the door starts. The pantry has the ability to be another 2 feet deep, but it is not."

Wells looked at what Max was referring to and quickly moved to help her. He glanced at the other cupboards in the kitchen. "You're on to something, Max. Look at this. The construction is slightly different on this pantry. The wood used on the inside isn't the same, looks like it was added later."

By that time, Max had the pantry completely unloaded and was poking around in the back. "Look, right there," she said, pointing to the corner. "It looks like a hinge."

Wells pushed where Max was pointing and the wall moved. Then he pulled on it instead of pushing. A moment later, the wall gave and swung open. He glanced back at Max, then pulled the two walls apart.

They stood facing a door.

"In here," Wells shouted out as he reached to turn the knob on the door in front of them.

As the door opened, Max and Wells stared into the darkness of the basement stairwell that faced them. Wells ran his gloved hand along the wall until it passed over a switch. He flipped it into the on position, and light flooded the stairs into the room at the bottom. Moving forward, they drew their guns and slowly moved down the stairway into the basement, Wells leading the way. Cortez appeared behind Max moments after they landed at the bottom, and soon the room filled with other officers. They found themselves in a room with a sofa, small table and large freezer, and they looked at each other, all recognizing the strong odor of bleach. Max tried to calm her racing heart. This was it. They hadn't found him, not yet, but they'd found where he murdered those people. She was sure of it.

Ahead of them was another door, and they cautiously proceeded forward. Wells reached out and turned the knob, swinging the door inward, and the smell of bleach nearly overwhelmed them. He flipped on another light, and the room lit up, displaying a stainless steel table sitting in the middle of what appeared to be a makeshift operating room.

"Clear," Wells called out, once again holstering his gun.

All the officers relaxed their stance, and Wells and Max moved into the room. She noted that the shelves were clear of any items, but it was obvious that this room had been used. Wells ordered the CSI agents to test for prints everywhere, as well as check the drain and all surfaces for any trace evidence.

Moving out to the main room again and over to the freezer, Max opened the door with some apprehension, glancing over her shoulder at Cortez, who was on her heels. The light came on in the inside of the freezer as the door swung open, and Max glanced in. She was almost relieved to find it empty. She hadn't realized until that moment that she'd been afraid they might find another victim, though she was pretty certain Jessica Jenkins had completed the process of trying to put his wife back together. She exhaled softly. Behind her, Cortez let out a sigh too.

Staring into the freezer, there was no way not to consider what and who had occupied this cold room. Max pictured his victims inside and the baggie with the hands and feet laying on one of those shelves. *Had he stored any of the victims in here? Was he keeping the parts in here? Was Jessica's face in this freezer once?* The coroner had not said anything about any of the victims being frozen. He took the parts he needed and then buried the rest.

Max turned to Cortez just as Wells approached. "Damn it, he's in the wind," she claimed, considering the missing clothes and the lack of anything in this freezer.

"Not necessarily, he could pull in the drive at any moment," Wells returned.

"No, he ran!" Max nearly shouted as she turned for the stairs, taking them two by two. With Wells and Cortez right behind her, confused by her outburst, Max hurried through the kitchen and returned to the master bedroom, staring at the closet again. She ran through the door to the bathroom, opening the drawers again.

"Look," she exclaimed, pointing into the drawers one by one. "Everything one uses on a daily basis is gone. Razor, toothbrush, comb, gel, toothpaste – all of it is missing. The only items left in these drawers are the things someone would leave behind if they were in a hurry and didn't need every day. And the closets, his and hers, are both partially empty. He took what he needed for 'them' and left with *his version* of a restored Hope."

Wells and Cortez stared down into the drawers, taking stock of the contents. Q-tips, lotions, dental floss, cotton balls … there wasn't a single item that was a must-have on a daily basis.

"Shit," Wells exclaimed, quickly turning from the room and heading out to the team. He gave directions to the CSI team to speed up the results on the car tire treads. "We need to know what kind of vehicles those treads go on. We have reason to believe the suspect has left the area."

The CSI agent responded that they hoped to know the make and model of the car that had left the other tread marks within the hour, and Wells nodded. "As quick as you can," he muttered. "We need to get after this guy."

Meanwhile, Max stood in the living room, taking in the activities of the crime scene investigators. Detective Adair was leading the collection efforts, and every detail of the home was being covered. He had emailed photos of fingerprints from within the home, to be compared to Jack Tyler's prints. He looked at Max and nodded in acknowledgement.

"We should have some information soon on the prints. If this guy is Tyler, we'll have a positive ID. My team is supposed to call me as soon as they have something."

Max looked at him and offered a small smile. "Thanks, Detective," she said, trying to not show the frustration and despair that was starting to creep over her. She had missed him at the salon, and now she may have lost him here. The house made her skin crawl, and for a moment she had to choke back the bile that built in her throat.

Wells entered the room and looked at Max with an understanding look on his face. "Max, we *will* find this guy. If it's the last thing we do, we'll track this bastard down. The CSI team is working on the tire treads, and while it may not be 100 percent conclusive, we'll get a list of vehicles that are a potential match. We're also canvassing the neighborhood. Agent James is talking to the closest neighbor right now. We're hoping maybe he saw something."

Looking at Wells, their eyes met and locked in. Max nodded not feeling the confidence her gesture indicated. That moment when their eyes connected there was a comfort that transferred between them. Max could read Wells. Cortez walked up then, and the three of them stood there for a moment, then headed back out into the night towards the car and some of the others. They'd made it as far as Wells's car when Detective Adair came rushing out.

"We got it," he said, not able to contain his excitement. "The fingerprints are a positive match to Dr. Jack Tyler."

Max sighed. "That's good news."

Wells jumped in. "Exactly. Now we know that Tyler is our guy, and with the surgical room in the basement, I'm certain we'll be able to connect him to the victims. Any idea how soon we might get tread analysis?"

"It depends. It might be morning before we get that. The team is processing those photographs now, and they have been informed to advise me the minute they have any information."

"Agent Wells, sir," Agent James said, approaching the group.

"Yes, James?" Wells responded. "What do you have?"

"The neighbor seems to be a bit of a voyeur. You know, the Gladys Kravitz type," she offered, referring to the nosey neighbor in the 1970's television show *Bewitched*. "He says that yesterday Enterprise delivered a white van to this address. He knows because the rental company had a car with the company logo on it. He saw that van leave early today and never saw it return."

"Good work, James," Wells praised. "Detective Adair, can you tell your team to narrow the tire tread search against only vans? Also, can you contact Enterprise and see if we can get the rental information, ASAP? Whichever gets us the answer faster, we go with."

"I'm on it," Adair said, quickly heading off.

Max, Wells and Cortez waited together discussing their options. Max decided it was early enough in Los Angeles to bring the chief up to speed so she made a quick call to him. He did his typical barking out commands, demanding her to keep him informed and then as usual hung up on her. She sighed, he sounded disappointed when she told him she had let Tyler get the slip on her at the salon. "Great," she muttered under her breath before returning to Wells and Cortez. As she walked up, Adair was coming up from the other direction.

"I have a little bad news. The rental company isn't open again until five in the morning. In the meantime, the team has matched the tires to a very common tread – 17-inch wheels that could fit several models of vans."

"Okay, thank you, Detective," Wells replied, unable to contain his disappointment. "What else are we finding inside the home?"

"Not much so far, I'm sorry to say. We have a lot of evidence that will likely tie Tyler to the murders, including some blood in the drain trap. Most of it was contaminated by the heavy use of bleach, but I think we have a good sample. All we need is to tie him to one of the victims, and we've got him. Unfortunately, we haven't found anything indicating where he may be headed. We do have a trace on his cell phone, but there hasn't been any recent activity, and the signal is showing somewhere near here. I have a team looking for it. I'm pretty sure he dumped it."

After a few moments of silence, Wells, Max and Cortez realized they were stalled until they had the information from the rental company. In the meantime, Jack was hours ahead of them and they had no idea where he was headed. With the search of the house winding down, they were running out of things to do as they waited.

Finally, Wells broke the silence. "I recommend we get four hours of shut eye. Tomorrow, as soon as we have the vehicle information for the rental, we can get a BOLO out on the van and track him wherever he's gone. I'm not giving up yet. But I need to sleep if I'm going to keep my eyes open tomorrow, and so do all of you."

Returning to the hotel together, the three of them boarded the elevator, along with Agent James, and rode up to their floor in silence. Wells and Max headed in the opposite direction from Cortez to their respective rooms, while Agent James stayed on the elevator for another floor. They agreed to meet right at five the next morning, hoping that Detective Adair would have some news from the rental car agency as soon as they opened.

When Max got to her door, she was surprised to see Wells stopping with her. He leaned close enough for her to hear his heartbeat, and whispered, "Stay with me tonight?"

Somewhat shocked by his request, she shook her head. Leaning in to him and looping her hand up around his neck, she pulled him down to her and placed a gentle kiss on his lips. "I'd like that but, we only have a few hours. And we need to be fresh. I'm hoping tomorrow is a long day."

Wells feigning a pout in protest, then leaned back down and pulled her into his arms, giving her a deep, passionate kiss before releasing her and turning to his own door. He looked at her one last time before slipping into his room and closing the door.

Max entered her room too, still savoring the kiss on her lips. All she really wanted was to crawl into his arms and sleep for the next few days, but she knew they couldn't do that until Jack Tyler had been stopped. Dropping into bed after merely pulling off her socks and pants, not even bothering to pull on her sleep clothes, Max fell into a restless sleep, her mind imagining catching and facing the monster that Jack Tyler had become.

Chapter Thirty-Five

Jack had arrived in Fayetteville a little more than two hours after leaving Oklahoma, and had gone straight to the storage facility. After he filled out the necessary paperwork, the elderly man behind the counter offered him directions to the specific refrigeration storage rental. He proceeded through the storage facility, following the rows of mini-garages down and around to the back. He was pleased to learn that the cold storage was at the rear of the facility. He had asked for a corner space, seeking the most privacy possible. As he worked his way past the other rows, he paid careful attention, looking down each one for signs of anyone else accessing their storage lot. He didn't see anyone and assumed that was because it was mid-day. Feeling good about the fact that he was apparently alone, he continued looking for the storage number. He also made a mental note that mid-day provided privacy, even though it was daylight. No one seeing him was more important than the concealment of darkness. He would be back here in a couple of months and wanted to remember this.

Arriving at the storage unit marked 7373, he smiled up at the numbers. When asked his preference of available units he'd chosen this one because he saw those numbers as a lucky sign. Not that he was a gambling man. In fact he had never stepped into the casino that sat within walking distance of the home in Catoosa. But he still occasionally found himself looking for the odd things that could be considered omens. This was a good omen, he was sure of it. Pulling the rear of the van up as close to the door of the storage unit as possible, Jack jumped out and removed the bag on the seat next to him. He'd purchased a heavy-duty combination lock from the man at the counter. It would be used to keep Hope safe. Tearing away the packaging, he tossed the empty box back into the driver's seat and opened the locker door.

Stepping into the storage room, he quickly assessed the temperature and made a minor adjustment, setting the thermostat to the optimal temperature. Before paying and accepting the rental lock or signing the rental contract, he'd asked what happened during power outages, and was happy to learn that the backup generators would keep Hope safe even during power failure. Short of a complete failure of the refrigeration system, this should be a perfect place for her until he could return. The storage room was equipped with built-in shelves on one wall that would serve perfectly for laying Hope down flat.

Returning to the van, he looked around again and noticed the surveillance cameras. He made sure that the van doors were up against the wall offering a block against the cameras positioned throughout the facility. He took one more look around to make sure that he was out of sight. Then he gently pulled back the tarp and the now thawing blanket, lifting Hope's body from the floor of the van and carrying her into the storage room, where he carefully set her on the middle shelf. Her body laid perfectly on the width of the shelf, and he tucked her arms close to her sides.

Bringing the blankets in, he laid one over her, covering everything except for her face, and stood staring down at her for a few moments before returning to the van, this time to retrieve the boxes of supplies, chemicals and surgical instruments. Finally, he put the bag with Hope's personal clothes and toiletries in the room. Once everything was inside the storage room, he closed the door behind him.

Now he moved over to stand next to Hope. He took the other blanket and folded it several times, transforming it into a small square. He lifted Hope's head, placing the blanket in a pillow-like manner so that her head could rest on it. In his mind, it was very important to make his wife comfortable. As he cared for her, he covered the moment with loving words and promises that he wouldn't stay away any longer than necessary. Before turning away from her, Jack leaned over and kissed her lips and softly brushed the hair from her forehead.

All he saw was the beauty that Hope had once been. He did not see the stitches, or the strange way the face sat over the eye sockets. To anyone else the strange sight would have been a horror. Repulsive and terrifying, but to Jack she was as perfect as Hope had ever been.

Leaving the storage locker was the hardest thing Jack had ever done. He had to force himself to stay focused on the next chapter. Carefully programming the date of his wedding anniversary as the code for the padlock, he double and triple checked the security of the lock. Once satisfied, he closed the van doors and walked around the van, ducking the cameras and sliding into the driver's seat. Pulling away, he left the storage unit and Hope behind.

He exited through the gates of the storage facility, smiling at the sign advertising 24-hour access. He could come back any time, once he returned. All he needed was the access code he'd been given after filling out the paperwork. He'd paid for three months advanced rent, not thinking he would be gone that long, but not wanting to have to worry about any payment issues while out of the country.

Heading through town, Jack began seeking the perfect place to leave the van. At some point it would be detected, and he only needed it until tomorrow morning when his flight would leave.

While Jack was safely tucking Hope away in storage, the task force in Oklahoma was pulling together information on him that would lead to the discovery of his home.

Jack had ditched his cell phone already, tossing it out the window before ever getting on the interstate in Oklahoma. As he drove along the street, he saw a Dollar General along North Gregg Avenue and pulled in, deciding to buy a throw-away cell phone. After gathering everything he needed, he proceeded to the checkout counter.

Placing the phone, a ball cap, and a pair of reading glasses with the minimum level of magnification in them on the counter, he paid with cash and then asked the clerk if she had a phone book he could borrow. Seeming a little annoyed, the twenty-something reached under the counter and handed Jack the small book. Flipping through the yellow pages, he committed to memory the number of a local cab service and, thanking the clerk, grabbed his yellow Dollar General bag. Seeing a dumpster at the side of the building, he pulled the printer out of the passenger side of the van and tossed it in the dumpster under some of the trash, then climbed back in the vehicle and continued down the street.

When he saw a small diner just off the road, he decided that it was a good spot to park. There was a wraparound parking lot and the place sat a bit off the road. Pulling into the lot, he drove to the back and parked in one of the spaces. Pulling out the new cell phone, he installed the battery and sim card, then powered it up and dialed the cab company, requesting a ride from his current location, giving the diner name as the pickup address.

Pulling on the hat and glasses, Jack waited for the driver to arrive. He collected his travel bag, travel documents, and laptop from inside the van and locked it up. The cab arrived about ten minutes later. As he saw the black car with yellow checkers in a triangle on the door pull into the diner parking lot, he approached the driver, requesting to be taken to the airport rental car center. The driver helped him load his bag into the trunk, and Jack climbed in the back of the car, keeping his laptop with him.

The ride to the airport was fairly short, taking only ten minutes, during which the driver never spoke. Jack was relieved to be left alone with his thoughts. As the car moved across town, his mind cycled through a checklist, making sure he had thought of everything. Mostly, that he had Hope safe in a place where she could stay until he returned. He pictured how he had left her, and sadness overcame him.

Paying the driver cash, Jack gathered his belongings and headed inside the rental center. He approached the Hertz counter and asked the clerk for a compact car for a one-way rental to St. Louis. Handing over a credit card and the driver's license, both in the name of Jackson Phillips, he secured the rental and headed out to the parking lot. There he found the White Chevy Aveo in the appropriate spot, placed his bags in the trunk and got in the car, quickly adjusting the seat and mirrors.

Once he was out of the parking lot, he took off the glasses, so as not to impair his driving vision, and made his way out of the airport, headed north. It was a five and a half-hour drive to St. Louis. To be safe he would make only necessary stops.

He arrived in St. Louis, just after six o'clock. It had been a long day, but everything was going according to his plan. He found a fueling station and filled the car with unleaded gasoline, paying with the credit card of his newest identity. Finally turning into the rental car return center, Jack put the glasses back on and pulled into the rental return. He asked the return agent to leave the charges. Receiving the receipt, he thanked the agent and headed to the shuttle van area, where he waited for the shuttle to the airport terminals and hotels. He carried his bags onto the shuttle and informed the driver that he was going to the Hilton Garden Inn then settled in for the ride. As he focused on his new cell phone, he smiled at the thought of how easily he was slipping away from the authorities.

Arriving at the hotel, Jack checked in, requesting a late checkout the following day, which was granted. He would be allowed to stay in his room until two o'clock. After making those arrangements, he proceeded to his room and ordered some room service, not intending to leave again until it was time to head to the airport. In less than twenty-four hours, he'd be on a flight to the Caymans, and they'd never find him. Or Hope.

Chapter Thirty-Six

Max rose before the alarm even went off, tired of tossing and turning. After she showered and dressed, she grabbed her laptop and hurried downstairs, anxious to get the day started and find out what the rental company had on the vehicle. Being the first one downstairs, she enjoyed the coffee and silence of the room. Apparently the fishing tournament was either over or they were already headed to the lake. As a child, Max had fished with her grandfather and remembered going out in the wee hours. According to her grandfather, fish would bite best before it got too hot. Based on that memory, she was betting the fishing teams had headed out a while ago.

After about twenty minutes of silence, Wells showed up, followed very shortly after by Cortez. As they were getting their daily breakfast and coffees, Wells's phone rang. Max looked at the time on her cell phone and saw that it was just a couple minutes after five. She held her breath, hoping that this was the call they were waiting on.

A few minutes later, Wells hung up. "Got it, we have the make, model and license plate number. We already have a BOLO out on the car and Tyler in all fifty states. Let's hope he didn't expect us to find out what vehicle he is driving right away. Anyone spots the vehicle, they're directed to arrest him on the spot."

Max looked at Wells and then to Cortez, nodding her head. "Once we get a hit on the vehicle, what's the plan?"

"If he's left the state, the immediate orders are to extradite him back to Oklahoma. In the meantime, we're waiting for the preliminary results on blood found in the drain trap at the house. We're hoping to have some information before noon. The CSI team is conducting a lab comparison of the blood found in the trap against the DNA of our six victims. We've requested a rush on the results, and Detective Adair has a personal connection to the coroner, so he's pulling some strings to get the confirmation of the connection between Tyler and the victims. When we find him, and we will, we can bring him back to face trial here."

"What about the crimes in California?" Cortez asked.

"Once he's convicted in Oklahoma, he could be forced to go to California to stand trial there," Max replied before Wells could, citing the interstate laws.

"So basically, both states get their day, just not at the same time?"

Wells nodded. "That's correct, but let's not get ahead of ourselves. We need to locate Tyler first."

Max couldn't sit around waiting on the BOLO to hit, so she and Cortez headed back to speak with Jack's employer Samantha, in the hopes that she or one of the other employees had heard Jack talk about going somewhere specific. After talking to each employee and then going over to speak to Melody again, though, they'd come up with nothing more than a handful of new names of fellow students that might have had conversations with Jack. Given that the people Jack knew best seemed to know nothing, they returned to the City Hall building to see how the rest of the task force was proceeding.

It was just after ten o'clock when they got in, and Wells brought them up to date immediately. It was becoming increasingly clear that they needed a hit on the vehicle, he said, because without it there was no indication as to where Jack was heading, and time was getting away from them.

Suddenly, Max had a thought, and she pulled Cortez aside. "The magazines we went through from Jack's play house. We have all of those places cataloged that he studied for years. Do you think he may be heading to one of those other places? After all, Tulsa was one of the primary locations. Maybe we can find another escape plan there."

Cortez looked at Max and immediately reached for her laptop. "It's worth a look. We aren't doing any good just standing here."

Max and Cortez sat down together in front of the computer and pulled up the files with the magazine information, including a photo of the wall in Max's home. As they drilled through the files, Wells got a phone call and the whole room stopped, waiting for any indication that they had received a lead.

Wells glanced around the room as he finished the call, giving the team the nod they'd all been waiting on. "We've got the van, two hours from here in Arkansas. Nichols and Cortez, you're with me and Agent James. We'll fly from Tulsa. Prepare to leave. We don't know where this will take us or how long we will be gone. The plane will be on the tarmac waiting."

A quick stop at the hotel to grab their personal items and check out, and they were off to the airport. The flight to Fayetteville took just forty minutes, and upon their arrival they were met by the local Sheriff's Department, who led the team to the car waiting for them and then to the diner where Jack had left the van.

"The owner of the diner called it in after the breakfast rush. The van was there last night, but he didn't think too much about it until it was still there this morning."

Max checked the doors but found them all locked. She stood there with her hand still on the door handle stunned. Again, Jack Tyler was ahead of them.

After Wells gave the word, the sheriff pulled the lock from the driver's door with a crowbar. A quick search of the vehicle showed that it was completely empty, other than a box from a disposable cell phone. On the box was an associated phone number for the throw-away cell. Max immediately dialed the number, waiting for the third ring before the phone call was answered.

"Hello," Jack answered smiling.

"Dr. Jack Tyler?" Max asked, her heart racing a bit at the thought of speaking with Tyler.

"Yes, this is he."

"Dr. Tyler, we found your vehicle, and we know your whereabouts," Max bluffed, wondering if she could get him to offer any indication of where he currently was.

"Doubtful," he said confidently. "And who is it I have the pleasure of speaking to?"

"This is Detective Maxine Nichols of the Los Angeles Police Department, and I'm here with Agent Mark Wells of the FBI. Dr. Tyler, it would be best if you surrendered."

"Detective Nichols," he said slowly letting the words roll off his tongue, "are you the stunning woman I saw at the Beehive?" Not waiting for an answer, he continued on. "Perhaps turning myself in would be best for *you*, but certainly not for *me*. You see, I have things to do. I'm sorry to disappoint you, but have a good day, Detective Maxine Nichols. And give my best to your Hispanic friend." The line went dead.

Max stood, staring at the phone. She knew he was right. They did not have his location. His confidence was remarkable. She could hear the smugness in his voice, and at the moment she wanted to punch something. Wells and Cortez looked on as she shook her head, indicating that he hadn't offered her anything that would be helpful. "Nothing, but I could hear what sounded like the airport in the distance. He must be near an airport."

A crime scene team arrived to run prints on the vehicle and to look for any trace evidence. They still needed something material to connect Tyler to these crimes. Wells asked Agent James to interview the diner owner and the employees, to see if any one saw anything that might be helpful. After interviewing several people, Agent James came back out, shaking her head.

"So far no one remembers anything about the van or the driver of the van. I did get some information. There is a group of men that meet here every day about this time. Yesterday they sat next to the window where the van's parked. It's possible one of them may be able to provide some details. They should be arriving soon for their daily gathering."

"Great, make sure you speak to them the minute they start arriving," Wells requested turning back to Max and Cortez noting that they were watching the collection of evidence from the van. The evidence team had already recovered some prints on the steering wheel, and there was some trace fibers in the back of the van. The tech had said these appeared to be some sort of thread from clothing or a blanket. While this was happening, several cars had arrived, and the team was subjected to curious onlookers as the patrons rubber-necked trying to figure out what the commotion was all about as they made their way into the diner.

Some of these people were the group of older, male diners. They started arriving a few minutes later, and Agent James was quick to start speaking with them. After several minutes, she returned to the parking lot with a bit of news. "One of the men, Manny, sat next to the window said he saw a man park and then unload some luggage from the back of the van. He said the driver then went out front and waited a few minutes for a cab. The cab came probably ten to fifteen minutes later and picked him up.

Manny said the driver was about six feet tall, wearing jeans and a white shirt, and a baseball cap, so he didn't see the color of his hair. Said the driver had on glasses. Not sunglasses, regular glasses."

"He's wearing a disguise?" Cortez asked.

"Possibly. It would make sense if he knew that we were on to him. We know he saw us at the salon, so he has to know we're trying to track him. Probably realized we were close to finding his house," Wells offered.

"Was the witness able to say anything about the cab service or which company it might have been?" Max asked, her mind running through the possibilities.

Agent James nodded, "Yes, he said the cab is the black one with the gold checkered triangle on the side, and the owner gave me some information. We need to get the logs to see who picked up here yesterday and where they took him."

Wells turned to the local officer. "Sheriff, can you assist us with this please? We need to know where the cab company took the driver of that van."

Max felt excitement growing. *We might have you yet, Dr. Jack Tyler,* she thought to herself. If they could figure out where he was headed, they could meet him there and catch him before he disappeared again.

The officer nodded. "You've got it," he said as he flipped open the cell phone. He punched in a number and waited for a moment, then started speaking. "Debbie, do me a favor and get a hold of the owner of the Triangle Cab Company. What's his name? James? We need to know right away who picked up from the Bluestem Diner yesterday and where they took the passenger. We'll also need someone to interview that cabbie."

Max, Wells and Cortez all stood and watched anxiously listening to the one-sided conversation as the sheriff worked to gain information on who had taken a fare from this location.

The sheriff hung up and offered the information, "We're getting the cab driver's statement, but he said he took the driver to the rental center at the airport."

Wells and Max exchanged a look. Why would Jack rent another car? Did he know they were right on his heels, or was he just being careful? Was this the airport she'd heard on the phone?"

"Good work Sheriff," Max said, walking quickly toward the car. "We need to get to the airport right away."

Max, Cortez, James and Wells raced from rental counter to rental counter, asking for information on whether a Thomas Jennings had rented an automobile in the past twenty-four hours. Each counter showed no records of a rental by that name. Max showed the Avis rental agent a photo of Jack on her phone, and the woman shook her head, not recognizing the man in the picture. Looking down the row of rental counters Max saw Cortez, talking to a young male with a sassy attitude at the Hertz counter and then saw her head outside through the rental doors.

Finding nothing with her person, she walked towards the exit where she had seen Cortez leave and found her walking back in, "What ya' got?"

"He said that he wasn't working the day before, but the person at the exit might recognize the photo. I went out to see but got nothing out there either."

In the end, Wells requested a complete list of all rentals from the prior day, between ten in the morning and four in the afternoon. At a couple of counters, he met some resistance, until he said he would get a subpoena. He described the process of what would happen and how they would have to shut down until the FBI had reviewed all of their records. With this information, each of the counters offered their rental names and contact numbers.

Now, with a complete list in their hands, the three of them each took a page and looked through the names. Narrowing the list down to only the males, Max quickly honed in on the name Jackson Phillips. Jack ... son. This had to be the one. Showing Wells, she quickly returned to the rental counter, asking the agent if they kept copies of the driver's license. The agent shook his head, saying that they recorded the number, but didn't make a copy of the actual license. After further questioning, he was able to inform them that the rental contract indicated the car, a Chevy Aveo was a one-way rental that was to be dropped at the St. Louis airport.

Wells immediately called the bureau with the driver's license number and requested the information on the identification. A few minutes later, a photo was delivered to his email. The photo matched that of Jack Tyler. Wells dialed another number, snapping, "We need to be in the air to St. Louis in thirty minutes."

After thanking the Sheriff and his team and letting him know they would be in touch, the team headed to the private runway across the jet bridge from the rental center, where they'd landed two hours earlier. Thirty minutes later they were in flight to St. Louis.

Chapter Thirty-Seven

Jack hadn't slept well and rose early, ordering another meal from room service and spent the morning replaying his conversation with the pretty Detective. It had left his mind racing over the details again and again. He wasn't really sure if she was bluffing, but he was pretty certain they could not have traced him that quickly. The uncertainty left him anxious and restless. He needed to leave but was safer here than roaming the airport for any more time than was necessary. Deciding it was time to start getting ready, he headed to the shower.

After showering and packing his items, he sat waiting for the departure time. He'd spent some time watching the news and now knew that the police had raided his home in Oklahoma. They had found his surgery room and the freezer. Oh well, so they knew who he was, but based on the brief report, they did not know where he was and seemingly had not gone completely national with their findings yet. They must be trying to sneak up on him, hoping that he wouldn't hear what was happening. He knew he needed to get out of the country soon. After the phone call with Detective Maxine Nichols, it would be a national search soon if it was not already. He had to get on that flight and out of the USA.

Once the flight crossed into international space, they wouldn't be able to touch him. Jack had been very careful in his search of areas to travel, and had chosen the Cayman Islands because they were in British Overseas Territory and didn't have an extradition treaty with the USA. Once he was on that plane, he'd be on his way to safety.

The phone call from Detective Maxine Nichols had been a fun distraction from the waiting. It had let him know that they were onto him and had confirmed that he had no options but to leave soon. Of course, he had no way of knowing if the beautiful detective had been bluffing when she said they knew of his location, but he strongly doubted that they could have tracked him that quickly. Still, it was definitely time to get moving.

Jack left the room, wearing his glasses and ball cap pulled low over his brow. He tossed the room key on the counter on his way out. He'd requested the shuttle the night before, and it was waiting for him on the curb out front. After loading his items, the stout, balding shuttle driver asked him for his airline information and made the short drive over to the terminal, dropping Jack on the curb and assisting him with his bag. Jack slipped a $5 into the man's hand, drawing a big toothless smile from the wrinkled face. He could tell the man had worked hard his whole life and he appreciated that kind of discipline.

Then Jack followed the signs to the flight departures and checked in for his flight at the self-check kiosk counter, scanning his passport. Opting to carry his bag on, he continued to the security checkpoint, checking the display monitors on his way. His flight was on time and due to board in less than an hour.

He made his way through security, offering boarding pass and passport as requested, and removing money from his pockets. He slipped off his shoes and deposited these items along with the ball cap in the tub. He laid out his laptop in another tub and pushed all the items onto the security belt into the metal detector. He waited patiently as the two people in front of him took their turns going through the body scanner. At the direction of the gloved airport TSA agent, Jack stepped into the body scanner and raised his arms placing his thumbs in the center of his head. His heart raced, as he stepped through, placing his feet on the mat with the pre-drawn out shoes waiting until he received the all clear. Given the okay he collected his belongings, slipped back on his shoes and followed the signs that indicated the direction of his boarding gate. Arriving at his gate, he checked the monitor, which indicated that boarding would begin in ten minutes. He took a seat and waited for them to start.

Chapter Thirty-Eight

During the flight to St. Louis, Wells had the Bureau checking all departing flights the prior day and through the next twenty-four hours for any manifest showing a ticketed passenger name, Thomas Jennings, Jack Tyler or Jackson Phillips. If Jack Tyler was traveling from the St. Louis airport under any of these names they would have that information by the time they landed.

"If Tyler hasn't left the area yet, we'll have the flight grounded," Wells explained to Max and Cortez.

"What if he's gone already?" Cortez asked.

"It depends on where he's gone, honestly."

Max knew what Wells was referring to. Some areas were off limits to the USA, due to treaty agreements. If he'd gone to one of those countries, it would be impossible to extradite him. "Certain places outside of the USA won't give him back," she said quickly. "Let's hope we're ahead of him."

Max could feel her stomach churning as the time in the air seemed like an eternal wait. No one spoke during the flight, but she could occasionally feel Wells looking at her. She was careful not to allow their eyes to connect. Her feelings were all over the place. During the flight she struggled with the feelings that vacillated between the anxieties of tracking Jack, the possibility of actually being this close and finally catching him, worrying that somehow he might once again be a step ahead of them and slip away before they arrived, and the feelings she had for Wells. She continued to try to throttle those feelings and struggled to understand what they really meant. With Jack in cuffs she could relax and then she only needed to work through her feeling for Wells. He had said they needed to talk once this was settled. She tried to picture that conversation, but she could imagine it going in two very different directions and pushed those thoughts back again.

Chapter Thirty-Nine

Jack looked up as the airline gate agent began the flight announcement. "Welcome to Delta Airlines Flight #4673. We'll begin boarding for our flight to Grand Cayman, beginning with our 1st class and premier passengers, through gate #43. Please have your boarding pass ready to help make the boarding process go smoothly. We do have a full flight today, so please place small items under the seat in front of you and only one roller bag in the overhead storage compartment."

Jack stood and made his way over to the gate and handed his ticket to the ticket agent. The slim woman, with her blonde hair swept up on her head, smiled at Jack, accepting his 1st class ticket. "Welcome to the flight. Mr. Phillips."

Thanking her, Jack took his boarding pass back and headed down the jet bridge. After entering the plane, he stowed his bag in the overhead compartment and placed his laptop under the seat in front of him, so he could retrieve it during the flight. The flight attendant approached him and offered him a drink, but he smiled and answered that he'd have one once they were in the air. He settled into his seat, trying to not fidget as he waited for the door to close.

The other passengers poured onto the plane and took their seats one by one. Jack watched, looking at the wide variety of people passing him. Apparently the Caymans were a destination hot spot for families, as several children passed him. He wished that he could have taken Hope with him, but he settled his thoughts, reminding himself that he had to do this in order to have the future with her.

Chapter Forty

When the flight landed in St. Louis, Wells received word that a passenger manifest showed a passenger by the name of Jackson Phillips on a Delta Flight. The time of the departure wasn't available, but as they exited the plane, they were to be met by a Delta representative. Wells found out that the woman would be waiting for them on the tarmac with the flight information.

Max wasn't sure what this meant but was grateful that they would have immediate information when they got off the flight. They had to be on time to stop this man.

Exiting the plane, they found a small black woman waiting for them. She extended her hand and introduced herself. "Agent Wells, my name is Darlene Jefferson. I understand you're interested in a passenger by the name of Jackson Phillips." She nodded acknowledgement to the others.

"Thank you for meeting with us, Ms. Jefferson," Wells replied. "What can you tell us about the flight he's booked?"

"Unfortunately, that flight departed on schedule. It's already entered international airspace, and we're not able to recall a plane once it has crossed over into British territory. I am afraid you're too late, sir."

Wells looked at Max. "I understand, Ms. Jefferson. Thank you for your cooperation."

Max stood there on the tarmac with the wind from the planes blowing her hair into her face, forcing the rage she felt down deep inside her. The bastard *had* gotten away.

Chapter Forty-One

Jack hadn't fully relaxed for the first two hours of the flight. He'd watched anxiously until the airplane monitor showed when they crossed out of the USA and then finally ordered Vodka on the rocks. Sipping his drink, he reclined his 1st class seat and popped open his laptop, deciding that he could now watch a video. Finally able to enjoy himself, he reveled in the fact that his plan had worked. Hope was safely waiting for his return, and he was out of the long reach of Detective Maxine Nichols and her attractive Hispanic partner. Where he was heading, not even her friends with the FBI could get to him. Jack put his ear buds in his ears, ordered another drink and settled back in his seat. When the time was right, he would return, reunite with his wife and enjoy the rest of his life protecting her.

Chapter Forty-Two

Wells could hardly stand the pained look on Max's face. Neither she nor Cortez had spoken since Ms. Jefferson had delivered the news. There were a lot of loose ends to wrap up, and it would take weeks before all of the evidence was fully processed. Both Max and Wells had to inform their supervisors. There would be a massive amount of reports to file and interviews to conduct. All of the forensics on each of the bodies in both California and Oklahoma would have to all be completed. There would be questions from peers, and there were the emotional aspects to deal with, accepting the fact that they had been too late.

Both Max and Wells knew that Dr. Jack Tyler had escaped them for now, but they also knew he would not be satisfied. There was no way this man could refrain from killing. He had successfully restored Hope, but he was unable to take her with him. They could only assume that he'd disposed of her somewhere. What was more, they knew with absolute certainty that if he wasn't able to keep this one, he would have to have another one. It was only a matter of time before he was forced by desire or need to take another life.

Deciding it was too late to return to California or Washington tonight, everyone agreed an attempt at a good night's rest was in order. Checking into a nearby hotel, Wells left the women alone for a while as he checked in with headquarters and updated Detective Adair in Oklahoma.

No longer on the hunt for a serial killer, the women all decided to order a bottle of wine. As they sipped their drinks each one began to relax, slowly shedding the reality that their guy had gotten away. They shared some personal stories, getting to know a little more about Agent James through the conversation.

Wells returned to the table and joined them in a drink. They sat sipping wine and nibbling on food until it got late. Agent James was the first to excuse herself from the table, turning in for the night, followed shortly thereafter by Cortez. They said their good nights, though Wells and Max stayed on for a while longer.

Once the ladies had left them alone, Wells offered, "I know you're disappointed."

"I am," she acknowledge without even trying to deny it. "I mean damn it, Mark, we were so close. We *have* this guy, we just can't touch him."

"Yes, we have him. But guess what? He'll come back at some point, and when he does we'll arrest him."

"You might, but I'll be back in California, working some highway shooter case."

"Hey, we got you involved this time, right?"

"Yes, but it won't be that easy in the future. The colder my case in California becomes, the less likely it is I'll be allowed to stop, drop and roll to chase Jack Tyler around the country."

"Ever think about joining the FBI? Then you'd get to chase guys like this all the time," Wells asked, his wine glass half raised to his mouth and his eyes fixed on her beautiful face.

Max laughed out loud. "What? You're kidding, right?"

"Not really. Max, you have great skills and an instinct that can't be trained. We need good agents like you."

"You *are* serious?" Max said considering what he was saying.

"I'm dead serious. Think about it."

Max watched Wells for a moment before taking another sip of the wine. She was on her second glass and starting to feel a little tipsy. Deciding she needed to head up to her room, she started to excuse herself when Wells grabbed her hand.

"Stay with me tonight," he murmured.

"Mark, we shouldn't."

"Why not?" he asked, looking into her green eyes.

Standing up, he offered her his hand and walked her to his room.

Epilogue

It had been three weeks since Max returned home from St. Louis. The chief had praised her efforts and simultaneously ripped her for being unsuccessful in apprehending Dr. Jack Tyler. She and Cortez had started a weekly "girls" night at Max's house on Fridays, when schedules permitted. Cortez was completely unrelenting on her teasing of Max on the topic of Agent Mark Wells, but Max shut her down every chance she got. Privately, she had to admit that the man was fully under her skin.

That final night in St. Louis, after a couple of glasses of wine, she'd found herself in his room and again in his strong arms. When he'd taken her hand, her body immediately began to respond to his touch. Once his lips touched hers, she was filled with an intoxication that had nothing to do with the wine and everything to do with his strong, clean and manly scent. After she succumbed to his kiss and her hands found the muscles in his arms and stomach, there was no turning back. Their kissing had led to at first passionate lovemaking, followed by tender and gentle kissing, and an exploration that left no parts of their bodies unexplored. After hours of releasing into each other the energy they had channeled towards finding Jack Tyler, they had slept together, bodies intertwined.

The next morning, Max had stared in amazement at Mark as he slept, then covered his chest with light kisses until his blue eyes locked on her face. A smile had crept across his lips. It was a smile of comfort and contentment. In the end, after promising each other that they would not leave things as they had the first time they connected, they'd been forced to peel away from each other in order to prepare for their individual return flights home.

Since returning to California, Max had focused her attention on a new case and had shared endless hours of conversation with Mark on the phone. Each call ended with his niggling at her to cast her application into the FBI. She left every one of those calls torn between her emotions, her career aspirations, the unknown, and her own fears of commitment to a relationship.

Now it was Saturday morning, and she was preparing a light, healthy breakfast, with plans of following it up with a good run to get her body moving. She always enjoyed the burn of a good workout routine of any sort, and it sounded like exactly what she needed today. She was pouring coffee when the doorbell rang. Surprised to have an early morning visitor, she wondered if Cortez had forgotten something the night before. They'd spent the prior evening sipping wine, talking about the men on the force, and occasionally speculating about what Jack Tyler was up to now.

When she opened the door, she was surprised to see Mark Wells standing before her with a lopsided grin on his face. "I was in the neighborhood, and thought I would swing by to see if you have time for breakfast," he said.

Max returned the smile and stepped forward, taking his hand and pulling him through the door.

***

A warm breeze came off of the ocean, causing little white caps on the glistening water in the Caymans. Jack sat with his now-tanned legs stretched out in front of him, sipping on a rum punch. Having restored Hope, he merely was biding his time until it was safe to return home to be reunited with his wife.

He'd been enjoying his time on the island but was beginning to get that feeling again. He wouldn't be able to fight it much longer, as only Hope's presence and the role of a surgeon had helped him resist the urges. He'd been noticing certain tourists lately … people who would be easy picks – those that frequently over indulged in alcohol. They would help tame the darkness and hold him until he could return to the United States. It was just a matter of time, not much longer.

He'd been tracking the news in the States, and his story had all but dwindled off. Based on this, he'd decided to wait at least one more month before returning. Until then, he'd enjoy his time here in the sun, while getting to know a couple of those overly intoxicated tourists.

Settling back in his chair, he took another sip of the sweet rum punch and smiled at his good fortune.

The End

Acknowledgement

There are several people who helped make this book possible. First, thanks to my partner, Lorea and to my children Maima and Akins for their patience while I spent hours absorbed in allowing my mind to take this journey. I also must thank my mother, Joyce Knupp for her honesty and encouragement as the first reader, editor and critic. She gave the nudge to keep writing.

To my editor Hollie Zunun, I thank you for what you brought to the final product, especially for your ideas and suggestions on the storyline. You did an amazing job of correcting my punctuation and challenging me all along the way.

A very special recognition goes to Jim Martin, a friend, co-worker and author of A Madman's Song, for generously sharing your discoveries on self-publishing. Your input saved me endless hours and made me realize I could do this. Read his book too, it is wonderful! Thank you so much!

About the Author

Valerie Knupp lives on 7 acres outside the Tulsa area near Inola, Oklahoma. She loves to travel and is an avid reader of anything with a grisly plot. When not doing one of these things, she enjoys spending time around the house with her partner and two adopted children. This is her debut novel and is the 1st of a trilogy. She is currently working on the 2nd of the Dr. Jack Tyler series.

Visit **www.thrillersbyknupp**.com to provide feedback, comments or if you found any errors while taking your first Dr. Jack Tyler journey!

www.ingramcontent.com/pod-product-compliance
Lightning Source LLC
Chambersburg PA
CBHW071249170626
46809CB00001B/137